Vows
of
Gold
and
Laughter

Tale One
of the
Immortal
Beings

EDITH PAWLICKI

ISBN: 9798576569151

Contents

Map: Earth

Prologue: The Last Acts of Bai the Warrior   1

Diagram: The Nine Colors and their Families   21

1   How Nanami Stole a God   22

2   The Useless Betrothal   53

3   How Xiao Worried, Argued, and Failed   78

4   How Bai was Recalled to the World   103

5   A Fight, a Talk, and a Song   128

6   A Drink, a Diviner, and a Decision   146

7   Power and Poison   172

Map: Sun Palace   194

8   How Nanami Met Justice   195

9   The Wanderer and the Willow   227

10   How Nanami Walked the Shadows   253

11   How Jin Was Rescued   277

12   How Xiao Realized His Strength   295

Map: Tsuku   317

13   The Sin of Destruction   318

Map: Sea Palace   344

14   How the Sea Dragon Roared   345

15   The Sleeper's Resting Place   359

16   How the Night Dragon Retaliated   379

17   How Four Fears Were Faced   400

Glossary   416

A Note About Language   430

EARTH
100,000 YEARS AFTER CREATION

This map shows the regions immortals use rather than the mortal nations of Earth. The only mortal creations drawn are their largest cities; other points of interest are immortal residences and magical sites made by immortal beings.

Map labels

LAND OF WINTER

GATE TO THE UNDERWORLD

KORIKAMI'S TOMB

ENDLESS SEA

CRESCENT MOON

TATOU

TSUKU

SEA PALACE

O'O

AH

NI

PO

STRAIT OF THE MOON

BANDO

DAEDO

BYEONG MOUNTAINS

CHEOLMUN PASS

SANCTUARY CAVES

GE MAN

MOAYI

ZHONGTU

SHUGAM RIVER

MOS LAKE

COLD PEAKS

ONDOR PEAKS

RUINS OF XILING

MIRROR RIVER

LAKE OF REFLECTION

WOOD PAVILIONS

JINGZI

GREAT WILLOW

LIUSHI

DOUBLE BAY

SOUTH SEA

EHKORON

FROZEN DESERT

WHITE MOUNTAIN

GREAT LADIES

SHUBRA DESERT

DATAA RIVER

KUANBAI RIVER

JEEVANTI

SHAHAR

CHATTAN KILE

ENDLESS SEA

Prologue

The Last Acts of Bai the Warrior

18,000 years ago

BAI leapt high, his calves burning from the demand. A broad spear head sliced under his feet, so close that he felt the breeze of its passing. He landed on the wooden shaft, and before it dipped under his weight, he decapitated the soldier holding it with an efficient swing of the Starlight Sword. He pushed off the shaft to avoid being entangled by the dead soldier, and this time his right leg protested his landing, spasming at the knee before giving out beneath him. Bai knew his end had come and closed his eyes in relief.

But no blow fell.

He slowly opened his eyes and scanned the pass, letting the Starlight Sword and the Water Shield—bound to his left forearm—drag his arms down.

Bai had chosen the narrowest section of Cheolmun Pass to defend, where men could fit no more than four abreast—if he rested his fingers on one sheer stone wall, he could just touch the other with his sword. Having studied martial arts for twenty-five millennia, he could easily defeat even four skilled fighters at any given time, but to do so for so long against so many...

When he undertook this task as a favor to his student, Gang, the God of War, he had accepted his death.

But Bai heard nothing besides his own harsh panting. The soldiers of Zhongtu were a mass of blood and tangled limbs beneath him. While fighting, he had been almost oblivious to the smells, but suddenly the putrid blood hit the back of his throat. His stomach revolted and his throat seized.

I cannot vomit on the dead!

Bai made a clumsy attempt to get down from the mounded bodies, resulting in a tumble where he dropped his sword. His hands bit deep into the rust-colored mud—*this was dust before the fight*—and he dry retched for some time.

When the heaves subsided, Bai sat back on his heels and regarded the dead.

It was impossible to count them, tangled as they were, but during the fighting the sun had set and risen again. Given the rate of the fight, he must have killed nearly three hundred soldiers. A mortal man might have collapsed from dehydration or exhaustion, but though it was unpleasant to endure, Bai could go indefinitely without nourishment and rest, a perk of having been a stone before he gained awareness and became the first immortal.

Perhaps there are some wounded who will live? he thought doubtfully. Having delivered every blow himself, he knew that he had struck over and over to kill as quickly as possible so that he might turn his attention to the seemingly endless onslaught.

But it had ended. And he was still alive.

Hands trembling, he fumbled at the strings that held his water flask. When he finally had it free and uncorked, he gulped desperately at the stale, hot water. He lowered the flask and looked to his hands, filthy and deadly.

When will it be enough? he wondered. *How do these men's' deaths avenge Noran? They were soldiers, not bandits.*

For the first time, he realized that he could not wait for some lucky warrior to slay him. If he was tired of this life, of slaughtering all challengers, only he could do something about it. He reached for the Starlight Sword, waiting haphazardly in the muck, and pulled it onto his lap. He had once thought it the most beautiful thing he had ever made.

He closed his eyes. "I am so ashamed."

"You should be," came a tart voice.

Bai's eyes flew open and landed on a heavily pregnant woman just past the edge of the bloody mud. Petite and fine-boned, her hands warily clutched her azure sari to a swollen abdomen that threatened to topple her. Her face was taut, and her jaw jutted aggressively, overcompensating for fear. Bai recognized her rich cerulean braid that hung over her shoulder and her eyes, bits of sky even from this distance.

"Neela?" Was he hallucinating?

Neela was only five thousand years younger than Bai—like him, she was one of the Colors that shaped the world. It was strange to think that while he had been destroying life, she had been making it.

"Congratulations," he said, indicating her belly.

Neela hissed. "Don't wave that butcher's knife at me!"

Bai flushed—he had gestured with the Starlight Sword without thinking. "I apologize."

"Hmm." Neela stared at him.

He cleared his throat. "Why are you here?"

"I was elected. Cheng thought if anyone approached you that you'd just cut them down, but Haraa thought my condition might make you pause long enough that I could get some words out."

"I can't believe Cheng would approve of such a gamble."

Neela tossed her braid over her shoulder with a sniff. "And why would that concern me?"

Obviously it doesn't. Bai empathized with his lovelorn friend, although Neela had always been clear that she didn't return his interest.

When Bai didn't reply, Neela looked past him to the pile of dead bodies. She pressed the back of her right hand to her mouth and looked away.

Bai said, "Haraa appears to be right though—it's beyond me to ignore a woman on the cusp of labor. Why don't we relocate before we speak? And I need to bathe."

She nodded. "Come to my camp when you finish. My wagon is by the mouth of the Kuanbai River, beneath the Great Willow."

"Very well." And that was no coincidence. He had created the willow fifty millennia ago—Neela was surely trying to remind him of another way of life. But he was no longer that man, and he could only move forward, not back.

"I'll expect you in an hour then." The sharpness in her voice made Bai wonder what punishment she thought she could mete out if he failed to appear, but he was in no mood for confrontation. As soon as she vanished, he turned to the dead and bowed at the waist.

"May you find peace in the Sea of Souls, and fate smile upon your families. I am sorry for taking your lives without knowing why you fought."

Bai teleported as he straightened and lost about ten minutes between. He was clearly exhausted—usually teleporting took him half that.

He reappeared on the shore of the Kuanbai River, not far from rich green foliage that danced lightly in a breeze from the ocean. He could feel the large grains of pale sand through his thin-soled boots, and the river drifted past his toes languorously. Tears pricked Bai's eyes.

He swallowed his emotions. A quick scan found no bystanders, for which Bai was thankful. The sight of him, clad in armor and blood, would ruin this peaceful place.

Bai set down his sword to unbind the Water Shield from his left arm. He set it on the sand and then he removed his leather armor. He shivered—it was a warm day, but the sweat that coated him and dampened his underrobe made the wind feel sharper than it was.

He studied the Starlight Sword for a moment, its dappled metal hidden by crusted blood. He had always cleaned it before tending to himself. He had forged it from the metal of two meteorites under the white light of the stars over a hundred nights, and it had its own power. But today he hated it.

Bai filled, drained, and refilled his water flask before stripping his shoes, trousers, and underrobe. He waded into the Kuanbai until the water reached his waist. Then he dove, swimming with deep strokes to the bottom.

What would happen if he just stayed here? He didn't need to breathe, but given enough time, would the water erode him away? He kicked away from the sandy bottom and his morbid thought.

Breaking through the water's surface, he glanced to shore, half-hoping, half-fearing that someone had discovered the Starlight Sword while he was submerged and made off with it. He didn't want it anymore, but he could not in good conscience let anyone have it.

But it was still there, ugly with dried blood. He returned to the shallows, where he used the coarse sand to scrub the blood from his body.

I'm not even injured. Not one of the soldiers he fought for the past day and night had managed to land a blow. He felt like his heart had been cut out.

When all the grime had been scoured away, he unbound his top knot and rinsed his long white hair. Then he ran his fingers through the sand until he found a simple white stone. *Those men would still be alive*, he thought, *if I had remained like this little one.* Both of them had once been a part of the White Mountain, until they were tumbled free by a mountain spring and washed down the Kuanbai River. But then their fates diverged. Less than a mile from here, where the river met the bay, Bai had suddenly become the first immortal.

He shook the memories from his head and shaped the stone into a comb. Detangling his hair was soothing—he kept his mind blank as he worked.

Finally he rose and dropped the comb into the river. He was ready to deal with the accoutrements of war.

His garments and armor would never be free of blood stains again. He might as well be rid of them. White sand, white sunlight. He focused, bouncing the white light off the sand to the clothes until they burst into flame.

While they burned, he scoured his sword and shield with wet sand. After he rinsed each for a final time, he set them to dry on a large stone. Then he looked for something from which to make cloth and found a dove tree, with large petals of purest white. He plucked a flower, discarded the pistils, crumpled its petal in his hand, and then shook it out into a drying cloth, which he used to wipe the remaining water and sand from his body before plucking six more. The first he stretched and folded until it became a pair of wide-legged trousers. The second became a wrap-around shirt. The third he tore into strips for ties, the fourth a loose overrobe with bell-like sleeves, and the last two each made one soft-soled boot.

He dressed himself and then returned to his belongings. After a brief hesitation, he sheathed his now dry sword and tied it with his shield to his back.

He wanted to lie down and sleep, but it had already been more than an hour since Neela had admonished him. He supposed he should see her first. Too tired to teleport, he pushed his way through the dense foliage to where Neela waited.

Her wagon was parked several paces from the willow's white trunk, where the long, thin branches of the tree caressed it at the breeze's whimsy. Now that Bai was dry and dressed, the breeze was mild and sweet. The silver leaves of the willow rustled a welcome. He held up a hand in return, and they kissed his fingers.

Looking down, it was as if the green undergrowth held thousands of tiny blue butterflies the same cerulean as Neela's hair. Having once been a dayflower herself, Neela was very fond of them. She must have been here some time to have grown so many. The undergrowth was broken only by a stone fire pit, which had been used so recently that heat still distorted the air above it.

Her blue ombre caravan was a whimsical affair, made of layered star and octagon lattices that changed from pale robin's egg to a deep cerulean. The roof was arched, and the windows were six-pointed stars. Neela was watching him from one of those stars, a beaten copper cup in her hand. The scent of hot buttered bread beckoned him.

"Door's open," Neela pointed out.

Bai mounted the narrow steps of a curved ladder and ducked his head to enter the wagon—the lintel was only five feet high, ample enough for Neela, but hideously low for him. Once through, Bai was confronted by swathes of royal blue, shimmering sapphire, and cyan embroidery on cerulean. It took him a few moments to parse the many textures and shades into familiar objects.

Neela was ensconced on a sumptuous velvet bench on one side of a narrow wood table. She was indicating the bench opposite with a smirk, as if she knew exactly what he was thinking. Perhaps she did. Just as Bai could always discern the essence of things, Neela had insight into the thoughts of sentient beings.

Once Bai was seated, Neela offered him a cup of opaque burgundy juice. Bai thanked her and traced his thumb over the dimples in the metal before taking a sip. His mouth puckered—the juice was both too sweet and too sour.

He gratefully accepted a plate of flatbread and yogurt from Neela and used the supple bread like a spoon to fill his mouth with tangy yogurt. His stomach rumbled its approval.

"Butchering mortals is hungry work, hey?"

He grimaced but continued eating.

"You said you were ashamed?"

"You're not my mother," Bai returned, around a mouthful of bread.

"No," Neela retorted, "you haven't got a mother, no more than I. But it seems like you need one, so I'll just have to do my best, won't I?"

Bai, despite his hunger, paused to stare her down. She met his gaze without flinching.

"So why were you ashamed?"

Bai gulped his juice, then set down the cup. He rubbed his eyes. "When Noran was killed..."

"You decided to purge the world of bandits. To kill the wicked and protect the vulnerable," Neela said dryly.

Bai's lips twisted. "Yes. Well. I..." He waved a hand, unable to find the words.

Neela sighed. "I am familiar with your unrequited love—Noran bragged about it often enough. And although I never cared for her, no one deserves such a death."

Bai closed his eyes, remembering Noran's bold, flirtatious manner. He had known she mocked his seriousness, his earnestness behind his back, but he had not cared. She had been everything he was not, and he had wanted her vivacity for himself.

He had given her a braided bracelet of his hair so that she might summon him whenever she wanted. And she used it regularly—whenever she wanted to make Aka, the second eldest immortal and her lover, jealous. After she and Aka had Gang—the first born-immortal—Bai didn't see the point in going to her anymore. That was why he had hesitated and arrived too late to save her that day.

When he found her dead, surrounded by mortal bandits, her crying son sheltered by her bloody body...

Anger and hatred had rushed through him and found a convenient target in the mortal bandits who had murdered her. But even after they were all dead, and Gang returned to his father, the rage didn't dissipate.

Bai started his third life that day, that of a warrior who

honed his body into a tool for destruction. He had mastered every weapon he encountered and invented dozens of new ones. Two thousand years later, Gang, on the threshold of adulthood, had come and asked to be trained, and so Bai had taught the God of War everything he could.

Gang wasn't just a warrior—he was a general. He had often called on Bai over the last score of millennia and sent him to the worst battles. Bai had always gone willingly, trying to obliterate the memory of the small boy huddled beneath his dead mother.

"It was watching your self-destruction that made me realize we are better off without great passions." Neela's words pulled Bai back to the present.

Neela had only casual affairs, usually with mortal men whom she could soon forget.

"Self-destruction?" he said. "I never thought of it that way before today. I thought the deeper I threw myself into the art of fighting, the more men I killed, the more whole I would feel. Somewhere along the way, I stopped caring about why there was fighting, just that there was. Today... I don't even know why I was fighting those men. Hundreds of men dead, and I don't even know why."

Neela took a slow sip of her juice. "I know why. Shall I tell you?"

Bai nodded once.

"Those men were reinforcements, coming to the aid of the Bandoan king."

Bai finished chewing a bit of bread and then said, "But the Bandoan royal family were Gang's first worshippers. Why would he turn on them?"

Neela fiddled with her cup. "His father was fighting the

Golden Phoenix, and the men of Bando tried to intervene."

"The Phoenix? But why? He's not like the other immortal creatures that Aka has locked away over the years."

"It doesn't make sense to you because you've never wanted anyone to worship you. But Aka would like to replace Phoenix in the hearts of the Bandoans." Neela took another sip. "I don't think Aka has been locking away the immortal creatures out of generosity—he has specifically been pursuing the worship of mortals. Regardless of whether the creatures are benevolent or wicked or simply are."

Bai considered this. "I can believe such of Aka, but," Bai shook his head, "surely Gang would not help with such an endeavor?"

"What, because you were his teacher? Or because Noran was his mother?" Neela shook her head. "You don't know him as well as you think.

"Early this morning, while you were still butchering mortals, Aka locked Phoenix in the Underworld. He was the last of them—the last of the immortal creatures."

"Are you certain?" Worry and disbelief sharpened his voice. "How could he have done that without our noticing?"

"Some of us *have* noticed—Cheng, Haraa, and I. And so have Zi and Hei for that matter—they've been helping him in exchange for a position at court."

"Court? What court?"

Neela smiled humorlessly. "The Court of the Heavens. You are now an imperial subject of the Sun Emperor. As are all who live in the upper realms."

Bai snorted. "I'd like to see Aka try to command me."

"Hmm. I wouldn't mind seeing that myself." Then she sighed. "Regardless of how much personal power you have, most are now subject to Aka's rule. Which isn't all bad—"

Bai cut her off. "But what are you proposing? You want me to fight him? That's why you sought me out?"

Neela suddenly looked old and tired, her tens of millennia showing in her eyes. "No. I want you to stop fighting. I sought you out so you *wouldn't* fight him. Can you imagine the destruction of an immortal war? You against Aka and Zi and Hei? All those little deities they've gathered around themselves?" Neela shuddered.

"I consider it done," she continued. "Aka is the Sun Emperor. I want you to accept it. That's why I found you."

Bai looked at Neela closely—about as closely as she was studying him. For the second time that day, he wondered just what she thought she could do to him. She clearly had some idea—but he was hardly going to provoke a pregnant woman nearing labor. He didn't want to fight Aka anyway.

Casting about for a different subject, Bai tried, "Who's the father?"

"I don't know."

Perhaps, all things considered, that was not surprising. "I could find him for you," Bai offered.

Neela laughed. "Not even you could find him—he must be eight hundred years dead. He was a mortal—I made sure of that."

"Ah—you thought you could have the child all to yourself."

Neela scowled. "And what's that supposed to mean?"

"It's good for children to have two parents—it brings balance. She'll look to others for guidance whether you like it or not."

Neela turned to him in excitement. "She?"

"Yes. It'll be a girl."

"Good. Then I'll name her Aashchary." Neela smiled to herself, dismissing his warning as pontificating. Bai shrugged—there was nothing he could say to convince her. Neela was as stubborn as they came.

"She'll be born soon—less than a week, I should think. Do you have a midwife?"

Neela tossed her head. "What do I need one for?"

Bai smiled. "It's easier to have a baby with support." He cleared his throat. "I'll stay nearby until the babe comes, if you like. I've caught a few."

"You? When?"

"When soldiers go to war, wives and other women follow. And inevitably..."

"So mortal babes then."

Bai shrugged. "The process is the same for us as it is for them, if longer."

Neela looked down, chewing her full bottom lip. "Well, if you want."

Bai smiled slightly. "I'll stay then. I need to think through all you've told me, anyway."

TWO weeks after little Aashchary entered the world, Bai teleported to the Gate to the Underworld.

Aka had built it in the Land of Winter, a lone structure on top of barren Mount Korikami. Despite being summer, a bitter wind mourned the Korikami, the fearsome creature that Aka had trapped in the Underworld a few millennia ago. The wind chilled Bai through his dove petal clothes.

Black gravel crunched beneath his feet as he circled the vermilion torii gate that now was the only way to enter the

Underworld. So fervently red that it almost glowed, the gate consisted of two thick columns on either side, two bars across the top, with a flaring roof above the upper. He had walked through it several times, but each time he had simply passed through to the other side—in fact, if not for his insight into the true nature of things, he might have believed it was nothing but a beautiful monument.

It needed a key to enter. An object that triggered the gate so that the other side was the Underworld. Aka must have the key. The same narcissism that had led the immortal to declare himself a god and now an emperor would surely compel him to keep such a powerful artifact for himself.

Bai had no intention of starting a war to free the creatures, but the gate was not fully closed and that troubled him. Energy was streaming through it, flowing most likely to the key. Without being able to examine the key, Bai could not identify that energy, but he suspected that Aka was draining power from the creatures he had defeated.

Even if only the foulest of the monsters that were trapped there, Bai could not abide such an arrangement. To steal another's power was wrong. Each being had a right to itself; he had learned that the hard way when Aka came to be.

It had been over fifty millennia since that day, and Bai had decided that it was not only futile to control other beings, but it was wrong. Everyone was entitled to their own self, to make their own choices poorly or wisely, to regulate their own bodies, minds, and powers—so long as they respected those rights in others.

The possibility that Aka might be violating that essential truth in regard to the immortal creatures filled Bai with a cold anger.

He needed to see the key for himself.

Bai transformed into a white egret, hiding the Starlight Sword and the Water Shield in his feathers, and took to the skies. He teleported midflight to the air above the Sun Palace.

When Aka claimed his divinity, he had rather pretentiously gathered the red rays of a rising sun and created a floating residence. Bai had visited it before, a guest of Noran and then later Gang, but he was surprised to see just how much it had changed.

The original residence's walls were still in place, creating what must still be Aka and his wife's personal living compound. Central was a nine-storied pagoda with red clay roofs and gold-leaf sides. On either side of the pagoda were pavilions centered in two large ponds with arching bridges granting access to them. Grand halls stood at both the north and south points of the enclosure, and several smaller buildings were set among the gardens. This was familiar.

But there was now an outer wall encapsulating as much space as the inner. There were new gardens being landscaped and a variety of colorful buildings—the residences of his court, perhaps. Three smaller circular compounds were also present—it was easy enough to see that each was for one of Aka's children. Bai briefly considered going to Gang's, near the north gate, but Bai no longer trusted his student as he always had. To see him and know Gang had changed—or worse, that he was the same, but Bai had never known him at all—well, Bai would simply find the key himself.

Bai opened his senses, looking for it. He knew it would have the same essence as the gate he had just studied.

Aka was having tea in one of the pavilions with two concubines. Dangling from a red ribbon around his neck was a wooden pendant carved into a sun with a hundred rays, painted deep vermilion like the gate—the key. *Kunjee,* it told Bai its name.

Bai's suspicions were correct; Kunjee was siphoning magical power from the creatures trapped in the Underworld.

Bai immediately decided to take it.

He flew to the Southern Gate, circling once before landing lightly on the polished pink marble slab before it. Two guards, clad in red leather with embossed suns on their chests, eyed him curiously. As Bai transformed, they both lowered their spears nervously. When he was once again himself—clad in the white dove petal clothes he had made by the Kuanbai River, the Starlight Sword and the Watershield on his back—Bai smiled at the Guards and bowed respectfully.

"I have come to see the Sun Emperor."

The guard to the left frowned and began, "The Sun Emperor—" but his fellow raised a hand, having noted Bai's pure white warrior's knot and the gleaming handle over his shoulder.

"Bai the Warrior, bearer of the Starlight Sword," he said and bowed. "Please wait while we send a messenger to his Imperial Majesty."

Bai nodded graciously. If he had to fight his way in, he would, but let them see if Aka would welcome him.

As he waited, he amused himself by studying the elaborate illusion of water that filled the circular gate, intended to conceal the palace grounds. With little effort, Bai looked through it to see a broad flagstone path edged with cherry trees—their leaves were a vibrant green with bright red clusters of fruit hiding amongst them. At the end of the path was Aka's Reception Hall, a massive wooden building with vermilion pillars as thick as a man was tall and a flaring red-clay roof. Very quickly, a large retinue arrived at the hall, Aka at the center and wearing Kunjee. Some minutes later, an official wearing rose robes heavily embroidered with silver peonies made his way down the flagstone path and through the gate. He bowed to Bai repeatedly, inviting him to enter the palace. Passing through the high arch of Southern Gate immediately brought the rich, sweet smell of ripe cherries and a noticeable warming of the air.

As they approached the large hall, Bai saw it was not entirely red after all—golden lattices decorated the top and bottom of the pillars and gold chrysanthemums were on the end of every row of roof tiles. Bai recognized Noran's designs immediately, and his heart, even after all these years, lurched sadly. They walked up a wide set of stone steps, and Bai's escort immediately genuflected on a marble floor that was as pure a white as Bai's robes. At the far end of the hall, Aka sat on a massive red lacquer throne carved with immortal creatures. To his right sat his Empress, the Goddess of Lightning, whom Bai had known before her marriage. She kept her eyes on her hands and her expression blank. To Aka's left was a young woman with eyes just a bit deeper red than Aka's—his daughter. She returned Bai's gaze with frank curiosity, and her ambition scorched him. He abruptly returned his focus to her father.

Aka's hands clenched his armrests when he realized that Bai had no intention of genuflecting, but he said nothing. The official glanced at Bai nervously—because of his master's anger and because he realized how powerful Bai must be to ignore Aka's rules. As he rose, he trembled like a leaf in the wind.

They halted twenty paces before Aka where a red-lacquered table had been set with refreshments.

The official indicated that Bai should be seated then backed away from the imperial presence on his knees, until he reached the pillars where other members of the court sat. Bai eyed them. "Perhaps a private discussion would be preferable?" he said dryly.

Bai could see hesitation, doubt, deep under Aka's façade, but the other man simply replied, "These are the record keepers of the Sun Court. They watch all my meetings."

Bai arched a brow but shrugged.

"I've come for Kunjee."

Aka stiffened. Before he could make a reply, Bai continued, "You've sealed the immortal creatures, and made yourself emperor, but the power it channels does not belong to you. You have no right to harvest it."

Aka scowled now. "And you do?"

"No. No one does. I will keep it safe so that no being can siphon the power of the immortal creatures."

Aka stroked the red sun pendant. "Did you really go to Cheolmun Pass?"

"I did. I killed three hundred mortals for your cause. I will accept Kunjee as payment."

Red fire danced over Aka's fingers before disappearing. "You would find me a more difficult target than those mortals."

Bai again arched a brow. "I am sure I would. And your death would reverberate throughout the realms more heavily than theirs."

Sweat beaded on Aka's forehead.

"I think we must let fate tell us if you or I should be the keeper of Kunjee," he suggested.

"A duel?" asked Bai, somewhat surprised.

"Not with weapons," answered Aka. "Let us play Jieqi."

The world game. Bai nodded his consent.

Aka waved his hand, and there was a flurry of activity as court officials set up the game. Brown ribbons were stretched across the floor to create a grid, with four blue ribbons crossing diagonally for rivers. The court officials donned masks— monkey, elephant, goat, peacock, deer, elephant, tiger, and dragon. They took their places as pieces, and Bai had to suppress a laugh at the sheer pretension. It seemed they were well-acquainted to this job though, as they elegantly and efficiently followed the instructions that Bai and Aka called out.

At last Bai prevailed. He watched Aka carefully as he captured the emperor's dragon to win the game.

Aka seethed beneath the surface as he removed Kunjee from his neck. He then blasted it toward Bai on a ray of pure sunshine that could easily have been deathly, but Bai froze the water vapor that hung in its path and used it to whirl away the heat before he caught the key.

"Thank you," Bai responded and almost teleported. But he sensed Aka's satisfaction and studied the pendant intently. Aka had woven an intricate protection that prevented any but himself from teleporting with it—anyone else who did so would leave the pendant behind. Bai thought he could break the protection, but he immediately saw the folly of doing so— such a protection would make it difficult for a thief to steal it. So, after a moment's thought, he slipped the ribbon over his head, gave a nod to the court, and walked out of the palace.

He summoned a wispy cirrus cloud at the gate and harnessed it as mount.

The men gaped as the cloud drifted away.

He sighed. He had never felt so old, as if all the millennia of his life were bearing down on him. He touched the sun pendant around his neck. *Kunjee.*

First, I must put you somewhere safe. Then... then I can lay down my burdens.

He steered the cloud to the White Mountain. *It is time to go home. To leave this world behind.*

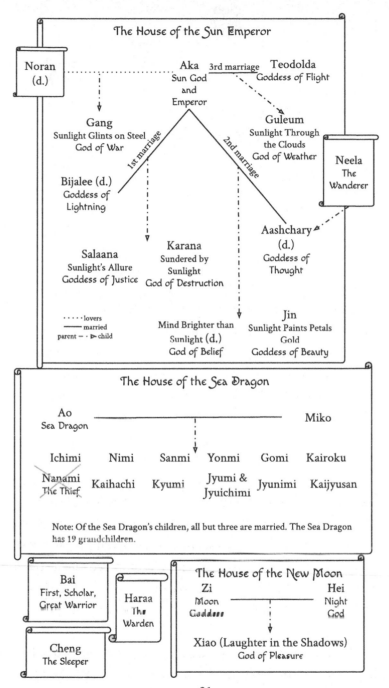

The House of the Sun Emperor

Noran
(d.)

Aka
Sun God
and
Emperor

3rd marriage

Teodolda
Goddess of Flight

Gang
Sunlight Glints on Steel
God of War

1st marriage

Guleum
Sunlight Through
the Clouds
God of Weather

Neela
The
Wanderer

Bijalee (d.)
Goddess of
Lightning

2nd marriage

Aashchary
(d.)
Goddess of
Thought

Salaana
Sunlight's Allure
Goddess of Justice

Karana
Sundered by
Sunlight
God of Destruction

· · · · · lovers
———— married
parent — · ▻ child

Mind Brighter than
Sunlight (d.)
God of Belief

Jin
Sunlight Paints Petals
Gold
Goddess of Beauty

The House of the Sea Dragon

Ao
Sea Dragon

Miko

Ichimi   Nimi   Sanmi   Yonmi   Gomi   Kairoku

Nanami
The Thief

Kaihachi   Kyumi   Jyumi &
Jyuichimi   Jyunimi   Kaijyusan

Note: Of the Sea Dragon's children, all but three are married. The Sea Dragon
has 19 grandchildren.

Bai
First, Scholar,
Great Warrior

Haraa
The
Warden

The House of the New Moon

Zi
Moon
Goddess

Hei
Night
God

Cheng
The Sleeper

Xiao (Laughter in the Shadows)
God of Pleasure

21

1

How Nanami Stole a God

Present Day

IT was before dawn when the tugging of summoning woke Nanami the Thief. Disoriented in the dark, she tried to sit up but was caught by bands around her waist and chest. Nanami remembered that she tied herself in the crotch of a tree for the night. She was still fully dressed, so it was but a minute's work to untie the bindings and teleport in response to the summons.

About half an hour later, Nanami arrived in a small circle of light cast by a fire burning on coarse sand. A thickset man sat by it, though he stood at her appearance. She took a moment to orient herself—the bitterly cold air told Nanami she was in the north, and she recognized Mos Lake, just a stone's throw from the fire. Mos Lake sat in a valley in the Cold Peaks, and those mountains surrounded her, outlined in a rosy glow. The man—her summoner—was bundled against the cold with thick furs. It was hard to determine his expression in the flickering firelight, but Nanami had the impression of great patience and control.

"A moment, please." She walked to the lakeshore and pulled up a thick rope of water which she shook out into a cloak. Once

22

it settled on her shoulders, it was warm and dry, bearing no resemblance to its origins.

She returned to the man and exchanged bows with him before settling herself in the fire's circle across from him.

"I see the rumor is true—" he began but stopped as Nanami tossed a small blue sphere into the flames. The flames turned bright blue and the smoke sweet.

"I insist on honesty from my clients," Nanami explained at his cocked eyebrow.

The man smiled faintly. "Then that is two true rumors."

"What is your name?" Nanami asked.

The man shook his head. "I wish to be anonymous. Is that acceptable?"

"Perhaps," Nanami hedged, "but it will make delivery more difficult."

"That's alright—I want you to steal something so the owner doesn't have it, not so that I do. Keep it, throw it away, sell it, whatever you wish."

The flames stayed true blue. Surprised, Nanami studied the man more carefully.

Between recognizing her as the Sea Dragon's daughter and having cast the summoning so well, he must be an immortal. His beard and hair were thick and reminded Nanami of rusty iron, with patches of gray and orange. He wore his hair in a simple top knot with no ornamentation; his beard was perhaps six inches long and flared out at the tips like the roofs on her father's palace. Deep lines marked his forehead, as if his brow was usually furrowed, and there were putty bags under his eyes. Life had been hard on this man.

He had no visible weapons (personally, Nanami had five

weapons concealed on her body), but he moved as if there was a sword at his right hip—his hand had moved there automatically when she had added the truth detector to the flames. He was very broad, but not fat, and Nanami suspected that weapons or no, this man would do well in a fight. He met her gaze boldly, giving Nanami a sense of directness and honesty—not common in the clients of a thief. She had to admit, she was curious about this job.

"So who's the owner?" she asked.

When his expression objected, she added, "I don't need a name, but at least their relation to you or..." She waved to indicate the variety of options.

He nodded once. "My daughter's future betrothed. The man's a drunkard. He has an earthenware jug that dispenses limitless alcohol. I want you to steal it so that when he comes to the betrothal ceremony in seven days, he's sober—or at least less intoxicated than usual."

Nanami frowned. "If you don't want your daughter to marry a sot, why don't you just stop the betrothal?"

"There's nothing I can do." The flames lost their brilliant blue, and Nanami arched a brow in challenge.

"Very well," amended the man, "there is nothing I am willing to do. The betrothal was arranged by my father, to strengthen the ties between our family and the drunk's. It would be worse for my daughter if I intervened directly."

The flames turned blue again, showing he believed his words.

"Very well, I can accept that. What are you willing to pay for this undertaking?"

"The means to complete it." He offered her a yellow leather

pouch, tooled with flowers. Nanami manipulated the bag for a moment—it was some sort of powder—and opened it gingerly. Although he could not have summoned her with malicious intent, anything valuable enough for her to accept as payment might be very volatile. The powder shimmered white in the firelight and smelled of the ocean.

Nanami's eyes widened despite herself. "Nishikai powder? I haven't had any of this in quite some time..."

"I would imagine not, given how angry your father must be with your vocation."

Nanami's lips thinned. "His loss is your gain."

"Indeed," replied her client lightly. "You'll need to shrink the Infinite Jug to carry it away—it's as high as your hip and must be at least twice your weight. But there is plenty of powder—what's left is your payment. And the Jug itself, of course."

Nanami nodded. "You are generous—which makes me wonder, what power does this sot have?"

"Nothing you need be concerned about."

The flames stayed blue, but Nanami pursued it further. "This isn't some petty squabble among minor immortals, not if you're paying with nishikai powder."

The man glared at her. She waited.

"He's a god," he conceded, "but only because he was born one. He is useless. He has been trained with a sword, but he is no warrior. He has no skills worth mentioning." Still blue.

Nanami considered. There were at least a thousand gods, most of whom had far smaller spring of power than Nanami. And she could sympathize with this man and his daughter; she could well imagine the humiliation of a drunk groom, especially in an arranged marriage. That had been the silver lining of her estrangement, that she no longer need dread such a fate.

To her client, she nodded and said, "I'll take the job. Describe the Infinite Jug in detail, please."

XIAO dragged the Infinite Jug across the wrap-around porch of his favorite guest house. The massive black jug scratched the wide wooden planks, but his hostess wouldn't care, and the jug was murder to lift. When the spigot overhung the edge of the porch, Xiao grabbed an earthenware cup that had been discarded in the shrubbery the day before. He rinsed it with the rice wine from the jug and dumped the cloudy yellow liquid and a decent amount of dirt on the ground. He then refilled his cup and took a swig.

Xiao's father had made the Infinite Jug, and since he rarely drank himself, it was perhaps not surprising that the wine it dispensed wasn't particularly good or strong alcohol. However, over the past millennium, Xiao had grown accustomed to it. Its comfortable taste eased the knots of Xiao's stomach and helped him greet each morning.

Xiao woke up feeling anxious most days, which was stupid. There was nothing about which he needed to worry. He had relatively few worshippers and their prayers were usually easily answered. No one dared threaten him or give him a hard time about anything since his parents were second only to the Sun Emperor himself in power. He spent most of his days on Earth, frittering away the time. Sometimes he'd visit Jin at the Sun Palace, but she always grew tired of his company in less than a month.

Well, so, perhaps this morning his anxiety actually had an excuse. The formal betrothal ceremony for Jin and him was exactly a week from today. Xiao sighed and drained his cup.

He sat down on the wide wooden steps leading up to the pavilion, refilled his cup, and rested his back against the jug. He didn't drink right away, instead looking up at the dawn sky through the branches overhead. They were only sparsely leafed this early in the spring, and the branches were silhouetted against the pink and blue sky. He knew they'd inspire Jin to write poetry or paint a picture or create some entirely new art form to record their beauty.

Xiao sipped at his drink again.

The first person who'd ever drunk with him was Jin. They'd both been adolescents, though Jin had already reached her full height and Xiao had been noticing for some time that other parts of her had been growing instead. Xiao, while taller than Jin, had been inches shorter than he was now and skinny as a reed. But after two cups, they'd both been rather giggly, and he'd decided to kiss her.

She'd turned her head at the last moment, so his lips had met her ear instead of her mouth.

"Don't!" Jin had said very sternly, almost angrily, before getting up and walking away. The weird thing was, he'd never wanted to kiss her again after that day. Their relationship had never transitioned past friendship... or rather kinship because although they weren't lovers, they were closer than friends.

Once the betrothal ceremony was held, that was it. They would have to get married or they'd lose both their magic and their immortality. If Xiao tried to kiss Jin now, would she still turn her face and order him not to?

He was more than half-convinced that she was asexual—as far he knew, she'd never even experienced sexual attraction. And if that was the case, maybe it was better that she marry him rather than anyone else because he'd love her anyway, but...

But that wasn't what he wanted.

A hand fell on his shoulder, startling Xiao out of his reverie.

It was a male immortal with a youthful face. He grinned at Xiao and said, "You do start early, don't you?"

Xiao smirked back, but the words hurt a little. Unlike the revelers who joined him wherever he went, he wasn't drinking for fun. He was drinking because he couldn't seem to stop. And yes, even though he pretended to be in control, to be indulging because he could, the little remarks that pointed to the truth were stings that only alcohol soothed.

"Want some?"

"Sure." And the other man leaned forward and kissed Xiao slowly. He leaned back and said, rather smugly, "That's enough for me."

Xiao laughed, even though he didn't really find it funny or charming. This man had a deep insecurity and craved Xiao's approval. Just like last night, Xiao couldn't deny him. For most of his life, he had been keenly aware of others' wishes and desires, and he found it almost impossible not to appease them if he could. He was, after all, the God of Pleasure.

BY the time Nanami's client left, dawn had stretched across the sky and the small fire had nearly burnt out. Although it was still chilly, she decided to change her clothes before leaving herself.

She transformed her dark blue cloak from Mos Lake into a simple woman's kimono of the same color. She made it hang unusually low in back to reveal her dragon claw tattoo. That was a bit dishonest, since she was disowned and her father would not avenge her death, but enough people had them that it wouldn't identify her, and her father was scary enough that it would protect her from casual violence. Besides, even though she didn't like being lied to, Nanami wasn't above bending the truth if it made her own work easier.

She walked to the lake and scattered a handful of water on the kimono. Silver blossoming plum branch embroidery appeared where the drops fell. Nanami removed her outer clothes, streaky gray trousers and wraparound shirt that were excellent for cat-burglary but ill-suited for socializing. She released her mid-length navy hair from her usual half-up twist and combed it out with her fingers. From the pockets in her knee length underpants, she took out a hair stick with a small, green-enameled waterlily on the end and used it to pin her hair in a bun at the nape of her neck. She drew the kimono over her underclothes and checked the lay to make sure her forearm sheaths and the throwing stars wrapped on her stomach were not immediately obvious. Being too blatant with one's weapons brought the wrong kind of attention. Nanami tied her spare clothes into a neat bundle on the end of a long stick.

With a grin, Nanami teleported.

Her excitement lent her strength—she spent only twenty or so minutes between before she reappeared on a dirt road surrounded by trees with budding leaves. A few hundred miles south of Mos Lake, the air was warmer and smelled of spring. It would take her about three hours to walk to the Wood

Pavilions, where her client was sure his prospective son-in-law was squandering his time. Enjoying the weather and the scenery, Nanami whistled an old bawdy song as she walked.

After a half an hour, she heard a cart approaching behind her, and Nanami moved to the side.

"Hello, Lady," called the mortal driver, a farmer by the looks of him. He slowed the donkey as they came abreast of her. "Headed to the Pavilion?"

"You have a keen eye, Uncle," Nanami said, acknowledging that she was indeed an immortal. The Wood Pavilions belonged to Haraa the Warden. Like Nanami's father, Haraa was one of the Nine Colors and very powerful. Unlike Nanami's father, Haraa had no ambition and no formality— the Wood Pavilions were where immortals and gods congregated on Earth for an endless celebration. There was only one rule: Don't damage the flora. It was not without its dangers, but Nanami enjoyed it.

"If you'd like, Lady, you could ride next to me."

Nanami smiled broadly. "Blessings on your house, Uncle, for your kindness." Like most immortal blessings, Nanami's wasn't worth much, but some mortals liked to collect them just the same. She was happy to offer it in exchange for a ride. The farmer stopped the cart and Nanami climbed on the back.

"I thought I recognized the tune you were whistling," said the farmer as the donkey resumed pulling. "Was it the Moon and Night's Monks?"

"Uncle has a good ear!"

He laughed. "I used to know all thirty verses! Let me see, how does the chorus go...

A silly lady's vow, a foolish man's word

No more would they plow, to please their Lords.
But were their Lords pleased? No, not a bit.
Not a bit, not a bit.
For what pleases the Moon, and what pleases the Night,
But two souls in a swoon, a tup in moonlight?"
Nanami laughed. "Well sung!"
The farmer grinned widely. "I always loved that story."
"What man doesn't?" asked Nanami dryly, and the farmer laughed.

"No, no, it's not the earthiness—I mean, maybe when I was a youth, but not now. I like how the monks are so sure they have to sacrifice their pleasure, but then the Moon and Night deities want the opposite. People always think they have to punish themselves—to suffer—to be worthy, but to my thinking the world is better when we're happy and loved."

Nanami smiled faintly. "A romantic, Uncle?"

He laughed again. "You've caught me! Been married twenty-six years, and still think my wife's the prettiest woman on Earth."

Nanami was envious. She was nearly twenty-six *thousand* years old, and she had never felt that way about anyone. "Then maybe I should pray to the Moon Goddess, too."

The man shook his head. "Actually, I prayed to her son."

"The God of Pleasure?" Nanami asked in disbelief.

"Yup—I was still just looking for a good time, rather than marriage and love, but I swear he brought me to my wife. I still thank him every prayer day—I say a good dose of pleasure is what any marriage needs."

"Hmm." The God of Pleasure was all about sex. It made an odd sort of sense, she supposed, since his parents, the Moon

Goddess and the Night God, were the patrons of romantic love. They had invented marriage, oh, almost fifty thousand years ago. But Nanami didn't like sex. She had gotten rid of her virginity after being disowned—an immature attempt to spite her father—and she had never seen fit to repeat the experience. "Thanks for the tip," she told the farmer, even as she thought she'd never pray to such a god.

They continued to talk about nothing and everything—the farmer was quite the philosopher—and it wasn't long before they reached the Wood Pavilions. Nanami could see the famous curved green roofs above the trees, but raucous laughter and joyful music would have told her just as clearly.

"Thank you, again, Uncle," she told the farmer as he stopped the cart. "Blessings on you and your wife." He waved and left.

Nanami left the road to follow a gravel path that wound beneath the trees. The air smelled green, it was so overwhelmingly lush here. Up ahead, she could hear the happy gurgling of a brook, which the path soon met at a bench with several long-handled drinking cups. The water ran fast and clear, so Nanami took one and reached down to fill it in the brook. The water tasted of spring and metal. She found herself smiling as she set the cup back on the bench.

Not much further along the path, Nanami met her first group of partygoers. The three immortal women were scantily dressed and smelled of alcohol, so she asked them where to get a cup of rice wine on the chance it would lead to the Infinite Jug. One of them shoved a clay cup at her with a giggle. "Here, have mine—I can get more from Xiao."

"Xiao?" asked Nanami.

"Xiao is the best!" said another. "He always gives wine to everyone! And he's so handsome. I hope he'll take us to bed soon."

Nanami deliberately spilled all the wine she had been offered as she accepted it from the woman's hand. "Oh, I'm sorry! I'll refill it, if you'll just point me in the right direction."

"We'll take you ourselves! We need more anyway," said the woman.

The Wood Pavilions were a maze. There were about thirty of them, spread out over fifty wooded acres, linked by gravel paths and stone bridges. There were streams and ponds and large boulders throughout the wild gardens, and the whole thing was laid out in a haphazard manner, Haraa adding pavilions whenever her guests filled the current ones. The pavilions themselves ranged from one to four stories, and their styles varied widely, though they all featured the green copper roofs that Nanami had seen from the road.

Winding along these paths with three silly women stretched Nanami's patience. They were very tipsy and took several loops, but she was playing the role of someone with nowhere better to be. Finally the four of them reached a three-story pavilion with a massive earthenware jar on the porch. It was an ugly thing, unglazed and dirty, remarkable only for the clever spigot near its base, that could be stoppered and unstoppered by the twist of a handle. It matched the description she'd received. People were helping themselves to the wine while watching two men wrestle in a small pond. They were topless and their wet trousers clung to their legs. They were both laughing as they splashed about and generally made a mess. Nanami almost called out to them to mind the waterlilies, for it would bring Haraa's wrath down on all of them if they ripped a flower, but one of them seemed particularly mindful of this, and kept his rival from doing any harm.

Nanami watched that man for a long time; she was a little embarrassed to admit she found him excessively appealing. He was well-muscled, and his hair was long and deepest black. He had a rich, merry laugh that made her laugh too—everyone seemed to find it equally engaging, as most of the crowd joined in. And when he laughed, two deep dimples appeared in his full cheeks as his eyes were lost beneath fat lids. With a high, pointed nose and expressive, full lips, every one of his features was almost a caricature of itself, and yet they balanced each other into a face of unparalleled charm and good will. Nanami could not imagine anyone disliking this man.

"Who is that?" she asked one of her tipsy guides.

"Oh, that's Xiao! It's his wine jug," the girl trilled. "We're all in love with him. But don't worry, he spreads his favors quite generously among anyone who wants them."

Although it wasn't totally confirmed, Nanami was sure that Xiao was going to be betrothed to her client's daughter in a week's time. The thought upset her, almost as much as the idea of him "spreading his favors" annoyed her. Swift on the heels of those emotions came irritation for feeling them.

Nanami decided to fade back, to observe rather than engage. But just then, Xiao succeeded in dunking his opponent. He stepped out of the pond, and several admirers rushed him. It should have been easy to slip away in the excitement, but Xiao looked directly at her and *smiled*.

Nanami was familiar with social smiles and children's smiles; smiles of amusement and self-deprecating smiles. This smile though... this smile was just for her. It snatched her breath and made her heartbeat faster. It was utterly ridiculous; it was embarrassing. She couldn't move. This smile promised love, unconditional, life-changing love, the type Nanami craved so badly that she had denied all interest in it.

Beneath those lazy fat lids, his lavender eyes never left her own as he made his way effortlessly through the crowd to her.

"Hello," he said, and his voice reminded Nanami of lying under the stars while sweet potatoes roasted in the coals. "Please, call me Xiao. Who might you be?"

"I'm—" Nanami just caught herself from making a proper introduction. "I'm not interested," she barked, and immediately regretted the words. His thick black brows climbed his forehead.

"Not Interested?" he repeated. "An unusual name."

The crowd at his back laughed merrily, and Nanami's face burned. She almost teleported away right then. Thankfully she caught herself—Nanami knew she wouldn't have enough power to return today.

"Please," he said, waving to a path, "won't you walk with me a way? Perhaps you can explain what you aren't interested in?" His smile was gone, but his solemn gaze was no less appealing.

Well, I need to confirm this is the man, Nanami told herself. But even she knew that wasn't the real reason she said yes.

THE woman's focus on him was so intense, it burst through Xiao's alcohol induced euphoria. He felt the disappointment of the crowd as he left with her, and though he hated to let anyone down, he just couldn't resist.

Between her not quite articulated desire, her repressed

sexuality, and her hunger for affection, she had responded to him on a deep level.

As they strolled through Haraa's wild gardens, Xiao studied her. She was shorter even than Jin, probably a foot shorter than Xiao himself. She was quite slender; the bun at her nape drew attention to the slimness of her neck. But she didn't seem delicate. Instead she moved with a deft grace that suggested martial prowess. Her hair just brushed her shoulders—far shorter than Jin's hair, which touched the ground unbound, and only half the length of Xiao's. It was a blue so deep as to be mistaken for black. Her loose bangs very nicely framed a round face with dark narrow eyes that constantly scanned their surroundings. Xiao suspected there was very little they missed. Overall, even if she wasn't a rare beauty like Jin, Xiao found her interesting and appealing, and his favorite feature was her full lower lip, which she was currently teasing with small white teeth.

When they were out of earshot of the crowd, Xiao finally asked, "So what aren't you interested in?"

She looked at him suspiciously, so he gave her his most innocent smile.

"I'm not—those women told me—no sex." Xiao could just make out a flush on her tanned cheeks and neck—he wouldn't have minded seeing where else it reached.

Aloud he said, "I didn't offer—yet. And you needn't worry—I only offer if it's welcome."

The woman snorted. "And like every man, I suppose you think you can tell?"

"Not like every man," he countered, "but yes, I can tell." His sensitivity was both burden and blessing.

She crossed her arms and rolled her eyes. Xiao liked that too—Jin would never do something so inelegant.

"Might I ask your name?" he said mildly.

"Call me Nana," she said after a moment. Then, unexpectedly, "Are you celebrating anything in particular?"

"Indeed—the last days of my freedom. My parents have arranged a betrothal for me." And he should be celebrating, despite his doubts. Besides being beautiful, Jin was the person to whom he was the closest, and she was also extremely nice. Maybe too nice. She would run herself ragged over an idle remark.

"You don't love her, then?"

Xiao took in Nana's calculating eyes and grinned. "I don't want to talk about my betrothed—let's talk about you."

She stepped back. "No, thank you—you should return to your alcohol. That crowd will soon have it empty."

"Not at all," he reassured her. "It never empties—perhaps I could offer you some?"

She snorted. "I'm even less interested in your alcohol than I am in you."

That wouldn't be hard, Xiao thought, *as you are very, very interested in me.* But as long as she continued to deny her needs, her urges... well, there wasn't anything for him to do.

He watched her walk away though. It was a pity she didn't want his expertise. He never understood why people were ashamed of their sexuality.

After she was out of sight, he returned to the Infinite Jug and drank straight from the spigot as his "friends" cheered.

ALMOST no light found Nanami stretched out on the upper

branch of the giant gingko tree. She was more than twenty feet above the ground, her feet braced against the trunk, toes clutching the thick ridges of bark through her cotton soles, and her hands were wrapped around the branch beneath her, carefully placed so as to not damage the new spring leaves. Her kimono had been returned to its original state, adding a little bit of Mos Lake to the pond where Xiao had wrestled, and she was once again in her streaky gray wrap-around shirt and loose trousers, bound tight at the waist and at her calves, cloth boots with a split toe, and a large kerchief that hid all of her face but her eyes. She was all but invisible in the dark of the night.

The gingko was fortuitously placed. When she turned her head to the left, she could see straight into the pavilion's third floor, which Xiao had taken as his bedroom. The room was plain. Branch lattices had green leaves stretched almost to transparency across them. The only furniture was a single low table that had been shoved into a corner. Every day, when he retired for the night, Xiao dragged the Infinite Jug in behind him and set it on that table, as it was now. The rest of the room was a swirl of silks and pillows that provided the perfect setting for Xiao's orgies.

And orgies he had. As Nanami's guide had claimed, Xiao was willing to partner anyone who asked, and he seemingly had no boundaries. Although Nanami's spying was intended purely for practical reconnaissance, over the past three nights, it had taken on voyeuristic overtones, like watching the pictures from a pillow book come to life.

It was as if Nanami had fallen through a trapdoor in her own mind into a secret room that had safely contained her sexuality until now. She felt ignorant and awkward—puberty all over again. *How is it that I still don't know myself?*

She had made a choice, so many years ago, to be detached from romance, from physical desire. She had always despised her parents for their blatant displays of affection; she had been contemptuous of the courtiers who had allowed themselves to be humiliated for the sake of "love." She had her one uncomfortable and unpleasant experience that had confirmed all her biases about sex. So why now, against her better judgment, against her own inclination, did she now feel such a keen yearning for something she had never needed before? Last night she had, in a moment of frustration and weakness, heeded that farmer's advice and prayed to the God of Pleasure, asking his aid in navigating this previously closed room of her own psyche.

It was all Xiao's fault.

His appeal, Nanami had realized, was in his total dedication to his companion's delight. A generosity of self that was too extreme, both frightening and alluring to Nanami. She supposed that sex must be another of this man's addictions—for as her client had said, he was indeed an alcoholic, living in a state of inebriation. And the only power that Nanami had seen was his improbable ability to continue his sexual exploits through it. Today he had four guests, all of whom seemed equally pleased to be present.

If you wanted, you could join them, a little voice whispered. Frustrated with herself, Nanami turned her face away from the escapades in the room. She continued to listen closely though, rationalizing that she needed to know when they fell asleep—she had determined that she had a solid hour once they all passed out to get in and extract the jar.

After a few hours, no more laughter or whispers came from the room, and Nanami looked back. A lamp was burning dimly, allowing her to see that everyone indeed appeared to be asleep. *There's no reason to wait another day*, Nanami admitted to herself. Everything had been very predictable, boring even, given that she had abstained from drinking.

Nanami rose and began to run down the branch—it bent beneath her footfalls, but she moved so quickly, that it hardly affected her. A flying leap and she was holding the windowsill.

Nanami pulled herself up and into the window, careful to keep noise to a minimum. Though, having witnessed their drinking all day, she was sure the five sleepers would not easily rouse.

She picked her way around the sleepers to the Infinite Jug, setting each foot down slowly as to not send tremors through the mats. She took the pouch of nishikai powder from inside her shirt and extracted a pinch. She flung it at the jug and willed it to be smaller.

The jug immediately began to shrink. By the time Nanami had replaced the nishikai powder in her shirt, the jug was no bigger than her fist. Nanami picked it up and examined it. She felt irrationally disappointed—she was not ready for this job to be done.

"That's not what you really want." Nanami's head jerked up and she found Xiao watching her. He was alone amid the sumptuous silks, smiling in invitation. Nanami's brow knitted.

"They were an illusion," he said apologetically.

But illusions didn't usually affect her—an inheritance from her father that couldn't be lost even if he disowned her. If this man had influenced her senses, he had far more power than the run-of-the-mill god.

Nanami slipped the Jug into her shirt and shifted onto the balls of her feet.

His lush lips quirked upward, revealing his dimples. "You're so beautiful."

Stunned, Nanami touched her face, but no, her kerchief still covered all but her eyes. She was immediately irritated with herself for checking—for a moment she had been unreasonably pleased by the compliment, but he was just a confused drunk.

"Not because of your face," he went on, as if he heard her thoughts, "it's you. The economy of your movements, the surety in your steps—it's almost as if you're dancing. You know exactly how to move, and you embody grace. Your competence is your beauty."

Throughout her childhood, she had believed herself plain—and compared to the potent, fulsome beauties of her father's court, her soft prettiness had indeed seemed unremarkable. Her eyes were even and narrow, slightly hooded, and dark as the deepest ocean. Her navy hair was thin with a slight wave, and did not work well with elaborate court styles, but now that she wore long bangs and tied it half up, it flattered her round face. She had a thin, straight nose, and small lips, the bottom just slightly plumper than the top. But Xiao, the drunk who supposedly had no particular skills, shook her with his insight. Her appeal came from her inner confidence. It was only after she left her father's court that she had learned who she was, and how to like that person, and so became pretty.

Nanami prepared to run, but Xiao said, "Don't move," and she was caught like a fly in honey.

"How?" she gasped. "How did you know I was watching? How did you cast an illusion? How do you hold me now?"

He blinked. "Because you want me. You prayed to me, worshipped me, gave me power over you."

"What! Of course I didn't!"

He rose and cocked his head. "Don't you know who I am?"

"Xiao!"

He started laughing. "The person who sent you after the Jug really didn't tell you?"

"He said you had no power that need concern me! It was the truth." Xiao walked close to her, steadier than she expected.

"Perhaps it was, before you yearned for me. I am Laughter in the Shadows. God of Pleasure." He laid a hand against her face. Nanami leaned into its warm strength and closed her eyes. She should be mortified, and yet he was right. She did want him. Badly.

His other hand snaked around her back and pulled her against him. Nanami leaned in, embracing physical desire for the first time in her life. The hand cradling her head jerked down the scarf covering her mouth, and then his lips brushed hers. She whimpered. His hand traveled down, caressing the side of her ribs, her waist, her hip. His mouth burned a trail of kisses to her ear, which he suckled gently. She gasped, her lips parting.

And then, when she had lost her focus and was wholly in his power, he made two mistakes. One, he returned his mouth to hers and thrust his tongue deep, sharing with her the bitter taste of cheap wine. Two, his hand slipped into her shirt and wrapped around the shrunken Infinite Jug.

Fury and disappointment broke his spell. Nanami wrapped

her right hand in his hair, spreading a few grains of nishikai powder that had clung to her fingers into it.

She willed him to shrink.

"What—" He tried to pull away from her, but she was holding him tightly.

"Let go of me," he commanded.

Nanami smiled bitterly. "You can't control me anymore— your alcoholism killed my desire for you." When he was no taller than her palm, she stuffed him into a very special white silk bag that was tied to her essence so that only she could remove whatever was inside.

"Grooms should be sober for their betrothals," she told the writhing bag. "I'm going to make sure you arrive that way."

TWO nights after his kidnapping, Xiao was still shrunken, smaller than his own hand ought to be. His captor had trapped him under a rough bamboo cage that he could have crushed, had he been full-size. He hadn't tried to teleport away yet because one, he didn't have nishikai powder of his own, two, he didn't intend to leave until he had a route to revenge, and three, because he was feeling terrible.

Yesterday he'd vomited several times (alcohol withdrawal, Nanami had smugly informed him, as if he didn't know), and the consequent reek didn't help his headache. He secretly had been a little alarmed that his body had reacted so strongly to a lack of alcohol. He knew, of course, that too much alcohol poisoned mortals, but it rarely impacted immortals. But then again, Xiao couldn't remember the last time he hadn't any wine in his system, so he supposed it wasn't shocking he had developed some sort of dependence on it.

That thought made him anxious, which made him really want his morning drink, and he tightened his arm around the bamboo bar of his cage until it was almost painful to distract himself.

He also glared at his captor. She sat a few feet away, boiling water over a campfire and ignoring him so studiously that it was obvious she was aware of everything he did.

"I'm thirsty," he called to her. For about the hundredth time. She never responded, but her shoulders almost always hitched a little higher.

This time was no exception, and Xiao decided to take a gamble. "*Nanami,* I'm thirsty!"

This time she whirled, and through gritted teeth snarled, "So drink the water I gave you!"

Xiao smirked. Annoying her didn't even come close to an adequate revenge but it was a start. If she had just stolen the Infinite Jug—that he would have forgotten soon enough. The shrinking was infuriating, but it was *locking him in a cage* that was unforgivable.

He hated, hated being locked up. The bars here reminded him too much of the ones on his bedroom windows, even though they were bamboo rather than black iron. Given his current size and strength, they were just as unbreakable.

So he would annoy her for now, and then, when he got out of here...

Well, he wasn't sure. He had never been this angry at anyone, except maybe his parents. But this deed would change her life forever, he would make sure of that.

"I want wine, not water."

"I haven't got any."

"Excuse me?" Xiao slapped a bar in his irritation. "What about my jug?"

Her chin dropped, and her lips parted. Xiao didn't doubt she was telling the truth when she said, "I forgot about the jug!" She pulled it out of her sash. "I need to deal with this, then I'll be back."

Panic hit Xiao right in the gut. What if something happened to her? What if he was stuck in this cage forever? "You can't leave," he blurted. "What if—how can I be sure you'll come back?" He tried once again to break a bamboo bar.

She stared at him a moment, and Xiao didn't mind the pity in her eyes, if it meant she let him out. "Even if I didn't return, someone would come looking if you didn't show up at the betrothal. The Moon and Night deities should have no trouble finding you."

Xiao scoffed and stepped back from the cage. "I wasn't worried. Just trying to get you to free me."

She bit her lip, shrugged, and then she was gone, the Infinite Jug with her.

Stress built in Xiao until he jumped up and down and yelled. He then took several big gulps of air. She was right. Even if she abandoned him, somebody would find him in less than a week.

He rubbed his face. What a horrid place to be stuck for a week. His robes were disgusting too, for he hadn't entirely missed them when he vomited.

"Well, at least that water will be good for something."

He stripped and washed away first the vomit from the ground, then scrubbed his robes and hung them to dry. He then sluiced water from the cup over himself, rinsing away any trace of bile and scrubbing dirt from his hair. He then collected one of the chestnuts that Nanami had left him and sat on the cloth bed she provided.

He did not need to eat, being of shadow and twilight, but he hated going without food. The fact that she had left him so much actually made him a little less mad at her—but would it have killed her to give him one cup of wine before making off with his jug?

The normally simple task of shelling the chestnut took him the better part of an hour and required hammering the stupid thing on a boulder—well, a stone that was bigger than his current size. But he finally managed and found that it tasted more delicious than any delicacy ever served in the Sun Court.

As he ate, he found himself thinking about the way Nanami had forgotten that she even had the jug—her official task. That suggested that she had forgotten the jug because of Xiao.

He turned the chestnut over in his hands. He knew that she had tumbled into lust with him the moment she saw him. But the way she took his kiss so personally, the fact his ulterior motives for seduction had upset her so much that she had abducted him—that seemed like more than lust.

Such an impulsive action didn't match the stories he had heard about her. Nanami was tens of millennia old, and she had evaded the Goddess of Justice for most of that time. She was said to steal only when someone deserved to lose what they had or someone else needed it more. Being caught by Xiao had only been because of the prayer she had sent him. Otherwise she would have succeeded. Even the fact she had prayed to him felt a little out of character, though admittedly stories could be wrong, and Xiao hadn't known her long.

Still, it suggested that she felt more than lust for him. Was her overreaction because she liked him? Even if it was simply infatuation, Xiao might be able to turn the tables on her.

NANAMI teleported the Infinite Jug back to Mos Lake, where this commission had begun. It was a relatively isolated place with plenty of water, which gave her options for dealing with the jug.

Her first choice would be to break it, of course, and scatter the pieces, because although she didn't object to alcohol generally, she didn't see any good coming from the possession of a limitless supply of cheap wine. The jug's purpose was clear—to feed an addiction.

Nanami knew a little about addiction, having struggled with her own kleptomania, and the very existence of the jug offended her. The fact that Xiao's father—if he really was the Night God, and given Xiao's powerful illusion, Nanami supposed he must be—had created such a thing for his son made her mad on Xiao's behalf. It also made her unsure if she could destroy the jug.

The Nine Colors were hundreds of times more powerful than other immortals and even Nanami, the daughter of one Color, couldn't match them. She'd tried to destroy one of their artifacts before and had failed miserably. Really, she wished that they'd give a little more thought to the long-term consequences before making immensely powerful objects that no one else could destroy. But perhaps miracles like the Great Willow and the Sanctuary Caves made up for abominations like the Sowon Gold and the Infinite Jug...

Nanami selected a large piece of driftwood and swung it

against the Infinite Jug. Wood splinters flew everywhere without even making a scratch. She tried a rock next. Despite being granite, it shattered against the coarse-looking clay.

She shaped a water whip from Mos Lake and lashed the jug to no avail.

She'd sink it then.

Nanami made the water of the lake solid beneath her feet and dragged the jug behind her. When she reached the middle of the lake, she stopped supporting the cursed jug. It sank mostly down and then bobbed near the surface with just the crown of the jug showing.

Fate was laughing at her today! The wine inside must be lighter than the water. Well, it wasn't lighter than air. Nanami jumped on the jug, creating an air pocket around herself and the jug. By driving the water out of the way in front of her, the jug plummeted down to the bottom of the lake, Nanami with it.

Soon the world was nothing but deep indigo and the temperature grew bitterly cold, but it exuded familiar comfort to Nanami. This was, in some ways, her natural state, at least on her father's side. It reminded her a little bit of the Sea Palace, a thought that she pushed away.

At the bottom, she pulled water over the top of the jug as if tying it to the ground. She changed the water to stone, a massive sapphire slab holding down the jug.

She almost wished her father could see her now—it was magic worthy of his daughter.

No, magic worthy of me, she corrected. Who cared if the Sea Dragon acknowledged her or not?

She stared at the slab for a moment, reluctant to go back to the God of Pleasure when she had used so much of her power already but...

She remembered his eyes when she said she was leaving. Despite his later claim to have been messing with her, Nanami was pretty sure that he was scared to be alone. He found being constrained deeply upsetting, and Nanami regretted her impulsive kidnapping. She rubbed her face. She'd feel a bigger fool if she just released him after all that pontificating she'd done about grooms being sober.

Just two more days, then she'd free him and never see him again, most likely.

Nanami moved between to return.

WHEN Nanami reappeared at the campground, Xiao had finished his preparations.

Using the charred chestnut shells and a bit of water, he had made a rough ink and written on one of the blankets she'd given him—a love story of the greatest thief in the world and the useless god she stole. When she returned him to full size, he just had to make sure the blanket changed with him, and he'd have the perfect binding for her.

In the meantime, it was carefully folded and hidden.

Nanami glanced at him when she returned to campground, and immediately flushed, her eyes lingering on his exposed chest. Xiao resumed his post at the bars, clad in nothing but his still damp underwear.

She started to turn her head away, but then she swung it back at him.

"Earlier, you called me Nanami."

Xiao grinned. It was amazing how much better he felt now

that he had gotten under her skin. "And you responded."

She gritted her teeth. "Yes, you're right, I am Nanami the Thief."

Xiao rubbed his lower lip with his thumb. "It was pretty obvious when I thought about it. The tattoo on your back, the water magic, the stealing, and oh, your desperation for affection. Who else could you be but the Sea Dragon's disowned daughter?"

Her face went totally stiff and Xiao knew he'd struck a nerve. "You aren't so wanted yourself, the useless God of Pleasure. I feel sorry for the Moon and Night deities—after such a disappointment as yourself, no wonder they didn't have more children."

Xiao laughed. "That's the best you can do, really? How trite." He had all of her attention now. "I'm curious though, what gives you the gall to steal whatever you want?"

"Because I can," she said. "Isn't power the only law in this world? Haven't your parents taught you that yet? Besides, it isn't what I want—it's what my clients want. I don't steal for myself."

"Really? I thought you stole me for yourself."

Nanami's mouth dropped, and Xiao gave himself a mental high five. "I didn't," she sputtered. "Your father-in-law asked me to make sure you were sober this fifth day. I simply realized stealing the jug was not enough to complete my commission."

Xiao wanted to poke that—did she believe her lie?—but there was something more pressing. "Did you say my father-in-law? As in, the father of my betrothed?"

"Yes," she said with the confidence of belief.

Xiao didn't know who had hired the thief, but he was sure

it had not been the Sun Emperor, despite her claim that Jin's father was her employer. If Aka had wanted him sober, he would have just burned all the toxins from Xiao's bloodstream. He'd done it once before, when Xiao had puked on his foot at a party.

Did Nanami not know who he was marrying? Well, he wasn't going to enlighten her—she'd find out when he brought her to the Sun Palace, and he would savor the surprise.

THE next two days passed both too quickly and too slowly.

Nanami was aware that Xiao had gotten the better of her when she revealed the identity of her client, so she refused to tell him any more about the job. This seemed to amuse him more than anything, but Nanami kept mute all the same.

When he wasn't trying to irritate her, Xiao made outrageous propositions. Nanami had been closer to accepting them than she liked to admit. And that irritated her more than his obvious teasing because she was pretty sure he knew how much he tempted her. So it was a relief when the day of his betrothal finally arrived.

Xiao asked to go in the morning, with the excuse that he needed to bathe and dress. She believed him, but she didn't trust him to follow through.

"I let you go now, you'll be drunk by evening."

He winked. "I'm reformed, Nanami. You've so moved me that I want to be a better man."

She'd snorted, though she wondered. He hadn't asked for wine since she'd hidden the jug, and the side effects from withdrawal seemed to have abated. There was something driving him, something that had at least temporarily replaced his cravings.

"I'll return you to your original size, if you don't teleport as soon as you're able," Nanami offered when the sky turned orange.

"Why would I leave your side a moment before I must?"

Fate, she pitied his betrothed. That mouth! Of course, kissing it might compensate for listening to it...

She lifted the bamboo cage and sprinkled some nishikai powder. He quickly regained his full size.

Xiao smiled at her, and Nanami waited for him to leave first, loathe to lose the smile that promised her everything.

She didn't expect Xiao to sweep a dirty blanket around her shoulders and snag her close. Nanami tried to teleport then, but she couldn't. He had bound her to him.

"I'd like to formally invite you to my betrothal ceremony," he told her with a chuck under the chin. Those lavender eyes sparkled with satisfaction. "There's someone you need to point out to me."

2

The Useless Betrothal

JIN paused on the crown of the vermilion bridge that arched high over a pond to the pavilion at its center. The day was fine, as it always was at the Sun Palace, the water glistening silver in the bright light. The circular pavilion had a series of slender vermilion columns supporting its gold roof, all set on black stone that rose out of the pond. It had two bridges leading to shore, and Jin stood on the apex of one. From her vantage point, she could see the tea things were set on the round table, but instead of waiting on his stool, as he usually was, Aka stood next to a balustrade, his back to her. His dark red hair hung loose, reaching his waist, just a few shades deeper than his red silk robes. They were unusually plain, devoid of embroidery. She couldn't see his face, but with the certainty she sometimes had regarding others, Jin knew he was pensive, caught in the past.

It unsettled Jin to see Aka this way, not so much because of the darkness of his mood, albeit unusual, but because for the first time ever, she felt keenly aware of his age. Oh, she knew he was the oldest immortal, older even than her grandmother Neela, but while Neela's hair was gray and her face lined, Aka didn't even look old enough to be Jin's father.

After a moment, Jin continued down the bridge, though she began playing with the pink quartz beads hanging from her waist to wake her father from his reverie.

He turned to face her and smiled, though his dark red eyes remained melancholy.

"Ah, Sunlight Turns Petals Gold, you make my garden more beautiful every time you enter it."

Jin blushed at her full name and his compliment—a rosiness that was highly visible on her pale cheeks. Jin was the Goddess of Beauty, so she ought to be accustomed to such excessive compliments, but she had never heard them from her grandmother growing up. Her grandmother always said that Jin lacked her mother's vivacity and that it was unfortunate she hadn't inherited her coloring. Most people disagreed though— Jin's brother Karana claimed she had looked perfectly adorable and elegant at every age.

Jin's hair was a warm chestnut, with hints of fire. Like her father, she wore it loose at present, with just two clips behind her ears as ornamentation so that it hung to her ankles. Her eyes were a gold so brilliant that no less than five famous poets had lyricized them, to Jin's secret gratification. Secret because both her best friend, Xiao, and her grandmother had told her how ridiculous and embarrassing it was. She had delicate features in a heart-shaped face, and a delicate build with an hour-glass body. She just reached her father's shoulder.

Aka took her hands in his, and he kissed her lightly on the forehead. Then he led her to her stool and waited for her to arrange herself before sitting.

Jin waited patiently as Aka heated the tea with his hand, added the bright green powder to the bowl, and whisked it to a froth. He filled two small cups with a ladle and handed one to

Jin. She rotated it carefully in her hands, admiring the painted red horses that raced on its sides. She met her father's eyes and smiled—she had given him this cup herself, when she had returned to the Sun Palace to live. They drank in silence; the tea was the perfect temperature, just hot enough to lend itself to small sips. It tasted of summer. Jin pictured the tea plant, growing on a mountainside, its vibrant leaves collecting sunlight so that Jin could taste it now.

When she had swallowed her last sip, Jin placed her cup on the lacquer tray that held the serving bowl.

"Tonight is your betrothal ceremony," Aka noted. "Xiao has long been your closest friend. Will you be happy to marry him, Jin?"

Jin was surprised by the question. Instead of answering, she asked, "Is that what was weighing on you earlier? You seemed so sad, Papa. Please, tell me what you were thinking about?"

His dark red brows arched; his ruby-red eyes widened. Then he nodded slowly. "Yes, I was thinking of your betrothal—and another betrothal, a long time ago."

Jin waited patiently for him to find his thoughts.

"The first time I saw your mother, she was attending a mortal festival. She was on a float pulled by two plain horses, and she was wearing simple mortal clothes, but she was the most riveting thing I had ever seen. She was playing a flute and dancing, you know—but it wasn't just that which caught my attention. And it wasn't just her beauty—there was something else, something intangible... power, perhaps. I asked a man, a mortal man, who she was, and he said, 'Don't you know the Goddess of Thought?'" Aka laughed. "I was wearing my glamour ring, you know, so as not to be recognized as the Sun Emperor."

Jin sat very still, hardly daring to breathe, afraid that he might change his mind and stop telling the story at any moment. Her father had never spoken to her of her mother before; no one had. Jin had asked Neela about her a few times, and Neela had shaken her head, unwilling to speak.

"Aashchary," her father murmured, then smiled, sad and far away. "She was willing to become my lover for a night, but she had no interest in joining my court, in marrying me." He grew very quiet then, regret palpable, but Jin said nothing, hoping he would go on. Finally, her patience was rewarded.

"I did something... I did something I will always regret. I used my power to make sure a baby came of our single union. She came here, heavily pregnant, and said she had changed her mind. I married her without delay, triumphant, thinking only of myself. And then..." he laid a hand over Jin's. Their eyes met, and his were sadder than ever. "Well, you know your brother died in infancy."

Jin, afraid to touch his confession, asked only, "How did he die?"

His hand tightened convulsively on hers. "Fever, from an insect bite. Haraa was summoned, but... After that, I spelled the entire palace to keep such pests out."

Jin frowned. "But it's so rare that an immortal—"

"Yes, it is. And your mother—it broke her heart. For a while, I thought she'd never recover."

Jin wanted to ask more questions, but with Aka's pain so pronounced, she sat frozen with indecision.

After a moment, Aka said, "She was so happy when you were born, Jin. Zi visited with Xiao—still a baby himself—and Aashchary joked that perhaps you'd fall in love and get married." He smiled, his eyes still far away.

"After your mother died, Neela suggested that we make a contract. Zi, Hei, and I were all agreeable—it was easy to see how close the two of you were. And yet...

"You love him, but you never fell in love, have you?"

Jin turned her hand under his and gave it a gentle squeeze. "It is rare to find true love in a marriage. I can settle for a deep friendship."

Aka smiled, clearly pleased with her answer. Although her father could read most people's feelings, he always accepted her words at face value. They went on to speak of trivialities—the beauty of the water lilies on the pond, the shapes of the clouds overhead. Jin treasured this time all the same. Neela had taken Jin from the Sun Palace when she was still a toddler, just a millennium old, and had not let her return until Jin reached adulthood and Aka had insisted it was time for Jin to take her rightful place as his daughter. She had seen Aka only a handful of times outside the Sun Palace—twice at New Moon Manor, and twice when he had visited Neela's caravan.

Aka again took her hands and kissed her forehead. "I love you, dear heart. I so want you to be happy."

"I am happy, Papa."

He smiled. "I want to preserve it then. That happiness is a gift to me—someday you will have children, and you will understand." He handed her a red silk pouch, embroidered with dayflowers in brilliantly blue thread.

"I had this made for your mother, for when your baby brother was born, but of course...any way, I held on to it, and I thought you might like it."

Jin opened the pouch and pulled out a golden chain. A pendant half-turned twice before settling so she could study it.

It was peacock, with sapphire feathers and carnelian "eyes"

in its tail, all set in gold. No, not true gold, she realized after a moment, but that even more precious golden metal that could be made only by the God of War—she had a seemingly indestructible tessen made of the same material.

"It's beautiful."

She met Aka's eyes and picked up that she reminded him of someone. Her mother, she supposed.

Aka said, "The peacock was your mother's symbol. She was very fond of those colors." He kissed her forehead. "May fate smile on you, Jin."

Jin smiled and kissed his cheek. "And you also, Papa."

Then she left the imperial presence, walking back over the high arched bridge to the dark gravel path. The stones crunched pleasantly under her feet as she wove her way through the fanciful garden, a little brook gurgling happily out of sight. The red maples were blossoming, their flowers like tiny maroon fireworks clustered on dark branches. The path led her around her stepmother's hall—she could see her youngest brother, Guleum, and his mother having tea inside—to the wall, a bulwark of stone and red plaster that was more than twice her height and nearly as thick.

Two guardsmen opened the round wooden gates to allow Jin through. The wall had always bothered Jin—it was a thing of war, of danger. Just who did Aka think he was keeping out? Only the Sun Emperor himself could teleport anywhere within the Sun Palace, with the notable exception of each child's own residence—there they had dominion over who could come and go. It wasn't far from the gate to her residence, enclosed by its own walls, which Jin had painted with animals and plants in bright colors, inspired by stories from Jeevanti. Her own wooden gate, also richly painted, opened at her touch, and the sweet sound of two flutes in duet met her ears.

Jin slipped inside and listened silently for a few minutes, appreciating the artistry of her two disciples. They played a love song, the two flutes calling to each other before their sweet voices mingled. Jin's throat tightened, and she wondered why she had not asked to break the betrothal.

Hadn't she wished and wished for a way out of it? Her father had been sincere in his offer, she knew... and yet, she had also sensed his reluctance, his hope that she would not accept. He wanted this alliance, a permanent tie to the Night and Moon deities, a blood connection to his oldest supporters. *And it's not just Papa who wants it,* she reminded herself. Neela had orchestrated the whole betrothal. She had often told Jin that nothing would make her happier than to see her and Xiao wed. She had even spoken of their hypothetical children.

And Xiao had always spoken of their eventual marriage with certainty. Surely he wasn't in love with her, but it would hurt him badly if she jilted him the night of their betrothal ceremony.

It was only Jin who had reservations. She didn't love Xiao— well, no, she did love him, but she was not in love with him. After the ceremony, it would be a mere year until they were wed, and Jin sent to live at New Moon Manor. The rest of her life would be prescribed by her in-laws, before she even figured out what she wanted from it. She did not know what her passions were; she had never fallen in love or had her heart broken; she didn't even know who she was.

As the song ended, Jin shook off the self-pity. She moved forward to greet her disciples, a smile on her face.

"That was beautiful, Luye, Yeppeun. Your interpretation has gained nuance—another dozen years and you'll be ready to perform in the Sun Court."

Yeppeun, who had been the first mortal worshipper of Jin before she had contracted a fatal illness at the age of twenty, beamed at the praise. "Thank you, divinity."

Luye, a minor immortal whose parents had intended for her to be a concubine to the Sun Emperor and had become Jin's disciple to avoid that fate, grimaced. "Oh, be still my heart, my greatest dream fulfilled." Jin laughed at her dry tone, as Yeppeun began to scold her junior.

"I think," said Jin, "it is time to get dressed for the ceremony."

Both ladies leapt to their feet and ushered Jin through her garden to the largest structure. Each side featured intricately carved cedar sliding panels. Currently they were arranged to maximize the flow of the fresh spring air through the building.

Stepping inside was like taking a tour of Jin's childhood, at least the three thousand years she had travelled with her grandmother. The interior of each sliding panel was covered in gold-leaf and featured paintings in the style of the Crescent Moon master with whom Jin had trained for thirty years. A low table in the center of the room was for both writing and eating; it was made with rare blonde wood from Zhongtu and surrounded by colorful cushions made of scraps and contrasting embroidery that Jin had sewn with a housewife in Jeevanti. The large bed she had commissioned when her father had summoned her to live in the Sun Palace was also of blonde wood, and its canopy was hung with variegated silks the colors of peaches. These she had embroidered whenever her grandmother had confined her to the caravan; the traditions ranged from the lush flowers favored in Bando to the spare, even diamonds from Land of Winter.

Although the room featured mostly warm colors, elaborate blue robes were displayed on a mannequin by Jin's full-length mirror. She had had difficulty deciding what to wear tonight, but in the end had settled on Xiao's favorite color. *At least NeeNee will approve*, she thought. Having spent three thousand years living in Neela's blue-drenched caravan, Jin almost never chose the color for her clothes or her art. This was both—with Luye and Yeppeun's aid, she had sewn and embroidered it over the past ten years.

Jin didn't dislike the robes precisely; they just weren't her taste. But she had felt that was the point. She was showing her willingness to make a successful marriage by putting Xiao's preferences first. As Luye and Yeppeun helped her strip, Jin wondered what Xiao would wear.

When she was naked, her disciples gave her a sponge bath that smelled faintly of jasmine. Jin closed her eyes and meditated while they did so. Yeppeun, who had once been a king's favored courtesan, had insisted that she and later Luye serve Jin as handmaidens. Jin had agreed because it had pleased Yeppeun, but she still secretly preferred to wash herself. After being briskly dried with strips of cotton, Jin applied a few drops of oil to her neck and wrists that Yeppeun had mixed for her— a delicate combination of jasmine and orange blossom.

From a chest of sandalwood drawers, Luye fetched some white silk underpants; they were gathered at Jin's waist then hung loose the length of her leg until being tied around her ankle. Yeppeun selected a rich coral breast cover, dominated by the character for happiness embroidered in gold thread.

"Oh, no, Yeppeun, it will clash!" protested Jin.

Yeppeun arched a brow. "A lady's undergarments are for her," Yeppeun scolded. "Unless you planned to show them to someone this evening?"

Jin flushed. "Very well then."

As Yeppeun held the garment in place, Luye secured it around her neck with a delicate gold chain with round clasps impressed with chrysanthemums. Once they were content with how it hung, the neckline just above Jin's cleavage, Luye tied the strings in back so that it lay close to Jin's skin; the triangular front just reached her belly button.

Next came Jin's undershirt, a deep blue silk so thin as to be sheer. Jin held her arms out as they slipped it on, and the long sleeves just brushed the floor, displaying embroidered constellations and starbursts in white and silver. The body of the garment did not fully close in front and only reached her knees. Luye and Yeppeun quickly knotted its ties to hold it close to her torso. They secured a long white silk skirt shot with silver about her waist then added a silver corset that covered her torso. Overall of this went a sleeveless robe of sky-blue silk with a stiff silver collar that emphasized Jin's elegant neck. It was cinched at her waist with a wide, deep blue belt beaded with silver and lapis lazuli. Strands of hollow beads dangled from it so that in addition to the rustle of silk, her walk was accompanied by a delicate chiming.

"Come, divinity," said Luye, "We are finished with your robes. Sit while we arrange your hair."

While they combed and tugged, Jin slipped on rings of white jade and lapis lazuli. She then stroked each fingernail gently, adjusting their length and polishing them to a beautiful nacre.

"We're done," declared Yeppeun, but Luye said "Wait! Divinity, your brother, the God of Destruction, sent this earlier." Luye offered Jin a red and black lacquer box. Jin opened to find a lapis crescent moon on a silver chain.

She smiled. "Which of you showed him my outfit?"

"I did," Luye confessed.

"Thank you," said Jin and donned the necklace. She stroked the smooth stone of the moon pendant for a moment. She was lucky to have a brother like Karana.

Jin rose and walked to the full-length mirror. Luye and Yeppeun had swept up her hair and then made two large loops entwined with a pearl and lapis lazuli chain which encircled her ears. On the top of her head, a large bun was enclosed in a silver cuff with more pearls and it was stabbed by a long silver hair stick with a lapis bead cluster on the end. Two smaller loops of hair nestled to either side.

Her face was fully exposed by the style, and free of any paint, as would be expected by the court who considered her allegedly perfect features evidence of her divinity.

"It's a work of art, divinity," Luye told her, while Yeppeun beamed silently.

Jin fought a smile before grinning. Just as she started to strike a pose, Yeppeun jumped backward with an "Eeeeah!"

Jin spun and found Xiao sitting on her bed. He wore nothing but worse-for-wear underpants, and an unknown woman wrapped in a rather disgusting blanket was tucked under his arm.

"Luye, Yeppeun, please leave us," directed Jin.

The two disciples scurried away.

The bundled woman was a rather hostile mixture of jealousy and pity, so Jin addressed Xiao first.

"I don't think you've taken advantage of my open invitation since you ate those mushrooms," Jin observed. Jin would hardly allow just anyone to teleport into her private residence, but she trusted Xiao with both her life *and* her privacy. This was the first time he'd brought someone else along.

"I didn't eat anything strange, though I don't blame you for thinking of that. I need your help confining this woman, Jin."

"What's her crime?"

"Kidnapping. She's been holding me against my will for the last four days."

Jin frowned. "Is this like the time—"

"No," Xiao hurriedly put in, "though I don't blame you for thinking of that either. Let me introduce you. Jin, meet Nanami the Thief, castoff daughter of the Sea Dragon. Nanami, meet Jin, my almost betrothed, the Goddess of Beauty." Nanami suddenly looked quite pale, and her hostility faded.

"Yes, exactly," Xiao said smugly at the change in her demeanor.

"Exactly what?" demanded Jin, starting to feel rather irritated with the whole situation.

"Nanami claims that your father hired her to steal my Infinite Jug—"

"Fate laughs at us, but are you *sober*, Xiao?"

"I—yes, but that is not the point—"

"I think it's relevant," objected Jin. "Did you steal the Jug?" she asked Nanami.

The other woman smiled. "Yes. And put it where it will never see daylight again."

Jin grinned. "That's wonderful. But not enough to make Xiao sober."

"No, I realized. So I kidnapped him and kept him in a cage to get all the toxins out of his systems—your father—er, the man who hired me wished for him to be sober." Nanami's eyes skittered away at the last.

"The relevant bit here, Jin," interjected Xiao, "is we all know very well that it wasn't the Sun Emperor who hired Nanami. So who did, and why was he interfering in our betrothal?"

"I don't see how it matters—he obviously was looking after my interests."

Xiao sputtered. "You don't know that. Maybe being sober—"

"—means you won't step on my feet during the ceremony? Or pull my hair ornaments out? Or vomit on my dress? Or pass out during dinner?"

"Oh, I'm not that bad."

Jin arched a brow. "Xiao, you're my oldest friend, but you are, quite frankly ruining the beauty in you with alcohol." Jin tapped the corner of one eye. "I promise, this I know."

Jin approached the bed and smiled at Nanami. "The way I see it, I owe you a favor." She looked at Xiao. "I really think you ought to free her from that trap you've wrapped her in."

Xiao pouted. "Well, I don't. And I don't see that there's anything you can do about it."

Jin sniffed. "That rag is really quite hideously ugly, don't you think?" She touched it, and the yellowish cloth became a golden brocade featuring swirling clouds. The black smears—ink?—became embroidered brown nuts accompanied by sprays of pink flowers. Xiao's spell was broken. "You wrote this with chestnuts?" Jin asked.

"What on Earth do you think you're doing?" roared Xiao, as Nanami began to laugh

"But we aren't on Earth," Jin pointed out. "We're in the Heavens. Making that rag pretty didn't ruin anything for you, did it? Now, Xiao, why don't you run along? We still have a few minutes before the ceremony—if you hurry, Luye and

Yeppeun might be able to find you some clothes."

"You—"

"You know how the Sun Emperor abhors lateness," Jin pointed out. "And if he can't burn the alcohol from your blood, he might burn something else. Papa has quite the temper."

Xiao shook his head fiercely, then hurried from the room.

"That was masterful," Nanami managed as her laughter faded. "I was feeling quite bad for you, having to marry him, but I now see you'll be just fine."

Jin smiled. She was tempted to point out that pity wasn't all Nanami had been feeling, but that was too impolitic. "Xiao was born one day before me. He might be the person I know best in this world."

"But you're not in love with him?" Nanami asked.

"No. We're too different. You see, we're both considered useless gods, but I spend all my time trying to disprove that label, while Xiao spends all of his trying to fulfill it." Jin sat next to Nanami and held one of her hands. "I would very much appreciate it if you were willing to stay until after the ceremony so we could talk. I'd like to know more about who hired you— although I teased Xiao, it worries me that someone interfered. I want to know why."

"He meant well," Nanami said. "I can only be summoned by those of good-intent."

Jin smiled faintly. "There's another reason I'd like you to stay. I have the feeling we could be good friends."

Nanami's lips parted in surprise, but then she smiled. "Very well. I'll stay."

XIAO stood next to Jin just below the first step of the Sun

Court's Reception Hall. Though Jin's disciples had managed to find him clothes, Xiao knew that he looked like a poor relation next to Jin. He couldn't help but feel uneasy about it, which he hated. If this betrothal were truly about Jin and him, it wouldn't bother him in the least—despite being the Goddess of Beauty, Jin was the least superficial person he knew. (Or perhaps it would be more accurate to say *because* she was the Goddess of Beauty—Jin often argued that visible beauty was the least compelling).

But this betrothal was not about them—it was about their parents. The Sun Emperor cared a great deal about appearances, as evidenced by the massive, violently red edifice at their backs. The memory of his own blood heating past bearing, so hot that Xiao thought he had died, made his gut clench in dread. As for Xiao's own parents... they were unpredictable. Mostly they ignored him, but when they chose to pay attention...

His mother had always orchestrated elaborate parties with thousands of guests on Xiao's centennial birthdays. Jin was often the only guest who came for him, and there was nothing about the parties that had been designed for Xiao. One year, when Xiao was still a child, less than two thousand years old, he and Jin had found a large cache of fireworks among "his" presents. Gleeful and foolish, the two of them had smuggled the fireworks away to the back courtyard of New Moon Manor. They had set them off with great delight, totally oblivious to the fact that the vibrant sparks and rich booms would be evident to the party they'd left behind. Unfortunately, Zi, the Moon Goddess had been in the middle of a speech when the ruckus began. Xiao had spent the next year locked in his bedroom without food or drink.

Xiao's hands quivered involuntarily at the memory, and he yearned for the cup of sweet rice wine that Luye had gone to fetch for him—unfortunately, Jin had dragged him to the hall before the handmaiden returned. He half-turned, thinking perhaps there was still time to fetch it before the first guests arrived. Jin's hand slipped through his, and she gave it a reassuring squeeze.

He met her eyes, and she bowed her head slightly toward the South Gate. Xiao looked, and sure enough, guests were now streaming through it and down the cherry lane to them. Compared to the delicate pink cherry blossoms, the guests were a cacophony of vibrant silks with elaborate embroideries and headdresses that crossed the line into absurdity. From behind them, playful music grated on Xiao's nerves; a guzheng and a pipa chased the sound of the dizi flute in a mockery of courtship.

"You would look quite dashing, if you would just smile and show those famous dimples," Jin murmured to him.

"If you wanted me to smile, you shouldn't have let the thief slip through our fingers." Even to his own ears, Xiao sounded petulant. He touched the small dark ring around his left pinky—it was a lock of Nanami's hair that neither she nor Jin had seen him take. With it, he should be able to track her anywhere. Reassured that he could still find the thief, he softened his tone to add, "You are being naive to think whoever hired her doesn't pose a threat. If he could convince her he was your father, who else knows what he lied about? We should have brought her to the celebration to see if she recognized her client."

"If he is here, I don't want him to know. But Xiao, do you really think I'd let the first woman who stirred your over-sexed heart just leave?"

Xiao flushed. "She didn't—" He finished processing what Jin had said and forgot to object. "Wait, is she still here?" His nerves settled some, forcing Xiao to admit that some of his turmoil was from the worry that he might not be able to find Nanami. Which wasn't because she'd "stirred his heart." She had put him in a cage, locked him up, the way his parents did when they were irritated with him. She didn't get to just walk away.

Jin was speaking. "She promised to wait for me—and I didn't actually lift the teleportation ban for her. You'd think that the God of Pleasure would understand that honey makes finer bait than vinegar."

"It's mostly sexual pleasure," Xiao said, as he thought about what to ask Nanami.

"Don't I get any gratitude?"

Xiao smiled at last, his attention returning to her. "Jin, you are, and always will be, my best friend."

She smiled back.

The first of the guests reached them, bestowing congratulations and gifts, the latter of which were swiftly carried away by lesser immortals who served the imperial family. The parade of felicitations finished after two hours, and Xiao and Jin were summoned into the hall itself, making them the last to enter. The large hall was full of low lacquer tables practically groaning with dishes, but a clear path had been left from the entrance steps to the Sun Throne, where the emperor sat.

To his left was the empress, the Goddess of Flight, a very pretty woman who had just reached her tenth millennia and who seemed as thoughtless as the bird she had been. Xiao doubted that she would have achieved divinity if Aka hadn't settled on her for a wife. Next to her was her son and Jin's half-brother, Guleum, the God of Wind. His round face on his scrawny neck reminded Xiao of a dandelion puff on its stalk. He might live up to his mother's beauty when he reached adulthood, but for now he had all the awkwardness of early puberty. Xiao met his eyes and winked; Guleum smiled and sat a little straighter.

Next to Guleum were Xiao's parents. They sat so close to each other that their shoulders touched. Both wore large smiles, but Xiao could tell from their narrowed eyes that they had noted his mediocre attire.

To the emperor's immediate right was Neela the Wanderer, Jin's grandmother. She was the only one of the line-up that Xiao genuinely admired. Powerful enough to be a god, she had never sought worship. Xiao envied her unfettered life; he wished his parents hadn't established his divinity at birth. She was happily chatting with Jin's eldest brother, Gang, the God of War. Xiao would have been hard-pressed to find two people more different, but as he considered their gray-hair and lined faces, the only two of the head row to show their age, he supposed they might have common experiences.

On the other side of Gang was Salaana, Aka's daughter from his first marriage, the Goddess of Justice, her fierce beauty and burning eyes making Xiao squirm internally. He still remembered when she slapped him as a child, though he no longer remembered his crime. Last on that side was Salaana's full brother, Karana, the God of Destruction. He had the same intense beauty as his sister, but the fire in his eyes was banked—he was as nice as Salaana was mean, until he lost his temper.

Jin's hand on his arm, they genuflected just inside the hall, paying their respects to their families at the head table. They rose and inched down the hall, allowing everyone to study their appearance and gossip about them. Finally, they stood directly in front of the emperor.

The emperor rose slowly, his rich vermilion robes sighing softly as he moved. He beckoned the Moon and Night deities with one hand, and Neela with the other. Xiao looked at Neela to avoid his parent's gaze and was surprised to see tears marking Gang's cheeks. *Ah, that's right*—rumor said that Gang's love had died the night he proposed. This betrothal must bring up painful memories.

The emperor stepped off the dais which held his throne, and the three other immortals approached from the sides. Xiao gritted his teeth and let his parents clasp his hands, one on either side. Across from him Neela, Jin, and the emperor served as a mirror. Neela gave Xiao a wink when their eyes met, and Xiao's forced smile became a little more sincere. He knew Neela had proposed this match, which had been endorsed by his parents and the Sun Emperor, and perhaps Jin's mother too, though he had no memory of her.

The Sun Emperor began his speech.

"Good fortune to all who have joined us today. It is my pleasure to introduce to you all my beloved daughter, Sunlight Turns Petals Gold, the Goddess of Beauty." He and Neela turned Jin toward the spectators for the expected sigh of admiration.

Personally, Xiao thought Jin's physical perfection was overrated. Yes, she was lovely, the same way a frozen waterfall was lovely. Better to look at than touch. And Jin was a little boring. It would be better to be unpredictable, to please oneself, to find one's own meaning in life rather than trying to please one's family... Xiao cut off his thoughts as he realized he was remembering how Nanami had run her nishikai-coated fingers through his hair.

"And we have the pleasure of introducing our son, Laughter in the Shadows, the God of Pleasure," said the Moon Goddess, and she and the Night God maneuvered Xiao to face the crowd.

"Since their births five thousand years ago," said Neela, "these two beings have been meant for each other."

"The time has come to formally pledge their troths," said the Night God.

"I, Aka, Sun God and emperor of the upper realms, pledge to give Sunlight Turns Petals Gold to the House of the New Moon in one year's time."

"I, Sunlight Turns Petals Gold, pledge to marry as my father wishes."

"And we, Zi and Hei, the parents of Laughter in the Shadows, pledge to take Sunlight Turns Petals Gold as daughter of our house and the bride of our son in one year's time."

"I, Laughter in the Shadows, pledge to follow my parents' dictates." Xiao felt the power of the vow course through him, an indescribable pleasure-pain. Should he break his word, he would lose his immortality and his magic. He summoned a smile for Jin. The one she offered in exchange was a little wan.

When the clapping finished, all six of them were seated. Food was served immediately, and several immortals moved to the center aisle to dance. Xiao abruptly realized he was not the only one feeling troubled when Jin ignored the dancers in favor of her food. Dancing was Jin's passion.

"Hey." He touched her knuckles gently with his own. "You

okay?"

Jin met his eyes, and after a moment said, "As okay as you are."

Xiao searched for a reply, but a crash and a shriek interrupted his thoughts.

He looked to the dais, where the empress was continuing to vocalize her terror. The Sun Emperor had fallen from his throne; broken dishes surrounded his unmoving form.

JIN was wishing so hard that something would interrupt the betrothal to which she hadn't objected that when she saw her fallen father, she felt a brief surge of relief.

A moment later it changed to horror—she dashed over to him while the empress fainted at his side. Jin had just ascertained he was still breathing when a powerful hand clamped on her shoulder.

"He's alive," she told her oldest brother Gang, noting dazedly that this was the first time she could remember him touching her.

"Move aside, young one," he said gruffly. Jin did so, and Gang gently scooped their father into his arms. It was a strange sight. An outsider would think that Gang was the father and the emperor the son from their apparent ages. Jin supposed being the God of War was a heavy burden.

Neela, Zi, and Hei had risen and were calming the guests. The God of Wind was attending his mother, the collapsed empress. Jin decided to go with Gang. Instinctively, she reached a hand out to Xiao. Faster than she expected, he was at her side, holding it, as they followed Gang out the back of the hall and through a gate into the emperor's garden. Sun disciples slipped around them, several offering to carry the emperor, but Gang just shook his head impatiently.

He took the shortest possible route to the Sun Pagoda, through the Concubine's Hall—which under other circumstances would have mortified Jin—and across the arching bridges to and from the other pond's pavilion. In the Pagoda itself, Gang managed the stairs with amazing speed for a man carrying another—Jin had to jog to keep up with him, and Xiao took the steps two at a time behind her.

Gang laid Aka on the bed at the top of the pagoda, and Jin tried to make him comfortable, loosening his robe around his neck. His skin had turned sallow and his breath was irregular.

"What's wrong with him? What happened?" she asked Gang.

Her brother had his lips compressed so tightly that they were bloodless.

He turned to six sun disciples that had followed them. "You," he ordered the highest ranking, "fetch Haraa the Warden. The rest of you, out."

When the room was empty except for Xiao, Gang and herself, Gang said, "I think he's been poisoned."

Jin struggled to form words. "But... why? How?" She blanched. "Because of the betrothal."

Gang mouth twisted. "The betrothal made a good moment for him to collapse in front of many witnesses, but it is not the reason he was poisoned. Father has many who hate him."

Jin's head spun. "*Hate,*" Jin repeated in disbelief. She remembered thinking she was flying as her father tossed her high into the air at New Moon Manor; him visiting Neela's tiny caravan to have tea with Jin despite Neela glaring at him the entire time; his insistence she come home, to his side...

Suddenly Jin's heart clenched in dread.

"NeeNee..." she breathed, unable to articulate more.

"No," Gang reassured her. "Not Neela."

"But she really dislikes him..."

"She always resented his marrying her daughter. But this would not benefit her, and it's not her style."

Jin tried to process that—did Neela have a style for killing people? And how did Gang know? For his words rang with truth.

Gang cocked his head, as if he realized his words had discomfited her. His gold eyes were luminous with unshed tears. "Father has always delighted in you. You love him very much, don't you, Jin?"

"Of course," said Jin in confusion, just as the door opened.

Haraa stepped in, her emerald hair wrapped around her like a sari. She was wearing only a cropped brown top and short skirt underneath it. Jin blinked; it was very strange to see Haraa outside of the Wood Pavilions. She hadn't even come to the betrothal celebration, though Jin was sure she had been invited and she was a close friend of NeeNee's.

Haraa walked directly to the emperor's side; Jin wasn't sure if the Warden had even seen them. Jin pulled away from Gang and stood behind Haraa, folding her hands to stop their trembling. Haraa's own hands were steady and graceful as they drifted a few inches above the emperor's body, her face lost in thought.

"It's a death curse," she said, her voice loud and ringing in the quiet room. "Nasty things." She looked at Jin and Gang, and shook her head. Jin could feel her judgment and her contempt, though Jin didn't know why. "It can be broken only with a black peony and the will of his blood. There's nothing I can do." And just like that, Haraa teleported away.

"Death curse!" cried Jin. She whirled on Gang. "How do we get a black peony? What does that mean, 'will of his blood'?"

"Black peonies grow in the Underworld," Gang replied. "As for the latter. Well, it means he can only be saved by a blood relative, showing extreme dedication to his life."

Jin rallied. "Papa has five children. Surely together—"

"Jin..." Gang cleared his throat. "I have seen three death curses in my life—and two came to fruition. One, because the Underworld was locked, but the other... The reason a death curse can only be broken by a blood relative is it can only be made a blood relative. The closer the relationship, the stronger the curse."

"Are you saying... one of our siblings..."

"Yes. The curse that was broken—well, if you really want to save Father's life, you had better go yourself to fetch the black peony."

"But..." Jin sputtered. "How do you know you can trust me?"

Gang looked away. "Casting a death curse is one of the ugliest acts there is. You couldn't have done it."

"Ah," said Jin. "Because I'm a useless goddess. If I don't have the power to cast the death curse, how do you think I could break it?" She looked at Gang suspiciously. "Why wouldn't you go?"

Gang touched his grey hair ruefully. "Most of this is from disagreements with Father."

"But the emperor has no gray," objected Xiao, reminding Jin of his presence.

"Perhaps if he did," Gang said slowly, "then I could summon the dedication needed for this undertaking. As it is...

I do not mourn this as purely as Jin does." His words added anger to Jin's roil of emotions, but she reminded herself that there was always beauty in truth. She could respect Gang's honesty.

"Besides," Gang went on, "you are far from useless." He cleared his throat. "You must know that your mother, the Goddess of Thought, was one of the most powerful deities that the Sun Court has ever seen. Do you know why your brother was murdered?"

"Murdered?" echoed Jin, adrift in a world she did not know. "He was *murdered*?"

"He was assassinated for being the God of Belief. Many feared the power he held over their own worshippers. And so your mother named you the Goddess of Beauty. She thought it a benign title that would keep you safe. But your potential is still there, even if..." Gang looked away, hiding his words from her. "You are far from useless," he finally said.

"Jin, I'm coming with you," Xiao said, taking her hand and squeezing it.

Jin could not see the look that passed from her brother to her betrothed, but Xiao's eyes flashed angrily, and he declared, "If Jin is not a useless deity, neither am I."

"As you say," Gang murmured. He cleared his throat. "You should both leave as soon as possible. I will keep the court from learning what has happened as long as I can—but of course, someone must already know the truth."

Jin hesitated. So far Gang's words had held the beauty of truth, but he had not denied casting the death curse himself. If he had, surely both her life and Xiao's were forfeit. Although her hand trembled fiercely at her side, she decided that she would rather end this here than have the God of War's hounds at her heels.

"Tell me," Jin said, "that you did not cast the death curse yourself."

3

How Xiao Worried, Argued, and Failed

XIAO felt paranoid. When Jin had demanded the God of War exonerate himself, he had thought that they were never leaving that room. But Gang had sworn that he had not cast the death curse. As the two of them hurried through the palace to Jin's residence, a thousand questions had bubbled into Xiao's mouth, but he had swallowed them all until they reached Jin's residence. Then he asked the most immediate one.

"Jin, how does one go to the Underworld? I thought your father locked the gate."

"Every lock has a key," Jin said, her stride quickening now that they were away from curious eyes.

He frowned and hurried to keep pace with her. "And it's here? At the palace?"

"According to the Sunrise Scrolls, he gave it to the Great Warrior to keep safe. As his final act, the Great Warrior carried the key to the White Mountain, where he gave his life to cast a powerful protection over it."

Xiao swallowed his snark—she always nagged him to read the Sunrise and the Shadow Moon histories—and asked, "So how do we get past that?"

Jin stumbled slightly, and Xiao's heart hurt for her. He'd be upset if his own father were dying, and Jin actually *liked* Aka. He caught her elbow to steady her.

"Legend says the key can be taken if one is skilled enough. I thought..." She looked toward her pavilion.

"Nanami." Xiao breathed out slowly. He didn't want to ask her for help. But of course his grudge was nothing compared to the issue at hand. "It seems that fate has been playing with us." Xiao let her pull him to the pavilion.

Nanami was sitting cross-legged on one of Jin's floor cushions, eating the same dishes that had been in the hall— Luye or Yeppeun must have brought her food. She looked up in surprise when Xiao and Jin entered. Her eyes went immediately to Jin's elbow, which Xiao was still holding, and her expression closed.

"I didn't expect the celebration to end so early," she said neutrally.

"My father collapsed," Jin explained impatiently, shaking Xiao's hand free of her arm. She took Nanami's hands in her own. "Please, Nanami, I need your help. I must go to the Underworld to have any hope of saving him, and—"

"The Sun Emperor collapsed? He's *dying*?" Nanami asked, her eyes widening and her brows lifting.

"Yes. Please, I need your help."

Nanami stood, her brows coming together and her lips pursing. "What kind of help?"

"We need you to steal a key from the White Mountain."

"The key to the Underworld," and Nanami's suspicion shifted to excitement.

Jin nodded, her eyes never leaving Nanami.

"Before I agree," Nanami said, "will you let me test your words?"

Xiao scoffed, angry at the slight. "You, a kidnapper who Jin helped, won't trust her words?"

Nanami narrowed her eyes at him. "I'm not the only kidnapper here."

Jin stepped between them, her palms raised. "Please, emotions are high. Nanami, I will take your test."

So a fat white candle was produced and set on Jin's low table. Nanami sat on one side, Xiao and Jin on the other. Nanami withdrew yet another of her pouches and removed a small blue clay ball from it. She crushed it with the candle holder, and the candle's flame turned deep blue.

"What's that supposed to do?" demanded Xiao.

"If you speak the truth as you know it, the flame will remain blue. Lie, and the color disappears."

"Wait," Xiao put in, "this is why you believed your client was Jin's father?"

Nanami nodded.

"But then it's useless!" he objected.

"No, it's not," Jin disagreed. "I'm familiar with these balls— NeeNee makes them. Did you get them from her?"

Nanami's brows knit. "The Wanderer made them. I buy them from a friend who gets them from her."

Xiao snorted. "Yes, Neela the Wanderer—NeeNee."

Jin frowned. "Then perhaps it really was Father who hired Nanami, as I have never seen NeeNee's truth detectors fail. Or Nanami's friend cheated her. But, while I know you want to investigate this, Xiao, it's not our first concern right now. Please, Nanami, ask your questions."

Xiao crossed his arms. It made no sense for Aka to have hired Nanami. He'd sooner believe that it was Neela, breaking her own spell. But no, Nanami said it had been a man, and

Neela couldn't cast any illusions as far as Xiao knew.

Nanami's first question pulled his attention back to the present.

"Why do you wish to have the key?" Nanami asked Jin.

"To enter the Underworld so I can find the cure for my father."

"What is the cure? Will you be hurting any of the immortal creatures?"

"The cure has nothing to do with the immortal creatures. I won't hurt them unless I need to protect myself."

Nanami cocked her head at Jin's answer, but shrugged, as if deciding the cure wasn't her business.

"And you, Xiao, why will you go with her?"

Xiao blinked in surprise—wasn't it obvious? "To protect her. I'm not going to let Jin undertake a quest alone!"

Still true blue.

Nanami looked at him a while, and Xiao thought she was going to ask another question. However, she finally blew out the candle without doing so.

"I will come with you."

Jin scurried around the table and flung her arms around Nanami. "Thank you, thank you. What do I owe you in payment?"

Nanami patted Jin's back as if stunned. Xiao was hurt that Jin so readily embraced a woman who had locked him in a cage, but on reflection he realized he shouldn't be surprised. Jin was anxious to please everyone else, but she often took Xiao for granted.

After a moment, Nanami said, "If we manage to find the key and learn what happened to the Great Warrior, I will consider that payment enough. If we don't, well, then I will have failed, and you owe me nothing."

Xiao frowned. "What if we find the key but don't learn the fate of the Warrior?"

Nanami's lips twitched, and she glanced around the room. "Did you make those yourself?" she asked Jin, pointing to the silks hanging from the bed.

"Yes," said Jin.

"Then I will ask for a scarf embroidered by the Goddess of Beauty herself," Nanami decided.

Jin smiled. "I will make you one either way." She stood and rubbed her hands together. "We'll leave tonight. Nanami, please, make a list of anything you require, and my handmaiden will fetch it for you. Xiao, you as well."

Xiao frowned. "Why don't we sleep here and go in the morning, Jin?"

Jin shook her head. "Time is short—why would we wait?"

"We should prepare—see what the library has on the Underworld or..." He sought for a neutral term. "... your father's ailment."

Jin frowned at him. "That sounds flat, Xiao."

When someone prevaricated, Jin claimed it sounded ugly to her, like an out of tune instrument. It was incredibly obnoxious. "Okay, fine. I want to rest so I can teleport again."

Jin put her hands on her hips. "Can you still only manage two teleports a day? I suppose you drained your power to bring both you and Nanami here? Never mind—I will bring you myself. It'll be faster anyway."

Jin had recently bragged to him that her teleports took only five minutes; even dragging him and Nanami along she ought to be able to make it to their destination in less than half an hour.

Xiao crossed his arms. "You're being ridiculous, Jin. It'll be dark wherever we go—why leave tonight just so we can camp? Or did you think there was a palace at the base of the White Mountain?"

Jin's jaw jutted stubbornly, then she sighed. "Fine. But in that case, we *are* going to prepare."

NANAMI sat on the ground, her legs straight out in front of her, her hands wrapped around her feet, stretching her hamstrings while Jin and Xiao debated their course of action.

The three of them were in a valley at the base of the White Mountain, where a mountain stream entered. The morning air was sweet and warm and filled with the soft buzz of honeybees industriously gathering pollen from the spring flowers that grew on the streambank. The lovely scene faded to the background though, when Nanami focused on the two deities standing in it, dissecting old legends.

Jin was now attired in the prettiest warrior's clothes that Nanami had ever seen. A rich purple wrap-around shirt was tucked into her orange split-skirts, with pink peonies and wide green leaves embroidered over both. A red sash wrapped her waist and a golden tessen was tucked into it. Gold might seem like a poor choice for a weapon, but Nanami had seen the God of War's seal impressed into its base and knew it must be both durable and deadly. Her hair fell like a waterfall from the back of her head in a thick, loose braid that reached Jin's waist. Xiao was no longer the drunken partier of the Wood Pavilions. He wore tooled black leather mail and long and short swords on his back, but it was the determination on his face that made the biggest difference. Given her client's assessment—*no skills worth mentioning*—Nanami wondered if he could really use those swords.

They looked ideal together, appearing both attractive and competent, with the easy manner of long acquaintance. Nanami remembered her first glimpse of Jin in her suite, when she had suspected she was Xiao's betrothed, but hadn't known her identity. She had been overwhelmed by beauty and elegance and had despaired of ever competing with such a being. And then Nanami had immediately seen how kind, how genuine Jin was, and she hadn't wanted to compete with her.

That feeling had lasted for all of an hour. By the time Jin and Xiao had returned to her, she found that whatever strange pull she felt for Xiao was in force again. He was such a flawed being, and yet he was powerful and charming. She wanted to know how he became the way he was; she wanted to be there to comfort him, to keep him sober.

Nanami rubbed her forehead. What a glutton for punishment she was. She was travelling with a newly betrothed couple, developing an infatuation for the man while his lady was literally the most beautiful being in existence. And she didn't even want to help them!

Although Nanami was disowned, twelve millennia of scorning the self-proclaimed Sun Emperor were hard to forget. So she didn't want to save him, but she wanted to go to the Underworld. The idea scared her—she had had nightmares about being chased by Bulgae ever since she had met them in Bando—but she longed for and worried about the Koch-ssi, a creature she loved like family.

Of course, this was probably all moot. Nanami had tried to find the key herself, about six millennia ago. Like others, she had done her best to find the First's fabled home, but as far as she could tell, he wasn't even on the White Mountain. Perhaps he had truly died and buried himself with the key, as Aka had claimed.

She had no reason to think Jin and Xiao would have more success than the dozens who had gone before—they seemed even more ignorant than most—but there wasn't anywhere else she needed to be, so why not torture herself with their company?

"Nanami," called Jin, "we're going to follow the spring. Are you ready?"

Nanami leapt quickly to her feet.

There was the hint of a footpath along the stream, though if anyone had made it purposely, it had been a long time since they maintained it.

The silence as they hiked felt awkward and heavy to Nanami, so after a moment she said to Jin, "I can't imagine what it was like to grow up in the Sun Court."

Jin squeezed the base of her tessen. "I didn't really. My mother died before my eight hundredth birthday. I don't really remember that time much, just bits and pieces, usually when something sparks them. I grew up with my grandmother, NeeNee."

Nanami blinked, and then laughed. "The Wanderer? In that case, your upbringing must have been far freer than my own. What was that like?"

"Wonderful," said Xiao. "I travelled with them for twenty years, just after we turned two thousand. NeeNee let us go everywhere and get into everything. I don't think she knows what a punishment is. Tell her about those monkeys we met in Bando."

"Have you seen Bandoan macaques?" Jin asked Nanami.

Nanami nodded. "They're cute, but they can be mean. I once saw them beat up a mortal selling bananas."

Jin winced. "I can imagine that, but fortunately, these macaques were quite kind to us."

"Perhaps even macaques know better than to harass deities," suggested Nanami.

Xiao grinned. "I'm not sure that they weren't harassing us— they were grooming each other in a hot spring, and nothing would satisfy them but for us to join. Totally ruined our clothes, but NeeNee just laughed."

"Well, it's easy for her to make new ones," Jin reminded him. "I don't think I had a single article of clothing that wasn't blue until I returned to the Sun Court."

Xiao snorted. "Some people would get mad even if it is effortless to make clothes. When I—" He changed his mind abruptly, waving the story away with his hand. "NeeNee is the best."

"Of course, I love her very much," Jin said stiffly.

Nanami looked curiously back and forth between the two of them. She had thought there was nothing they couldn't discuss easily with each other, but it seemed parents—or grandparents—was a difficult subject. Which made her want to know more.

Before she came up with another question, Jin asked her, "How did you become the best thief? I can't imagine that's a skill the Sea Dragon has his children taught."

Nanami barely stopped from flinching. Hoping her tone was casual, she said, "I started stealing things just before my six thousandth birthday. Out of boredom, I suppose. I didn't take things that people needed or were very valuable. Little things, like a hair tie or a pair of socks."

"You wanted to see if anyone would notice if they were missing," accused Xiao.

Yes, Nanami admitted silently, *I wanted to see if anyone would notice me.* Nanami was one of thirteen, none more than two thousand years apart. Her parents had first had five daughters, then a longed-for son, then Nanami, then another son. Sometimes she had hated her brothers for making her invisible. Aloud she said, "One day I stole a hair stick from a guest. It was very plain, made of wood, but it had a magical property—it cast an illusion over the wearer. I was caught almost immediately because I put it in my own hair. My father disowned me, and I left the Sea Palace." Jin and Xiao had become very quiet, and Nanami was a little annoyed with herself for speaking so openly. And yet, she kept going.

"I am not the best thief," she told them, "I just have a reputation. The best thief, I believe, is He Who Walks in Shadow. He does not steal for anyone but himself."

"But you don't steal for yourself at all," interjected Jin.

"That's right."

"Why?" asked Xiao. Nanami glanced at him, surprised by the genuine curiosity in his voice, but he avoided her eyes.

She caressed her belt, feeling beneath the cloth her pouch of nishikai powder, four throwing stars, and the spelled bag with which she had trapped Xiao. She remembered the Light Hands hunting her through the deep forest in Zhongtu and she clasped her hands, reassuring herself that they were both still there. "I like the act of stealing, the thrill," she said lightly. "The first time I stole, I expected to get caught immediately, but I didn't. It was thrilling and so I did it again. The thrill would wear off sooner and sooner, and instead I would feel this pressure building until I couldn't think about anything but taking something and getting away with it.

"When I first entered the world, I still felt compelled to steal constantly, and that scared me. I wanted—needed—to regain control over that impulse. So I made a rule to never steal unless it was for a job."

"You are an addict," Xiao said shortly, angrily.

Nanami nodded.

"That's not fair," argued Jin. "Stealing isn't a drug. It's not like Xiao's drinking."

Nanami shook her head slightly, but she didn't argue the point. Instead, she turned her attention to a rock wall ahead, where the stream they followed transformed into a waterfall.

"That'll be a difficult climb."

"At least an hour. Perhaps we should teleport past it," said Xiao.

And just because she felt a little bad for them, for they truly didn't seem to know how many had sought the First before them, she said, "I know legend says the Great Warrior died along this stream, but we aren't the first to make this climb. Do you really think it matters if we scour each inch or if we teleport around?"

Jin, who seemed to have been entertaining Xiao's suggestion, straightened. "It matters. My father made the key, so I should have an affinity for it. We must move carefully so that I can feel it."

"What will you do if we reach the top without feeling it?"

"We'll consult a seer."

Nanami grimaced. Seers were crazy mortals who reeked of chicken blood and spoke in a nonsensical language largely of their own invention. Oh, yes, they had some sort of insight into fate, but what was the point when they couldn't share it?

And so they climbed laboriously along the waterfall.

They were perhaps a third of the way up the mountain when they established their camp for the night. Jin had chafed at the need to stop, but Xiao had reminded her that as a quarter flower she needed nourishment. Nanami's own grandfather was once a deer, so she also needed to eat and rest as much as any mortal.

Xiao had impressed them by catching two fish from the stream while Nanami made a fire and Jin scavenged for edible plants. They had a warm dinner with a small salad of wild greens and fell asleep to the soft gurgle of water.

When Nanami woke in the morning, she smiled at the sight of a sleeping Jin and Xiao and reflected how nice it was to be travelling with companions. As soon as she finished processing the thought though, she lost her smile. She had worked alone since fighting with He Who Walks in Shadow six millennia ago. Being alone meant she was free, and she wouldn't be disappointed by others. This was just temporary, to satisfy her curiosity as she had too much time on her hands.

Nanami went to the stream to wash up. She shivered at the bite of the water. It was rather cold this morning, and she knew it would get colder yet. The White Mountain wore a snow cap even through the hottest summers. She quickly made herself a thick cloak from the stream, and after a moment, made one for each of her companions. It would be rude not to, she rationalized.

Jin was particularly thrilled with the thick, dark blue cloak and made Nanami blush with her praises.

The day passed much like the previous, telling stories of their lives to each other. When they stopped for the night though, they had reached the snow. Jin and Nanami were both vulnerable to the cold, so Nanami made blankets from the stream while Xiao built a fire.

"Hey, Jin," he said as he worked. "You know what'd make us feel warmer? Some spicy chicken skewers from Maoyi. What do you say?"

"Uh—"

"Come on, Miss-Five-Minute-Teleport. You could get a flagon of Dragon's Flame to go with it."

"Hard liquor on a frozen mountain in the middle of a dangerous quest," Jin said dryly, "You always have the best ideas, Xiao." She bit her lip, then added, "But the skewers—sure. And some fruit. Any requests, Nanami?"

Nanami shook her head. "I'll eat anything."

The moment Jin disappeared, Xiao turned and grinned at her. "Alone at last," he said.

Nanami felt a flush creep up her neck, but she ignored it. "Is there something you want to say to me?"

"You now concede that the man who hired you wasn't Jin's father?"

Nanami hesitated. "It wasn't the Sun Emperor who hired me."

Xiao's brows snapped together, and he frowned. "What are you suggesting? That the emperor isn't her father?"

Nanami shrugged one shoulder. "The only person I know of who can flummox the Wanderer's truth detectors is Cheng the Sleeper, and I don't see why he'd wake up for you."

"I don't know who that is, but don't change the subject. I want to know who hired you and why!"

"And I have already told you everything I know," she snapped back. "Look, I crossed a line kidnapping you, I know that, and I'm sorry. I just wanted to help—"

Nanami cut herself off and stared at her hands. She thought she could feel Xiao's gaze on her.

"You just wanted to help me overcome my addiction because you fell in lur-ve with me. Is that really what you were going to say?" His voice was weird—like he was trying to sound scornful but couldn't quite summon the proper feeling. Nanami looked up at him.

"Awfully vain, aren't you? Look, I said it yesterday. I know what it's like to be controlled by an addiction. And you kind of remind me of myself, before my family cut me off. I do want to help you, believe it or not."

"Okay," he finally said. "I'll believe you—that doesn't make me any less pissed. You have no right to interfere in my life." Nanami was seeing another side of him again. The inner him maybe, the vulnerable part that he hid beneath charm and partying. "If you want to do shit like that, you have to earn a right to do it. You have to be my friend."

Nanami rubbed her lips against each other. "I'd like to be your friend."

He crossed his arms. "And that doesn't mean lover. I'm betrothed now, and I intend to be faithful."

Nanami glared at him. "Who asked to be your lover?"

Xiao snorted knowingly and she wanted to—fate should curse her, but she found his awareness of her attraction strangely appealing.

Jin reappeared, accompanied by the smell of chili and mango.

"Now that's what I'm talking about!" Xiao cheered, as if their conversation had never happened. He snatched two bamboo skewers from Jin's hand. "Still warm," he acknowledged. "I guess all that time you spent practicing might have been worthwhile."

Jin handed Nanami two skewers of her own before slicing up the ripe ochre mangos she had wrapped in a scarf. Their conversation stayed light and focused on food.

That night, the three of them slept close, sharing the blankets and their body heat. Nanami could not stop thinking about the orgies she had witnessed, and almost against her will she briefly imagined what it would be like if these two beautiful beings were both making love to her. She was forced to feign sleep for several hours before she finally attained it.

AS Jin entered her room, she saw a lump under her covers. She pulled the blankets back and found a small baby there. Only after she picked it up did she realize it was dead. She tried to scream for help, but she couldn't make any noise. The baby said, "But I died a long time ago. Why are you trying to help now?"

Her eyes flew open, and Jin gasped for breath. Gradually she became aware of the two warm bodies pressed to either side of her, though her nose and ears were cold. She looked to her left and saw Xiao; suddenly she remembered where she was. And she knew the baby of her dreams was her brother, the one Gang claimed had been murdered. She blinked rapidly to stay imminent tears.

She sat up carefully, hoping for a few minutes alone to collect herself, but Xiao's eyes opened immediately.

"I don't think we've slept like this since those years in NeeNee's caravan," he mused quietly.

Jin nodded, unable to find any words.

"Hasn't changed much, has it?"

Impatient with him—of course it had changed!—impatient that her father was dying while she trudged slowly up a mountain chasing a myth, impatient with Gang who had dumped this mess in her lap, Jin got up without replying. She pulled the cloak Nanami had made her more tightly around her shoulders and walked away.

She didn't get far before Xiao caught her, wrapping an arm around her shoulders and snagging her in close.

"What's wrong?" he asked.

Jin struggled to answer.

"Worried about your father?"

Jin turned her face into his shoulder, finally accepting the comfort that came with his strength and warmth. "Yes, and other things," she admitted.

Xiao rubbed her back lightly, and Jin sorted through her thoughts.

"Do you think that my brother was murdered? That my mother deliberately tried to make me a 'useless' goddess to protect me?"

Xiao rested his chin on top of her head. "I have no special ability to tell when one speaks the truth, but I thought you did."

Jin closed her eyes, trying to bury her doubt. "It sounded true. But—I just don't understand. How could I have not known that? Maybe Gang was mistaken."

Xiao didn't reply, but her magic picked up his thoughts, so Jin knew he was skeptical. He thought she was in denial.

"Do you think NeeNee knows?" Jin closed her eyes. "If she does—if she believes that—that must be why she insisted on raising me away from the court, and maybe why Papa let her." She then tried to peer at Xiao's face, but she couldn't see much besides his chin.

"There is little that NeeNee doesn't know," Xiao conceded. "But I'm sure she had her reasons for keeping it from you."

Jin hissed her frustration, then her next concern. "Why did Gang reveal it? Why now?"

"He said he didn't cast the death curse, and that he would do all he could to keep you safe. I assumed that was also true, since you then immediately began to make plans?"

"Yes. Yes. I've been thinking. It must have been Salaana or Karana who cast the death curse, don't you think? Surely not Guleum."

Xiao squeezed her. "I also doubt Guleum cast it. He's not even full-grown."

Jin leaned into him, accepting his comfort. "Yes. It would break my heart if it were him. But... if it is Salaana or Karana... well, that frightens me."

Salaana and Karana were full siblings, children of the Goddess of Lightning. Salaana was the Goddess of Justice. Jin knew her better through the eyes of her worshippers than as a sister—she was a well-known goddess, a champion of innocence and very harsh with all others. She was the patron of magistrates and prefects, but even they only called on her in dire situations. Salaana would take the tongue of a liar, the hand of a thief, and the life of a murderer without regard to their circumstances. If Salaana had cast the death curse, Jin was afraid to learn the reason. But even if Salaana had cast it, could she really be right to kill their father?

Karana was the God of Destruction. Destruction and death of course went hand in hand, but it clashed with Jin's impression of him. One of Jin's few clear memories from before her mother's death was of "feeding" Karana a meal she had made of grass and mud. Karana visited at least once a year when she lived with Neela. He had helped with her swimming lessons and convinced Neela to let Jin stay with the painting master. It hurt to think he might have cast the curse and forced her to acknowledge a side of him that Jin tried to ignore. Like many immortals, Neela had insisted on watching the burning of Xiling, the former capital of Zhongtu, which Karana had razed to the ground a few hundred years ago. Jin had never really understood why he'd done it, but she still had nightmares about the screams of the people and the smell of burning flesh.

"Either Salaana or Karana would move against us if they cast the curse," Xiao observed.

"I know," Jin whispered. "I feel like the world is not the one I knew a few days ago."

Xiao snorted lightly, and she broke free of his embrace to look at him. "Say it," she commanded.

His full lips pouted well. After a moment, he whined, "The world was never the one you knew."

"What do you mean?"

"Have you ever starved?"

"Of course not. Have you?" she threw back at him.

"Yes, as a matter of fact, I have."

"Pfft. When?"

"Regularly. Whenever Zi got mad at me. Sometimes I hated the fact I could not die from hunger." Zi was born of twilight and Hei of shadow; like his parents, Xiao needed nothing to sustain him. But it was extremely uncomfortable for any immortal to go without food or drink.

Jin felt cold. "Why didn't you tell me?"

"What could you have done?" Xiao shrugged. "That's probably why Neela didn't tell you about your brother. There's nothing you could do about it. It just hurts you."

Jin spun away from him, hurting for him and grasping at anger to cope. "So are you saying Gang just wanted to hurt me? That you just want to hurt me now?"

"No! That's not why I told you—I was just trying to make you accept reality. As Gang was."

Jin held on to the anger for a few more moments, then took a deep breath.

"I'm sorry, Xiao."

"Don't."

"Don't be sorry?"

"I—look, I don't know. I don't like to think about it. It just sort of popped out. I don't want you to think about it either. We're both upset and stressed."

Jin suddenly snorted. "I can't believe a few days ago I was agonizing over whether or not you'd let me take lovers." She had expected him to laugh too, but he became very quiet instead. "Xiao?" she asked when the silence stretched too long.

"You want to take lovers?"

"I -well, you know. I've never fallen in love. I was hoping... down the line... if I met someone... I mean, aren't you going to sleep with whomever you please?"

"Whomever *I* please? I never—the point is, marriage is a sacred union. It is meant to be monogamous." He shook his head. "My parents invented marriage, Jin!" His left hand began to chop through the air, punctuating his words. "Of course I would honor it! I mean, I know you think I'm lazy and irresponsible, but this... this... it's like who I am. The product of the first marriage. A living symbol of love."

"I—" Jin examined his expression closely, wishing the sun had finished rising so that she might see more clearly, "—well,

I know all that, but... we're not in love."

Xiao looked at the ground. "No. We're not. Did you have someone in mind?"

"No! I just..."

To her surprise, Xiao reached out and took her hand. He squeezed it gently. "Maybe we shouldn't get married."

"But our parents—"

"I don't care about pleasing them."

"To break a vow means to give up your immortality," Jin murmured.

Xiao hesitated. "That might not be so bad."

Jin pulled away slightly to look at him better. "Are you so unhappy then?"

"I'll fetch breakfast." And he was gone.

Jin covered her face with her hands as uncontrollable giggles escaped her. When they finally subsided, she peeped through her fingers at their camp.

The fire had died to small orange coals, their glow half-hidden under the gray ash. The smell of smoke from the fire mingled pleasantly with the cold, sharply fresh air, reminding Jin of travelling in the Cold Peaks with Neela. Neela preferred the southern coastal areas, but Jin had loved everywhere they travelled equally. She began stoking the coals and added two small pieces of wood. It would be more than an hour before Xiao returned so they might as well be warm.

Nanami sat up as Jin worked, and Jin could feel her eyes on her.

"I was also surprised that Xiao wants a monogamous marriage." Nanami finally said, and Jin almost dropped the stick with which she stirred the coals.

Jin looked at Nanami out of the corner of her eye. "I guess

we got pretty loud."

Nanami looked down. "Sorry. I couldn't really help but overhear. And he told me as much when you went to get dinner last night."

"It doesn't make sense," Jin griped, partly because she felt guilty for hurting Xiao. She had not understood why Xiao felt so frustrated with the match, as she had once told him that she wouldn't interfere with his pleasures. But now, remembering that conversation, she recalled his sarcastic gratitude. Jin had supposed he meant to imply she *couldn't* interfere with what he did, but now she realized it was that it hurt him she didn't want a monogamous relationship with him. "I know he likes you. I thought..."

Nanami looked gobsmacked. "Likes me? More like hate. He is furious that I trapped him."

Jin nodded. "Yes, but only because it meant something to him. Xiao rarely loses his temper. He generally just laughs everything off."

Nanami frowned. "I'm not sure—I think something about the kidnapping triggered him. I don't think he was moved."

Jin tapped her temple. "I'm not as good at listening to thoughts or feelings as my grandmother and father, but some comes through. Xiao isn't just angry at you—and the anger comes from other feelings."

Nanami stared at her, and Jin couldn't help but hear her thought too.

"No, it doesn't bother me," she told Nanami. "He's like a brother." She wrinkled her nose. "We had to get betrothed for our parents, but I thought... well, you heard my expectations."

Nanami bit her lip and looked far away. Jin tried to hear her thoughts, but they were a bit confused. "What are you thinking about?"

"I—well, I don't know. It's just, you say you love Xiao, but aren't you a little too hard on him?"

Jin was shocked and a little offended. "In what way?"

"You're very unsympathetic about his addiction, and pretty demanding. I mean, he did volunteer to go on this quest with you. Shouldn't you be a little more... grateful?"

Jin almost scoffed, but Nanami's words unsettled her, which might mean they were right. "I'll reflect on it. I'm going to wash up now."

Nanami nodded, and Jin moved away. When she returned, she had thought of a safer topic and asked Nanami to tell her about the Great Warrior.

"The Great Warrior—the First, I always called him. He wasn't like anyone else." And the being Nanami described did indeed seem peerless.

Nanami had ample time to tell the story of the ice duel he had had with her father before Xiao returned, nearly two hours after he left. Jin immediately smelled the strong fumes of fermented rice on his breath.

Jin clucked her tongue. "You stopped to drink?"

"I just had a little while our food was made," he said, unwrapping hand rolls filled with salmon and daikon sprouts. "It would have been rude to refuse."

"No one offered you sake for breakfast," complained Jin.

"Ah, but it's lunchtime in O'o."

Jin crossed her arms. "Well. You didn't need to go so far."

"Salmon is my favorite," he countered and took a massive bite of his roll.

When they resumed their hike along the stream, the going became more difficult as the snow deepened. Finally, they reached a sheer, ice-covered outcropping that was an impossible climb even for Nanami.

"We'll have to go around," suggested Xiao, and the two women agreed.

They had just managed to crest it from the side when Xiao, in the lead, sighed. "I guess this was a dead end. We should have started with the seer."

"Why, what do you see?" asked Jin, trying to peer around her companions.

"The spring is frozen. It's surrounded by snow."

But Jin had managed to see past their shoulders and gaped. "Snow? That's jasmine! This must be it."

The spring was burbling freely, not a trace of ice, contrary to Xiao's claim. White jasmine blossoms dotted the greenery around it so thickly that it almost—*almost*—looked like snow. But instead it looked like summer. A large block of white quartz was exposed on the mountainside; a door had been carved into it.

"Why, you are right! And I see a little temple back there," exclaimed Nanami in surprise.

Xiao blinked. "I see it too. Was it an illusion? Why did Jin see through it?"

Nanami shrugged. "I'll go first, in case of booby traps."

And so Jin stood back with Xiao, watching Nanami cautiously approach the flowered area. A moment later, she was walking back to them. Her lips parted in surprise, but she quickly pressed them shut and spun to face the spring.

After the tenth time that Nanami tried to reach the spring, only to walk away from it, she admitted, "I've never encountered magic like this. I can't even tell there is any, except that it keeps turning me around! There's nothing I can do here."

"I will try," said Jin, "I could see through the illusion, after all."

"Then I'll come with you," said Xiao.

"No, let me try alone."

He grabbed her elbow. "Jin, I'm here to protect you. I know it looks pretty, but it must be dangerous."

Jin looked at the flowers again. "Maybe the protections are made to allow those who truly need the key to find it. In the end, this is my quest."

She began walking, and Xiao started to follow her, but a moment later she was alone. She looked back and saw Xiao had been turned away much as Nanami had. Jin shrugged and continued.

The temperature rose pleasantly as she approached the spring. The snow disappeared quickly, and Jin paused to hang her thick water-cloak on a convenient pine tree burl. The alluring scent of jasmine was brought to her by a soft breeze, and Jin smiled unconsciously. As she walked, her view sharpened, as if a haze were burning away, and she suddenly saw an old man with white hair balancing on a rock within the spring. He was on one leg like a stork, his other knee bent so sharply that his foot was planted on his inner thigh. His arms reached up to form a vee, his palms supplicating the Heavens. Jin made her way to him eagerly, picking her way through the jasmine.

Her steps faltered when she was just a few paces from the man, and her throat went dry. Though his hair was indeed as white as the flowers around them, it was thick and full, framing a youthful face of startling beauty. He had full lips and a straight, delicate nose in an oblong face, made masculine by a strong chin and straight white brows over his closed eyes.

Jin was accustomed to beauty, however, and it was not his face that made her mouth go dry. He wore loose, undyed hemp trousers, but his torso was totally bare. It was a thing of valleys and ridges, and sweat beaded on it, slowly making its way down his trim stomach to the waistband of his pants.

She had a bewildering impulse to touch her lips to his chest and taste it. Before she could analyze or understand such a bizarre notion, his eyes snapped open—they were gray fire, and drove every thought from her head.

4

How Bai was Recalled to the World

BAI felt someone enter his garden, and he felt a surge of excitement and annoyance.

Excitement because isolation was sometimes tedious.

Annoyance because it would be a lost mortal whose desperation to survive had allowed them to stumble into this place. His magics only let in those whose essence was distilled to a single, all-consuming purpose. They had in fact been keeping out a thrill seeker all morning.

He would spend the next week nursing them to health and hearing about the world from their very limited perspective. It would be both too little and too much information. He would be tempted to leave his mountain and see how things had changed for himself, but he was better here, with no great attachments, and no need to take another life. So he braced himself and opened his eyes.

The most attractive woman he had ever seen stood before him. Her dress blazed in his white garden, a sunset of orange and violet, splashed with pink embroidery. A red sash about her waist, revealing a figure that even Zi would envy. Her hair, chestnut with hints of cerulean, was swept back from her heart-shaped face, and what a face it was. Lips the color of crushed plum blossoms, slightly pouty in their fullness, and eminently kissable. Her eyes were liquid gold, tilted up, with thick dark lashes.

He, who had disdained to take a lover for nearly fifty millennia, suddenly remembered the fierce joy of joining with another, and for the briefest moment imagined pulling her close and making passionate love to her amongst the jasmine.

He was horrified, then suspicious. He looked at her more deeply, trying to see her essence, to find her core.

It was like falling through fire—red, orange, yellow, and blue flames devoured him, burning brighter and fiercer as he fell.

He felt she was earnestly trying to show him her essence, even as he looked for it. He finally tore himself free and tumbled inelegantly into the spring.

He pulled himself out with much awkward splashing, ignoring her offered hand. He sputtered, "What are you?"

Those golden eyes blinked. "I am the Goddess of Beauty."

In a flash, Bai understood. "Beauty is in the eye of the beholder."

The woman shook her head. "No, I am the arbiter of beauty. I can make things more or less beautiful."

"Exactly my point," returned Bai.

"I don't understand," and Bai could see that she didn't.

"Why are you here?" he asked, his voice turning gruff.

A delicate flush kissed her slanted cheekbones.

"I am seeking the key to the Underworld."

He felt irrationally disappointed. He had been half hoping that this potent, beautiful woman had been looking for him.

"You can't have it," he said gruffly. "I won't let anyone use it."

"But I must go to the Underworld!" she insisted, taking a step closer to him, her hand hovering inches from his arm. "I need a black peony. My father's life depends on it. Please, you were brought here by the Great Warrior, weren't you? To protect the key? How can I prove myself to you?"

Bai looked at her in disbelief. The Great Warrior? Surely that was him. Perhaps he had lived in isolation too long if people no longer recognized him. He felt strangely reluctant to enlighten her though and settled for, "Tell me what you know of Kun—the key."

She nodded earnestly. "After the monsters that plagued Earth were all locked in the Underworld, the gate was locked, and its key was given to the greatest warrior of all. He was slowly dying of his wounds from battle, but he carried the key to the White Mountain. He gave his life to cast a powerful protection over it."

Bai knew she spoke the truth as she knew it. Cautiously, he examined her again, looking past the raw power into which he had sank, but he could read nothing. "How old are you?"

"I—I will be five thousand in the summer."

"Five thousand?" Bai repeated. "You're a baby!" When Bai was five thousand years old, he had not even thought of himself as a man, but as a stone. He had wandered Earth, abandoned by Aka, trying to understand who he was. He didn't even meet Cheng until he was six thousand...

"You don't seem all that old yourself," she frowned, "even though your hair is white." Her eyes flashed, and Bai was unnerved by how much he liked that. "Stop delaying—does this garden hold the key or not?"

"The key is here."

She smiled, and Bai heard his own heartbeat. Her hand

stopped hovering and wrapped around his arm. "Please, tell me how to prove myself."

Bai's eyes were drawn to that elegant hand, warm and soft against his skin, and he thought of several replies that had little to do with worthiness. Before he could find any words, he felt another twinge—a second intruder had entered his garden.

This one was a man, possibly young as well, but with the early signs of dissipation in his face.

"Jin?" he called, his eyes scanning the garden frantically. "Jin, can you hear me?"

"Of course I can hear you—I'm standing right here," she snapped in irritation.

To Bai's surprise, her will to be seen undid his effective invisibility, which she had extended to herself when she touched him.

The man gaped then quickly drew his long sword. "Release her," he demanded.

"I'm not holding her," Bai pointed out dryly.

The goddess—Jin—dropped her hand from Bai's arm, and he immediately placed his own where it had been, as if he could catch the feel of her fingers before it faded.

"Xiao, don't be obnoxious!" Jin scolded impatiently. "The key is here. He is its guardian."

Xiao lowered his sword but didn't sheath it. He moved quickly, interposing himself between Jin and Bai, and Bai allowed him to do so.

Warily, after his last experience, Bai looked for Xiao's essence and his gut clenched. It seemed Zi and Hei had forgotten his warning; this man was their child. He reminded Bai of a rabid wolf, no less dangerous for the rot at his core.

A man as tangled as this one shouldn't have been able to

enter Bai's garden. How had he found the clarity of purpose to do so? "And you are?" Bai asked, just to see what Xiao would say.

"Who are you?" Xiao countered.

"You can call me Trang. I live here."

Xiao frowned over his reply, but Jin nudged him in the ribs. He looked at her. As his expression softened, Bai understood. Xiao's love for Jin, pure and strong, had clarified his essence. It seemed Bai was not the only one she had manipulated, albeit unconsciously.

"I am the God of Pleasure."

"Pleasure?" echoed Bai in disbelief, and Xiao stiffened.

"Yes," he returned, and Bai realized he had offended Xiao. So, like Jin, was he unaware of the depth of his power? Oblivious to his own essential self?

"Search for the key, then," he told them, "if you find it before I return, perhaps I'll let you leave with it."

"Return?" asked Jin, her brow knitting.

Bai smiled at her expression before catching himself. "Yes, there's someone I want to talk to." He commanded his garden to hold them and teleported to New Moon Manor.

"WHAT just happened?" Xiao demanded after the stranger disappeared.

"I think he set a teleportation ban so we can't leave before his return."

Xiao began running back the way they'd come, only to find himself turned in the same manner as when he'd first tried to approach the spring. Trang had banned more than teleporting.

When he reached Jin, he started to look for another route

of escape, but Jin caught his arm.

"Xiao, we're not ready to leave yet anyway—we should be looking for the key. He said he might let us have it if we find it."

"How can you be so naive, Jin?" Sometimes Xiao found it hard to believe that Jin had travelled with Neela for three thousand years. Neela was always suspicious and hung out with many strange characters—so why did Jin always assume the best of people? "He might never return. The key might not be here. Perhaps he's fetching reinforcements."

Jin placed a slim-fingered hand on either side of Xiao's face, forcing him to meet her eyes. She smiled gently. "Xiao, the key is here. You think I'm naive because I trust people, but actually, truly malicious beings are the exception not the rule. And Trang is the most beautiful being I have ever met. We can trust him."

"What?" Xiao scoffed. "You're judging him on his looks?" *Sure, even I wanted to stroke those abs, and I thought I'd seen everything! But my face is better than his! Maybe I should try going around without a shirt.*

"I'm judging him on his soul," corrected Jin. "He is honorable, with a strong sense of duty to the greater good."

"The greater good, huh? That sounds fine and dandy, but what if we aren't a part of it?"

Jin dropped her hands. "How can you say that? We're trying to save my father's life."

"Which is in danger because one of your siblings is trying to kill him. You and I both suspect Salaana the most—but wouldn't that mean his death is just?"

Jin stepped back, as if he'd hit her. Xiao felt a pulse of guilt, but he didn't apologize.

"I'm going to look for the key," she told him. "You can help me or not."

She spun on her heel, her wide orange pant legs swirling, and strode toward the door in the mountainside. Xiao made a half-hearted attempt to grab her thick braid and pull her back, but he missed. He waited several minutes, hating that he upset her and worrying what she might have found. Finally, he followed.

He arrived in a small empty foyer, its stone walls devoid of decoration. There were two tunnels off it, one straight ahead and one to the right. Both were dark and unlit. "Jin?"

There was no answer. "Jin, which way did you go?" he called more loudly. Still no answer.

He went straight. As his eyes adjusted to the gloom, Xiao moved cautiously to a strange glow from across the room. When he reached it, he realized that he was by a small fireplace that had already been laid. Still using the glow as light, he found some flint tucked in a niche in the mantle and lit the fire.

The firelight revealed an all-purpose room. The white stone walls were unadorned, though a long wooden shelf was stuffed to bursting with scrolls. Both the shelf and a low table were made from peeled branches and live edge slabs, pale and alien in the sterile room.

"Does he hate color?" Xiao muttered to himself. He turned to the source of the glow and was surprised to find a sheathed sword—its hilt had been the source of the light—leaning against the rough mantle. Based on the black streaks up the sheath, he guessed that Trang was using it as a poker.

Xiao lifted the sword to examine the hilt, and his breath caught. It was a dark gray metal; the grip was a slightly textured column with a plain oblate spheroid on the end. The crossguard was made of the same material and featured an intricate pattern of starbursts. He had seen a sketch that looked like this once. With fingers that trembled, he slid the sheath off the blade.

The most intricate patterning Xiao had ever seen in person was revealed, mimicking the starbursts on the crossguard. Xiao caressed the flat of the blade before testing it on his sash.

The silk parted so effortlessly, it was almost erotic.

"That idiot is using the Starlight Sword as a fire poker!"

Xiao resheathed the sword reluctantly, then slid the sheath halfway off again. It truly was the Starlight Sword; he was sure of it. *The Great Warrior must have brought it here with the key.*

Xiao liked the look of the hilt in his hand—he knew how to use a double-edge sword, even if he was more proficient with his short and long curved swords. He imagined how Jin would react when he told her he found the blade, her eyes round and her lips parted in admiration. She would see that no matter how "honorable" Trang was, he lacked insight—the fact he couldn't just look at the blade and see its power!

"Nothing annoys Jin more than obliviousness," he said with satisfaction.

After tying the sword to his back, he continued into the next room. "Jin?" he called softly.

JIN entered the mountain and paused just past the doorway, her lips parting in delight. A soft, white light had filled the space as soon as she entered. It came from swirling lines that covered the stone, evocative of clouds. There were three tunnels off the foyer. The one on the left was lit, the swirling lines extending into it.

Almost without conscious thought, Jin followed the light.

In sharp contrast to the pure whiteness of the foyer, this hallway was lush with color. To her right hung a variety of cloths—brocade silks, dyed cotton, embroidered hemp—traversing the rainbow from a bright scarlet to deep violet. To her left were hanging scrolls. Curious, Jin stepped closer to the first and blinked in recognition. Her father stared back at her, large as life, though never before had she seen such a sullen expression on him. Her eyes darted to the calligraphy on the side—it was odd and old, a predecessor to modern characters. But the stamp on the bottom was familiar, and she almost touched the black ink before catching herself. She had seen this stamp before, on her painting teacher's most prized possession, a painting of a school of carp so realistic that the fish seemed to swim. It was the mark of the Scholar, an ancient immortal who had invented writing, painting, music, and mathematics. She looked into her father's face again, taking in his smooth skin and his deep red hair—he looked barely older than Jin herself, both in this portrayal and as she'd last seen him, slowly dying in his bed. She had known, of course, that her father was the oldest being there was, but for some reason it had never occurred to her that he might have met the Scholar. What else could he have taught her about if she had only bothered to ask?

Jin dashed tears away from her eyes. She refused to believe it was too late. She would save her father from this curse, and there would be eternity to hear stories of his youth.

Jin moved on to the next portrait, an unfamiliar man with vibrant orange hair and eyes like embers. Like the first, it was stamped as the Scholar's work. Then there was a woman, striking rather than pretty, with the palest hair that Jin had ever seen and gold eyes much like her own. Jin quickly identified the next as Haraa, the Healer, though she looked a few years younger and several pounds lighter here than she had in the Emperor's bed chamber. The next portrait, a woman with brilliantly blue hair, made Jin frown. The face was very familiar and yet surely she would remember that hair. The woman clutched a bouquet of dayflowers, and Jin gaped in sudden recognition. Could this possibly be Neela?

The next man was unknown to Jin, but he was followed by her future mother-in-law, the Moon Goddess. She had reached the end and turned to face a solid black curtain. She drew it aside, but there was no passage, only a blank scroll hanging on the wall. Jin turned, thinking to return to the foyer, but to her surprise, that doorway was gone as well. In its place was the largest, smoothest piece of silver Jin had ever seen, reflecting her and the whole room perfectly. Jin strode purposefully to it and tried to push it aside, but to no avail. "Xiao?" she called. Then, when there was no answer, "Trang?"

When her throat grew tired, Jin returned to the scroll. Although that wall was as immovable as the mirror, Jin's inspection of it revealed a brush and a pot of black ink.

So I should paint something, Jin mused. She looked back along the wall. *Or someone.* Jin preferred flora and fauna to faces, but her master had insisted she learn—if only she knew who to paint.

Thinking of the mirror on the other end, she impulsively did a self-portrait. It wasn't too bad—after all, the most available model for an art student was oneself. But no sooner had Jin finished the portrait then it disappeared, with no change to her predicament.

Jin paced the hallway again. As she looked at the three unfamiliar faces, she worried that she had never seen the person she needed to record. A nervous giggle escaped her, and Jin had to take several calming breaths.

You know four of these people—what do they have in common? Some were deities, some weren't. Some lived in the Heavens, some on Earth. *They're all very old.*

Jin wasn't sure of their exact ages, but she knew that Neela was older than Zi. Her gaze fell on the unknown man with indigo hair between Neela and Zi—he was short, with the same round face as Nanami. Could he possibly be the Sea Dragon? If he was, almost all the really old immortals that Jin knew of were here. The only one missing...

Feeling rather ridiculous, Jin painted a portrait of the Night God, Xiao's father. It looked ridiculous—although she knew what he looked like, she had over-exaggerated all his features. It looked unfinished. The magic seemed to agree with her, for nothing happened.

Well, if there is one thing I can do, it's make things look good. She placed her palm at the top of the scroll and dragged it down, replacing her rough strokes with an exact likeness of the Night God. As she lifted her palm away from the scroll, it and the wall it hung on disappeared. She looked back—the mirror was still blocking the other way. With a shrug, she walked on.

And dropped to the floor in a split to avoid a white blade of light, swung by a featureless golem of white stone. The golem managed to pull back its swing before the light sword met the wall that had filled the doorway. It turned its head, as if to look at Jin, though it had no eyes.

With speed earned through millennia of dancing, Jin pushed off the stone floor and past the golem. She removed her tessen from her sash, keeping it closed. She wasn't sure what that blade of light could slice through, but she thought the fan's metal ribs stood a better chance against it than her body.

The golem moved again, almost too fast for Jin to track—she settled for dodging again.

Within a minute, it was clear to Jin that she was outmatched. She was panting from the exertion of avoiding its attacks, and though she appeared to be slightly faster than it, that advantage was quickly fading for the creature seemed tireless. She should have attacked it immediately, pressed her advantage—but she had seen no opportunity. Jin could defeat most mortals in single combat, but she was far from the mastery with which someone had imbued the golem.

Well, as NeeNee says, if you can't win a fair fight, make it unfair.

Golems tended to be simple creatures with a single purpose. When Jin was very small, NeeNee used to make golems and challenge Jin to decipher them. Jin had loved the game, but one day after finding a golem's purpose was to pick berries for NeeNee, Jin had tweaked it so that it would pick berries for her instead. NeeNee had been furious; they had never played the game again. In fact, Jin had almost forgotten it.

Taking a deep breath, Jin snapped her tessen open and caught the golem's sword between the tines. It was a stupid maneuver—the golem was far stronger than she. But she only needed the golem to be still a few moments while she explored its thought.

Its purpose was, predictably, to kill intruders. Jin pushed on the kill and found it surprisingly easy to change into defeat.

The golem twisted its blade, ripping the tessen from her hand, and Jin knelt on the floor, stretching her palms before her and exposing her back.

"I surrender," she said meekly.

The golem's sword vanished, and it stepped back into the wall, seemingly rejoining the stone.

Jin waited a few minutes, catching her breath, but nothing else happened. She sat up. The golem did not reform.

She looked around her—although the threat was gone, no doorway had appeared. She stood and retrieved her tessen, tucking it into her belt.

"I'm not stuck," she said aloud. "And if I were, Xiao and Trang would release me." *But*, she realized, *if Trang frees me, I won't have found the key. And my father will still be dying.*

"I am powerful. I am the daughter of the Sun Emperor. I am the daughter of the Goddess of Thought. A mountain cannot defeat me, Great Warrior or no."

She marched up to where the swirling light on the ceiling disappeared into the wall. She placed her hands on the white stone and closed her eyes. She imagined fire burning through the wall, creating a beautiful arched doorway. When she opened her eyes, there was indeed an asymmetric arch with glass flames, shifting from a rich cerulean at the base to crimson at the tips.

Jin was so excited that she didn't even notice the room beyond for a few moments. When she did, her breath caught.

The room was circular and brilliant with swirling white light that threw rainbows off the white quartz walls. In the middle was a pedestal of the same rock, and on it was a vermillion sun, no bigger than Jin's fist. It felt so strongly of her father, that she caught herself looking around for the man himself.

Jin walked to the pedestal slowly, waiting for another test or trap to appear. When none did, she reached for the sun. Her hand closed, and she felt the pendant, warm and appealing in her hand. And full of power—oh, so full of power, a dam filled to bursting, power unfamiliar and different from her own, but no less alluring for its strangeness.

The white light blazed more fiercely, and Jin closed her eyes against a blinding flare. It was as if flame danced on her face, and her clothes felt hot and painful. She reached into the pendant, preparing to pull its power into herself, to use it to put out the light before it burned her alive.

But as Jin touched the power, she heard a scream. Raw, pained, and she knew this power belonged to someone else. If she seized it, took it, she was seizing their essence, violating them in the most intimate manner possible. And not just one person but many. This power belonged to a thousand or more beings.

Jin trembled. Although she feared death, and although she wanted to save her father, she could not put their lives above so many. She could not steal the essence of strangers, even to save herself. If she did, she would not be a person worth saving.

Jin not only released the power, she reached into the pendant itself and fixed the hideous flaw within that allowed such power to be drawn through it so that no one could ever violate the natural order through it again.

Fire seared through Jin's veins. As she fell to her knees, she realized the screams echoing around her were her own.

BAI reappeared at the Crescent Gate of New Moon Manor. Beneath his feet was darkest basalt and before him was a familiar amethyst arch of two crescent moons bent inward. Less familiar were high basalt walls capped with slate tiles. Between the moons were two massive iron doors. The last time

Bai was here, everything had been open to reveal austere rock gardens.

He hesitated, wondering if he was prepared for the other changes he would find. After reflection, he was certain that he could handle anything. There was a large violet bell, also new, mounted near the gate, so Bai rang it.

Moments later the gate swung open to reveal two men, one in violet robes and the other in black, both with swords at their waists. They did a double take when they saw Bai, and he felt relieved that someone recognized him—until the violet fellow asked stiffly for his name and business.

"I am Bai, the First, and I would speak with Zi or Hei."

His answer brought frowns to their faces and they conferred in whispers.

"Isn't he dead?"

"But just in case—"

"Yes, I'll ask."

Black robes hurried away, and his partner watched Bai through narrow eyes. "You aren't carrying the Starlight Sword," he stated.

Since no reply seemed necessary, Bai said nothing until black robes returned. "We are to show you to the reception hall." Both men stood aside and ushered him through the gate.

The building had at least doubled inside, and the rock gardens had been replaced by plants and a pond. They traversed a wide basalt path to the central hall, a circular structure that looked much the same as the day Zi and Hei had married fifty-odd millennia ago.

The interior was unchanged as well, walls of silver with the moon in all its phases surrounding him and a million obsidian stars set in the gleaming walls. Equally unchanged were Zi and

Hei, sitting slightly apart, a stone's throw from him.

Zi's hair was deepest violet and finagled into a monstrosity atop her head whereas Hei's black crew cut was even simpler than Bai's hair. Their robes matched their hair—Zi in layered silk with an overwhelming amount of embroidery, and Hei in black cotton that looked almost mortal in its lack of ornamentation. Their eyes were closed in unlined faces, their heads cocked as if listening intently—and Bai supposed they were. Incense burned in front of each of them, a soft lavender smoke carrying prayers to Zi's ears and a heavy black smoke for Hei's. Their hands moved busily, dividing the smoke as they granted some requests and refused others.

Zi and Hei had set themselves up as the arbiters of love. Given the right opportunity, Zi could influence emotion and Hei essences. The rush of interest, of attraction made people susceptible to Zi, and once they were in love—well, love was the greatest transformative force any being could experience. And thus the reason Bai avoided strong emotion.

Bai cleared his throat, and their eyes snapped open. Hei immediately frowned, clearly annoyed, but Zi smiled smugly, an expression that Bai found far more unsettling than the glare.

"It's considered polite to wear robes," Hei growled.

Bai glanced down at his bare, still damp chest. It had been a long time since he had worried about things like appropriate attire, but he belatedly realized that this had been the reason for the guards' odd reactions at the gate.

"But you never really cared about being polite, did you, Bai?" Zi observed. "I remember you once said, 'Why would I waste time fulfilling an arbitrary expectation from others?' when Noran told you to say please. Of course, your reply took far more time."

"But was it a waste?" Bai drawled. He stepped forward. "I have met the God of Pleasure."

Zi smiled more broadly. "You warned us that a child would lessen our power, but you were wrong."

"Why do you say that?" Bai asked.

Hei snorted. "Because it's true."

Zi added, "It's a simple matter to claim his power."

Bai stiffened. They were keeping their own son's power for themselves?

This was exactly why he had never liked Zi and Hei. They were the most deeply selfish beings he had ever met, much worse than Aka.

In his long life, Bai had come to believe that it was respect for other beings that made existence worthwhile. Perhaps it was because he had been alone, in a way that Zi and Hei as the youngest Colors never had, but he valued other beings. He would fight when challenged, he would kill to ensure his own survival, but he tried to let other beings live the way they wanted. He would never steal power, and he would not initiate an attack.

Truthfully, he had discouraged them from having children not because he cared if they split their own power or because he feared their offspring, but because he had known they'd be terrible parents. Telling Zi and Hei that they were unfit as parents would not have affected their decision to have children, but he knew how much they valued their power, their worshippers. So he had told them that any child they had would have both their powers and thus become the true God of Love.

"So you steal his power. What else did you do, ignore him? Beat him? Confine him?"

Bai shook his head angrily at their silence, reading his answer in their very essences.

"He's five thousand years old," Bai pointed out. "You think that just because you managed to suppress him so far that he won't one day surpass you? You have not curtailed his power, simply delayed its realization. And when he does realize it, will he temper that power with the kindness and gentleness you showed him as a child? Will he demonstrate the self-control and restraint you taught him as an adult?"

Bai slapped his forehead. "Oh, I forgot. He's an addict constantly struggling for self-control who wears the emotional scars of his childhood on his sleeve."

"How dare you!" hissed Zi. She rose and purple sparks danced on her hands. "You are not a parent—don't act as if you know everything!"

"You treated one of the most powerful beings to ever enter this world as worthless trash, so that is what he is becoming." Bai shook his head. He was angry, but what was done was done.

Bai tried to teleport then, but to his surprise, he couldn't break the ban they had laid on New Moon Manor.

Bai stiffened in shock. Bai was used to winning power struggles—only Gang, who had all of Noran's power and half of Aka's, had ever beaten him. Each Color formed with the same amount of raw power, but Bai had always been the strongest willed and the most creative with it. And even if they siphoned power off Xiao his power, some must leak through to him, so their pool must be smaller than Bai's. So how did she hold him like this?

Zi smiled. "Wondering how I overpowered you? Worshippers, Bai. If you had become a god, you would understand that though one mortal's belief isn't worth speaking of, every million double my power."

Million? How many mortals are there?

Zi continued to speak, lecturing Bai on the folly of entering their territory, but Bai shifted his focus to Hei. He might not like them very much, but he knew them well. Anytime Zi grew particularly exuberant, it was to divert attention from her husband.

Sure enough, just like the shadow he had once been, Hei was unobtrusively making his way toward Bai, the Night Sword held ready and low.

Bai's confidence in his magical power had been misplaced; he wasn't so foolish as to test his martial skills just because he could defeat Hei eighteen millennia ago.

So he spun and sprinted for the door.

Shadows writhed in the corners of the room, twisting together to form a golem, but Zi and Hei had been foolish to use so much silver in their decorating. Bai focused the light on those reflective surfaces, and the shadows were banished.

He shattered the wooden door with the palm of his hand, and then he was running across the wide basalt path from earlier. The black iron gate loomed in front of him; Bai knew it would be much harder to break than the wooden door of the reception hall.

He cut across the shrubbery toward the wall, thrice repelling Night and Moon disciples who tried to block his path. He heard the fast steps of Hei at his heels, but Bai was faster still.

He leapt as he reached the wall and changed into an egret. A few powerful wingbeats cleared the teleportation ban. So shocked was he at the increase in mortals that Bai was tempted to tour the world so that he would not be caught off guard again. However, he also now questioned whether his own essence trap that he had set for the young gods at his hermitage would hold.

Bai changed back into a man, and as he began to plummet, he teleported.

Five minutes later, he landed on the ground of his garden. As he caught his breath, he determined that the unknown thrill seeker still waited outside while Xiao and an oddness that was surely Jin were within the mountain. He rose and brushed himself off, heading for his door. When he entered the foyer though, he paused in surprise. Jin and Xiao had taken different routes. Jin had somehow seen the left-hand tunnel, the one he had tied to Cheng's essence—or so he had thought.

A cold knot formed in his stomach—the route to Kunjee was dangerous, and he could tell she was in the final room. He began to run, admitting to himself that he would regret her death.

But she was not dead. She sat on the floor, her legs inelegantly sprawled before her. Kunjee was in her hand; she examined it the way a child looked at their first seashell.

As he entered the chamber, she lifted her head and blinked those glorious gold eyes.

"I found it," she said.

JIN was exhausted. She had never used so much power in such a short time, not to mention whatever that searing light had been. She felt as if her very essence had been scoured.

When Trang entered the room, still shirtless and sweating, she had been slightly dumbfounded. Unable to think of anything else to say, she showed him the key in her hands.

"Yes, I see," he told her, a single brow arched high. He touched the key lightly. "What did you do to it?"

"I fixed it. So that no power can be drained through it."

"You fixed it. And you are both a master painter and warrior?"

Jin snorted in surprise. "Hardly! Well, I am a very good painter. That puzzle in the first room really confused me for a while. I'm still not totally sure what it was about—it just seemed like the Night God should be there if his wife was."

Trang nodded slowly. "And the golem?"

"I cheated. I tweaked its purpose, and then I made my own door in the wall."

Trang scratched his chin with his pointer finger. "You influenced it and reshaped my wall." He expelled his breath. He smiled at her. "How many mortals worship the Goddess of Beauty anyway?"

"Oh—maybe a million. I'm not that popular. Why? Does it change your mind about giving me the key?"

He stared at her blankly before he started to laugh. Jin had no idea what had amused him, but its richness swept her up and she chuckled in bemusement. "What's so funny?" She asked when the laughter faded.

Still smiling, he shook his head. "I'm not sure if I can explain. Just that this is the most confused I have been in, oh, seventy millennia. It's intriguing."

Jin suddenly bolted to her feet. "Seventy millennia? But— but I thought—who are you?"

"I'm Bai," he told her.

Jin waited patiently for him to elaborate.

"Um—you don't know that name? I'm the First."

"The first what?"

Trang—or rather, Bai—blinked. "The first being. The first immortal."

Jin couldn't help but frown, for his words sounded true, but, "My father, the Sun Emperor, is the first immortal."

He stepped back. "Aka is your father? And your mother?"

"My mother was the Goddess of Thought, but she died long ago."

"I didn't know her then." He shook his head decisively and caught her hand. "Come with me."

Jin followed dazedly, looking at his hand holding hers. It was rather bold of him, but she didn't mind. Actually, she liked the way it felt.

He led her through the flame door she had made and back into the first room. He waved at the eight portraits, including the one that she had painted. "These, including myself, are the Nine Colors. The first and most powerful immortals."

He pointed to the Night God first. "You are obviously familiar with Hei, Black, as this is an excellent likeness."

Jin almost told him that the Night God would soon be her father-in-law, but she found she didn't want him to know she was betrothed. So instead she said simply, "I'm not actually much of a portraitist, but I used my magic to fix it."

"Hmm. And Zi, Violet."

"Yes, the Moon Goddess."

He pointed to the next one, but Jin had to shake her head.

"This is Ao, Indigo."

"The Sea Dragon? I've never been to the Sea Palace. He and my father don't get along."

"At least some things have stayed the same," Bai muttered. He moved on to the next.

"Isn't this Neela the Wanderer?"

"Yes, Blue."

"Her hair was beautiful." Jin lifted her hand as if to stroke it, but she didn't quite touch the painting. "And she looks so young." Jin sighed. "Mother's death must have aged her."

"Mother—the Goddess of Thought?"

"Yes—she was NeeNee's only child."

"I'm sorry, is Neela your grandmother? Was the Goddess of Thought named Aashchary?"

"Yes. You knew her, too?"

Bai cocked his head. "It would be too much to say I knew her, but I—I met her once." Jin picked the rest of the thought from him.

"You delivered my mother?" If his age had shocked her, this left her feeling totally off-kilter.

He flushed. "You are Neela's granddaughter, indeed."

Jin looked at the next portrait herself, not wanting to dwell on the fact the man that she was attracted to had watched her mother be born. "Haraa has only changed a little bit. She couldn't help my father."

"What happened to Aka?"

Jin hesitated. Gang had wanted her to keep it a secret. "He's dying."

"You said as much earlier. You don't want to tell me more?"

Jin flushed. "It's not that exactly—my brother said that—it's just—"

"It's alright." He stepped in front of the next portrait. "You probably haven't seen Noran before. She was yellow, and the mother of your brother Gang."

Jin looked at the painting again. "The Scholar must have enjoyed painting her, don't you think?"

Bai, who had been standing close to her shoulder, jerked

away. "What do you mean by that?"

Jin turned to look at him in surprise. "Just—the feeling is a little different, isn't it? There's more emotion in her expression—her eyes almost sparkle."

Bai stared at her a long time, and Jin wondered what ignorance she had revealed now. Finally he pointed to the black stamp at the bottom on the side of the painting. "You recognized this?"

Jin nodded. "Yes. I've seen some of the Scholar's paintings before." She suddenly realized that Bai probably commissioned these portraits. "You've met him, haven't you? What was he like?"

"He—he's standing next to you."

Jin looked to her other side before realizing her mistake. She looked back at him, her face burning. "You are the Scholar?"

Bai nodded. "Some people called me that."

Jin nodded slowly. "It makes sense. The Great Warrior would feel comfortable leaving the key with you."

He had started laughing again. "That was simply another one of my titles. When you live as long as I have, you accrue quite a few."

Jin wanted the ground to swallow her. He must think her the stupidest being he'd ever met!

She practically shoved her finger at the next portrait. "I don't recognize him at all."

Bai's laughter abruptly ended, and his brows knit. "Cheng? Orange? But this chamber was keyed to Cheng's essence, so I thought..."

Jin shrugged. "I've never heard that name before."

Bai rubbed his chin. "Maybe he went into isolation like me." The frown didn't leave his eyes, but he gestured to the last painting. "And obviously you know Aka. Red."

They had reached the far wall, and he called forth the silver mirror. "And Bai, White.

"We each have dominion over our own color; we also have our fundamental power. I know the essence of things. There is little that I cannot understand." There was the slightest pause, which Jin only noticed because his speech was usually so composed and deliberate, before he added, "Cheng could counter my power, as well as Aka's and Neela's."

He turned back to her. "I think we should go find your friend, Xiao. The three of us have much to discuss."

5

A Fight, a Talk, and a Song

XIAO heard footsteps, so he was facing the mountain when Trang and Jin exited it. Trang was alert, his eyes scanning the garden, clearly seeking Xiao until they settled on him. Jin was a step or so behind Trang, her face flushed, her focus wholly on him. Or perhaps, more precisely, on his bare torso. She leaned toward him slightly, her interest in him blatant.

Xiao clenched his jaw. He had spent the last two hours turning Trang's home inside out, trying to find a trap door or hidden room. He had shouted himself hoarse calling for Jin, then for Trang when he had given up on her responding.

He blinked slowly. Jin hadn't responded to his calls, and she was with Trang? Xiao met Trang's gaze, letting his anger show in his eyes, and waited for them to reach him.

But Trang's eyes shifted suddenly, to the Starlight Sword on Xiao's back, and his neutral expression shifted into disapproval.

"Give that to me," he commanded.

"You'll have to get yourself a new fire poker," Xiao drawled. "This sword was never meant for such."

One of Trang's eyebrows cocked. "Return it, or I will take it."

Xiao snorted and drew the sword. "I'd like to see you try."

"What in the Heavens—"

"We aren't in the Heavens," Xiao told Jin, pleased to be able to throw her words back at her. "We're on Earth. And if he wants the Starlight Sword, he'll have to take it by force."

Jin's eyes narrowed and she looked more closely at the sword he had drawn. Jin wasn't a warrior, but she would remember the Starlight Sword.

"Jin, stand back," Trang ordered her. Xiao scowled—as if he cared more for Jin's safety than Xiao did.

Xiao moved onto the balls of his feet as he spread them wide, his knees bending slightly. "Where's your weapon?" he asked Trang.

But instead of replying, Trang simply ran toward him. Xiao swung the Starlight Sword, but somehow Trang landed on the flat of the blade, forcing it down. Before Xiao could react, Trang hit his wrist hard. Xiao let go of the sword. Seconds later, it was in Trang's right hand as he wiped the blade clean with a scrap of white cloth.

"The sheath?" Trang's voice was dry.

Xiao fumbled at the sheath's ties—his right hand was numb from the hit to his wrist. Silently, he proffered the sheath.

Trang sheathed the Starlight Sword.

"Now," said Trang, only to pause awkwardly.

"Now what?" asked Jin.

"The thief who attempted to enter earlier—they're with you?" replied Trang, seemingly out of nowhere.

"Yes," said Jin.

"They are trying to enter again—I'll let them in."

Nanami ran into the garden moments later. "Are—are you alright?" she asked Xiao. She touched his shoulders briefly, and was apparently reassured, for she whirled to face Trang.

Nanami pressed her hands to her mouth, then dropped them to reveal an awed smile.

"The Immortal Bai," she whispered, the admiration in her voice unmistakable.

Trang—Bai?—gave her a half-bow.

"You know who he is?" exclaimed Jin.

"Of course," replied Nanami in surprise. "The First Being, the Scholar, the Great Warrior—I remember you visiting my father's court when I was a child. I'm glad you're still alive."

Bai looked at her more closely. "You're one of Ao's?"

Nanami nodded.

Bai snorted in amusement. "Then you must be the seventh. Nanami."

Xiao, fleeing his own embarrassment, threw out the first thing that came to mind—not that it improved the situation. "You're supposed to be dead!"

Bai's eyebrow rose again, a habit that was quickly beginning to irk Xiao.

"Why does everyone think you're dead?" Xiao demanded.

"Well, given that I have been living here for the past eighteen millennia, you would be better equipped to answer that than I."

"The Sun Emperor," interjected Nanami. "He claimed that he gave you the key to the Underworld to protect it, and that you sacrificed your life for the cause."

"The cause? What, of locking away the creatures?" The disbelief in his voice was clear. "And he didn't *give* me the key. I—" His gaze darted to Jin, and Xiao could see him revise what he had been about to say. "Aka and I have never seen things quite the same way."

"Ak—" Xiao choked on the name. "You claim to be older than the Sun Emperor?" he asked. He looked at Jin, expecting her to denounce the lie. She didn't. Instead, the way she looked at Bai made Xiao want to break something.

"What's that in your hand, Jin?" Xiao asked instead.

This gambit worked far better than his first—everyone's attention was diverted.

"The key to the Underworld," Jin told him, raising it so he could see. Jin smiled at him alone, and Xiao smiled back.

"Then what are we waiting for? Let's go," he told her.

To his annoyance, Jin turned to Bai, as if for permission.

"I won't try to take it from you, and I won't hold you here any longer," he said, and Jin's smile widened.

Jin tugged a gold chain out from her robes, revealing a peacock pendant that Xiao had never seen before, and hung the sun pendant next to it.

When she had put it back on her neck, Xiao stepped forward to take her hand. "Well, then, I guess this is where we say farewell. Nanami—you'll be seeing me again. Bai—hopefully not."

Jin elbowed him hard at those words. "Nanami, Bai—thank you. May fate smile upon you."

"And you," Nanami said, her face a picture of frustration. Bai simply nodded, a faint smile on his lips that Xiao didn't like.

It was a little more than half an hour later when Xiao found himself facing the vermillion gate to the Underworld. It was as cold here as Bai's garden should have been, a fierce wind howling above the snow-covered ground.

His hand was clutching empty air. That wasn't too strange, Jin must have beat him here. But as he looked around, Jin was nowhere to be seen. His stomach dropped, and he turned to face the vermillion gate. Had she entered without him? Xiao ran straight at it, only to pass through as if there were nothing mystical about it.

"Jin!" he shouted for what must have been the hundredth time that day, but his cry was carried away by an angry howl of wind. Xiao fell to his knees. How could she have passed through the gate without him? After some time, he decided to teleport for help. His first thought was the Sun Palace—he tried to go to Jin's residence, but he couldn't. Teleporting here had exhausted his power. He growled his frustration, then tried to return to the garden, again to no avail.

Never had he felt so useless. Never had he despised himself so much.

A moment later, a hand fell on his shoulder.

"Jin!" he exclaimed, whirling to face her.

But it wasn't Jin; it was Bai.

"What are you doing here?" Xiao demanded angrily, forgetting that a moment ago he had intended to go to this man for help.

"Jin thought perhaps you weren't able to teleport back," Bai said.

Xiao blinked. He was so upset that it took a moment to process the words. "You know where she is? She's in the garden? Didn't the key work?"

Bai frowned without replying, and Xiao considered shaking the answers from him. Finally, "Yes, she's in the garden. It's impossible to teleport with Kunjee. When she realized it was missing, she returned for it."

Xiao let out an explosive breath. "You knew, and didn't warn us?"

Bai shrugged.

"Why didn't she come to fetch me herself?"

"I volunteered," Bai admitted. "She worried whether she would have enough strength to bring you back with her."

What exactly had Jin done in the mountain, that she was so low on power?

Aloud, Xiao groused, "But you have plenty, even though you've teleported at least twice."

"As you say," agreed Bai. He offered Xiao his hand. It almost killed Xiao to clasp it. As soon as he did, they moved between. It took them less than ten minutes to reappear in the garden, and Xiao didn't feel the least bit grateful for the speed. When they arrived, Jin was just studying the key in her hand intently, apparently unconcerned that her supposed best friend had been stranded on the other side of the world.

"Jin?" Xiao managed to keep his tone neutral.

"Oh, good, you're back—apparently Father protected the key to make it more difficult to steal."

"Mmm." Xiao drew deep on his patience. "So what are we supposed to do?"

"I'll have to travel like a mortal," Jin said. "Will you still accompany me?"

What Xiao wanted to do was to tell her off. What he said was, "Of course."

"I'll come with you as well," Bai said.

"What? Why?" demanded Xiao.

"I've spent the last eighteen thousand years on this mountain, my main purpose to protect the key. Why would I stop protecting it now?"

"Because it has other protectors," asserted Xiao.

That cursed eyebrow cocked again. "I'm not convinced of

their abilities."

Xiao humphed. And because he didn't like the idea of Jin having an admirer, he said, "Nanami, won't you come too? We could use your experience in navigating the Earth."

Nanami's eyes met his and narrowed.

"You seemed eager to leave me behind just moments ago," she pointed out.

Xiao dimpled at her. "I wasn't eager—I simply couldn't think of an excuse to invite you. Now I have."

Nanami's lips twitched; it was a relief to see that he could still charm *someone*. "I suppose I might as well travel with you until someone wants my services."

ONCE again Nanami found herself remembering how young Xiao was—he had a fifth of her years. Something about Bai had ticked him off and he was acting like a spoiled child who had been denied a second helping of dessert.

Bai, who looked younger than when she had last seen him, acted oblivious to Xiao's animosity, but Nanami was sure he was keenly aware of it. In the years he had spent at the Dragon Palace, he had discussed her habit of petty theft with her, intervened when her brother Kairoku tried to take advantage of a servant, rejected half a dozen love confessions without giving offense, and helped her sister Ichimi overcome the embarrassment of her husband's desertion. Nanami was sure that very little escaped him, even after years of isolation.

The tension made Nanami remember why she had chosen to be on her own—yet it wasn't enough to drive her away. Not yet.

She had wondered if she should leave as she waited, but she

had been curious about the garden and the key and whether Jin would be successful. And if she was a little too relieved to be invited by Xiao to continue on with them—well, she was free. She had no obligations to anyone; why shouldn't she journey to the Underworld if it suited her? She did want to see the Koch-ssi...

Nanami's eyes darted to Xiao, looking unfairly adorable as he pouted, and she suggested, "The fastest way to reach the Land of Winter is by water."

"Water?" Jin echoed. "But surely the shortest route is across northern Zhongtu."

Nanami shook her head. "You've never been in a rush before, have you? It's true—that route is shorter, but it's slower. With good mules and cooperative weather, it'll take three months. But if we go down the Kuanbai by boat, and then a fast ship over the sea, we can make it in two."

Jin brightened. "I had no idea we could get there so quickly!"

"There's much to discuss. Why don't we sit down?" Bai suggested.

"And maybe you could feed us?" Xiao suggested dryly, "Or does a legend like you not bother with food?"

"I would be happy to prepare something," Bai said and led them into his hermitage.

Nanami studied his common room with interest. It was plain with many natural elements, creating a similar atmosphere as her grandfather's home in Tsuku, and Nanami was reminded that Bai had once been good friends with him.

"You've sailed on the Kuanbai recently?" Jin asked when they were crowded around Bai's small table.

"Yes," Nanami admitted. "Just ten years ago."

"Please tell us about it."

While Bai prepared a soup over the fire, Nanami found herself scrambling to recall all she could about the Kuanbai River and its boat culture.

The Kuanbai River was fed by several mountain springs, including the one they had just left, and became suitable for boating near the foot of the White Mountain. It wound its way through the Great Ladies mountain range, supporting several villages and serving as a common pilgrim's route because mountains were the closest mortals could come to the Heavens. The Great Ladies were the tallest in the world, and the White Mountain was first among them. That section of the river was full of small flat-bottomed boats, carrying goods, news, and pilgrims from village to village.

"The villages here are isolated, and they are very fond of their traders. It's an insular group though—downriver traders can't break in easily. The traders know as many generations of their family as the Bandoan royal family," Nanami noted with amusement. "If you ask their name, prepare to wait as they recite their entire lineage."

"So we'll pay for passage with a family then?"

"Yes," Nanami agreed, "and we'll have to pay extra so that they don't dawdle in every village along the way—I knew a trader who spent six months just getting to the foothills of the Ladies."

As the river left the Great Ladies behind, it quadrupled its width and served as the border between Jeevanti and Zhongtu, supporting some of the finest farmland in both countries. Men frequently looked with avarice upon the other side, resulting in frequent trade of the territories, and now the locals identified more as Kuanbaians than nationals of a country. Nanami loved travelling the Kuanbai in this region. The foods of Zhongtu and Jeevanti fused here to create such local specialties as crispy mango duck and curried noodles -

"Yes, I know," interrupted Jin with a smile. "My grandmother bloomed on the Jeevanti side of the river, and we lived there several times during my childhood. For all my familiarity with the area though, I know little about the traders. Grandma had no time for boats because she couldn't fit her caravan on them."

So Nanami described the larger flat-bottom boats on the lower Kuanbai, which often doubled as traders' homes.

"The living quarters aren't all that different from a caravan's," said Nanami. "Families all sleep on top of one another, although if you have the money to spend, some riverfolk specialize in passengers, and have quarters designated for them. They're still small though."

Jin smiled. "That won't bother me—and it certainly won't bother Xiao. He often shares a bed with four others voluntarily."

"I know," sighed Nanami before she caught herself.

"Hey, what's wrong with that?" Xiao demanded.

Just then, Bai set a steaming pot on the table. Nanami found his face suspiciously blank and wondered if they had embarrassed the famously chaste immortal.

As Bai set four bowls around the table, Xiao demanded, "Don't you wear a shirt to eat?"

Bai blinked, and touched his chest as if surprised to find it bare. "Excuse me," he said, his pale face turning quite red. "I'm not used to having guests."

Jin touched his arm reassuringly. "Not at all. We're sorry to discommode you."

"We all know that's how *you* feel," muttered Xiao, only to wince a moment later. Nanami thought Jin kicked him under the table.

"Not at all," Bai said, ignoring Xiao. He went through a doorway at the back of the room and Jin's eyes followed him.

Oh, dear, thought Nanami. *She obviously doesn't know that Bai has spent the last fifty millennia pining over Noran.*

Jin turned quickly to Nanami. "You mentioned payment a few times—what will they want?"

Nanami began outlying the various requests traders usually made of immortals, but Xiao cut her off.

"We should disguise ourselves as mortals."

Nanami frowned. "Why?"

Jin and Xiao looked at each other.

"We had better tell them," Jin suggested.

"Gang told us not to," Xiao ground out.

"But it could be dangerous..."

Feeling this was for them to hash out, Nanami tried her soup—it turned out to be miso and was extremely tasty. Did he grow and ferment his own beans? She supposed he must.

Bai returned as Jin and Xiao finished their ambiguous argument, and Jin won. Nanami was beginning to feel a little bothered by how often Xiao gave in to her—not that it was her business.

Once Bai was seated, Jin announced, "My father is under a death curse. That means at least one of my siblings is against us. Not Gang, though."

"Oh," said Nanami, feeling a little light-headed. "I'm so relieved we don't have to worry about the Sun Guards hunting us down—just the Light Hands and their flaming swords."

"I know Gang," said Bai, "but who are your other siblings?"

"There's Salaana, Goddess of Justice, and Karana, God of Destruction," said Nanami.

"And Guleum, God of Wind," added Jin, "but he's not a threat. I suppose we should hope he is the curser, except that would be too upsetting."

"Mmm," agreed Xiao.

"Why are you sure it's not Gang?" asked Bai.

"He told me so. Truth has an intrinsic beauty; it chimes sweetly to my ear. When someone is lying or misdirecting, it sounds dissonant. He swore to me that he did not cast the spell."

Nanami thought that over slowly. "Even if he didn't cast the spell, he might still know who did."

Jin's eyes widened, and she bit her lower lip.

"But Gang also promised to protect Jin," added Xiao.

"If he intends on moving against us, it cannot be immediately," Jin added.

"Unless you already have what he wants—the key to the Underworld," suggested Nanami. "Maybe he needs it and knew you would be able to fetch it. After all, you were the only one of us who could enter the garden—well, at first."

"The key to entering the garden was simply clarity of purpose. Gang could enter himself, if he wanted. But only Cheng should have been able to find that passage. And you don't even know who he is..."

"They're too young," Nanami said. "Cheng disappeared— oh, a little after you did. I've never heard a reason why nor rumor of his whereabouts."

Bai looked away from the group, and Nanami thought he must be worried for his old friend.

"To get back to our plans," Jin interjected, "if you are both willing to proceed despite the risk, we need to figure out how we'll pay for our passage."

"Well, if we are trying to pass as mortals, gold is good," said Nanami. "Just about anything the traders can sell, but we'll want small items of high value if we're persuading them to prioritize speed."

"I didn't bring much we can use," Jin admitted. "Xiao -?" He shook his head.

"Surely you could go home to get something," said Nanami.

"Ah, no, I won't be returning home any time soon."

To Nanami's surprise, it was Bai who nodded knowingly, not Jin.

"Could you steal something?" Jin asked Nanami.

"I never steal from mortals," said Nanami, a little more harshly than she intended. Jin cocked her head, and Nanami knew her claim hadn't passed Jin's truth test. "Not anymore, anyway," she amended. She cleared her throat. "But I know a way we can make a lot of money quickly. There's an inn not far from us that caters to Zhongtuese nobles in exile. It has some of the highest stakes gambling around, and we'll be able to find passage there as well."

"I know it," said Xiao. "The White Tiger, isn't it?"

"Yes, that's right," agreed Nanami. "It's been around about fifty years. You've been there?"

"Mmm, I have a temple nearby."

"But we don't have money," Jin said. "How can we participate in high stakes gambling?"

Nanami grinned. "We don't need to gamble—you and I will be luck-bringers."

"That could work," said Xiao.

Sensing Jin's puzzlement, Nanami explained how gamblers,

particularly those who played high stakes, liked to have pretty women on their arm to bring them luck. "It's customary for them to split their winnings with you, a percentage agreed on beforehand. With your beauty, you'll be in high demand."

Jin's smile looked nervous.

AFTER five days of travel, the four companions reached Bailaohu Village on the southern slope of the White Mountain, nestled in a curve of the Kuanbai River. The village had less than four hundred locals; it had sprung up to support a temple—Xiao's apparently—and then later, the White Tiger Inn. Even if Nanami and Xiao had not been there as guides, Bai would have immediately gone to the inn. It was by far the largest building. It was quite sparse, made of rough-cut wood with no ornamentation—a typical mortal dwelling, Bai believed. He had asked Jin if she was itching to tweak its appearance. To his surprise, she had replied, "No, I like it very much. Its rusticity is appealing."

She had turned to face Bai fully and smiled at him. "Actually, there is beauty in most things, and it is the infinite variety that allows us to see it."

Bai had been thinking about that since, but he wasn't sure he saw the beauty here. The inn's one story sprawled lazily, haphazardly from its sizable common room with no clear thought of aesthetic or function. The windows were small and high and covered with animal skins, making it necessary to burn lamps nearly all day.

One side of the common room led to the courtyard kitchen, where large iron kettles swung over smoky fires. The common room was filled with low tables, perhaps originally intended for food, but the exiles had found a different purpose: gambling. Most tables were covered by hand carved tiles, their rapid clicking standing in for conversation. A few had carved boards with small balls where players went heads-up, though they attracted crowds of spectators. Bai had thought he had a good grasp of mortal gambling from knowing generations of fighters, and he was fairly sure the tile game was a descendant of one he had known, but the play here had little in common with the casual games of the battlefield.

In addition to the exiles, who were mostly men, there were many luck-bringers of the type Nanami had described. Bai suspected "luck" was not all they were selling. He hoped, although it was hardly his business, that Jin would not join them in offering more.

When they had introduced themselves to the innkeeper, he had been pleased to see both Bai's guzheng and the two ladies.

"Music makes the nobles less surly," he'd told Bai, "And there are always more men than women," he told the ladies. He'd frowned at Xiao. "What do you do?"

Xiao had grinned. "Drink."

Nanami had laughed, "Always a joker, our Bhuti. He's our guard." The innkeeper had shrugged in reply.

Then they had split three ways: Jin and Nanami disappeared into a room to wash, Xiao—actually, Bai wasn't sure where he'd gone—and Bai began setting up in the common room.

Bai had a good view of the proceedings from a raised wooden stage in the corner. He sat, tuning his guzheng. It seemed almost obscene to be coaxing its strings to perfect harmony for this lot, tipsy mortals more interested in the tiles before them than music. So he bent his head over it, ignoring the room. He could always play for himself, and the innkeeper had agreed to pay him a silver piece on top of whatever tips he earned. Bai was willing to contribute that money to the hiring of a boat, even though he had silently withheld other aid from his travelling companions—for example, they didn't need to know that they could reach Mount Korikami (or the Korikami's Tomb, as Jin had called it) by cloud in a mere week. After all, this wasn't his quest and he wasn't worried about Kunjee anymore, not now that Jin had "fixed" it. If anyone somehow seized it and travelled into the Underworld—well, the Underworld was a far bigger threat to them than vice-versa. He was really travelling with them because he wanted to understand Jin.

A commotion broke his focus, and Bai looked up from the guzheng and saw that Nanami and Jin had entered the common room. Both had availed themselves of wash water to scrub away the grime of travel and wore relatively simple robes that Bai and Nanami had created and Jin had altered. There the similarities ended. Nanami wore extravagant makeup and a knowing smile. She immediately garnered attention and was quickly drawn away from Jin and into negotiations as a luck-bringer.

Jin looked beautiful, of course, her face free of makeup and her expression shy. But for the first time, Bai didn't think she looked alluring. Instead, he found himself comparing her to a frozen waterfall—nice to look at, not to touch.

Bai frowned—that thought did *not* originate with him. A frozen waterfall? He wasn't sure he had even seen one. Jin was manipulating perceptions again—she didn't want the gamblers to find her appealing. The minutes wore on, and it became very clear that no one intended to ask her to be their luck.

Bai began to play his first song, and the din quieted. He had been wrong—these exiles appreciated the music more than the tiles after all. When he looked up from the strings, it was to find Jin watching him, her joy in his play making her seem more approachable. Almost before he realized what he intended, Bai stood, got off the stage and walked to her.

"You must sing or dance—or perhaps play the flute? Why don't you join me?" he suggested.

Jin's lips parted before blooming into a smile. "I would love to. I am a better dancer than musician, although I have some skill in both."

"What do you like to dance to?"

Jin glanced over the crowd. "Do you know 'Lost Sands'?"

Bai shook his head. "I've never heard of it—I don't suppose you know any old music?"

Jin blinked. "But 'Lost Sands' *is* old. It's popular in the Sun Court, and I think it was written more than thirty millennia ago."

"Hum it for me."

The sweet, fast melody caught Bai off guard. He had written it himself, or at least the antecedent. He had called it, "Noran's Song." *Lost sand, indeed,* he thought sadly. "I know it after all," he told her.

"Oh, wonderful! It's my favorite song," she told him, and Bai was absurdly pleased.

Soon he was glad that he could play this particular tune effortlessly, for it allowed him to watch Jin.

At first she exhibited the same control and power as a martial artist, slow movements, full of nuance and intention. Her silk scarf became an extension of her—no, more like it took on a life of its own, dancing at the end of her arm as if in duet. As the melody shifted, and Bai's fingers danced over the guzheng strings at an almost frenetic pace, her movements sped up as well. Still subtle, still controlled, but with a rawness, a passion that Bai would have frowned on in a soldier. Some of the audience began to throw coins at the stage in appreciation—that was why Bai did not notice the throwing star until after it sliced Jin's cheek just below her left eye.

6

A Drink, a Diviner, and a Decision

NANAMI was enjoying the White Tiger Inn. A rather handsome, slightly intoxicated mortal had agreed to give her a fourth of his winnings in exchange for setting his arm about her waist and her tapping his tiles for good luck. She had never been a good luck charm before, but she was embracing her attraction as a woman, and she rather liked it. She had felt bad when no one had invited Jin to be theirs, and she couldn't understand why. Jin looked so perfectly beautiful that Nanami hadn't even been able to bring herself to apply makeup to her face. Anything she added would have simply detracted.

But then Bai had invited Jin to dance, which she did well, and several members of the crowd were throwing coins to them. So Nanami leaned a little into the mortal, enjoying his warm, strong arm and the fact he so clearly found her appealing.

Suddenly Bai stopped playing, mid-song if Nanami wasn't mistaken. She glanced to the stage and saw Jin holding her golden tessen, its ribs spread. The hairs on the back of Nanami's neck stood up, and she scanned the crowd. What had they seen?

Bai resumed playing with a different song, and Nanami

supposed Jin was dancing again as the people began to throw more coins. A young man of delicate build who certainly *looked* like a Zhongtuese noble caught Nanami's attention—his face was bored, but his body was ready for action. As she watched, he also threw something at the stage—a shuriken, not a coin.

Nanami pulled away from her patron, but he caught her back.

"Hey, you can't leave," he said. "I'm in the middle of a game."

"Oh, I just need..." she hesitated. If she said to relieve herself, why would she walk deeper into the crowd? "I want to talk to my friend..."

"The dancer? She's busy. You can talk when the game ends, and I don't need you anymore." He hauled her roughly back into his lap, and Nanami found those arms a lot less appealing. She looked back to the young man, but he was gone. Teleported? Or just disappeared into the crowd?

Nanami shoved at the arm. "I need to talk to my friend. It'll just be a moment." She had a dagger up her sleeve, but she was loath to escalate the matter.

Suddenly, though the music continued, Jin was there. "Is everything alright?"

Nanami looked up at Jin and noted the tiny cut across her left cheekbone.

The mortal scowled at Jin, no more inclined to listen to her than Nanami. "It's fine. Don't tell me you ladies would break a deal?"

Jin's hand tightened on her tessen. Nanami decided to switch gears. She giggled. "Oh, that's alright. Jin, I just wanted to tell you that I saw that young noble who kissed your cheek in the crowd—he was wearing blue and gray. If you hurry, you might catch him. There, see that's all I wanted to tell her—I am happy to be your luck, sir."

Jin frowned; Nanami knew her lie must have sounded flat.

"I saw him leave—*very quickly* when he saw me," Jin told Nanami, "He's not worth my time—I'd rather keep dancing." She turned her focus on the man. "Good luck, sir." And then she returned to the stage.

Very quickly, was it? Nanami supposed that meant he had teleported. She looked around the room for Xiao, but he had still not appeared. Where had he gone anyway? He was supposed to be protecting Jin. If he'd been here, maybe they could have caught the immortal.

Nanami made herself sit patiently on the man's lap, but he lost his game, so when he finally released her an hour or so later, it was without any payment. "Good riddance," he muttered as she walked away.

Jin was no longer dancing. Instead, Bai had produced a wooden dizi flute and Jin was playing with him. Nanami was impressed that Jin had handled the attack so calmly; she doubted any of the mortals here had noticed anything amiss. And Bai and Jin were doing far better earning money than she—she would look for Xiao.

She strode through the inn for some time, checking the kitchen courtyard and each wing, but there was no sign of him. She finally went out, circled around, and checked the stables. A boy was working in the latter, currying horses.

"Can I help you, lady?"

"I'm looking for a member of my party—a young man wearing blue robes and two swords, with his hair in a very long plait."

The boy thought for a moment. "Does he like to drink, lady?"

Nanami's gut immediately knotted. "He does. Do you think you've seen him?"

"I saw a man like that take two wine jugs down to the river, probably three hours ago." The boy hesitated. "Lady, the master's wine is brewed at the temple. It is very strong."

"Thank you," Nanami said, before making her way to the river.

XIAO came awake suddenly, sputtering and wiping cold water from his face. When he could finally see clearly, he found Nanami standing over him, having used one of the empty wine jugs to pour half the river on him.

"What are you doing?" Nanami demanded, showing an unwarranted degree of emotion.

"Shouldn't that be my line?" Xiao asked as he struggled to sit up. "Why did you dump water on me? And why are you so angry?"

Nanami sputtered, then said, "This isn't the way to impress her."

"Her? Jin?" Xiao snorted. "Why should I impress her? Besides, she has eyes only for Bai."

Nanami bit her lip, and Xiao thought she must agree with him. She said, "You've been sober a week and a half—are you really going to throw that away? You *could* win her. She cares about you. You're extremely handsome. How can you concede to him without a fight?"

Xiao reached for his second jug—he had only finished one before taking a nap. Nanami knocked the jug away from him, spilling the wine into the dirt. Xiao glared at her—she was still presuming too much. He knew she felt connected to him, a sort of problem child bond, but that didn't mean he had to choose the same path she had. He reached for the jug again. She snatched it up and began pouring it out.

Xiao roared and lunged at her, but Nanami was fleet-footed. Xiao ended up slamming into the ground. "Who do you think you are?" he demanded.

Nanami hesitated. "I'd like to be your friend."

Xiao paused. He could feel, beneath her neutral words, a keen vulnerability, the same yearning that had alerted him to her attention in the Wood Pavilion. His eyes darted to the jug in her hand, still pouring wine but surely close to empty.

Xiao let his lids half-close and his dimples show. "Nanami, of course you are my friend. Can't we be reasonable about this?"

Nanami glared at him. "Your addiction has never been clearer than in this moment. Only desperation would allow you to change from raging bull to charming monkey so quickly."

Xiao's smile, just a thin veneer to begin with, cracked. "It's my addiction. Why won't you just leave me alone?"

Nanami lowered the jug—it was empty. "I'll help you earn Jin's affections," she suggested.

"Because you think that's the only thing I want more than alcohol?" he returned bitterly.

"Because you deserve them," she countered.

He shook his head. "You're wrong. I don't deserve them." Xiao saw the pity in her eyes, but he continued before she could reply. "No one deserves another being's affection—that's not how love works. You don't earn love. Love is a gift, and gifts aren't earned.

"The best thing for me," he added, "would be to give away my love. To love another being wholly and without conditions. But I can't."

"Why?" asked Nanami, her curiosity genuine.

"Because I don't love myself. Until I do, I can't sustain a love like that."

Nanami's face showed shock, and she turned away from him. Xiao started to rise, intending to get another jug. But then Nanami whirled around. "How about I help you love yourself then?"

Xiao met her dark, fierce eyes and knew some of the fire there burned for him. He really didn't understand why; maybe Nanami didn't either. Even though her words moved him, he leered at her and said, "If you want to sleep with me, just say so."

Nanami flushed, but she didn't back off. "That's not what I'm talking about, and you know it."

"So what are you talking about?"

"I'm talking about—about your purpose. Protecting Jin!"

Xiao snorted. "She hardly needs me, not with Bai around."

"Well, if you had been there earlier, maybe she wouldn't have gotten hurt! Or at least we could have caught the culprit." Nanami threw back at him.

Xiao barely heard the second part. "Jin's hurt? Why didn't you tell me immediately?"

"Because you were passed out!"

"I wasn't—never mind!" he snapped and began to run back to the inn.

"Wait, wait," Nanami latched on to his arm. "It's a small cut. There's nothing to be done right now. Let me tell you what happened."

Xiao shook her off impatiently, but he stood still. "I'm listening."

So Nanami described the immortal who threw a shuriken at Jin, clearing intending to hurt, if not kill her.

Xiao rubbed a hand over his face. He felt guilty, yes, but contrary to Nanami's accusation, he doubted that it would have played out differently if he had been present. Still, he shouldn't have been here, drinking wine and sleeping. So where should he have been?

The answer came to him surprisingly quickly.

"I can be useful on this quest, but not as Jin's bodyguard. I should be at the Sun Court, figuring out who cursed the emperor and who is sending men after her."

"We know the enemy must be one of Jin's siblings," Nanami said.

"Your point being?"

"I haven't met them, but I know enough about them to realize I wouldn't want any of them as an enemy—well, maybe the God of Wind wouldn't bother me. But the rest are dangerous. Powerful."

"Yes, and one of them is already Jin's enemy. So I need to learn as much as I can about their plans."

"What do you know about espionage?" she challenged.

Xiao felt his cheeks heat. He was sick of being dismissed. "You'd be surprised what I learn—pillow talk and all that."

"Oh, so you'll just seduce the Goddess of Justice?"

"Not that one," Xiao disagreed. "I'm not her type."

Nanami frowned, clearly confused by his answer. When Xiao didn't elaborate, Nanami said, "I was just trying to say that you might find the help of someone who knows the shadows useful."

"I thought you were a thief, not a spy."

"There is some overlap of skills."

Xiao nodded, "I suppose that's true, but... I don't trust you. And not just because you stuck me in a cage for a week. The more I think about it, the more I realize we have only rumors to suggest your trustworthiness. You might very well have known it wasn't Jin's father who hired you—or maybe *no one* hired you? Did you know the Sun Emperor would be cursed, and you wanted to be there? Maybe you are how they found us—"

"Stop! Just stop, okay?" Nanami stared at him; she was angry, her nostrils flaring. Xiao was glad to see that, actually— it was the reaction of an innocent person, and... he wanted Nanami to be innocent.

"I will prove myself to you. I will break one of the Wanderer's truth detectors—you can ask me anything you want."

Xiao crossed his arms. "Magic provided by you? How can I trust that?"

"You saw me use it!"

"It also let a man masquerade as Jin's father, according to you."

Nanami waved her hands impatiently. "What would you have me do?"

Xiao could ask Jin to play truth detector. But... he didn't want to. Jin wouldn't let him ask the questions he wanted; she would view them as offensive. And he definitely wanted to ask more about Nanami's recent client, which Jin was not ready to do.

"Come with me to my temple," Xiao said. "There's a diviner there."

THE idea of being questioned before a diviner did not thrill
Nanami, but she had to admit she was curious. Diviners did
more than detect the truth. They heard things unsaid; very
powerful ones could sometimes make foretellings of the future.
She had been surprised to learn that there was a diviner who
worshipped the God of Pleasure.

"You shouldn't be," Xiao had scolded her, "Don't you know
how many mortals want to know if their partner is faithful? Or
if they are honest? A diviner who specializes in relationships is
in high demand."

The temple had a purely ornamental wall enclosing a lush
flower garden, filling the air with sweetness. There were several
small shrines—it looked like prayers could be offered to the
Moon Goddess and the Night God here as well—in a line
behind the flowers. Without hesitation though, Xiao walked
past the clearly public area of the temple to the bunkhouses
behind. He went straight to a monk who was both short and
plump.

"Choden," said Xiao, his voice warm. The woman, who had
been weeding a vegetable garden, stood with a vibrant smile.
She held out her hands, which Xiao took and kissed,
disregarding the dirt.

"Divinity!" she exclaimed. "I did not think to meet you
again in this lifetime." She stared at Xiao's chest, and Nanami
abruptly realized she was blind. "May I assist you, divinity?"

"Yes, Choden, I have need of your skills," Xiao told her. "I
have brought a woman with me. I would like to question her
with you present so that you can verify or correct her answers."

Choden nodded, still smiling. "It would be my honor to
help, divinity."

She must have lived at the temple for some time because, despite her blindness, she led them confidently to a small shack at the back of the temple. Choden pushed through the curtain, and Nanami followed her.

The small interior smelled strongly of cloves and anise from the burning incense. The diviner took a seat near one wall and asked Nanami to sit opposite her. Xiao settled to the left of them where he could easily look at either's face.

"I must ask her a few questions, divinity, to establish a baseline."

Xiao looked at Nanami, who nodded. "Please, Choden, go ahead."

"What is your name?" Choden asked.

"Nanami."

"What is your favorite color?"

"Blue," replied Nanami.

"No, you like lavender," corrected Choden.

Nanami flushed. Xiao's eyes were lavender; she hoped he did not make the connection. Choden smiled knowingly.

"What do you like to eat?"

Nanami shrugged. "Most things. I love noodles."

"Especially spicy ones."

Nanami nodded automatically, then blinked.

"Divinity," Choden said to Xiao, "please begin your questions."

"Who hired you to steal the Infinite Jug?"

"I don't know his name," Nanami said. She described his appearance as best as she was able.

"And what exactly did he say about his relationship with Jin?"

Nanami closed her eyes, remembering. "He said you were

betrothed to his daughter. That his father had arranged the marriage, and that he could not stop it without making the situation worse for her."

"The Sun God," said Choden.

Xiao turned his attention to her with a frown. "The Sun God hired this thief?"

"No," said Choden. "The Sun God is the father of whom the man spoke."

Xiao looked at Nanami, and she knew he had figured out who hired her, though it didn't narrow her list down at all. She had realized that it must be either the God of War or the God of Destruction the evening of the betrothal. "You think the person who hired me cursed the emperor?" she asked.

"I am asking the questions here," was all Xiao said.

Nanami chewed her lip as he thought.

"Do you want Jin to succeed in her quest?"

Nanami hesitated. "I am not part of the conspiracy to kill the Sun Emperor," she tried.

"But she would be happy if he died," added Choden.

Nanami couldn't stop herself from glaring at the woman.

"So you are trying to sabotage the quest?"

"No—I don't know," Nanami confessed. "I like Jin. I like— I like—you. I haven't yet figured out what I would do if there were an opportunity."

Choden let this stand.

"Could I trust you to help me and not betray me to the curser?"

"Yes," Nanami said firmly.

"She would never betray you," said Choden. "Never, never, never."

Nanami leapt up. "That's excessive," she said. She couldn't

meet Xiao's eyes—had she really been thinking that? Or was the diviner making a forecast?

"No, it's not," argued Choden, and Nanami scowled.

"Please sit back down." Xiao's tone was dry.

She did so, reluctantly.

Xiao was quiet for so long that Nanami finally looked at him. His eyes were very soft. He seemed more vulnerable than any time she could remember, except perhaps when he had been vomiting uncontrollably during his withdrawal.

"Would you hurt Jin?"

"No," said Nanami.

"What if it turned out our enemies were conspiring with the Sea Dragon?"

"My father has no desire to be emperor," objected Nanami.

"It's been a long time since you've seen him," pointed out Xiao. "Perhaps he's changed. What if it turns out he is allied with them? What would you do?"

Nanami frowned. "I owe him no allegiance."

"But she is still loyal. She loves her family," whispered Choden.

"But I wouldn't help them hurt innocents! I wouldn't stand with them against you or Jin."

"She'd just run away instead."

Xiao snorted. "I can accept that." He tapped his knee. "I have no objection except..." He shook his head. "No, I have no objection. If you truly wish to come with me to the Sun Court, I will accept your aid." He paused then added, "My friend."

Nanami felt tears prick her eyes. "Well, don't act like you're doing me some great favor," she scolded him. "Shall we go to tell Jin? And Bai?"

Xiao nodded. "Indeed, we should tell Jin. And Bai."

XIAO walked beside Nanami in silence as they returned to the inn. He wasn't embarrassed for not trusting her; in fact, given her divided loyalties, he felt validated. But he was surprised at what had been uncovered.

First—could *Gang* be Jin's father? If the man who hired Nanami was truly Jin's father and a son of Aka, it must have been Karana or Gang. Did Aka know one of his sons had cuckolded him? Xiao shuddered at the idea of telling him. The description had matched Gang, but Karana had always been the most involved of Jin's siblings in her life. He might have disguised himself—but then, if one of them had fathered Jin, wouldn't he have hidden it by staying away from her? How frustrating, to be handed the answer yet be unable to trust it. If only Choden had been able to determine the man's name.

Second—Nanami liked him more than he realized. Maybe more than she had realized. He felt strange; he was betrothed. He wasn't looking to fall in love. And Nanami pissed him off. Except... except when she didn't, and he found her appealing— knowing that she felt more than lust made things... confusing.

"I haven't totally forgiven you but... I guess we're friends," he said aloud, startling her.

"So you said." Her brows raised.

Xiao swallowed his embarrassment. "Yes, well, I—actually, I don't have many friends, and I was figuring out how I feel."

"How you feel?" echoed Nanami. "Is that a thing you often think about?"

"Well, yes. Don't you?"

"No," she said confidently. "I just... am."

Xiao laughed. "That sounds nice, but also... uncontrolled?"

Nanami tucked a loose strand of hair behind her ear, and

Xiao decided it was time to change the subject. "So what's our story?"

Nanami frowned. "What do you mean?"

"At the Sun Court. I can teleport in and out of Jin's residence. I could stay there, if I were by myself, but I'm not sure how it would be taken if you did as well."

Nanami bit her lip. "Everyone will assume we're lovers."

"Yes," Xiao agreed. He thought a few minutes. "How about becoming one of her disciples?"

"A disciple of beauty?" Nanami's disbelief was clear in her tone.

"Not *really*, just as your disguise. You can be a young immortal that Jin found on Earth. A former butterfly, perhaps, or a flower."

Nanami scoffed. "You're serious?"

"Yes."

Nanami let out a big breath. "What will we say when people ask us about Jin's whereabouts?"

"Hmm, yes, it's too bad you can't masquerade *as* Jin. I suppose we'll say there was a beauty emergency—an acne breakout among courtesans."

"Oh, be serious," Nanami scolded him. Xiao just laughed.

"We'll ask Jin what to say." Xiao looked at her again. "Are you sure you want to go?"

"Yes, why?"

Xiao couldn't tell her the real reason—that he didn't want to leave Jin and Bai alone together—not when the diviner had all but confessed Nanami's interest in him. So he said another. "It will be dangerous."

"Life is dangerous."

Xiao blinked. "I don't think most immortals agree with

you."

"Most immortals aren't the disowned daughter of the Sea Dragon or professional thieves."

"Hmm, I suppose that's true. What's the Sea Dragon like? Why doesn't he ever come to the Sun Court?"

Nanami fiddled with the bit of hair that had once again fallen out from behind her ear. "Because he and the Emperor have too much ego to fit in one room. He's... hmmm. He's overwhelming. He's not a very large person, physically, but he's full of energy, and it's very intense to be the focus of his attention. He's fiercely loyal when he's on your side." She kept fiddling with her hair. "You know I'm one of thirteen, I suppose."

Xiao nodded.

"Did you know we are numbered? That's what our names mean—one sea, two sea, three sea... Anyway, my first brother is six sea, then me, then my next brother."

"Ah."

"Ah," she repeated, "as if you understand, just from that?"

"You could say I'm a student of relationships and emotions. Were your parents very eager to have sons?"

"When I knew them, yes. Ichimi—that's my oldest sister— said they were quite happy to have daughters, until they started suspecting they would *only* have daughters. It's not that they didn't love me, it's just that...sometimes they forgot me."

Wanting to comfort her, Xiao slipped his hand in hers and squeezed gently. Nanami fell silent, looking at their joined hands, so Xiao looked too. Hers was smaller than his, her fingers slim. Her skin was a slighter deeper tan. Her nails were cut very short, shorter than his. It was a nice hand, strong and neat.

"How do you do that?" she asked in wonder.

Xiao blinked. "Do what?"

"Touch people so easily. Like it's no big deal. I've always been afraid to touch people—at least since I left the Sea Palace. Maybe before." She frowned. "That sounds strong—*afraid*—but it's the right word. So I started telling myself I didn't want to touch people. It wasn't until I met you that I realized I'd been lying."

Xiao was still holding her hand and he brushed the back of it with his thumb. Nanami saw him as he really was—flawed, lonely, but with something to offer.

"Thank you," he told her.

"For what?"

He smiled. "For reminding me that I'm not useless."

"Oh."

The inn was soon in sight, and Nanami jerked her hand away. Xiao rubbed his fingers together but said nothing.

"There they are," announced Nanami, indicating to Jin and Bai sitting in the grass not far from the inn. They were each eating a bowl of rice; there were two more between them.

"Are you hungry?" Jin asked, offering the bowls to each of them.

"Yes, thanks," said Nanami, sitting and immediately starting to eat.

"Thank you," Xiao said, taking the bowl a little more slowly. When he didn't sit right away, Jin flushed a little. She held out a small flagon to him. "Rice wine."

Xiao blinked—he was both touched and hurt. He knew, *knew*, she was offering it to be nice, since he had disappeared all day, and yet none of the rest of them were drinking. He stared at that flagon a long time—if it was the same wine as earlier, it would be sweet and satisfying. And yet...at this exact moment, when he felt hopeful...he didn't need it. He wanted to be fully present in the world, daring to try his best.

"That's alright, I'm all set." He sat down and focused on his rice, though he could feel Nanami's gaze burning into him.

He pushed the rice around with the chopsticks Jin handed him, then said. "Nanami and I are leaving. We are going to the Sun Court, to find whoever poisoned the Emperor. We'll keep you updated on what we learn." He looked at Jin closely, and found the hairline cut on her cheek. "I'm sorry you were hurt, Jin, and I'm sorry that I went off drinking instead of staying nearby to help."

Jin set down her empty bowl of rice and looked at Bai. Xiao didn't know if she read anything there, but the other man's face looked totally blank to him. She looked at Nanami, who was chewing her lip. Then she met Xiao's eyes again. She got up on her knees and leaned forward to hug him.

"Thank you, Xiao. You are right—we need to know who our enemies are. Bai and I were just discussing it—but this is a far more elegant solution than any of ours." She sat back on her heels. "And thank you, Nanami. You can teleport in and out of my compound at will now."

Xiao closed his eyes briefly. He had anticipated this, but it still shocked him how trusting Jin was. Thank goodness he had taken the time to interrogate Nanami earlier.

Bai apparently shared Xiao's concerns. "You should not trust someone so readily," he scolded Jin. "You must make sure Nanami is worthy of such trust."

Jin blinked. "But you like Nanami," she protested.

"But why would you trust me?" he said.

Jin laughed. "Perhaps because you are arguing with me

about this?"

Xiao enjoyed Bai's loss of words.

"Jin—Nanami and I may both be able to enter the Sun Palace through your residence," Xiao said, "but won't it look odd if we are at the Sun Palace without you? I thought perhaps Nanami could pose as your disciple..."

"Can you shapeshift, Nanami?" Bai asked.

"Shapeshift?" she echoed, clearly surprised.

"Shapeshifting is a myth," objected Xiao.

Bai shrugged. "Nanami's father can shapeshift—at least he used to."

"I've never seen it," Nanami said. "And I don't know how."

"Well," broke in Jin, "it wouldn't be too hard to arrange for you to be my disciple, but my disciples spend most of their time in my residence polishing their arts. You'd be better off as a servant. Or one of Salaana's disciples, come to think of it."

Xiao stiffened in alarm. It was true that Salaana was a prime suspect, but... "Are you crazy? The Goddess of Justice will cut Nanami's hands off!"

"Only if she knew who I am." Xiao didn't like the look on Nanami's face, that of a thrill seeker who knew that death was possible. "How does one become her disciple?" asked Nanami. Xiao glared at her, but she just smirked back.

"Well, I really mean aspirant," said Jin. "Salaana expects immortals to serve her for a thousand years or so before she'll elevate them to full disciples, but she accepts aspirants regularly. You must go to the East Gate and prostrate yourself before her statue for two days. You cannot eat or drink during that time. Then you will be allowed into her residence and put into training."

"That sounds awful," Nanami said.

"It is," Xiao assured her. "You don't want to do it."

"But I'm going to anyway," Nanami declared. "Now we just need to figure out why Xiao would be at the Sun Court without Jin."

Jin considered. "Someone already knows where we are, and possibly what we are doing. If your story is too far from the truth, you will immediately draw suspicion to yourself. What you really need is an explanation for why I am travelling like a mortal."

"Pilgrims," suggested Bai.

Jin nodded. "Yes, what better reason to undertake a pilgrimage than an ill father?"

"But most people travel up the Kuanbai to the White Mountain, not the other way around," objected Nanami.

"Most people—but not the most important," said Xiao. "When the Sun Emperor sought his divinity, he started at the White Mountain and travelled to the Korikami's Tomb."

Bai choked, and Xiao frowned at him as he coughed. "I suppose you're going to say that's not really what happened."

"He did travel from the White Mountain to the Land of Winter," said Bai, "and it culminated with him becoming a god. But to call it a pilgrimage—" Bai shook his head. "It doesn't matter. If that is how it is seen, it would be a good explanation. Jin is following her father's route in hopes of finding a cure."

"And why isn't Xiao travelling with her? Unless we want to advertise that Bai is?"

"No, I don't think so," said Bai. "The man barely looked at me; he might have even thought I was mortal. If he comes again, the element of surprise is not to be underrated."

Xiao nodded. "As to why I'm not protecting her, it's easy—

we play up my incompetency."

"You'll tell people you failed?" Nanami frowned.

"No, I will brag to them that Jin trusts no one else to keep vigil over her father and asked me to stay at the Sun Court while she completes her pilgrimage—all while acting like a drunken sot and flirting with everything that breathes."

Jin nodded. "And they'll all assume I really asked you to stay at the Sun Court so I didn't have to deal with you."

"How can you say that?" exclaimed Nanami, glaring at Jin. "Xiao is more than a drunk!"

Her offense on his behalf surprised him—but it also gave him a warm feeling in his belly. Until she said something, he hadn't even realized it that Jin's quick agreement had hurt just a little bit.

Jin's eyes widened. "*I* know that. But that is how he's viewed at the Sun Court."

"Jin is right," Xiao told Nanami.

"Well, you shouldn't have to act like a layabout if you don't want to. Why don't you masquerade as a servant or a soldier?"

Xiao shook his head. "This way I don't have to worry about a disguise being uncovered, and I know how to be a drunk."

Nanami's lips compressed angrily; Jin looked at him uncertainly. He winked back at her and she smiled. He slightly resented the exchange—why did he always feel the need to reassure Jin, make sure nothing upset her? Even when *he* was upset?

"I suppose there is no reason to delay our departure," Nanami finally said, "unless you need help selecting a boat?"

"No," Jin shook her head, "I can haggle with the best." Then she blushed to Xiao's amusement. "I mean, I think—"

"It's fine, Jin," he interrupted. "You are allowed to describe your own skills accurately without fear of boasting."

Jin bit her lip, but Xiao pretended not to see. He stood. "Nanami, there are a few preparations we should make before leaving."

She nodded, also rising.

"I'll help," Jin said, but she paused when she was only half-risen.

"What's wrong?" asked Xiao.

"Oh—my leg is just a bit stiff. I guess dancing after all that walking was too much."

"Then you should just rest. There isn't much for us to do," he told her.

"But I can help Nanami look like an aspirant that will win Salaana's favor—"

"Simple, pretty, and conservative? I know Salaana and the Sun Court as well as you," Xiao said.

"And you have a lot more walking ahead of you, if you are really traveling as a mortal. You should enjoy your rest," Nanami assured her.

Jin's brow knit, but all she said was, "May fate smile on you."

"Good fortune," Nanami and Xiao echoed back.

As they walked toward the inn to fetch Nanami's belongings, Xiao told Nanami, "You had better leave your tools of the trade with me, if you are serious about trying to join Salaana's household."

Nanami's brow knit.

"Now who doesn't trust who?" Xiao teased.

"*I* didn't question *you* before a diviner—so of course I can't trust you."

Xiao chuckled, and after a moment Nanami grinned.

"You're right, though," Nanami conceded, "But if I find out you've used my powders without me..."

"Make myself a tiny lover, hmm? I don't know, I think I prefer the full-size version."

She blushed, as he intended.

"We'll go our separate ways when we leave, won't we? I'll teleport to the East Gate, and you to Jin's residence?"

"I suppose."

"So how will we meet again?" As she asked, they entered a door on one of the inn's wings and made their way down the dim hallway.

Xiao looked down at her; was his daring thief nervous? *Not yours*, he reminded himself. "It is better if I do not see you during the petition." He hesitated, then held up his left hand, showing her the small dark ring on his pinky finger. "With this, I will always be able to find you."

Nanami frowned in puzzlement and reached out a hand to touch the ring. She focused on it briefly, then gaped. "Is this made from my hair? When did you..."

Xiao grinned. "When Jin refused to keep you captive, I cut a lock of your hair. I've had it since before the betrothal ceremony."

Her brows knit. "You shouldn't have done that without my permission."

He shrugged. "You shouldn't have kept me in a cage for five days."

She pouted, but then relented. "Fine, then we're even."

"Not yet, dear thief," he told her, "but we're getting there."

"Hmph." She stopped at a door and opened it. Xiao slipped inside behind her.

"I'm going to change," she objected.

"And I'd love to watch," Xiao returned, "but I need to advise you on your clothes first. Nothing you have now is suitable." He turned her toward a warped metal mirror. "But this kimono is a good start. Salaana favors Jeevantian immortals, like her mother, but anything is better than Zhongtuese. However, you need to raise the back. In fact, do a high collar, so that it touches here," his finger stroked the middle of her nape, "and wraps tightly in the front."

"Only children wear it that way," Nanami objected.

"And Salaana's would-be disciples. Although you'll be given a sari if you're accepted as an aspirant."

Nanami's mouth twisted petulantly, then she shrugged. Her hands swept over the collar, fixing it so that it hugged her neck closely.

Xiao stepped back to examine her from a distance. "Get rid of the embroidery. And your obi—it's too elaborate. Can you get rid of the bow in back?"

Nanami rolled her eyes. "Not without it falling off, but I know what you want."

She shook her skirts once; the embroidery was gone, the only trace it left behind were some water droplets on the floor. Xiao wiped them up while Nanami fiddled with her elaborate bow. He saw what she meant when she finished; the obi was still tied, but now instead of several feet of loops it was one tight knot.

"Good—your hair—will you let me style it?"

Nanami tossed up her hands and took a seat on a barrel that had been left in the room for that purpose. Xiao rifled through Jin's bag and took two carved wooden combs. "Jin won't mind," he told Nanami.

She snorted. "Did you forget who you're talking to? As long

as the former owner won't suffer undeservedly, theft doesn't bother me at all. People are too attached to their possessions anyway—losing them is a reminder that everything is ephemeral."

Xiao paused, much struck by her attitude. But he did not wish to engage in philosophy, so he simply started untying her hair knot and said, "Taking the Infinite Jug caused me to suffer a great deal."

"*Undeservedly*," she repeated. "You must have missed that when I said it earlier."

He stuck his tongue out at the warped mirror; Nanami saw it, just as he intended. She smiled, then half-closed her eyes as he began combing her hair.

Xiao wanted to ask how long it had been since another person had done this, but her expression in the mirror was too vulnerable, her tongue nervously touching her plump bottom lip and her lashes forming dark crescents against her cheeks, hiding her eyes. Only when Xiao finished brushing and began to braid her hair did she look up again.

"How did you learn to do this?"

He gave her a lascivious smile and said, "Surely you can imagine." She immediately dropped her eyes, and her shoulders stiffened.

"I've been doing my own hair most of my life, of course," he told her, pulling forward the long plait he had chosen for travel. "Mostly trial and error though I picked up a lesson here and there."

"Oh!" And he saw her small smile before she hid it. So his experience bothered her a little. Because she was jealous? Or insecure? Surely not prudish—he still remembered that desperate prayer she had sent him. No, not prudish, though perhaps shy.

"Salaana doesn't like men much. She has almost no male disciples, and she only takes women as lovers. Daddy issues, I've always thought."

"I've heard Aka's wives have a convenient way of dying when he tires of them, so that's understandable."

Xiao's hands stilled in her hair and he met her eyes in the mirror. "You must never, never say that at the Sun Court. Do not criticize or scorn the emperor in any way."

"Not even to please Salaana?"

"She'll think that's why you said it and despise you for it." Xiao resumed braiding. "Salaana assumes the worst of everyone." He hesitated. "Jin wouldn't like that I am telling you this, but I remember—it was before her mother died, so I suppose we must have been about seven hundred years old. For some reason, we were having tea with Salaana. I think our mothers were there, and I know Neela was, because years later I asked her if it really happened and she confirmed it, but all I remember was that there were these absolutely delicious honey sesame cookies. Jin and I each ate ours—we had only been given one—and I noticed that Salaana's was untouched on her plate. I wanted it, and Jin told me that Salaana didn't like sweets and said she'd get it for me. She stood next to Salaana's side and looked cute. I mean, she and I both knew that was what she was doing, and she asked for the cookie. Salaana turned to her—and this I can't forget—said, 'Look at you, already mastered the skills of a whore.' And then she burned the cookie." Xiao blinked. "I don't think I could have known what whore meant then, but Salaana's face was so scary and it seems like I have always known. The point is, Salaana is the type of person who calls a little girl a whore."

He refocused on Nanami's face; it was nearly expressionless. "What did Jin's mother do?"

"I don't remember. Actually, I remember Aashchary as being soft and warm and singing the most beautiful songs, but I can't even recall her face or any specific interaction."

Nanami smiled tightly. "Memory is funny like that." She sighed. "Salaana always assumes the worst. I knew that already, from the legends that I've heard. But she's also far from infallible."

Xiao twisted the braids up and secured them with the two carved combs. "This'll do. You must win her approval by appearing humble, demure, and hard-working."

Nanami's lips curled into a smile—not quite bitter, but not happy either. "I know just who to emulate."

"Good," said Xiao. "I'll wait outside while you finish packing."

She looked down. "There's no reason to wait for me to change, if you wish to go now."

It was obvious that she wanted him to wait. "Yes, there is—you have to give me your powders and tools, remember?"

"Oh—right."

Outside the room, Xiao leaned against the lintel. He could barely hear Nanami inside—even when she wasn't sneaking, she moved quietly and deliberately. Xiao rubbed his mouth and thought about the wine Jin had offered earlier. His mouth was dry. He should have taken it. After all, a little bottle like that wouldn't even impair him.

He closed his eyes. No, he had better not drink, even though he would be playing a drunk for the Sun Court. It wasn't just himself he had to worry about now—his thief was going to live in justice's house.

7

Power and Poison

BAI didn't understand why Jin trusted him so fully. Even though she had heard of his accomplishments, she didn't know his character. He wished that she would be more wary, even though her faith was in his own favor. It made it easy enough to persuade her to stay longer at the inn while he accustomed himself to the modern world. But why was she willing to travel alone with him?

"Because you are nice. Even when Xiao had your sword, your priority was to reclaim it without hurting him. And because you worry about things like me trusting you too much."

Bai froze, his spoon of rice only halfway to his mouth.

The two of them were eating an early dinner, provided by the innkeeper, so that they might play as soon as the paying guests came down to eat. He had agreed to give them room and board for two more nights, and let them keep the tips they earned, in exchange for their performances. The food was a bit lacking though—Bai enjoyed the rice, not having had it since he lived alone, but the side dishes were made up of odds and ends, things the nobles would scorn to eat.

But they are good enough for a goddess, mused Bai.

"How much of my thoughts do you hear?" he asked aloud. He kept forgetting that she was a mystery to him, but the reverse was not true. "As much as Neela?"

Jin wrinkled her nose—it was ridiculously adorable. "No. NeeNee always seems to hear everything. With me, I can tell when you lie or if you aren't speaking but thinking about something very hard, like you were now, then I usually hear it." She grinned. "Why? Do you have secrets?"

"More than you have years," he told her.

"No, that was a lie. Or at least an exaggeration," she told him. "You're like me—you don't like to keep secrets. Xiao says people don't tell me things to protect me, but I think it's because they know I will tell everyone."

"But you learned secrets recently?"

"Two. My father confessed that he trapped my mother into marriage with a pregnancy she didn't want, and Gang told me that the baby, who died shortly after his birth, was murdered. And I have always known that my mother was murdered shortly before she was to give birth again.

"Do you think I must bring bad luck, to be surrounded by such unfortunate events?"

"No. If anything, you must bring good luck, to have escaped that fate."

"But why should I share it? Why would anyone want me or my brothers dead?"

"Power," said Bai. "The reason for most heinous acts in the world."

"I'm not very powerful," she argued.

"I heard you say that before, as we travelled down the mountain. You and Xiao called yourselves useless. And yet I saw you transmute many things, regardless of color. You even made my hair black! I can't change it back you know—I tried. I think you have more raw power than even Gang."

Jin's brows knit, and Bai felt the urge to comfort her. "Because I changed your hair? I don't understand."

"Color is the fundamental building block of our world. All immortals are limited in what colors they can influence—except you, it seems." Bai hurried on, realizing he was not quite ready to tell her his suspicions regarding that. "Born immortals inherit all the abilities and needs of their parents—and grandparents. That is why you sometimes hear thoughts like Neela, and sometimes feel emotions like Aka. And that is why you must eat and drink daily. Like you, Gang also inherited power from two Colors—Noran and Aka. Many other immortals feared him as a child and sought his death. If it had not been for both Aka and I protecting him, he would surely have died."

Jin bit her lip and looked at the ground. "Gang told me that my mother tried to protect me by naming me Goddess of Beauty, something harmless."

"Mm. She was wise indeed—beauty may be mistaken for being harmless, but it is certainly dangerous and powerful. You just haven't fully embraced your powers yet. I will teach you, as I taught Gang, so that soon you will be able to protect yourself."

"Why? Why help me?"

Bai pushed away the real reasons, not wanting her to hear it in his thoughts. "I hate to see things wasted. Besides, aren't you going to help me? It's easy enough to pick up new mortal languages, but I feel somewhat adrift on Earth. Too much has changed—you promised to teach me."

Jin laughed and pulled some coins they'd earn yesterday

from her sleeve. "Yes, and I promised to start with money. You see this mark? This shows it was minted by a Zhongtu monarchy. It's a guarantee it has the same weight as all the others like it…"

It was hard for Bai to believe that mortals he had seen mark sticks to count their livestock had now developed mathematics that let them manage economies and build palaces, but of course he knew Jin's words were true and he loved listening to her explain. Her fondness for mortals was evident—Bai realized that not only mortals had changed, but deities had as well, if others cared for their worshippers as Jin did.

That night, as he watched her twirl and bend to his music, Bai admitted to himself that he wanted to protect and teach this being not because he was worried about her wasted power, but because he didn't want to leave her side—and he wanted her to feel the same way about him.

THE day was fine. The weather had finally warmed and the riverbank seemed to grow greener as it slid by. The water lapped gently against the wooden riverboat that they had hired—it was a typical craft, perhaps four times Jin's height in length and not quite wide enough for her to lay across. The family who owned it consisted of a father, mother, and son. The father stood to the rear, sculling with his long oar, and listening happily to the sweet trill of thrushes on shore. The mother and son were working at the prow, weaving new raincoats from dry rushes. In the middle of the boat was an arched canopy made of woven bamboo. There were six wide planks beneath, currently two were lifted and stacked in the center, forming a table and benches. Jin sat on one side and Bai sat opposite, his hand resting on his guzheng case beside him. Bai's eyes were closed—he was probably meditating.

In addition to darkening his white hair to a soft black, she had lengthened it so he could wear it in a bun on his crown. His clothes were rough hemp, a gray wrap-around tunic and brown trousers, as befit pilgrims. Even with his appearance altered, she found him deeply appealing.

The riverboat family believed that he was her husband, that the pilgrimage was to address infertility. It was a practical deception; mortals, particularly in this area, acted as though unwed individuals were totally at the mercy of their uncontrollable sexual urges while married individuals were granted both more respect and freedom. The trouble was Jin kept wishing—ridiculously, frivolously, naively—that it was true.

Last night, the first they had spent on the boat, the two of them had unrolled their blankets in the prow of the boat, while the family slept under the arch. They had fallen asleep with a few inches separating them. She had awoken tucked against Bai's side, her cheek on his shoulder, his arm a band of warmth down her back. Unwilling to move, she had feigned sleep. He had extricated himself perhaps fifteen minutes later and Jin had "woken" shortly after that.

She had felt ashamed of herself, but she couldn't quite control her feelings. She had finally found the something she'd been seeking since her four thousandth birthday—a spark of interest, a compatibility, a likeness of spirit. She wanted to lean in, to let herself fall deeply, wholly in love with Bai. But Xiao had admitted his hope for a monogamous, true marriage. Jin didn't want to hurt him. She couldn't like herself if she hurt her closest friend to pursue a potential romance. And the idea that

Bai would reciprocate her feelings verged on absurd. He was the first being, a master of the arts, the greatest warrior in existence, and—according to Nanami—he had spent the last fifty millennia being loyal to the memory of his lost love. Surely he thought her ignorant and immature.

"Jin?" Bai broke into her thoughts. "Are your legs hurting?"

Jin jerked her eyes back to his and followed his gaze to her hands, which were absently kneading her thighs. She folded her hands in her lap. "Not at all," she said.

Bai's eyes narrowed as if unconvinced.

Flushing, Jin admitted, "Well, I'm a bit sore. It's nothing of concern." His brows knit, and Jin thought of how effortlessly he had risen on the boat, without a hint of stiffness, before doing some stretching that revealed both flexibility and strength.

He glanced at the riverboat family, and when he spoke again, it was in the tongue of immortals. "We should start the lessons I promised you."

She glanced at the family as well. "What can we do without disturbing our hosts?"

Bai hesitated. "We can work on your beliefs—they are severely limiting your abilities."

She laughed. "My beliefs? How could my beliefs change how much power I have? Is it not an objective fact?"

Bai smiled, crinkles appearing at the corner of his eyes. He seemingly withdrew a piece of string from the loose sleeve of his robe, though Jin suspected that he had in fact just made it. He handed it to her. "Could you tie this in a knot?"

"Yes, of course."

The string shortened in her hand. "Now?"

"Yes?"

The string shortened until it was perhaps a half an inch long. "Now?"

Jin tried, but the string was too thick and short. "I can't tie it," she told him, thoroughly puzzled.

"But you can, I promise you."

"Truly?"

He touched his heart in sincerity.

Jin frowned at him a moment, then rubbed the string between her fingers. It frayed. She seized the ends and pulled it apart—now it was twice as long, if in two segments, and she tied it. She sent him a questioning look.

He was smiling. "If you believe you cannot do something, you will never do it. If you believe you can..." he shrugged. "Often you will find a way."

Jin looked at the small knot she held. After a moment, she tucked it into her sash. "Very well, I accept my beliefs limit me. What should I try to do?"

Bai indicated the mother and son working at the front of the boat. "Tell me, how does the boy feel?"

Jin was embarrassed. "I only pick up feelings sporadically."

"Knowing others' feelings is Aka's fundamental power. It is not random. You simply have not mastered it. You probably pick up only on particularly strong feelings. Focus on the boy. How does he feel?"

"He's bored," Jin said, then laughed. "But anyone could guess that. Just look at his face."

"So how else does he feel? Come, you can read him."

"But I only have domain over beauty," she told him.

"So? Are emotions not beautiful?"

"Emotion can be beautiful..." Jin murmured, focusing again on the boy. For a moment, it was as if she had slid inside of him; she felt his boredom powerfully. *I wish I was sculling. If only mother and father would let me.*

"He's wistful," Jin says. "He wants to be sculling." She grinned, feeling proud of herself, and she looked for Bai's approval. But he looked more surprised than anything.

"That's a thought, not an emotion," he told her.

"Oh—right—sorry."

"Don't be. You find it easier to read thoughts?"

Jin nodded. "NeeNee—my grandmother—taught me to read golems' thoughts. That was how I figured out the task yours was set to. Reading the boy was similar."

Bai frowned. "You said you tweaked my golem—what did you mean?"

"I influenced his thoughts."

Bai went very still and stared at her hard.

Jin shifted uncomfortably beneath his gaze. "Is that very bad? NeeNee got very angry with me when I did it as a child."

"It's not bad—it's just not a power you inherited from Aka or Neela." He clapped a hand over his mouth. "Red, orange, yellow, blue," he muttered to himself. He started laughing.

Jin found herself chuckling too, his laughter was so engaging. "What's so funny?" she asked.

"I've been suspecting something for a long time—I thought I couldn't read your essence. But I can, it just confounded me." He suddenly grew serious. "Red, orange, yellow, and blue," he said once again.

"What does that mean?" she asked.

Bai sighed. "Those are the colors of your essence. Blue is from Neela, red is from Aka."

"So who's the orange and yellow from?"

Bai raised an eyebrow at her. Jin thought. "Cheng and

Noran? Those immortals in the paintings?"

Bai nodded.

"But how? My unknown grandfather?"

"That would be a logical conclusion."

Jin shifted uncomfortably under his gaze. "You seem to think it's a bad thing."

He looked away from her, lost in thought. "About thirty millennia ago, I taught warfare to a man of Zhongtu."

Jin blinked at the seeming non sequitur. "You mean Chao the Conqueror? His fort later became the first city in Zhongtu."

"Yes, Chao. When I met him, he was a noble young man. Very fair, very honest, eager to improve the lots of those around him. But when he became a warlord, he also used his power to force the daughters of those he conquered to his bed. He became focused on bettering his own lot, and let his followers starve. They eventually killed him, chanting, 'Power corrupts.'"

Jin stiffened. "And you agree with them?"

Bai shook his head. "No, but I feel there is something to learn from the story. I am very powerful, you know. There have been times when I have been ashamed of how I used that power."

He looked at her very intently, those eyes blazing, even though they were dark now rather than gray, thanks to Jin's magic. "You will be much more powerful than I am one day. I suppose I am telling you to be careful. Power may not corrupt, but if the powerful are corrupt, we can do so much more damage than others can."

Jin studied him. He looked serene, kind; his patience and thoughtfulness were almost palpable. It was hard to imagine him doing anything shameful. His soul was beautiful—no, she realized abruptly, that wasn't what she was seeing. She was feeling his emotions and his thoughts. That was what had initially attracted her to him, his sense of calm, a deep inner peace. Even when he told her that he had made mistakes, that he didn't know the answers, she could feel that peace. She yearned for it, as a ship yearns for a safe port during rough seas.

"What was Noran like?" she asked abruptly, then blushed. She was curious about her heritage, but that was an excuse. Nanami had identified Noran as Bai's great love.

"Noran?" he echoed, perhaps the first time Jin had heard him speak without intention. He looked down at his hands, drawing Jin's attention to them as well. They were fisted, the knuckles white. They slowly relaxed beneath her gaze. "Of course, you must be curious about the grandparents you never met."

She nodded, squashing her guilt.

"Well, you saw the painting I did. You do look a bit like her—the same pale skin and the same gold eyes."

Jin squeezed her hands together—that was not what she wanted to hear.

"She was once a grain of sand on the coast of Bando...the first female being." He hesitated. "She claimed that she fell in love with Aka when he slept on her beach, and so made herself someone who could impress him."

Jin blinked. "*Aka*? But I thought..." she flushed.

Bai looked surprised. "Yes, Aka. Remember, she is Gang's mother?"

"Yes—I just—" Jin bit her lip, wondering just what his relationship with Noran had been. She knew he had trained Gang in the art of war... "But to be my grandmother—was she Cheng's lover as well?"

Bai shifted, visibly uncomfortable. "I met Noran at Zi and Hei's wedding. I only know what others have told me of her earlier life."

That was over fifty thousand years ago, ten times longer than Jin had been alive. "What happened at the wedding?"

Bai looked out toward the river, and Jin thought she had been too intrusive. "I'm sorry," she said, "you don't need to answer that."

Bai looked back at her, his face unreadable. "Noran flirted with me, but she wasn't truly interested."

"She used you to make him jealous," Jin said, and her face burned.

"I think so," admitted Bai. "It took me a long time to understand that, actually, but it is what I believe now. Anyway, she and he built the Sun Palace shortly afterward."

Jin's eyes widened. "I can't imagine it not existing. I must seem like a child to you!"

So quickly that she wasn't sure she hadn't imagined it, his eyes flicked down, over her body. "You are young, but you are not child-like," he said. He cleared his throat. "Come, let us try another exercise."

"THIS is the end of our route, but we've gotten here at the best time. Today is the Flower Festival. Actually, because of that, we'll stay here tonight if you wish to sleep on the boat," the father of the riverboat family announced as they tied their boat to a small wooden dock. They had reached the foothills of the Great Ladies. There was a thriving market town here, where the Kuanbai River widened significantly. Bai and Jin would have to find a larger riverboat to carry them to the sea.

"Thank you," Bai told him. "I think we'll take quarters in town, assuming we can find some." He disembarked first, then turned to watch Jin. It was hard to believe that she had the power of four Colors; she barely reached his shoulder and looked as delicate as an orchid. He cringed inwardly as he realized that was much the way he had always viewed Noran. *You old fool,* he thought to himself, *have you learned nothing in fifty millennia?*

What good was fighting efficiently, stretching the capabilities of his body, or calming his mind when he still didn't understand other beings, couldn't connect with them? Bai didn't take his eyes off Jin as she disembarked, and so he was able to catch her elbow when she stumbled. He didn't think he had squeezed too hard, but she flinched from his grip. Bai frowned. The graceful, strong dancer who had captivated him in Bailaohu had been replaced by a stiff and sore young woman doing her best to hide the pain she was in.

"Shall we find somewhere to rest?" he asked her.

"We've done nothing but rest for days," she told him. With anyone else, Bai would have said they were complaining, but Jin's tone was light and cheerful. "I'd much rather walk or even—you said we might do some exercises on shore...?"

"Yes, certainly," but he watched her carefully as they walked down the wooden dock. She stumbled again before they reached land—she seemed to be having trouble lifting her feet. He tried to read her essence, but, as always, it made no sense to him. The brilliant colors swirled in his mind; he tried to set them aside, forcing his knowledge upon them but to no avail. He learned nothing new. Perhaps she really was just stiff from sitting.

He dragged his eyes from her to the town before them. The

path to the dock widened quickly and vendors lined the sides, creating a far denser grouping of mortals than he had ever seen. Buyers and sellers haggled over cloth and carved goods; those stalls bore a symbol that Bai hadn't seen before, a circle enclosing several slashing lines of varying length. Old women cheerfully called to passersby, tempting them to try fried fish and spicy pastries, egg chatamaris and honey doughnuts.

"Mmm, that smells wonderful." Jin tilted her head back, her eyes half closing in appreciation.

Impulsively, Bai said, "Why don't we buy some food?"

She grinned at him and nodded.

Soon they were sitting on a small stone bench, eating chatamaris, and watching humanity swirl past.

"I had forgotten how nice it is to eat food prepared by someone else," Bai said after a few bites.

"It nourishes the soul as well as the body," Jin agreed. "I miss NeeNee's cooking now that I live in the Sun Palace."

"You didn't always?"

"No, after my mother died, NeeNee brought me traveling with her."

Bai chewed his bit of chatamari slowly, thinking. "In her very blue caravan?"

"Yes," Jin laughed. "You've seen it?"

Bai laughed as well. "To my regret."

"We went all over the world in that caravan, never in a rush to get anywhere. 'It's the journey, not the destination,' she'd always say." Jin bit her lip, and her eyes were far away.

"What is it?" Bai asked, leaning a little closer to her despite himself.

"Apparently my mother hated being Sun Empress. I suppose she would have liked to live like NeeNee did. I was feeling guilty about what my father did to her..."

Bai almost rested his hand on her back, but he changed his mind. Instead he said, "What Aka did is beyond apology, but you should not feel guilt for it."

"But he's my father."

"Well, he's my blood, but I do not feel responsible."

"Your blood?" Jin echoed. Her eyes came back to the present and latched on his face. "What does that mean?"

"I used to be alone in the world..." Memories rushed to him. There hadn't even been animals when he first came to be. One day, when he was exploring the Crescent Moon, he had seen an eruption to the north. Curious, he had set off to see what it was—at that time, he hadn't known what a volcano was nor how dangerous it would be. A few weeks later saw him at the caldera of the Korikami's Tomb, and he had tried to climb down a ways to inspect the lava.

He had slipped, and Bai had realized that the magma would be his death as little else could be - it would melt him. He had grabbed frantically for a handhold, and he had found one, but he badly sliced his hand in the process. Blood had been all over the stones, but Bai had disregarded it for he was focused on scrambling to safety and then bandaging himself.

It had not been the first time Bai had bled, but it was the first - and only - time that his blood had become another being. Bai had never seen something so similar in structure to himself, although the coloring had been quite different. Hair the color of coals almost extinguished and eyes the exact shade of Bai's blood.

Aka.

Aka had spoken first, but even then Bai hadn't understood that he was a being with thoughts and opinions as unique as his own - that idea had been too new, too inconceivable. Bai had tried, unsuccessfully, to control him, like a limb that had suddenly detached itself.

He laughed at his own folly, and turned to look at Jin.

She was looking back as if he had just changed into a monster.

"Anything can become an immortal, you know," he felt defensive.

"Yes, but—does this mean you're my *grandfather*?"

"No! As fate laughs at us, no. No more than a dayflower is your great-grandmother. When my blood left me and transformed, it became a totally separate being that really had nothing to do with me. It took me a long time to understand that, though. I spent a few hundred years trying to control all aspects of Aka's being, before he rebelled and left me. I didn't see him again for..." Bai had to stop and think. It wasn't until Aka declared himself a god and collected human worshippers that Bai had encountered him again. "... about twenty thousand years."

"I just can't understand your scale of time. How old are you?"

Bai shrugged. "I never kept track of time until Aka formed. But my best guess is seventy-five thousand years."

Jin passed a hand over her eyes. "Haven't you been lonely?"

"Yes, frequently," he admitted.

He very much wanted to hear her response, but just then a shout rose in the marketplace.

"Thief! Thief!"

Two emperor's men, dressed in red and black with swords at their waists, pushed their way to the shopkeeper, a man selling embroidered goods. His finger, thin and long, pointed at a child huddling against her mother, both of them held in place by the crowd. The mother held her child with one hand, and the other clutched a colorful pendant.

"My daughter's not a thief!" protested the mother loudly, but Bai could hear the lie in her voice, and the fear. Bai looked away, but to his surprise, he saw that Jin had risen and was watching the scene closely. He looked back to see what held her interest so.

"Check her pockets!" howled the merchant. "She stole a little blue purse."

Sure enough, the purse was produced. The merchant determined it ruined, covered in grease from the child's hands.

"She didn't mean it! She doesn't know better!"

"It's your responsibility to teach her better," scolded one of the emperor's men. "I'm tired of your excuses, Goodwife Sonam. If you won't teach her not to steal, we will."

The emperor's men each seized one of the girl's arms and pulled the girl from her mother. Her face made Bai pull back in shock. Red and splotchy from her crying, her forehead was too large and her features too small. Bai recognized her as a Forever Child, and he knew that despite her small stature she might be fully grown. Bai shifted uncomfortably. Forever Children, in addition to retaining a childlike appearance, had a simplistic view of the world. As her mother claimed, she might not have understood the wrongness of taking the purse. Bai turned away, unwilling to witness any more. But Jin moved into the crowd, transforming before his eyes. The darkness in her eyes leached away, leaving them gold and glowing. He didn't think she changed either her hair or her clothes, yet he suddenly found himself thinking her impossibly grand and beautiful. The crowd agreed. They prostrated themselves as the

Goddess of Beauty moved among them.

Jin held her hand out to the merchant, who rose onto his knees to offer her the embroidered purse.

"It is beautiful work. The needlewoman was skilled," she said. She turned to the Forever Child, still standing, no longer crying. "Beautiful things call to each other, don't they?" She handed the purse to the Child, who clutched it to her heart. Jin then let several coins trickle into the merchant's still open palm, glittering like water in sunlight. Bai had enough presence of mind to realize this was more of her manipulation.

"This market is full of lovely goods. I am proud to have my mark graven on so many stalls." Briefly the mark that Bai had noted earlier, the circled bars, flared everywhere it was carved or branded. "But you must remember, the greatest beauty of all comes from the good thoughts of humans. Jamyang's kind heart and happy soul is a blessing upon this town. She sees beauty everywhere, and so has mastered the most important skill of my followers." Jin touched Jamyang's cheek, and Bai had to admit that her innocence and great joy made for a particularly beautiful smile.

Jin then surveyed the crowd. "It is common to cringe away from the unfamiliar, to reject those who are different from ourselves. But, to see the infinite beauty of the world, we must keep our minds open and unafraid. To ask before we accuse. Jamyang, will you share your eyes with this town, and help them see the beauty that surrounds them?"

Jamyang nodded and Jin's mark gleamed on her forehead, marking her as a chosen of the Goddess of Beauty, whose prayers would always be heard. Behind Jamyang, her mother pressed her mouth as tears streamed down her cheeks.

Jin smiled and made her way from the crowd, holding them

in place with her overwhelming beauty. Bai did not move for
fear of breaking her spell. Once she was out of sight, the people
rose, and slowly returned to their business, though many cast
sidelong looks at Jamyang. Bai waited a few minutes longer,
then hurried after Jin.

He found her clutching a wall in an alleyway, face white,
breath harsh, looking nothing like the Goddess who had just
awed the crowd. Jin tried to take a step toward him, but her leg
crumpled beneath her.

JIN closed her eyes, unable to find the strength to catch herself,
but she needn't have worried. One of Bai's arms wrapped
around her shoulders and the other caught her under the
knees. He swept her up, and her head lolled on his shoulder.
He was just as strong as he looked.

"What's wrong?" he demanded, his brow furrowed in
concern.

Jin tried to smile to reassure him but ended up coughing.
"I—I don't know," she managed.

"You used too much magic helping that mortal." He shook
his head, even as he started walking briskly. "If anything
happens—because you helped a *thief*!" The words burst forth
from him, wholly unlike his usual manner. "No one will
remember her in thirty years."

The harsh words might have upset Jin, if she hadn't felt his
deep worry beneath them—from his thoughts, that worry was
for her.

"She might not be remembered by history or create
anything of cultural significance, but every day she will bring
sweetness and joy into those who surround her. Her mother

prayed to me for help, and she did not deserve ten lashes." Jin coughed again, though she tried to suppress it.

"I may have used a lot of power, but I've never had a reaction like this before, even when I used more."

Bai's hold on her tightened. "I don't suppose you'd be willing to leave Kunjee behind so that I could take you to Haraa."

Jin shook her head. "I could wait for you."

Bai scowled fiercely, and Jin felt a spike of adrenaline. "I'm not leaving you," he said.

He began to stride quickly out of town, following the river. People passed them, and though they moved out of Bai's way, they barely seemed to notice them.

"What did you do?" asked Jin curiously.

Bai followed her gaze to a mortal woman carrying jugs past them. "You're not the only one who trick the eye. I call it whiting out. It makes it hard to focus on me." He walked faster. Jin tried to move her legs experimentally but could not.

"I can't feel or move my legs," she said, "and the rest of me hurts."

Bai's eyes flicked to hers and then back to the path. "I think you've been poisoned."

"The chatamaris?" she asked in disbelief.

His mouth twisted. "I don't think so. It's just a guess, but I think the reason we haven't seen your assailant again is he knew he had succeeded in his task—the throwing star must have been poisoned."

"But—it's been over a week..." Jin protested.

"And you've been feeling poorly for much of that time." He shook his head. "I'm sorry. I should have realized sooner. I'm so used to reading poison in a person's essence... If I had to guess, the poison is triggered by your use of magic. The poisoner probably expected you to teleport immediately, which would have led you to this state much sooner. Our small use of power on the riverboat kept you feeling ill, then—" He swallowed.

Jin swallowed as well. Bai's obvious fear for her was contagious. "If you can't read my essence, then you can't know it was poison. Perhaps I did overexert myself."

He didn't need to speak to make his opinion clear.

It appeared he found whatever he was looking for, as he turned off the path and settled her on a stretch of slightly muddy beach beneath a tree with large white flowers. A dove tree, Jin thought it was called. Bai plucked two of the petals and, faster than Jin could follow, he had made a riverboat. It was nearly identical to the one that they had purchased passage on, except it was as white as bone.

Bai stared at the boat a few moments, then plucked another six petals. "We might need them later," he explained when Jin made a questioning sound.

"But—can you steer this?"

His serious, almost frightening aspect softened as his lips twitched. "The Kuanbai River would never do me ill," he told her. "It carried me as a stone when it first formed, and I watched it mature from a trickle to a river."

Jin, who was trying to imagine a small stone becoming the man before her, made no objection as he lifted her onto the boat, and launched them. As he had implied, the river seemed to steer the boat for them and allowed Bai to examine her, his hands floating mere inches above her body. His frown grew ever fiercer, and Jin couldn't summon her voice to ask him what he was learning.

Finally, he touched her cheek, his finger skimming where the shuriken had cut her.

"I'm sorry," he said, producing a small blade. "I need to reopen the wound."

Jin closed her eyes and held very still. When she opened them, he was examining a drop of her blood on his index finger.

"It is poison," he confirmed, "triggered by magic use. It will paralyze you and put you in a coma, but it will not kill you."

"How...?"

"I can still read the essence of the poison, even if I can't read yours."

"Do you know the antidote then?"

He shook his head. "It needs to be removed from your body. If there is an herb or medicine that would do so, I don't know it." He sighed, meeting her eyes. She found them no less fiery for being black rather than gray.

"I have no affinity for blood. But you do—red has dominion over blood, and blue in a more limited way. Have you ever seen Aka clean someone's blood?"

Jin remembered it vividly: Xiao had fallen to his knees, screaming, when Aka had burned the toxins from his blood. "Yes," she admitted reluctantly.

"Then you must do it now, before the poison progresses farther."

Jin flinched. The idea of causing the pain that Aka caused, even if only on herself... "No—no, I can't do that." To cover her fear, she argued, "What if I fail? Surely the poison will be quickened."

"You must believe you can," Bai said fiercely. "Imagine your blood flowing through your body, then imagine it purifying, cleansing itself."

Jin closed her eyes. But she couldn't imagine the blood; she certainly couldn't burn away the impurities. She was the Goddess of Beauty, not blood nor healing nor fire.

"This won't work," she told Bai.

Bai glared at her, making Jin feel worthless. "Not if you have that attitude! You—"

"Stop!" Jin scolded him. "Stop yelling at me. We need a solution that is viable."

"Leave Kunjee here," he suggested again. "And I will bring you to Haraa."

"No," said Jin. "I have a different idea." She took a deep breath. "What has blue to do with blood? How is that possible?"

Bai shook his head impatiently, but he held up his hand. "See the veins? They are blue. When we see our blood through our skin, it's blue."

"Then Neela could cleanse it."

"Yes, but who knows where she is?"

Jin laughed despite herself. "I do. She's my grandmother— of course I can summon her. But are you sure she can help? I don't want to bring her here just to see me..."

Bai seized her hand and squeezed it. "Summon her."

Jin closed her eyes. Just as she had a thousand—no, a million—times before, she sent out a tendril of thought. *NeeNee? NeeNee? I need you.*

The last thing Jin heard was a querulous voice demanding, "What's going on here?"

SUN PALACE

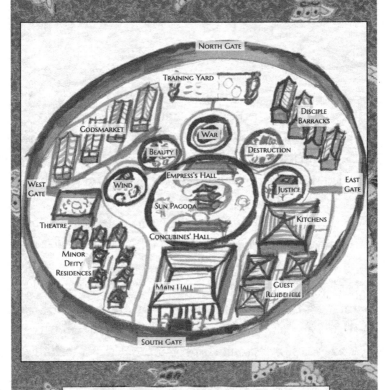

The central residence for the emperor was built by Aka and Noran fifty millennia ago. Each of his children was granted their own residence when they approached adulthood. Including disciples and minor deities, the palace is home to over a thousand immortals.

8

How Nanami Met Justice

THE East Gate, Jin had called it, but the characters above the gate itself read "Lightning." To either side of it were life-size bronze statues—the Goddess of Justice and the God of Destruction, by their accoutrements. Nanami wondered if they were accurate likenesses. There was certainly a family resemblance—both were lean and tall with patrician noses and sharp cheekbones. Perhaps any bronze statue would seem forbidding, but Nanami found Salaana's expression particularly severe.

Taking a deep breath, she walked before that statue, and prostrated herself, toes tucked under her heels and hands spread beneath her shoulders. The ground was a warm grey marble—not immediately unpleasant, but hardly forgiving. She felt vulnerable and uncomfortable.

Within five minutes, Nanami heard people walking through the gate. Some paused by her, as if she were placed for their entertainment and openly scrutinized her as the Goddess of Justice's latest petitioner. Others hurried past, one nearly stepping on Nanami's calf, she was so beneath her notice. Nanami resented both reactions, her gut roiling and her fingers tense against the marble. Even though it was a mere two days she had to lie here, the time stretched eternal.

XIAO arrived in Jin's empty bedchamber. Through a half open sliding door, he could see Yeppeun and Luye sitting in the garden. Some purple flowers, like grapes, dangled from a canopy over their heads. They were both holding flutes, though they appeared to be speaking rather than playing.

His first impulse was to call out to them—to tell them of the quest's progress and seek their help in uncovering Jin's enemy. He quelled it. The less people who knew a secret, the easier it was to keep. He took a deep breath and stumbled into Jin's low table-desk, knocking a blue and green vase to the ground, spilling water and white flowers across the wooden floor. He cursed loudly.

Yeppeun and Luye both turned their heads toward the building; moments later they entered.

"Divinity, have you returned?" Yeppeun called. She caught sight of Xiao and froze. "Oh. Hello."

Luye peered over Yeppeun's shoulder. "What're you doing here? Where's her divinity?"

"Oh, fine, fine, she's just worried about dear-old-dad, so she sent me to check on him." Xiao lurched toward the two women. He worried he was overacting, but they cast each other resigned looks and moved to steady him.

"Why, thank you ladies." He attempted to drop a kiss on Yeppeun's cheek— she smelled the rice wine he'd drunk, and her nose wrinkled in disgust. She turned her face so that his kiss landed in her hair. "Which of you wants to get me a drink?"

"Don't you want to see the emperor first?" Luye bit out

sarcastically.

Xiao laughed. "I doubt he cares one way or th'other." He shrugged away from them. "I'll just make my way down to the theater district and catch up on the gossip. You ladies make the bed ready for my return, won't you?"

"We aren't *your* disciples," said Luye.

"Well, I'm marrying your mistress, aren't I? Better get used to me as a master." He gave them each a swat on the bottom, then made his way to the gate, walking just a bit crooked.

He glanced back to see the unhappy disciples arguing. *Well, I daresay everyone will know Jin sent drunk Xiao back to get him out of her way by tomorrow.*

Xiao meandered between the outer wall of Jin's residence and her younger brother's, the small smooth stones crunching beneath his feet. The Palace had not changed during the past several days, yet its opulence now seemed ominous. It was a struggle to maintain his tipsy and relaxed facade. *A drink would have steadied my nerves.*

Guleum, the God of Wind, stepped onto the path with two attendants behind him. Guleum was too young to have disciples; these were servants assigned to him by his parents.

"Hello, Xiao," he said. "Rumor said we wouldn't be seeing you anytime soon, but we barely had a chance to register your absence before you came back!"

Xiao clapped a hand on Guleum's shoulder. His servants stiffened, though the young god seemed unperturbed by the contact.

"Little Gu! Are you old enough to drink yet? Why don't you join me, and I'll tell you all about it?" Xiao might not *want* to believe Guleum had cursed the Sun Emperor, but he was still a possibility.

Guleum grinned. "I've got something stronger in mind than spirits—mortal dreams! Why don't you join me?"

Xiao didn't have to fake his stumble, he was so surprised. "Mortal dreams, you say? You already have worshippers on Earth?"

Guleum shook his head. "Don't need 'em. You can buy your pick of dreams at the Godsmarket for next to nothing."

Xiao couldn't completely keep his disgust from his face, but Guleum, with the self-absorption of adolescence, didn't notice.

When a worshipper had a dream that was pertinent to their god, it came to the god's house just like a prayer. However, while prayers tended to be deliberate and limited to words, dreams were an immersive experience that often revealed subconscious desires. Xiao personally had ignored mortal dreams for almost five hundred years—he believed that some things should not be shared, even with a god.

That some gods sold their follower's dreams offended him deeply.

Xiao dredged up a lazy smile and said, "Lead on, Gu."

The Godsmarket was arrayed between the West and North Gates. Its canopied stalls lined either side of a broad brick avenue. The stalls themselves were of gold and silver, the silk awnings vibrantly and expertly dyed. There was no shouting, no hawking goods, instead just the plaintive song of several stringed instruments. Everyone seemed to know exactly what was sold where—Guleum certainly did. He walked boldly to a stall of silver with a multi-colored canopy. The symbol for dream was etched into the metal and colored candles of various shapes stood in neat rows. The seller was a grim-faced woman dressed in all black—Xiao supposed she must be a disciple of his father, who took a percentage from the sale of dreams, as the God of Night.

Guleum clapped his hands in delight. "I'll take four of the white-threaded-red. The wolf, the two swords, and the snake."

There were many white-threaded-red, almost a quarter of the table. "What do the colors mean?" Xiao asked.

"It indicates the type of dream," Guleum told him. "These ones are adventure—lots of fighting. The shape of the candle is a kind of preview." The seller made no comment, though the question had been intended for her. She wrapped the four candles that Guleum had chosen in thin rice paper and placed them in a bag. She then held out a glass vial and a needle.

"Two drops each."

Guleum frowned. "It was only one drop last time."

"If you don't want them..."

Guleum stabbed his thumb and squeezed eight drops of blood into the vial. Xiao stiffened. Only a young idiot like Guleum would think their *blood* "next to nothing." Xiao wasn't sure exactly what could be done with it, but his father had once lectured him about never letting another immortal have any blood, hair, or spit from his body saying they could use it to gain influence over him. Xiao watched Guleum hand the vial back to the merchant and considered snatching it or knocking it to the ground.

Guleum blithely wiped his thumb, still bleeding sluggishly, on his robe's collar, probably ruining the complex geometric embroidery.

"Do you want anything, Xiao?" asked Guleum. He started explaining the genres of the different colors—an olive green with yellow specks for food, a pearlescent pink for flying, purple for falling in love, purple-and-black for sex -

Xiao lost his struggle to maintain his tipsy-and-relaxed

facade. He grabbed a purple-and-black candle shaped like a man's torso, ignoring the merchant's protest.

"Where did you get this?" he demanded.

The merchant crossed her arms. "That's privileged information. If you aren't paying, give it back."

Xiao leaned forward. "I am the God of Pleasure, and this belongs to me. You will tell me where you got it now."

Sweat beaded on the woman's brow. "I will not answer—"

Xiao crushed the wax torso in his hand. "You will answer."

"What is going on here?" demanded a new voice, calm and sure. Xiao half-turned and found five Sun Guards surrounding them, their gold armor gleaming over red tunics.

"Nothing, nothing," Guleum put in, his face pale. "It's the God of Pleasure, he's just a bit drunk."

The Sun Guards relaxed slightly as they recognized Guleum and Xiao. "Divinity, if you'd please—"

Belligerent drunk? So be it. Xiao let his chin jut and swept his hands out, knocking over the candles that were so carefully aligned on the table. "These candles are made of *my* worshippers' dreams. They belong to *me*. You should be hasslin' her, not me! Find out how she got 'em!"

The guards looked doubtfully at each other. The merchant shifted her weight from foot to foot, her lips folded uneasily.

The lieutenant turned back to Xiao, his hands raised placatingly. "Divinity, we will confiscate the goods in question and open an inquiry. Would that—satisfy you?"

Xiao could hear the words he reconsidered—*would that calm you down?* "You're takin' 'em? How can I trust you?"

"Divinity," the lieutenant said, clearly shocked. "We are the Imperial Sun Guards."

"Oh, so you never have a little extra fun with the goods you seize?" Xiao sneered.

The lieutenant's expression hardened. "If you prefer, we can take you and the goods together."

"Oh, no, no, surely that isn't necessary," put in Guleum. He was sweating like he'd run a mile. "C'mon, Xiao, let the guards do their job. You can talk to my brother later if you aren't happy with the outcome."

"He can talk to me now," came Gang's deep rumble. The God of War was flanked by two more of his men—this little section of the market had become impassable. Despite Gang's offer, he looked toward his lieutenant, not Xiao. "What's all this?"

"The God of Pleasure believes this woman to illegally be selling his worshippers' dreams."

"Then confiscate the dreams in question and begin an inquiry."

The lieutenant flushed. "I was trying, divinity, but the God of Pleasure—"

Gang waved a hand, cutting the man off. "I will deal with him." And one of Gang's over-sized hands closed on Xiao's forearm.

As angry as he was, Xiao made no objection beyond a scowl.

"See you later," he told Guleum as Gang towed him away.

Xiao was hauled into a spartan office, featuring only a plain desk made of a dark wood. There were no windows, but several glowing yellow sconces were mounted on the walls. Gang dismissed his disciples and watched Xiao through narrow eyes until the sounds of the guards' footsteps had faded away.

"You're drunk?" Gang demanded.

It was probably unwise, but Xiao was sick of everyone treating him like a fool. "How could I be, when you hired a thief to steal the Infinite Jug?"

Gang's nostrils flared at "hired a thief," but otherwise his face remained impassive. "I don't know what you are talking about."

Of course Gang wouldn't admit it readily. "I captured the thief and consulted a diviner," he drawled.

A vein popped by Gang's left eye.

Xiao swallowed but persevered. "I can't believe you didn't bother with a disguise—even if the diviner hadn't confirmed your identity, I could have just from Nanami's description. Who knows you cuckolded—"

Gang slammed Xiao against the wall, one hand grasping the front of his robes, the other covering his mouth.

Gang closed his eyes. Xiao would have thought he was praying except—well, to whom would he pray?

After a few moments, Gang released him. Xiao nearly fell but caught himself on the wall.

"We may speak freely now. You said," Gang rumbled, "that you were going to help Jin on her quest. Why are you here?"

"Jin doesn't need me for a bodyguard, not with Bai following her like a lost puppy. I'm here to identify her enemy, make a proactive strike."

Gang looked surprised, his bushy eyebrows lifted, his mouth an O in his fierce beard. If he weren't still so scared, Xiao would have laughed at the expression.

"Bai—what nonsense are you spouting?"

Xiao shrugged. "You know," he dropped his voice to a whisper, "your old teacher. White-hair, likes to go around shirtless."

Gang took a seat behind the desk. After a moment, a red patch on the floor rose up, creating a stool, and he waved Xiao to it.

"If you talk about your suspicions to anyone, I will take your tongue," Gang announced, as he lowered his hands.

"If you won't admit to being her father, are you going to confess to attacking her?"

Gang's massive hands immediately became fists, and Xiao felt more confident he had the right brother. "What attack? Describe it clearly."

"An immortal chucked two throwing stars at Jin. Cut her cheek. Luckily, it wasn't too bad."

Gang released his breath; he must really care about Jin. "I promised that I would protect Jin to the best of my ability. I meant it."

Xiao nodded slowly. Then, "Protecting Jin doesn't mean you aren't working with whoever cursed the Sun Emperor."

Gang snorted. "I am not working with my siblings—indeed, I am preparing for the civil war that will surely come when he dies."

Xiao stiffened. "That's why you didn't suspect Jin—not that load about her beautiful soul. You said, the more blood the curser shares, the stronger the curse. And so you knew the curse hadn't been cast by a grandchild. But that means... even if she gets the black peony, could she lift the curse?"

Something flickered in Gang's gold eyes—for the first time Xiao was struck by how similar they were to Jin's and yet how little their expressions had in common. "Magic is unpredictable."

Xiao sneered. "So you don't think so." He rubbed his face. "Jin will be devastated."

"Don't tell her," Gang ordered. "She's far from court. It is safer than here, where she will surely return if she knows the quest is fruitless."

"So everything you said, how she is more powerful than she knows…"

"If I were lying, she would have known. There were simply other factors I chose not to mention."

Xiao stared at Gang's stony expression and felt suddenly afraid. "What are you going to do to me?"

Gang watched him silently.

"It's not a good idea to kill me."

A small humorless smile twisted Gang's lips. "Isn't it though? I don't think your parents would mind."

"Jin would," Xiao asserted.

"But she doesn't want to marry you," Gang pointed out.

"No, but I'm her best friend." Xiao's hands fisted in his lap. He remembered how quickly Bai had disarmed him. Did he stand a chance against Gang if it came to a fight right now?

Gang sighed, and his whole face drooped. "I'm not going to kill you, Xiao. Believe it or not, I hate killing. I only use it as a last resort. You're here to glean information on my siblings, fine, that suits me, as long as you share what you learn. That being said, I need some insurance."

"Insurance?"

"I will accept a pledge of obedience."

Xiao stiffened. His immortality, his powers, gone if he ever went against Gang's orders? He had no thought of thwarting the God of War, but if civil war were coming, how could he subjugate himself to another man?

And yet, did he have any other choice? Did death or imprisonment await him if he refused? Xiao remembered the long hours of his childhood, locked in his room. And yet, even then, he was still an autonomous being, not a puppet.

*And I would rather be physically chained than have my free
will overruled. And if Gang plans my death... well, I will fight
until the end.*

"No. I already have one vow hanging over my head that I
want to break—I'm not making another."

Gang laughed bitterly. "You're wiser than I was at your
age."

Then his hand darted out and seized Xiao's wrist. Quicker
than the eye could follow, he pricked Xiao's thumb with a
dagger and squeezed three drops of blood from it. They fell on
a white sheet of paper below it. Gang released his hand.

"I will accept these instead of a vow. You may go."

Xiao rubbed his thumb uneasily, but he stayed seated. Gang
cocked his head. "I would have thought you'd scurry from my
office."

Xiao grit his teeth at Gang's disdain, but managed, "I have
other business with you. You said your men will investigate the
dreams. I'm supposed to just leave it there?"

Gang's gold eyes bored into him. "Do you really not know
who's selling them?"

Xiao flushed—Gang acted like he was an idiot or a child or
both. "How would I?"

"Affinity. Not just anyone could collect those and distill
them for sale. In fact, given what you are, there are only two
people, working together, who could manage it."

Xiao's heart was in his throat. "I see." *I suppose I knew it was
them, didn't I—that's why I was so angry.* "It still violates the
Sun Emperor's second edict—no god may pretend to be
another."

Gang arched one of his bushy brows, in a way that
reminded Xiao of Bai. "So you want me to arrest your parents?"

Xiao squeezed his hands together. "Could you?"

Gang's barking laugh made Xiao twitch. "Possibly. But not without great risk."

"I'll deal with it myself," Xiao said, not sure if he was lying.

"RISE, faithful one, and meet your seniors."

Nanami did not immediately process the words. She was too uncomfortable for true sleep, but she had entered a trance-like state where her hunger, thirst, and discomfort could be held at a distance. However, a foot nudged her elbow, and she abruptly realized her petition had been accepted.

She attempted to rise, only to discover her limbs were stiff and painful. She felt needles all over. Two sets of hands grasped her by the shoulders, and she was brought to her feet.

There were three disciples present, all women, though she wouldn't have noted it if not for Xiao's comments. They were dressed in the uniform of justice, white saris edged in with crimson and bodices of the same color. Between that, their identical expressions, and neatly bound dark hair, it was difficult to distinguish them, even though their faces and builds really weren't that similar.

The disciple who wasn't helping her stand offered Nanami a white porcelain cup, which Nanami accepted gratefully. It held warm water, slightly sweetened with honey. Nanami forced herself to drink it slowly.

"I am Aarti, the third disciple of her divinity, the Goddess of Justice. This is Nika, the forty-second disciple," the woman to Nanami's right inclined her head, "and Eun-ji, the forty-eighth disciple," the woman to Nanami's left bowed. Aarti retrieved the cup. "What are you called?"

Nanami had to cough once to summon her voice. "Nana."

"Are you able to walk?"

Hesitantly, Nanami let her weight settle on her feet and took a few steps.

"Good," Aarti smiled in approval. "Welcome to the Sun Court, Nana."

The disciples moved slowly out of consideration for her, giving Nanami plenty of time to absorb the sights of the Sun Palace. Passing through the East Gate's water illusion, they entered a grassy park cut by broad, straight paths and neatly trimmed boxwoods. Despite it being spring, Nanami saw no flowers. Directly ahead was a rusty red building, and behind it was an immense vermillion wall.

"Those are the kitchens," murmured Eun-ji. "The wall encloses the imperial residence. She pointed to the left, where Nanami could just make out colorful roofs past rolling hills. "Those are where guests stay, if they are not invited into the main residence of their host."

The four of them went the opposite direction. The path passed a wall painted with wild swirls of red and white, evoking flames.

"The God of Destruction's residence."

When they came even with another wall of red and white, this one painted with mandalas of recursive squares, the ladies paused. "This is our lady's residence. Her first twenty disciples, including Aarti, live within. You, Nika, and I live in the servants' quarters just ahead." Nanami could see more rust-red buildings.

"Usually you will eat with us there, but your first meal will be in our lady's home. Nika and I will wait for you here."

Nanami looked to Aarti, who waited a few steps ahead—

impatient, Nanami thought. Nanami stumbled a little as she hurried to catch up. In front of a large white door featuring red starburst medallions, Aarti bowed from the waist, so Nanami did the same, stifling a groan as she did so. The door swung open.

The inside of Salaana's residence was austere and almost frightening. If it took any aesthetic from Jeevanti, it was the Shubra Desert, which Nanami had seen only once, briefly, by her own preference. Carefully raked sand filled the open spaces, accented by gray stepping stones and carved benches, several of which were occupied by more of the uniformed disciples. Nanami had to fight the impulse to run through the neat lines of sand and spray it on the focused disciples.

Aarti led the way over the stones to the largest structure, a rather humble building of untreated wood, and indicated they should remove their shoes. When they entered, Nanami gasped in surprised pleasure. Contrary to her expectations, the interior was simple and homey. The floor was tatami mats and there were blue and white zabuton cushions stacked in the corner. Like any wealthy Jeevanti home, there was an inner courtyard but this one featured a large koi pond with a bamboo fountain. The fish themselves were the only red Nanami saw. They were rather small, but all were splotched with red and white.

Aarti cocked her head. "You are from the Crescent Moon, aren't you? What do you think of the space?"

Nanami was startled by the question, so she took her time replying, making a show of examining the room. "It is lovely," she said at last. "It reminds me of home."

That was clearly the right answer, and Aarti beamed. She then led Nanami to the low table and set down a zabuton for each of them. She offered a huge array of snacks to Nanami—fermented soybeans, seasoned nori, sweet rice cakes, sesame cookies—and solicited Nanami's opinion of each item. Indeed, Aarti seemed almost frantic to please her. At last another disciple interrupted to announce a petitioner, and Nanami was relieved.

Aarti led Nanami back into the sand garden, directing her to line up with the other disciples while Aarti listened to the petitioner. Nanami moved to obey and narrowly stopped herself from doing a double take. Dressed in flowing formal robes of violet and lavender, hair braided with silver, and flask in hand was Xiao. Despite his attire, he looked a mess—he had spilled something on his skirts and from the smell, Nanami thought it was soju. His eyes were bloodshot as they swept past her. Nanami would have thought he hadn't even seen her if he hadn't touched the small dark ring on his left pinky before speaking.

"I wish to speak to *Salaana*," he insisted, with the belligerence of a man who'd had too much to drink. Nanami studied him closely, trying to decide if it was acting or not, while Aarti bowed deeply in apology.

"Her divinity is gone at present, but I will listen to your petition."

"And who are you?" he demanded.

"I am the Third Disciple of the Goddess of Justice. While she and the head disciples are absent, I act in her name."

Xiao sniffed, repeating "Third?" in an all too audible mutter. More loudly, he said, "Well, then, you need to punish the dream vendor in the Godsmarket. She is selling my worshippers' dreams without my permission."

"In the Godsmarket? And what did the Sun Guard say

about it?"

"The Sun Guard! Fools. They acted like I couldn't even recognize my own dreams. They gave them back to that unscrupulous merchant this morning."

Aarti's lips thinned. "I'm afraid that the Godsmarket is the Sun Guard's jurisdiction. If they found no wrongdoing, there's nothing more to be said about it."

"You tell Salaana I'll remember this," he sneered before the disciples managed to hustle him from the premises.

Nanami was likewise dismissed shortly after. The forty-eighth disciple, Eun-ji, showed Nanami her living quarters and then gave her a fuller tour of the palace. Nanami had little interest in the ornate gardens though. It was only when they came to the Godsmarket that she perked up. It was easy to find the dream vendor, as she was dressed in the robes of the Night God and had the symbol for dream etched on her silver stall. Eun-ji was willing enough to let Nanami stop and look at the candles and explained the red and white ones were Salaana's.

"Bringing extra dreams here for sale may be one of your duties in the future," she said.

"What makes a dream extra?" Nanami asked.

Eun-ji nodded approvingly at the question. "Mortal dreams are repetitive. We only need one dream per mortal to enact justice. Sometimes they even dream of justice that has already been delivered. All of these we sell."

"I suppose dreams of justice help spread the teachings of her divinity."

"Yes—and they are also very popular because they are exciting and satisfying. Immortals are willing to pay well for such dreams."

"Oh? What is the cost of a dream?"

"For our Lady's, a drop of blood."

Nanami just stopped herself from showing her revulsion. "Blood? I am surprised that many would pay that."

Eun-ji smiled and bought a dream shaped like a snake from the vendor, which she gave to Nanami.

"Perhaps after you feel it, you will understand."

Nanami nodded, hoping her expression was thoughtful.

That night, when most of the palace slept, Nanami slipped out of the building that housed Salaana's lower disciples and aspirants. She made her way to the Godsmarket. Several Sun Guards were patrolling, but their patterns were regular and after an hour of observation, Nanami crept through the market confidently until she found the dream vendor's stall. Nanami spat into her hand and made two lock picks from the fluid. Five minutes later, she filled a small satchel with the black and violet candles that must be Xiao's.

Jin's residence was the closest to the Godsmarket. Nanami was overconfident as she made her way there, and almost walked into a Sun Guard patrol. But the guards clearly didn't expect any chicanery and didn't even notice her duck under a bush. Nanami held her breath as they passed her, though she doubted they would have heard her anyway.

Nanami paused before scaling Jin's wall. She had deliberately paid little attention to it during her tour, but up close it was hard to ignore the fanciful paintings that covered the walls. The soft glow of torches revealed a peacock spreading his glorious tail of turquoise and gold and strutting for a peahen who surveyed him critically from a peony bush. Nanami smiled, thinking the peacock was not unlike a certain someone.

Reluctant to step on either bird, she finally found a section of wall that was only ferns. Taking it at a run, she reached the roof and pulled herself over the red terracotta tiles. She perched briefly at that top, refreshing her memory of the residence.

She quickly and quietly made her way to the main hall where Xiao would be sleeping, giving the disciples' huts a wide berth.

Xiao was indeed asleep, limbs askew, in Jin's bed. Nanami found that his ease there bothered her less than she would have expected. Feeling mischievous, she plucked a branch of azalea blooms from the vase on Jin's low table and used the flowers to tickle Xiao's cheek. He twitched slightly but continued to sleep. Nanami frowned and leaned forward to sniff his breath—had he passed out from drink?

But when she was bent over him, his hands suddenly seized her waist and flipped her under him. He smirked.

"Oh, dear, what would Salaana say if she knew her aspirant stole into her sister's residence to see said sister's betrothed?"

Nanami stuck her tongue out at him.

"Did you find something?" he asked.

"If you get off me, I'll show you."

So he let her up, and she removed the candles from her satchel.

Xiao's eyes widened with shock. "You stole my dreams?"

"Didn't you want them? I thought that was why you came to petition Salaana."

Xiao picked up a candle and examined it. "I came to see you and make sure all was going well. It didn't occur to me that you'd recover these." He met her eyes. "Thank you."

Nanami nodded, unable to reply. Xiao set the candle down and swept his arm over the lot of them, and the wax became smoke and faded away.

"So how did the vendor get these, anyway?"

Xiao grimaced. "My parents."

He wouldn't meet her eyes. Understanding how he felt, Nanami didn't push further. Instead she retrieved the white and red candle from her pocket. "One of Salaana's dreams," she told Xiao.

Xiao stiffened. "You stole from the Goddess of Justice? Nanami—"

"No," she reassured him. "I came by this honestly. A present from the forty-eighth disciple. Apparently they are very popular. And immortals pay blood for them."

Xiao winced. "Yes, I know. Guleum is one of the buyers." He turned it over in his hands. "Shall we feel the dream then?"

Nanami nodded.

The lit candle released a thick smoke smelling of cardamom and ginger which soon enveloped her, filling her ears with the rustling of cloth and obscuring her vision.

Nanami blinked. She was in a sunny market square, somewhere in Bando, she suspected. Vendors were hawking their goods, mostly bolts of cloth and embroidered pouches. A man was making his way from booth to booth, collecting money from each. He turned to Nanami and smiled, baring fanged teeth and slit eyes. A thin serpentine tongue darted out of his mouth and retreated. He turned away from her and Nanami leapt into the air. With a sharp cry and whirl, Nanami descended toward him and sent him flying backward. She landed lightly on the ground and punched the air several times before his gang showed up, tongues flickering. Nanami quickly beat them into submission, leaving them in a pile. The townspeople began to cheer and clap, and Nanami bowed humbly.

"It was nothing, nothing," she murmured.

Just then, the ground around her began to ripple, and the square fell silent. Nanami turned to follow the ripples, her fists ready and her heart in her mouth.

A massive emerald snake burst from the ground, sending dirt flying everywhere. It wrapped its coils around Nanami, threatening to suffocate her. Nanami began to grow, until the snake was but the size of her arm. She seized the monstrosity behind the head and cracked its spine. She dropped the snake to the ground, and she was suddenly normal size again. A beautiful girl threw her arms around her neck and gushed her gratitude.

And then Nanami was back in Jin's suite, laying on her back and slightly breathless. She could hear Xiao's pants beside her.

After a few minutes, she managed, "It was so vivid—so intense—more real than life, if that makes sense."

Xiao laughed. "That was your first mortal dream, huh? Yeah, that's why some people become addicted to them."

"Is Guleum?"

"Maybe."

Nanami patted his back awkwardly. He must feel particularly sensitive about addictions, and he was clearly worried about Guleum.

Xiao glanced at her hand and smiled. He then launched into a summary of his meeting with Gang.

Nanami observed, "These children of Aka really like blood, don't they? Aka has a particular affinity for it—do you know what they can do with it?"

"Probably a compulsory summons. Clean my blood at a distance—not sure why they'd want to."

"I wonder... if they could clean your blood, could they also poison it?"

Xiao stiffened. "Now that's a scary thought." He rubbed his face. "Well, he has my blood now. We'll have to wait and see."

OVER the next week, Xiao was not able to see Nanami frequently, but the court embraced his drunken antics with open arms. Of course, he wasn't really drunk, and pride in his deception helped him maintain the pretense of drinking. He told himself that everyone had been worried about nothing. He was in control of his urges. But his enjoyment in his success was tempered by worry. He worried about Jin and Nanami (he was not in the least worried about Bai) and about confronting his parents.

He also found himself trying to understand what Nanami meant to him. The fact that she had taken his worshippers' dreams from the market—well, it hardly dealt with the root of the problem, but it had meant a lot to him. He was grateful. He liked spending time with her, and he had already realized that it felt effortless compared to being with Jin. But—he was to wed Jin in less than a year.

Xiao finally went to see Aka, his nominal charge, with young Guleum. They entered the emperor's room at the top of the Sun Pagoda, and Xiao found Aka looked exactly as they'd left him, though someone had lit a great many red candles around him.

"My mother lit those," Guleum said. "None of my siblings could be bothered. I don't understand why she did either— she'd be better off if he died."

Xiao's jaw might have hit the floor, but he caught it. "Why do you say that?"

"He doesn't love her. Spends all his time with other women, while she suffers alone."

Xiao blinked in surprise. "The Sun Emperor has always had concubines and mistresses, with all of his wives."

Guleum eyes flashed angrily. "I know. And then he simply disposes of them when he wants a new one. My mother didn't want to marry him, you know—but how does one refuse the ruler of the world?"

Xiao had to admit he was surprised by this conversation. He hadn't realized that Guleum thought about anything serious. "I'm not sure anyone does," he admitted softly. "It is a shame, isn't it?"

"Yes," said Guleum fiercely, angrily.

Xiao hadn't realized how thoroughly Guleum resented Aka. "But now your mother has a chance to be free."

Guleum smiled. "Yes, I—well, I should not mind if he never wakes up." But there was a pride in the words, a gloating that struck Xiao as strange, unless Guleum was in fact the curser.

Xiao, searching for a way to solicit Guleum's confidences, asked, "I wonder why he collapsed. Do you think it was poison?"

Guleum hesitated. "If it were poison, I'd suspect Gang. My mother told me he has a plant that can make a god sick or comatose or dead, depending how you use it."

Xiao filed that away and pressed on. "But you don't think it was poison? Do you think Salaana or Karana did this?"

"If Salaana had anything to do with it, it's justice," said Guleum firmly, and Xiao found himself thinking that the boy had felt too many of Salaana's dreams. "I hope she wins the fight with Gang. She'd make a fair ruler."

"What about you or Karana?"

"I wouldn't want it, even if I stood a chance against the rest of them. As for Karana... He's Salaana's dog. He'll support her bid."

Xiao had not seen Salaana nor Karana all week. Perhaps they were seeking support outside the court?

"Anyway, there's dear old dad. Did you want to do anything else?"

"Um, no, doesn't seem like there's much I can do for him, does it?"

"No. There's nothing anyone can do for him."

And Guleum seemed alarmingly satisfied by that.

A FEW days later, the sky was a deep midnight above them, speckled with white stars. The theatre gardens, where they lounged, were well-lit by red lanterns strung between tall poles. The acrid scent of wine (which Xiao had imbibed just a little of appearing to drink a great deal) and spicy perfumes (that were almost as intoxicating) combined to assault Xiao's nose. He had needed a little wine to brace his nerves tonight, for Salaana had at last returned to the Sun Court. The wine might have been a mistake, for it had been shockingly difficult to dump the next cup down his sleeve instead of in his mouth. It had tasted so familiar, and the other partygoers were all indulging themselves on Salaana's generosity. She was hosting a light show in celebration. Nanami was not present, of course, being a mere aspirant.

Salaana sat on a dais around which the crowd was spread in a half-circle. She looked beautiful and intimidating in simple red robes with white accents. Her rust-colored hair was piled high with a silver headdress that must weigh a ton. Although servants wove among her guests, offering small glasses of potent wine, candied petals, and pillow-soft rice cakes, Salaana sat silently, observing them all. Xiao was tempted to give her some tips on hosting a party, but he had a strong attachment to his tongue, so he resisted the urge. He had been to her light shows a handful of times, and though he found Salaana as scary as a beast escaped from the Underworld, he was looking forward to the spectacle. As was the rest of the large crowd, so he supposed that she didn't need his hosting advice after all.

Just then the torches in the garden went out, and the crowd silent. Xiao looked to the dais and saw thin lines of red light assembling high above it—he could just make out Salaana's concise movements below, directing the light. A few lonely, melancholy notes plucked from a guzheng mimicked the light. As the light suddenly changed from an abstract swirl to a woman's form, the notes became a song, and the crowd sighed its pleasure. Like a play, the story of two women falling in love, but kept apart by circumstance, unfolded in the night sky.

Xiao leaned close to Guleum and murmured, "Oddly romantic for Salaana, isn't it?"

Guleum's eyes were wide. "It's her story. Mother told me that Salaana asked for permission to marry, but the emperor refused. He said the purpose of marriage is to have children, and they can't have any."

"So this is an opportunity to follow her heart."

"Yeah, I guess. You see that woman there?" He indicated a petite woman about forty feet away, then snapped his eyes back to the sky. "That's Ichimi. She came back with Salaana, and all the Light Hands have been bowing and scraping to her."

Although the show was impressive, Xiao found himself frequently regarding its living subject. Like her name, something about Ichimi struck Xiao as familiar, but if he had met her before, he could not remember where.

I want to talk to her, he decided suddenly. Ichimi, with her delicate prettiness, and clear awe at her lover's talents, seemed far more approachable than Salaana.

An opportunity did not present itself that night, but the next morning Xiao woke with a sense of purpose.

"Luye! Yeppeun!" he called into the garden. The two women arrived together, their expressions sullen and their arms crossed.

"You hollered, divinity?" asked Luye, her voice so dry that Xiao was tempted to empty a cup over her head to rehydrate it.

Instead he gave her his best, two-dimpled smile. "Wonderful ladies, I would like to meet Lady Ichimi this morning. Do you know where I might find her?"

The two women exchanged looks. Luye smirked. Yeppeun turned back to him, and in a much sweeter tone said, "Lady Ichimi is at the practice grounds of the Sun Guard. If you wish to spar with her, I'm sure she will welcome it."

"Ah, hoping I'll break my ass in the sand, are you, Yeppeun?"

"I'll settle for your head," the woman said with a sniff.

Xiao laughed, and started removing his robes to don trousers. The two disciples exclaimed angrily, then scurried from the room.

"I don't mind if you want to watch!" Xiao called after them.

Less than a half hour later, Xiao entered the Sun Guard training grounds.

He walked leisurely through the grounds. There were several dozen soldiers drilling, the rhythmic tap of their staves and their synchronized "huhs" almost musical. He paused for a while to watch the Sun Guard archers at target practice. They used longbows, taller than the archers themselves, and their arrows thudded menacingly into the bullseyes of the painted targets, over a hundred yards away.

Could civil war really be brewing, Xiao wondered, when Gang commands the Sun Guard? How could even Salaana expect to defeat him in a bid for the throne?

Xiao felt very cold. For the first time he realized that he did not expect Jin to succeed in her quest. Surely there would be a new emperor within the year. He reviewed Jin's three older siblings. He could not like the idea of any of them on the throne for they were all ruthless. *It should be Jin*, he thought. *Of all of them, she is the most reasonable, the kindest...*

It occurred to him that if Jin were empress, he would be her consort. Xiao felt panic and abruptly walked on.

He found Ichimi training with a group of women, probably Light Hands. They were fighting with tessen, the deceptively beautiful fans that Jin favored, rather than their usual swords. Xiao grinned. He was best against a tessen, having practiced with Jin more than anyone else over the years. Ichimi might defeat him, but surely it wouldn't be as humiliating as his defeat at Bai's hands.

"Excuse me, ladies," Xiao called into the group. "I don't suppose any of you would care to give me some practice this morning?"

Ichimi looked even more delicate and feminine up close— she only reached Xiao's chest and even her smile was sweet and demure. "I would be happy to spar with you...?"

"Xiao," he told her with a grin and a wink.

"And I am Ichimi."

Soon they were alone in the practice ring, surrounded by the other women. Xiao held his long sword ready as he and Ichimi circled each other.

Her tessen met Xiao's sword with a sharp clang. Then he almost tumbled in the dirt as she deflected his return strike. He soon worked up a sweat, and realized he was thoroughly enjoying himself. Despite Luye's smirk, it seemed that he and Ichimi were evenly matched.

Finally, she did overcome his defenses—Xiao lay on the ground, the sharp edge of her tessen at his throat. She was smiling.

Xiao grinned back. "I concede, Lady Ichimi. I must thank you for a pleasant practice. Perhaps you'll allow me to escort you to a mid-morning tea?"

One brow raised, and the lady nodded.

"Yes, divinity, I would be happy to accompany you."

There were protests from the other women—apparently, Xiao wasn't the only one eager to befriend Ichimi, but she waved them away.

Xiao thought about her address—she knew who he was. She must want the same thing from him that he wanted from her: information. Feeling that Ichimi would respond better to polite flirting than his usual boldness, he began with small talk.

"A lovely spring morning, is it not?" Xiao asked.

"Indeed, a thrush woke me this morning with her sweet song."

"Ah, the palace's songbirds are truly one of its treasures."

Ichimi nodded, her eyes smiling. "Yes, and they are so new to me."

"Indeed?" asked Xiao. "Where did you live that didn't have songbirds?"

"Beneath the sea," said Ichimi.

"Beneath the sea?" Xiao had to pick his jaw up off the ground. "Are you from the Sea Dragon's court, then?"

Ichimi nodded.

"No wonder you are so skilled with the tessen. I have heard all the ladies of that court are expected to master it." He abruptly recalled Nanami lamenting her father's conceit, *Did you know we are numbered? That's what our names mean—one sea, two sea, three sea.* Ichimi might mean "one sea"—and know that he thought of it, hadn't Nanami said her oldest sister was named Ichimi? Xiao's gut knotted, even as he pointed to a tea house run by the Goddess of Patience. It was a small, wooden building that would not be out of place in the mortal world, though it was an oddity on the palace grounds.

Ichimi dipped her head in consent. Xiao stepped through the narrow door first, letting the black flaps of linen brush his shoulders.

One of the goddess' disciples greeted them and settled them in the inner garden by a small bamboo fountain.

Xiao was politely silent as they took the time to appreciate the running water and waited for their tea. He was trying to organize his thoughts. He felt almost certain that Ichimi was the Sea Dragon's eldest daughter—now that he looked, he could see Nanami in her features. Her very dark, narrow eyes; the small lips, the bottom just a bit plumper. Nanami was taller and projected more strength and Ichimi's face was oval where Nanami's was round, but they looked like sisters nonetheless. Had she seen Nanami among Salaana's aspirants? And if so, would she expose her sister to her lover's judgement?

When the tea arrived, Xiao went through the motions of inhaling its steam and admiring its color before he took a small sip. Then he asked, "You haven't been at court very long, have you? Last night was the first time I saw you."

Ichimi smiled. "You don't have to be shy with me— someone pointed you out to me last night as well, the first being betrothed to any of the Sun Emperor's children. Salaana and I met three thousand years ago but I was only allowed at court after your betrothal ceremony." Despite practically declaring that the Sun Emperor's collapse had been to her benefit, Ichimi seemed calm and secure. Xiao suddenly suspected that she had deliberately gone easy on him during their sparring earlier. Contrary to appearances, this woman was neither soft nor gentle.

"I am sorry to hear that. I daresay you and Salaana would have been happier than Jin and myself at such a ceremony."

Ichimi nodded. "There is something particularly *unjust* about marriages arranged by parents without considering the principals' feelings, don't you think?"

Was Ichimi suggesting Salaana would help him break the betrothal? In exchange for what? Xiao tried to think of a way to turn the conversation back to Nanami, but Ichimi clearly had a plan for this conversation.

"I wonder, where is the Goddess of Beauty now?"

Xiao waved a hand languorously. "I do not keep close track. She is undertaking a pilgrimage in hopes of atoning for her father's sins and so change his fate."

Ichimi's mouth thinned. For the first time, she did not look pretty at all. "Then she will be a pilgrim until the end of her days."

Xiao shook his head, "I doubt she will continue after her father passes."

Ichimi sipped her tea and then asked so casually that her

interest was painfully obvious, "And what plans does she make for such a time?"

Xiao cocked his brow. "She doesn't. She still refuses to believe it will come to pass."

"But you're a realist," Ichimi suggested.

Xiao's mouth twisted. "If Jin is an expert on beauty, I am one on desire. Desire can be very ugly." He cleared his throat, trying to figure out how to steer the conversation where he wanted. "What plans does the Goddess of Justice make for such a time?"

Ichimi laughed lightly, a bell-like sound. "You know exactly what plans she makes. Karana stands with her—and perhaps your young friend. Since Salaana helped him overcome the greatest injustice he knew."

It took Xiao a moment to understand who she meant. When he did, he almost spat out the tea. Was she admitting that Salaana had cast the death curse to aid Guleum?

He realized Ichimi was waiting for his response. "And you fully support the goddess in her pursuit of justice?"

"Of course. Salaana is the family I have chosen." Ichimi studied him.

"Justice is a popular topic lately," Xiao noted.

"The Sun Court has lacked it for too long."

Xiao swallowed. "There have been many aspirants for justice lately. The goddess will have more disciples soon."

Ichimi seemed annoyed by his attempt to change the topic at hand. "Aspirants are not always what they seem. Salaana is dismissing her most recent one even now. As for Jin—"

"Dismissing? Why?" Xiao's heart seemed to be beating in his ears.

"She is not who she claimed to be. I identified her myself."

Ichimi waved a hand impatiently. "Salaana wishes to speak to Jin. Can you help us contact her?"

Xiao rubbed his face. He didn't want to squander this opportunity, but his energy for subtlety was exhausted by his worry about Nanami. "You really don't know where she is, do you? I wonder, could your lover be keeping secrets from you? Or would Karana act on his own?"

Ichimi looked briefly angry, then intrigued. "Was Jin threatened? If so, look to the God of War. Karana is very fond of Jin, and Salaana won't hurt her unless she has to."

Xiao desperately wished he had Jin's ability to know the truth. Ichimi seemed so sincere, but Jin herself had verified that Gang wanted to keep her safe. What was he missing? Did yet another enemy lurk in the shadows?

"I want to speak to Salaana myself." Xiao suggested.

Ichimi nodded. She actually looked pleased by the idea. "Let's go now."

The disciples at Salaana's gate were a little more hesitant though.

"Her divinity is dealing with the thief," they told Ichimi.

"Thief?" the hairs on the back of Xiao's neck stood up.

"The aspirant," Ichimi said. "I told you she wasn't who she claimed. Don't worry, it won't be long."

Xiao stared at her, then kicked open Salaana's gate. He ran into the residence, barely noticing the shocked cries of the disciples. Fine white sand sprayed beneath his urgent feet.

Xiao took in the scene before him in a moment: Nanami, kneeling before Salaana, hands outstretched in supplication. And Salaana, her hands full of lightning.

He took it in and understood it in a moment, but even that was too long.

THE pain was so intense, so searing, that Nanami did not understand what had happened. She gaped at her hand, or where her hand should be, but there was just an angry, shiny stump. She looked past it, trying to find her hand, but there was nothing but a molten glass in the white sand.

Then Nanami finally understood that her hand was gone, burned away by Salaana's bolt of crackling heat.

"Why...?" she asked, holding her forearm, as if it too might disappear.

"You must pay the price for your thievery. If you still wish to join my sect, you may. But know that if you steal again, I'll take the other one." Salaana indicated Nanami's remaining hand.

Before Nanami could even think of a reply, strong hands caught her and swung her upwards. She blinked at Xiao's face. He was saying something, but Nanami was having trouble listening. She clutched her handless arm and let her head fall against his chest.

9

The Wanderer and the Willow

THE intrusion of the old woman's voice made Bai look over his shoulder.

The immortal behind him hunched slightly with age. Her hair was almost as white as his own usually was, and deep crow's feet stretched beside both eyes. The only thing that reminded him of the Neela he had known was her sky-blue eyes and her brilliant blue sari—even her essence had changed drastically.

"Get away from my granddaughter, you lecherous old man!" she barked at him.

Startled, he released Jin's hand. Maybe Neela's essence wasn't that different.

"Jin's been poisoned," he explained. "It's in her blood."

Neela pushed past him and began to touch Jin everywhere.

It was only then that Bai realized Jin was unconscious. He fought the urge to return to her side and let Neela complete her inspection.

"I don't know what to do," Neela told him, a quaver he had never heard before in her voice. "The poison is in her blood, but I can only purify her veins."

"Blood follows a cycle," he told her. "All of it will eventually pass through the veins. So clean it in stages."

Neela held Jin's hands and concentrated. Bai counted to ninety-seven before Neela turned to glare at him.

"I cleaned her blood. Why hasn't she awoken?"

Bai clenched his jaw briefly. "The clean blood will have to circulate. May I?" He indicated Jin.

After a moment, Neela reluctantly moved aside.

Bai could not read her essence, but he had spent a couple of centuries studying anatomy. Based on her breath and pulse, Bai could tell she had entered a natural sleep. He sighed, the tension leaving him. "She'll be fine."

"Then we need to talk." Neela seized his arm roughly and pulled him to the prow of the ship.

Bai had to force himself not to shake her off. "I don't know what you're thinking—"

"You forget, I hear your thoughts!" she snarled. "My granddaughter is betrothed!"

"I know, I've met Xiao. I don't intend—"

"Don't you though?" She narrowed her eyes at him. "And what happened to, 'A warrior must never feel deep emotion'?"

Bai crossed his arms. "I'm not the only one who's changed."

Neela narrowed her eyes. "And what is that supposed to mean?"

Bai, who had been referring to her aged appearance, said instead, "I heard about Aashchary. I'm sorry."

Neela looked out over the river. "Parents shouldn't outlive their children."

Bai had no reply.

Neela turned back to him, her eyes guarded. "What are the two of you doing on the Kuanbai anyway? When did you leave your mountain?"

"A little over two weeks ago. Jin and Xiao came there, looking for the key to the Underworld."

Neela's brow furrowed and she shook her head. She opened and closed her mouth twice, as if she couldn't even decide what to ask first.

"Perhaps I need to back up. You know that Aka is under a death curse?"

Neela didn't look surprised. "Haraa told me."

Of course, Bai thought wryly, *the original gossips.* "Jin is trying to go to the Underworld to fetch a black peony. She hopes to save him."

Neela crossed her arms. "And you're helping? Bringing the key for her?"

Bai hesitated, not sure he wanted to tell Neela everything. But of course, with Neela, one doesn't always have the choice.

"Jin is carrying the key? You trust her?"

And what exactly did Neela know about the key? "What's there to trust?"

Neela snorted. "I know that you can pull power from the immortal creatures through it—Zi told me."

Neela must be closer to Zi than she used to be. Bai wondered what else had changed. "I don't have to trust her. She fixed it so that no one can channel the immortal creatures' power ever again."

Neela stared at him, but she said nothing.

Eighteen millennia ago, Bai had always felt that he, Cheng, Haraa, and Neela were of like minds. But if Neela was now close enough to Zi to learn secrets... "Why did you lie to me? You claimed Aashchary's father was a mortal when he was in fact Cheng."

Neela's face froze. "No one can lie to you."

"Cheng could," Bai argued. "I wouldn't have expected it to transfer, but somehow carrying his child gave you the ability as well."

Neela barely seemed to breathe as she replied, eerily calm, "I didn't lie. I believed her father *was* a mortal—then."

"I don't understand."

Neela's eyes were scanning the area around Bai—it almost seemed aimless, as if she was too embarrassed to meet his eyes, but there was a hint of desperation in it. "You know that Cheng weakens my power, as he does yours?"

Bai nodded.

"Well, then you know as much as I."

That couldn't be the whole of it. Why did Neela seem so upset? "Then how did you find out? Did you confront him?"

Neela sighed. "You know, just because you're the oldest doesn't mean you have the right to know everything. But when I couldn't read my own daughter, I suspected."

"What did Cheng say?"

"I got no answers from him. No one has seen him in several thousand years."

Bai felt like someone had poured lead in his gut. He had already heard as much from Nanami and Jin, but he had dismissed their words. When Neela said it, he knew something must have happened to his friend. "You think he's dead?"

Neela shrugged. Bai felt like she had slapped him—she didn't seem to care one way or another. She looked at Jin's still form on the pallet. "You read essences—you could tell that Jin is related to Cheng?"

"As sure as I can be, without confirmation from the man."

"Did you read anything else?" Her voice was too careful, and Bai stated his hunch as fact.

"Gang is her father."

Neela scoffed—a harsh, angry sound. "So that's what this is about—you've decided to accept Noran's granddaughter in her place. Jin does have her eyes—but they've nothing else in common."

Bai took a deep breath. He was furious—partly because he worried Neela was right. Was he still obsessed? Had that initial attraction he'd felt for Jin simply been because he saw Noran in her?

But Neela was right that they weren't alike in personality. And he liked Jin's personality.

Bai struggled to turn his thoughts. "If Aashchary married Aka, how did she come to bear Gang's daughter?"

Neela rolled her eyes. "Surely even you can figure that out on your own. To answer your real question, Aka knows. Knew, perhaps I should say." Neela grabbed his hand. Her gnarled fingers dug into his palm, clawlike. "Gang and I are the only others that know he fathered her. I am the only one who knows about Cheng. Please..."

Bai stared at her, unsure of how to respond.

"Bai, you are the one who protected Gang! So many immortals feared his potential, the combining of two Colors, that he would have been killed if you hadn't. And he has never tried for dominion, has always been content to live in his father's shadow. Jin doesn't even know her own potential. Aashchary very cleverly limited her by naming her Goddess of Beauty... You won't hurt her? Please, keep this secret! She means everything to me..." And Neela, for the first time that he had seen, cried. Fat tears caught in the crevices of her face. Snot ran from her nose.

"She has the power of *four* Colors, Neela. We would both

be wise to be frightened of her. And she's betrothed to Xiao—can you imagine their children? It's almost as if someone was trying to combine all the colors." Bai looked at his hands trying to hide his thoughts.

But Neela's tears calmed, and after a few sniffs, she said, "You're lying to me with the truth. You don't think Jin is dangerous." She snorted suddenly, darkly amused. "You are infatuated with her." She hit him repeatedly. "You dirty lecher! She isn't Noran come to life!"

Bai held up his arms to block Neela's blows and let her rant.

His forearms were stinging when she finally stopped hitting him.

She panted for a few moments before saying, "As long as you keep her safe, and your breeches tied, I will accept your infatuation."

Bai shook his head. "Am I that much worse than Aka?"

Neela burst out laughing. "You think I wanted Aka for my daughter? It's never been more obvious to me that you never had a child."

Bai blinked, then grinned. "I suppose she didn't give you any say in the matter."

Neela snorted. "You're still such a know-it-all."

"Yes," he agreed. The tension had been cut, and Bai almost felt like he was with his almost-friend from years ago. So he dared, "Why do you think you have a say with Jin?"

Neela shook her head. "Grandparents are respected while parents are rebelled against. And Jin was never wild the way Aashchary was."

Neela was rubbing her hands. Bai hoped she didn't hurt herself when she was hitting him. "The last time we spoke, after Aka sealed the Golden Phoenix in the Underworld, I thought you might kill him yourself," she mused. "Surely you don't intend to aid Jin in this fool's quest to cure him?"

Bai was very quiet. "I haven't decided anything. I've been detached from the world for so long that it's going to take me awhile to make up my mind."

Neela walked closer to the canopy and peered under it. So softly that Bai wasn't sure if he was supposed to hear, she said, "I wish she wouldn't do this—not just because it is clearly dangerous for her, but because... Aka doesn't deserve her aid."

Bai shrugged. "You can tell her that when she wakes. Perhaps she'll listen to you." Bai didn't believe for a moment that Jin would change her mind about her quest, grandmother or no grandmother.

Neela gave him a wry look, and he knew she'd heard his thought.

"Neela—who do you think poisoned her?"

"Someone who doesn't want Aka cured. She doesn't have any enemies of her own."

Bai clenched his teeth. He tried again. "It has to be someone who could find her." He hesitated. "I didn't think Gang would do something like this, but then again, I never expected his betrayal with the Phoenix."

"Gang loves her. Jin's all he has of her mother."

Bai frowned. "I hope he also loves her for her own sake."

"Mmm," said Neela, still focused on Jin.

Bai admitted there was no point in picking her brain any further. "I'll go ashore for a while, so you can have your privacy. I'll return in a few hours." He moved between.

IT was dark when Jin opened her eyes, and she was disoriented by a gentle rocking. The songs of frogs looking for mates was the first thing she recognized. Then she recalled the boat Bai had made and the poisoning. She sat up slowly, sending her awareness through her body. She seemed fully recovered from whatever it had been. A deep blue light flared up around her.

Jin warded off the sudden brightness with her hand. She blinked twice to adjust her eyes, then smiled. "NeeNee! You came. Thank you." Jin shuffled on her knees to her grandmother, who sat cross-legged under the arched canopy.

Neela allowed Jin to hug her, but she did not return it and her face was set in a sulk. "Why are you angry with me?" Jin asked, well accustomed to Neela's moods.

"What if I hadn't come? You might have died. Shouldn't I be angry?"

Jin knelt, taking her grandmother's hand. "You are worried."

"Of course, I am worried, you fool girl! You are on a quest to enter the Underworld! And if that weren't dangerous enough, you are making enemies to do so."

Jin studied Neela's face in the eerie blue light. Her nostrils were flared, her expression all sharp planes and angles, as if her skin had been pulled taut. Her eyes were narrow and unfathomable. Jin was not prepared for this level of anger, "Enemies? You mean whoever cursed my father?"

Neela tsked in exasperation. "Not just who cursed him! Don't you know how many people he has offended over the millennia? How many are pleased by his collapse?"

"No, I don't," Jin replied calmly. "Was it one of them who killed my mother's son?"

Neela pulled back sharply. Then she relaxed slightly and asked succinctly, "Which son?"

Jin was confused. "Hadn't she only one?"

"Mind Brighter than Sunlight, and your unborn brother, who had yet to be named."

Jin digested that. "You are saying both my brother and my mother were murdered?"

"Yes, and Aka is to blame!"

Jin jerked back, frightened by the true belief that strengthened Neela's words. "Why have you never told me about this before?"

"I was trying to protect you! But you've put yourself in danger anyway!"

Jin clenched her jaw—Neela's logic was exasperating. But she didn't want to delve into a fruitless argument of should-haves. "Why do you blame Papa? Because he failed to protect them?"

"He wanted your brother dead! Aashchary rubbed it in his face that her son was more powerful than him!"

Jin stared at her grandmother, feeling as though a stranger was before her. She had never seen her grandmother so angry—indeed, Neela had eschewed deep emotion for as long as Jin could remember. Sometimes, when Jin had been seeking praise or love as a child, Neela's casual, negligent affection had almost hurt. That she had so much anger, such belief of betrayal, coiled in her...

"Are you saying Papa killed my brother? My mother?"

Neela's lips twisted. "Yes, he did! So why would you save him?"

"NeeNee, you just lied."

"He might not have been the main agent of their deaths, but he was complicit! Your brother's death was blamed on a sickness—the most powerful god of all time, struck down by illness? I don't think so! Karana spelled him. I am sure of it! But Aka protected his son—his lackey!"

Neela believed what she was saying. Jin felt sick. Could this really be true? Or did everything she said have to be discounted because it came from a place of such rage and pain that no rational thought was left?

"And my mother?"

Neela hunched abruptly, as if her strength had been exhausted. "Your mother was slain by one of Aka's courtesans. The woman claimed that she had to kill Aashchary so that Aka would be free to marry her. He executed her immediately, making it impossible for anyone else to question her."

Jin crossed her arms tightly over her body.

"You really do believe that he had her killed."

Neela nodded. "So why would you save him, Jin?"

Jin stared at the planks of the boat. "He's my father. He loves me. I will not allow him to be killed like this, not without hearing his side."

"He's *not* your father."

"What? What did you say?"

"Aka is not your father! After her son was murdered, Gang comforted Aashchary."

Jin clapped her hands over her ears. "Stop!"

Neela seized Jin's wrists in a bruising grip and pulled her hands from her ears. "They became friends and then lovers. Only Aka knew, and he chose to allow it."

Jin tried not to listen, but Neela's words would not be denied. "When Aashchary became pregnant a second time, she and Gang decided to take you and leave the Sun Court for good. That's why Aka had her murdered—he ignored their love out of guilt, but he was too embarrassed to let anyone else find out about it."

Jin shook her head.

"You know I'm telling you the truth!"

"I'm continuing my quest."

"It's too dangerous!"

"Bai will help me."

"Don't you understand he's only interested in you because of Gang's mother? You look like her! He's been obsessed with her longer than you've been alive! Why would you trust him?"

Jin felt tears run down her cheeks. Neela nodded, and began to move between, pulling Jin along with her.

"No!" Jin barked, stopping the teleportation. Neela frowned and pushed harder. Jin pushed back.

"I'm your grandmother! I raised you!"

Jin refused to feel guilty. She was an adult. She would not just let her father die. But it frightened her how easily she was able to match Neela's strength. Never before had she thought she might be stronger than her grandmother.

But Neela fought on, straining desperately. *She doesn't realize how much stronger I am than her.* Jin pulled her hand away and stopped holding Neela back. Immediately, Neela moved between. Jin flooded the area around her with power, blocking Neela from coming back. It felt cowardly, and yet, Jin felt sure what they both needed was a little time. Neela to calm down, Jin to consider her claims. Her eyes watered suddenly, and Jin dashed at them with the back of her hand.

She investigated the boat, but it was empty, even though it still moved down the Kuanbai through Bai's magic. Jin sat in the prow, wrapping her arms around herself. She didn't believe that Bai had abandoned her. She had felt how deeply he cared about her as he carried her through the town.

He probably just left to give Neela privacy.

Jin dropped her head to her knees and cried.

WHEN Bai returned to the stern of the boat, he was immediately disconcerted by the silence. He peered under the canopy. Neela was nowhere in sight, but Jin was seated in the prow, her chin resting on her knees. As if sensing the weight of his gaze, she glanced back, and their eyes met.

Bai slid a strap off each shoulder, setting the earthenware jars and woven bamboo baskets beneath the boat's canopy, then made his way to her side. They sat without speaking for some time, making the bird calls along the river seem unnaturally loud. When Jin finally spoke, it was not a question he'd anticipated.

"You didn't make a boat when we left Bailaohu Village. Why wait?"

Bai hesitated. "This is your quest, not mine. I'm just along for protection."

"Kunjec wasn't at risk when you made this boat."

Bai bit his lower lip. "No."

"So it's me you are trying to protect."

He nodded reluctantly.

"Why? Because of Noran? Because you loved her, and she died?"

Bai stiffened. So, his caution earlier had been pointless. "I was infatuated with her."

"Nanami said you slaughtered a million bandits because of her death. That she was the reason you became the Warrior."

"Nanami seems to have said a lot," Bai said dryly. Then, "They weren't all bandits. By the time I stopped fighting, my motivation had been confused or twisted. Even now, sometimes I don't fully understand it myself. But I was angry and in pain... and Noran had named her son the God of War. I suppose I made myself useful to him. I think... I think I was pretending to be his father, something he neither needed nor wanted. We were friends though—still are, I hope, though it has been a long time."

"So that's why you are protecting me—just as you trained Noran's son, you want to train me." Jin's lips pressed together firmly. "I don't want it. Teach me for myself or not at all."

Bai hesitated. It would perhaps be wiser to let Jin think his only interest was in a long-gone relative. But if that meant she scorned him...

"I had no idea you were related to her when..."

"When?" she prompted.

"When you burst into my life. When you shook my complacency. When you made me want to live again."

"What do you mean?" There was the slightest tremor in her voice. Her lips remained slightly parted. Bai wanted to pull her into his arms to reassure her, to confess his feelings, his hopes for the future. But what were his feelings? And what were his hopes?

He spoke carefully, keeping his hands by his side—his arms seemed awkwardly rigid. "It's difficult for me to articulate. Do you remember what I said about beauty?"

She thought for a moment. "'Beauty is in the eye of the beholder.' But I disagreed."

"No—you said you are the arbiter of beauty."

"How can both be true?"

"You don't make something objectively more or less beautiful—you change the way it is perceived. You influence others. If you weren't limited by your divinity, you would have far more power to change perceptions than you do." Bai looked down at his lap. "Nonetheless, you affect others quite frequently without even realizing it. When we first met, I saw—" he shifted, too embarrassed to describe his first impression of her. "Well, how did you want me to see you?"

There was a silence, followed by a sharp gasp. Bai risked a look at her face—she had covered it with her hands.

He cleared his throat. "I realized fairly quickly that the way I was responding to you was due to your influence but—" he coughed. "Well, when I realized that, I was intrigued by your power. Then, I saw how you presented yourself to others, and I felt honored that you wanted me to see you... differently."

She lowered her hands just enough to peer at him through her fingers. Bai wasn't sure what she saw, but after a few minutes, she lowered her hands.

"Why? I know—Nanami said..."

Bai arched a brow.

Jin frowned at him, then continued. "Nanami told me that you've always had plenty of admirers. Why should my... crush affect you any more than theirs?"

Bai shrugged. "Perhaps something must be said for being the most desirable being I have ever seen."

Jin's eyes widened, then she flushed. Her eyes darted away, but she brought them swiftly back. She drew herself up.

"I am betrothed. I have made a vow to marry Xiao in one year."

Bai felt his lips twist into a self-deprecating smile. "I know. I also know that you want him to see you as sexless—beautiful but aloof and cold. Frozen water, I think it was?"

Jin stared at him. "Oh, fate judge me. I am a bad person."

Bai half-reached to her before he stopped himself. "No—why do you say that?"

Jin twisted her fingers together. "You aren't, perhaps, the person I should confess this to, and yet, I want so badly to confide and... you see so much." She cleared her throat. "Perhaps a thousand years ago, when Xiao and I became adults, he tried to kiss me. I was...upset. I wanted very badly for him not to see me that way—and then he didn't. But I didn't realize—I had no idea that it was because of something I had done. I have been cursing our betrothal because I thought our marriage was doomed because he seemed to view me—almost as a child, I suppose. And now, to realize I am the one sabotaging it—"

"But that hardly makes you bad—you weren't even aware—"

"No!" She held up a hand, stilling his words. "I am bad because now that I know I am sabotaging it, I don't want to stop. I want..." Her voice trailed off, but the look of longing on her face completed her sentiment.

Bai didn't know how to respond. He wanted that too—and yet, her power, her very life was on the line. To imagine this being, this fascinating woman, limited by mere mortal years made his heart hurt.

"Why?" he asked. "Why didn't you want Xiao to desire you? Was it just that you were young? Inexperienced?"

THIS conversation was running away from Jin—no, it had been a runaway horse to begin with, but she had grabbed the reins anyway.

If she answered Bai's question, was that a betrayal of Xiao?

But hadn't she already betrayed Xiao, with her earlier confession? What was one more secret of her heart?

"It was not inexperience." She cleared her throat. "Xiao once told me that his favorite thing about love is that it brings out the best in people. It makes them stronger, kinder, more thoughtful... What I did not tell him is that that is only when the love is good and healthy. I have seen love bring out jealousy, spite, pain, and make people petty and weak. Xiao is my friend, but there are parts of him I do not like. If he was my partner... my other half, I would hate those things. That would hurt him, and he would become worse, creating a downward spiral for both of us. I did not—I do not want that." Jin wasn't sure she had managed to capture her thoughts—nothing was wrong with Xiao except that he was wrong for her.

"Then why did you go through with the betrothal?" Bai's question was almost a whisper, but Jin flinched from it. She could hear the sorrow, the disappointment he was trying to hide.

"I didn't know you existed," she said. That he existed—what a silly way to say that she had given up on finding someone that she wanted a true partnership with, that she had settled for pleasing her family and looking for romance outside of her marriage. And how cowardly it seemed now, when she felt what she might have had!

But Bai didn't seem confused or upset by her words. After a long pause, he reached out and grasped her hand. Their fingers interlaced. Jin fancied she could feel the beat of his heart through their palms.

"Bai," she began, then cleared her throat to dispel the tremor in her voice. "Bai, I do not know what future I can offer you. If I marry Xiao, you will be pushed to the side. If I don't...

I'll have only a handful of years left."

He smiled, and for the first time that day, it was a true smile. Its sweetness made Jin want to weep. "For now, it's enough that you even want to offer it."

Jin squeezed his hand gently. She took a deep breath.

"I'd like your opinion. Neela tried to teleport me, but I overpowered her."

Bai nodded slowly. "That must have been upsetting."

"It wasn't just what she did. She said—" Jin choked on the words.

"I think I know what she said," he admitted. "She told you that Gang is your father. I asked her myself, earlier."

Jin jerked her hand away from him, as if that pleasant warmth might scald her. "How did you...?

"I'm sorry. I let you believe that your grandfather might have been a son of Noran and Cheng, but I knew no such person existed because Cheng is my friend." His hand remained stretched toward her, but he had the wisdom not to touch her. "You must be very shocked. I'm sorry."

"But then... do you think Neela is right? That Pa—that Aka plotted my mother's murder?"

Bai shook his head. "I know nothing, and don't want to speculate. The only way to truly know is to ask Aka."

Jin thought of Gang, on that surreal night when he told her that she was powerful, that she might be able to save the emperor when he could not. *I do not mourn this as purely as you do*, Gang had told her.

Jin suddenly threw herself at Bai's chest. His arms wrapped around her immediately. She was crying. She couldn't seem to stop. Xiao was right. The world had always been different than the one she knew. How could she trust anyone?

Finally, when her head ached and no more tears came, Jin told Bai, "I still want to travel to the Underworld, to find the black peony. I shall confront Aka after I save him."

"And if he's guilty?" Bai asked softly.

"Then I will turn him over to the Goddess of Justice."

EVEN as Jin was filled with inner turmoil, she was surrounded by peace. On the lower Kuanbai, the land rolled in low hills away from the river, and its banks were lush. Willows wept into the water, their branches thick with leaves. The air was warm and humid enough that Jin was glad of her coarse linen pilgrim robes, which were cool and light compared to the many layers of court dress. She and Bai quickly fell into a routine. During the cloudy mornings, Jin practiced magic. Under Bai's tutelage, she learned to shape anything red, orange, yellow, and blue to her will. He tried to teach her to change herself into a bird or a fish, but the trick of it eluded Jin.

After lessons came Jin's favorite time of day, when the inevitable drizzle began at noon, and they sat under the canopy, eating steamed fish as a thick white mist obscured the outside world, and Jin found her worries obscured as well. They told stories—or, more accurately, Jin cajoled stories from Bai. He told her of his youth, when the world was just stone and water. One day, shaping the thick mist with his will, he showed her how he rode the Sea Serpent, an enormous monster that made coastlines treacherous before it was banished to the Underworld. Jin even convinced him to describe his early forays into art, how the other immortals had laughed at his strange, colorful paintings until one day they became recognizable and people held their breath in awe.

"You've done so much. Don't I seem very boring to you?" she had asked him in a burst of insecurity.

A smile had played on his lips. "I've always thought boredom was a choice."

She had laughed and scolded him for his unchivalrous answer.

When the sun burned away the mist and drizzle in the early afternoon, Bai taught her the unfamiliar exercise that she had seen him practicing that first day in his garden—it was about control and strength and was far more challenging than even her tessen practice. It amazed Jin how being still could be harder than moving.

They did not speak again of their feelings for each other, even when the stars came out and the frogs began their love songs, but they did not need to. Jin could feel how Bai felt about her, and it seemed he could read her expression almost as easily. They rarely touched and slept at opposite ends of the boat—an unspoken agreement to respect Xiao. They had a year to settle what was between them. There was no rush.

When the Kuanbai widened dramatically, Bai declared they had better hire a mortal ship to carry them over the sea, as he did not have the same affinity with it as with the Kuanbai. So they sold their boat to mortal rivermen when they docked in Liushi, the City of the Willow, that great port where the Kuanbai met the Double Bay.

"Will its magic fade?" Jin asked as they walked away from the boat's new owners, who were eagerly exclaiming over the quality of its craftsmanship.

"It will last far longer than any boat made of wood and it will always find safe passage on the Kuanbai," he told her absently. "It will probably be famous in a few years."

ALTHOUGH it had been six hundred mortal generations since Bai was last here, he was shocked by the changes. Instead of a thick wilderness with a few isolated communities, the mouth of the Kuanbai was now the largest single collection of mortals that Bai had ever seen. Buildings, some many stories high, stretched as far as Bai could see. They were built in a higgledy-piggledy manner, so that the streets frequently bent out of sight.

"This is amazing," he said.

Jin looked about her for a few moments before turning back to him with a knit brow. "What is?"

"I—this city. It is larger than the Sun Palace, I should think."

"Well, yes," Jin agreed. "After all, there are far more mortals than immortals."

Bai almost gaped at her. Instead, he said carefully, "There are?"

Jin looked at him for a moment, then grinned. "I forget sometimes that you haven't left your mountain for longer than I've been alive. You must have thought that little market town was large! Perhaps three thousand years ago, mortals began to live in larger and larger groups. In Jeevanti, in the city of Shahar, there are one million mortals."

Bai studied her carefully. Was she teasing him? "I can't tell if you are telling the truth," he finally admitted, embarrassed to have his power fail him.

Jin's eyes widened, and she laughed merrily. Several mortals turned toward the almost musical sound. "I'm telling you the truth!" she protested. "Liushi itself has nearly a hundred thousand."

"But—how do they get food? There's no room to hunt, not enough land to farm..."

Jin shook her head. "We can't go straight to the docks. I must show you some of the triumphs of mortals."

She took his arm, her hand in the crook of his elbow, and gave him a general history of mortals as she dragged him through Liushi. Bai felt like the pilgrim he was impersonating—a country yokel who could barely keep track of his feet, his eyes were so glued to the sights. They climbed a thousand steps to the Sun God's temple, an edifice remarkably similar to the reception hall in the Sun Palace. But this one was built by *mortals*. It impressed Bai even more than money had.

It was in the entertainment district (yes, these mortals had enough buildings dedicated to music, theatre, and gambling that it warranted an entire district) that Bai finally recognized a landmark. The Great Willow, with its white bark and silvery leaves.

"It's still here then," he smiled at the tree, which was nearly as old as himself. He stopped at a metal fence that was clearly intended to keep admirers at bay. Physically, it was just as Bai remembered, but magically, there was something quite different about it. He cocked his head, trying to understand the new power that gathered in it.

"The Great Willow? Oh, yes, it's practically worshipped as a god in Liushi. See that temple?" She pointed to a white stone building, and Bai realized that the willow's power had been amplified through the belief of mortals, just as Zi and Hei's had. "There they sell a tea made from its leaves that is believed to grant insight. My fa-father really doesn't like that temple." Bai glanced at Jin, but her face was carefully blank, and he decided she didn't wish to discuss her angst over her parentage at present.

"I imagine it would. I planted the willow—made it, perhaps is a more accurate term. It's not quite a normal tree." Its roots ran deep into the earth, just as its white branches stretched high into the sky, and he created it to magnify his fundamental ability so that he might know the entire world as he sat in it.

He lost his smile as he remembered the first time that he sent his powers coursing through the tree and out into the world. He had found an unknowable pocket, an essence that he could not distill or understand. Curious, he had gone to investigate it and met Cheng.

Perhaps because Cheng had also been alone when he formed, magma that refused to cool into stone and so had become an immortal, he was far more like Bai than Aka had been. They had explored the world together, eager to teach and to learn. Cheng had been a friend—to think that he had disappeared, was presumed *dead*... He thought that perhaps he should use the tree to search for Cheng, but the idea that he might find nothing kept him from moving.

A light laugh shook him as surely as an earthquake. Jin had her index finger pressed to her lower lip. Her eyes were full of awe as she stared at the tree. "So when you say the boat we sold would be famous..." She looked back at the tree. "There must be hundreds—no, thousands—of miraculous artifacts scattered over Earth from your casual creation of them."

Bai shifted uncomfortably. "Well, now there is at least one because of you."

She snorted. "I think I must punish you, for being so cavalier about it all. We shall go watch *The Death of the Great Warrior*, and you shall tell me how much is true and how much is fiction."

Her hand slipped into his, and she pulled him away from the willow.

Bai's eyes locked on their hands. Hers was almost totally enveloped in his. It felt warm and surprisingly strong—just like her.

"The Death of the Great Warrior?" he forced himself to ask.

Jin indicated a young man dressed in bright strips of cloth containing all the colors of the rainbow. He was juggling equally brilliantly colored balls and shouting. "Come one, come all! Watch *The Death of the Great Warrior,* as done by the world-famous Rainbow Troupe!"

He shouted praises for the show, then began his announcement at the beginning again. Bai had seen a few other youths like him throughout Liushi, but he hadn't paid them very much attention.

"It's a very famous play," Jin told him, "where you defend a tiny pass from a thousand soldiers."

"Well, the death part is fiction then."

"Mmm, so I recently learned," she said with a smile.

Bai smiled himself. He wasn't particularly interested in seeing a play about himself, greatly exaggerated or not, but he did want to make Jin happy.

Soon they had exchanged a small amount of the coins from their sale of the boat to buy two seats at the rear of a large indoor theatre. The seats were cleverly contrived so that each subsequent row was slightly higher than the one in front of it.

The stage was low in front of them with a large painting of mountains as a backdrop. It was perhaps crude, but it charmed Bai anyway. The first scene was of a monstrous golden creature attacking many peasants. There were no words, but a small band of musicians narrated the tale with their instruments.

"What on Earth is that?" Bai asked Jin in a whisper.

"The Phoenix," was her soft reply.

Bai looked back at the stage in disbelief. It was golden and feathered, yes, but all resemblance to the Golden Phoenix of Bando ended there. The Phoenix had been a beautiful bird; awe-inspiring, yes, terrifying, no. This horned creation with its bulging eyes and absurd fangs was hideous. A man in red arrived to fight the monster. Bai didn't need Jin to tell him this was Aka. Suddenly soldiers arrived—at least Bai thought they were soldiers. They looked like two-legged versions of the monster. They harried the red man, but then "the Great Warrior" (wearing all white) and the God of War (a bearded fellow with red armor) arrived, riding on a large cloud. They forced the soldiers back so that Aka could continue his fight. The God of War directed the warrior somewhere off-stage, and the scene changed.

This is Cheolmun Pass, I suppose. The actor playing the Warrior was surely a magnificent dancer. He leapt and twirled with boundless energy. A silver silk scarf served as the Starlight Sword, but the man manipulated it so cleverly that it truly seemed to be a steel blade as it lashed his enemies. As they were injured, their wounds were simulated by red silk that burst everywhere as if with a mind of its own. Finally, the great battle ended, and a translucent red screen came down in front. The Warrior stumbled around on stage for a bit before summoning a cloud and the scene changed.

Aka, through the musicians at the side, praised the Warrior and handed him a large literal key. The warrior once again took his cloud mount to a land of flowers—as represented by lady dancers. There was a slow dance where the dancers pulled a copious number of red scarves from the Warrior and the actor made it clear he was dying ("What, are the flowers killing him?" muttered Bai. Jin did not respond).

Finally, the flowers abandoned the fallen warrior alone on stage, with the oversized key. There was a hush, and then the audience began a polite, synchronized clap, which Jin joined. Bai did not.

"Very little of that was true."

He expected her to laugh, but when Jin looked at him, her expression was guarded, her mouth pinched. "Yes, but... I always thought it was simply fantasy, but on the river—you shaped the mist with your hands. So I have to ask—can you really travel by cloud?"

Bai almost answered yes without thinking, but he suddenly realized why she looked so troubled. If he could travel by cloud, why weren't they doing so?

"Travelling by cloud would certainly be convenient, wouldn't it?" he managed a laugh. He thought he had struck the right balance of wistful and amused, but if anything, Jin looked more upset.

"You are very good at making me think that you've answered my question without lying and yet, leading me to believe something false—just like you did with Cheng and Noran."

Bai cleared his throat. "Yes, I can travel by cloud—"

"Then let us go to the gate now. Surely we could reach it in a matter of days."

Bai hesitated.

"Well?"

"No—I think we should—"

"Why? Don't you trust me?"

When he didn't answer right away, Jin whirled away from

him. Bai caught her arm. "I do trust you, Jin, I trust you to be fair and generous. But I'm not sure you know what is fair. Your view of the immortal creatures is wrong—like that supposed Phoenix—"

"Then why wouldn't you just tell me that? Why would you hide things from me?"

"I don't—I've only known you a month—"

"If you don't trust me, why should I trust you?" she looked down at her arm. "Let go of me. I need to think. *Alone.*"

He released her instantly. As she walked away, he felt a brief panic. "I'll be at the willow," he called, just before she disappeared into the crowd. He was fairly certain that she heard him.

But he waited at the Great Willow until it grew dark and light again, and still she did not come.

10

How Nanami Walked the Shadows

INDIGNATION and outrage were writ on Luye and Yeppeun's pretty faces, their arms crossed and their feet in a fighting stance on the wide portico of Jin's house. The rice paper doors were closed at Xiao's back, but he still feared they'd disturb Nanami, who he had set inside on Jin's bed. Fate had already cursed her enough today, so Xiao raised his hands in supplication.

"You cannot bring your lovers here!" insisted Yeppeun.

"Shh—she's not my lover, you know her."

"Yes, you brought her here on the day of your betrothal," said Luye over crossed arms.

"Yeah, and she's Jin's friend."

Both women gave him equally disbelieving looks, and Xiao rubbed his temples in frustration. "She stole and destroyed the Infinite Jug."

The disciples looked at each other. Luye's brows raised and Yeppeun's knitted.

"So why is she here?"

Xiao hesitated. "She tried to spy on Salaana for Jin. But she was exposed as a thief, and Salaana took her hand." He swallowed. "You may have heard of her—she's the Sea

Dragon's seventh child."

Both women simultaneously craned their necks, as if they could see through the rice paper to the woman within.

"I'll get her some food," said Luye.

"And I'll visit the Wood Pavilions for burn ointment."

Luye scurried out the gate, and Yeppeun disappeared into between.

Xiao frowned. Why should being the Sea Dragon's daughter matter? They thought she wouldn't condescend to take him as a lover? *Well, she pursued me,* he thought waspishly. Then he admitted that wasn't entirely true—but she did notice him first.

Xiao re-entered the hall.

Nanami was curled around her arm on Jin's bed. She in no way acknowledged his appearance. He wasn't sure if she was aware of him. He crossed to her and knelt, placing a hand on her shoulder. Her eyes opened and flashed to his. They were dull with pain and reddened from tears. As she looked at Xiao, a few more tears leaked free.

"Come to say, 'I told you so'?" she asked.

Xiao shook his head. "I came to check on my friend. Nanami—I am so sorry. I wish I hadn't let you come to the palace."

Nanami smiled weakly. "And just who do you think you are to have stopped me? No, it was my decision. And you had tried to warn me—that's been echoing in my mind the past few minutes. 'Salaana takes the hands of thieves,' you told me. I was too arrogant." She closed her eyes, and Xiao rubbed her back gently, unable to think of any other comfort to give. He looked at the stump of her arm, a painful looking burn where her hand should be.

Nanami said, "I'm sorry, I can't enter her service."

It took Xiao a moment to understand her, he was so surprised. After her hand had been cut off, she had considered moving forward with the plan.

"Of course you can't. That's common sense," Xiao said, surprised by how thick his tongue was. Words were heavy and cumbersome. As improbable as it seemed, in just three weeks, Nanami had become someone who mattered to him. Somehow her strange combination of raw need, complicated honor, and calm competence was a balm to his soul. She had more to offer him than his usual lovers who took all he could give with little in return, and yet, unlike Jin, she wanted to lean on him.

Nanami turned her face to his hand that rested on her shoulder and pressed her cheek against his knuckles.

Xiao moved to the bed and pulled her into his lap.

She opened her eyes in surprise. She bit that plump lower lip. They stared at each other for a few moments, Nanami tense in his arms. He waited for her to sort through her feelings.

More quickly than he expected, the tension ran out of her and she leaned against him, her eyes closing.

She breathed deeply, as if smelling him and said, "Tell me what you've learned since we last spoke. I need a distraction."

"Well—Ichimi said—"

"Wait. Did you say Ichimi?"

"Yes, your sister—" Xiao suddenly caught himself. Nanami's voice was *too* calm. He swallowed. "You don't know."

NANAMI heard her blood rushing in her ears. Her voice sounded oddly distant as she asked, "Know what?"

"Ichimi is Salaana's lover. That was why Salaana was gone from the court—she was fetching Ichimi. Ichimi saw and identified you."

Nanami suspected the betrayal as soon as he said Ichimi's name. But in a fog of—anger? shock? *hurt*?—she found herself replying, "Are you sure?"

Nanami wasn't certain what Xiao saw in her face, but it must have been frightening given the way he blanched. "She told me herself. I was speaking to her just before..."

Nanami nodded slowly. She was aware that her face was wooden, but she couldn't seem to make it relax.

"Are you okay?" Xiao asked.

She shook her head. "I just thought... I know my father disowned me, but I would've thought..."

Suddenly his arms were tight around her, her face pressed against his chest. It felt so good to be held, to not be alone.

But would this have happened if you had kept to yourself? came a little voice. But even if it didn't happen, she told it, *the potential would still be there. I would still be abandoned by my family.*

And I would still be a thief... a thief...

XIAO didn't notice Nanami fall asleep, but he noticed the fever.

Surprised, he checked the burn where her hand had been. Was it infected? Did infections happen that fast?

He was no healer, but it looked more like a scar than anything else. And the fever seemed too hot and sudden. He laid her out on Jin's bed and watched her eyelids twitch.

"A true dream," he realized. He had heard of them, but

never seen an immortal having one before. Xiao was too young to have them himself, but Nanami was over twenty thousand years old, so he supposed it was reasonable that she would.

True dreams came when an immortal could not reconcile their past with who they were now. After all, over thousands of years, people changed a great deal.

Xiao took her remaining hand in his and was startled to realize he was sweating. He was scared, he realized. Why now? Did she feel guilty about her thievery after all? Some part of her must feel she deserved to face Salaana's justice. What if she couldn't face whatever it was that she'd done? Would she die right here in front of him? Should he fetch help?

He squeezed her hand tighter. No, he knew there was nothing to do to aid a true dreamer. Nanami was strong and adaptable. He had to believe she could face whatever it was that she'd done.

6,000 years ago

IT was late afternoon when Nanami reached the massive banyan tree that He Who Walks in Shadow had chosen for their reunion. She settled in a partially enclosed nook among its roots, and dropped two heavy, bulging sacks on either side of her. She then pulled out a little polished tiger's eye stone. Smaller than her thumb, it was delightfully smooth, and she rolled it in her palm, enjoying the feel of it. It had sat on the bedside table of the head monk and had been harder to steal than the gold that He Who Walks in Shadow had wanted.

Nanami closed her eyes, remembering how dry her mouth had been as she crept into the bedroom as the monk slept. How she had seized the stone like a viper striking a mouse. The flush of triumph and success when she walked back out of the room without the monk waking.

"Did you get it?" came her master's gravelly voice.

Nanami opened her eyes and found him standing in front of her, his stance taut as if he might explode into motion any moment.

Nanami tucked the tigerseye back into its pouch. She grinned and held up a bulging bag with each hand. "Did you doubt me?"

"You know I don't trust anyone but myself." He Who Walks in Shadow dropped down next to her under the massive banyan tree. Her master was a little shorter than she was and equally slim and wiry. His youthful face was plain and pockmarked, which was odd for an immortal, but his dark eyes were intense and shrewd. They'd worked together for almost seven thousand years—he was her family now, if anyone was, and Nanami immediately passed him the bags, knowing he wouldn't be content until he had examined the goods himself.

"So what's so special about this gold anyway?"

"Does the apprentice need to know all that the master does?" he asked, as he removed a piece and examined it closely. He smiled at last. "You really got it. You are worthy of being my student."

Nanami rolled her eyes. Her master was an excessively vain man, but that was part of the reason he was comfortable. He was too self-absorbed to trouble her own heart.

"So are you going to give me some of that back? Or do I have to steal it?" she joked.

To her surprise, his smile faded and he glared at her. "We aren't going to spend this gold. Its value lies elsewhere." He seemed to realize he had upset her and moderated his expression. "I'm sorry, do you need some money to go play? Here." He handed her a string of silver and copper coins.

"Thanks," Nanami muttered, and teleported to the largest market in Jeevanti.

She took a deep breath of the hot, spice-filled air. Laughter and shouts buoyed her up from all sides, and Nanami let other marketgoers jostle her as she stood still, enjoying the energy of the crowd. She did catch one little boy's hand as it wrapped around her string of coins at her waist. "Sorry, can't let you have those," she told him.

The boy darted away, and Nanami tucked the string out of sight. Then, just because she could, she pulled the gold coin she had hidden in her sleeve out and flipped it once. He Who Walks in Shadow might be her master, but she was not a dog. He had to give her a reason if he wanted her to obey. Now, what was worth gold?

As she strolled through the market, vendors kept pressing samples on her—rose water sweets, spicy roasted chickpeas. Nanami kept trying to pay, but they kept insisting it was free. When she admired a very beautiful and elaborate sari, the merchant gifted it to her. Nanami was unnerved. She was dressed plainly; there was no reason for these people to be currying favor with her. She pulled out the gold coin once more.

About the size of her eye, it was rich in color, a true yellow gold. One side bore a chrysanthemum, the other the character for yellow. Nanami didn't feel any magic about it, but she was sure that there was some. She rubbed the character with her thumb.

Yellow. Noran? The lost Color?

Anything made by a Color would have immense power. Most legends had an artifact of the Colors at their core.

Nanami didn't know much about Noran, given she had died long before Nanami was born, but she knew the God of War had inherited his ability to manipulate other's thoughts from his mother.

So this coin makes people want to please me? To give me what I want?

Nanami thought back to the monastery where the gold coins had been. The monastery had been for women only and though it only served minor deities, someone had placed a powerful teleportation ban on it, one that not even Nanami could bypass. That was why He Who Walks in Shadow had asked her to commit the theft, because she could enter as a petitioner while he could not.

The gold had been in a forgotten storeroom, locked in a box. The monks would not miss the gold, not even knowing they had it.

And Nanami suddenly felt she ought to have left it that way—this wasn't a power that should see the light of day. With it, her master...

Nanami teleported back to the banyan tree, but there were just roots at its base.

Think, Nanami. Where would he have gone? What would he want that he couldn't have stolen?

IT took her a year, but when she found He Who Walks in Shadow, he had established a whorehouse of sorts. It was disgustingly trite, and the way the whores bent themselves to his every whim horrified Nanami.

She had tried arguing and pleading, but both failed to stir his conscience. So Nanami did what she did best. She stole the gold back.

But He Who Walks in Shadow sought revenge.

NANAMI was bathing in the stream near her home when she heard wood shatter. She pulled the water around her and stepped from the stream fully clothed. She stood on the bank, listening, and over the whisper of the water came voices.

"The house is empty, but it's full of stolen goods. This must be the right place."

"Fifteen through twenty—fan out in the woods and look for her. Neha and I will wait here, in case she returns, and sort through the goods."

Nanami had not spent the last seven thousand years sneaking around for nothing—she now climbed the closest tree and ran along the treetops as quiet as a squirrel. She saw one woman in a red and white sari pass beneath her, never thinking to look up. She stopped when she had a clear view of her home, standing on a branch and hugging the trunk of its tree.

Two more women in white and red saris stood in her courtyard, going through her things as if they belonged to them, like -

Like thieves.

Nanami's hands dug into the bark of the trunk she was gripping, hurting her fingers. Her first impulse was to confront the women, but she saw the glaives on their backs and thought better of it. Still, she lingered, not quite ready to abandon her home of the last few millennia.

"What will we do with all this?"

"Most of these were reported stolen to her divinity over the years—we cross check the prayers, and what we can return to its rightful owners we will. The rest will be donated to justice temples."

How convenient, thought Nanami. *Given that most of the owners are long dead mortals, they'll have a nice haul. But they aren't stealing, just enacting justice.*

"This belongs to the Sea Dragon," said one. Nanami's heart sank—she was holding Nanami's green enamel water lily hair stick. It *was* stolen—Nanami had taken it from her mother when she visited Nanami's grandfather in the Crescent Moon. And she couldn't bear to lose it.

Disregarding her own safety, Nanami leapt down into the yard and snatched the hair stick right out of the disciples' hands. Nanami wasn't so foolish to gloat and teleported away even as a glaive swung toward her.

NANAMI found it easy to stay one step ahead of the Light Hands that hunted her. In truth, she could have avoided them all together, but curiosity got the better of her. Would they really return what she had stolen to the "rightful" owners?

And so she went temple to temple, locating objects that had come from her collection and following the mortal monks as they went on pilgrimages to return the goods. What shocked Nanami was that the monks would return something if the disciples were even able to locate a descendant of the original owner—once a whole millennium distant.

And most of the recipients were impoverished. Often, there would be a local legend about how the family had been ruined because of the theft of their greatest treasure. Nanami had never really considered who she was stealing from or how the theft would affect them—certainly He Who Walks in Shadow had not.

As Nanami watched an old grandmother sobbing on her knees in gratitude as two monks returned the jewelry that had been her dowry—and resulted in a divorce when it went missing—Nanami felt ashamed of herself.

She was wicked, just as her father had said when he had thrown her out. She had hurt people. She deserved punishment.

But wasn't losing what she had taken enough? Did she really have to lose her hand too?

Couldn't she redeem herself another way?

Present Day

XIAO was in the middle of pressing a damp towel to Nanami's forehead, having cared for her continuously the past two days, when her eyes suddenly flew open.

"What—what happened?" she asked, her voice raspy.

Xiao poured water in a small pink porcelain cup and helped her drink it before answering.

"You had a true dream."

She drank the water. "A true dream—yes, I suppose it must have been." She rubbed her eyes. "I'm getting old."

How can I help her relax? Xiao leaned close and examined her hair. "I don't see any grays."

She scoffed, then giggled.

"Are you okay?" he asked, reading the shadows of her eyes intently.

"Mmm." Her eyes darted from his, breaking his concentration.

Xiao hesitated before asking his real question. "What did you dream of?"

Nanami arched her brows before saying, "The theft that changed my life. It caused a break between my master and me, and he exposed my house to Salaana. I never lived anywhere longer than a few years after that, and I stopped stealing for myself."

She cradled her stump and sighed. "I thought I had let go of the guilt long ago, but I guess I hadn't."

Xiao tried to think of something to say, but she suddenly stood. "I need to relieve myself."

Xiao half stood, thinking she might need support, but she left the room on her own. After a moment, Xiao smoothed the red silk cover of Jin's bed and sat back down on it. He'd have to ask Yeppeun and Luye to wash it later—it smelled a bit after days of enveloping a feverish Nanami.

When Nanami walked back in the room, she declared, "If Ichimi is actively supporting the Goddess of Justice, so is the Sea Dragon."

Xiao was more interested in making sure that Nanami was truly well than discussing her family, but he said, "Oh yeah?"

"That's the way my family is. Tight. Loyal. And the Dragon is utterly in control."

"Mmm." She seemed okay. He wasn't sure what he expected—for her to continue to cry and mope? That didn't seem like her. "Don't you think things might have changed since you were there last?" he asked, just to keep her talking.

Nanami's lips twisted as she plopped next to him on the bed. "Your parents are equals. My father chose my mother partially because he was so much more powerful than she is, and she was raised to be demure, submissive. She has never challenged his authority. Of thirteen children, only I ever went against his dictates."

"But Ichimi might have been sent from the Sea Court, too."

"I think, if she had, she wouldn't have been so intolerant of me."

Xiao put his arm around her, and she leaned against him slightly. "Tell me what Ichimi said."

Xiao laughed. "I know that for you this just happened, but I've been taking care of a sick person for two days. Let me see..." He recounted his conversation with Ichimi as best as he could remember.

"She's probably right—we should be looking at Gang. After all, it wouldn't be easy for Salaana, Karana, or Guleum to find Jin. But Gang could track her effortlessly."

"How so?" Xiao realized that he was stroking her arm idly, but he couldn't seem to stop.

"He's almost definitely her father."

"That's right—so of course he could find her." Xiao considered, then shook his head. "He was genuinely distraught by the idea of her being hurt—and he vowed to protect her."

Nanami tapped her lip. "The first time my mother caught me stealing, she locked me in my room. For my own protection, she said."

Xiao's gut clenched—that was uncomfortably familiar. His arm tightened around Nanami, and the warmth of her against his chest helped him stay calm. In fact, his voice sounded detached as he said, "I could believe Gang wants to lock her up, to keep her out of the conflict, but that man *attacked* her."

"He left pretty easily though—and I doubt he was running

from Bai. He wouldn't have recognized him. So—maybe just cutting Jin was his aim. Maybe—maybe the shuriken was painted with something."

And Xiao had thought he was paranoid. "What could affect an immortal in such a tiny amount?"

Nanami rubbed her lip. "My father told me that the God of War has a poison like that."

"That's the second time I've heard such a rumor in recent days. But if he had such a thing, why not knock me out when I was uncooperative?"

"I think you underestimate your parents' reaction."

Xiao snorted. "My parents are selling my worshippers' dreams without my consent. They don't care about me."

Nanami's lips twisted, and was that pity in her eyes? "Well, they care about those dreams, don't they? Without the God of Pleasure, those dreams would be lost."

Xiao grimaced. She might be right, but that didn't make him feel better. He would definitely need to confront them soon—how to do that? Storm into the hall? Maybe he should bring Jin with him...

"What are you thinking?"

Xiao glanced at Nanami and found her utterly focused on him. "I'm thinking I want to confront my parents, but..."

"But?"

"I don't stand a chance against them."

Nanami crossed her arms. "How come you can't shape things?"

Xiao stiffened. "Can you do everything the Sea Dragon does, then?" he challenged.

"I think so. Not as well, most things, I suppose, but I have the same abilities. The skill will come with time."

Xiao didn't believe her. After all, "Bai said the Sea Dragon can shapeshift, and you said you can't."

Nanami frowned. "Yes—well, I've never seen him do that. My grandfather is the only one I have ever seen change shape."

Xiao was shocked. He leaned closer, eager to know more. "The Moon Deer? He can really shapeshift?"

"He can become a deer—his original shape."

Wow. What would it be like...

Nanami poked him in the arm. "Stop using shapeshifting to avoid the issue. You should be able to do what your parents do."

He was tired of this. So he grabbed the finger that was poking him, winked at her, and kissed its tip. Nanami yanked it back, and that deep flush he had first seen at the Wood Pavilions spread over her neck.

A throat cleared from the door, and Xiao turned to find Luye glowering at them.

He removed Nanami from his lap. "Calm down," he muttered, "I was just comforting her."

Xiao needed a little space. "I'll leave you to Luye's excellent care," he told Nanami and headed out of the pavilion.

That wasn't enough, so Xiao went through the gate of Jin's residence.

Several Light Hands were waiting just outside, including his favorite third disciple. He started to slouch as if he were drunk, but he gave up almost immediately. He hadn't dumped any soju on himself today because, ever since that little slip at Salaana's light show, he had found the scent of alcohol harder to resist. So let them know he was sober and not useless. He had broken through Salaana's will effortlessly to aid Nanami; these women clearly had seen that themselves or heard of it, based on their wary stances.

"What do you want?"

"Our lady would speak with you."

"I haven't any interest in speaking with her though, and you can tell her that Nanami the Thief is a friend of Jin's. Let her chew that over."

He brusquely pushed past them and made his way to Guleum's compound, where he pounded on the door.

A servant opened it immediately, but when Xiao asked for Guleum, the man apologized and said the young master was busy.

"Feeling dreams?" Xiao drawled.

The servant's eyes darted away, and Xiao took that as confirmation.

"I'll wait inside." He brushed past the man's a token protest and strode through Guleum's pretty, if boring, garden to his house. Guleum was stretched out on the floor, his big head creaking his too thin neck, like a flower stalk that had failed to support its bloom. His eyes were closed, and red smoke clung to him, filling the air with an overwhelming scent of cinnamon. His limbs lay askew, and Xiao might have feared that he was dead if it weren't for his hands—thin and long, they twitched periodically, like a dog's legs as it dreams. Xiao sat down beside him.

He felt a bit nauseous. Was this how he looked like to others, after a night of partying? Was this how Jin had viewed him over the years? No wonder she was reluctant to marry him. But Nanami had seen him like this at the Wood Pavilions and still found something worthwhile...

About ten minutes later, Guleum's eyes opened. His breathing was irregular and he struggled to sit up, so Xiao helped him. He seemed mildly confused by Xiao's presence, but he smiled. "Hey, what brings you?"

Xiao should have spent the time waiting planning what to say, but he had been too emotional to think. He tapped his knees, then, "Let's be straight with each other. The Sun Emperor is dying. Gang and Salaana both want the throne. You favor Salaana. Will you offer her aid, whatever that might be?"

Guleum's mouth hung open for a moment before he shrugged and agreed.

"But Salaana's overly harsh. She sees the world as black and white," Xiao told him. "She just burned off the hand of my friend."

Guleum crossed his arms and looked smug. "Your friend is a thief?"

Xiao scowled. "She's a thief, but she only steals from those who deserve it."

Guleum snorted. "Deserves it? Not sure you'd be saying that if she stole from you."

"She *did* steal from me. That's how we met. And I deserved it." *And not for Jin's sake,* he admitted for the first time. *For my own. Because I was drinking my days away, and I deserve better than that.* And there it was—the reason he was working so cursed hard to stay sober at the Sun Court. He liked it. He wanted to be seen as a power, to be able to offer his challenge of Salaana from a place of equality.

Guleum scratched his nose.

"Look, Xiao, Salaana did me a big favor. I owe her my loyalty."

Xiao leaned forward. "Is that you or your blood talking?"

Guleum frowned. "I don't know what you mean."

"How many drops of blood have you given Salaana? Fifty?

A hundred?"

"I don't know. What does it matter?"

Xiao wanted to smack him. "Your family has an affinity for blood, you idiot! When you give someone a piece of you, they can use it for spells, curses—the Sun Emperor is under a death curse right now, cast by one of his blood! Salaana may have used the blood you gave her to cast it—so you will look like the culprit!"

"She didn't do that!"

"How do you know!"

"Because I cast the death curse!" Guleum leaped to his feet. "I killed that old bastard before he could kill my mother! He deserves to die, he's a murderer! And you and everybody else is always underestimating me! I thought you'd understand because they call you the useless god. But you're just like everybody else. Get out! Get out now!"

Xiao stood his ground. "I know what you're doing, okay? I get it I get overwhelmed too. When you find something that can make you feel good, that keeps the stress at a distance, of course you want to embrace it. But long term, it doesn't make the problems go away. In fact, they get harder to deal with, more overwhelming until it feels like you don't have any other choices—"

Guleum shoved him hard in the chest. "I'm not like you! You're a drunk—a useless god! I can handle my life—dreams of justice are just inspiration."

Suddenly the air began to move faster and faster around the room, buffeting Xiao with alarming force.

"I control the air! What can you do?" Guleum shouted.

Something snapped in Xiao. He grabbed Guleum's shoulders and found the fear at the root of Guleum's anger. He magnified it until it enveloped Guleum.

"I can control you," growled Xiao.

Guleum knelt before him, tears streaming down his face. His shoulders shook beneath Xiao's hands.

Xiao pulled back, horrified at himself. He had seen his mother do this many times—take someone's emotions and twist them to her purpose. He had always hated it.

"I'm—I'm sorry," he stuttered, before turning and running.

"XIAO." Nanami was knelt next to where he had passed out on the mossy bank of Jin's pond and shook his shoulder. No response. She pressed a hand to her face—this close, the harsh fumes of hard liquor and acrid vomit nearly overwhelmed her.

He looked a mess—it was hard to believe he was the same tender caregiver whom she had seen this morning.

She cast another glance at Jin's disciples. The two women reminded her of birds, with their anxious movements.

"Do you know when he returned last night? Where did he drink?"

One of them bit her lip and the other said, "Not in the palace. He stormed in here and teleported. We don't know when he came back."

Nanami's remaining hand fisted in Xiao's robe. She forced it to relax.

"Please, would one of you bring me tea and a bowl of rice?"

When the shorter disciple returned with her requests, Nanami pulled water from the pond, dumping it on Xiao. He woke sputtering, but Nanami offered him a cup of tea before he could fully process what had happened.

"Are you okay?" Nanami asked him.

He gulped some of the tea. "This dumping water on me seems to be becoming a habit of yours. A bad habit."

Nanami shrugged. "I tried to wake you up through other means first."

"You could have let me sleep it off."

"I could have, but I wanted you to know I was upset. And I wanted to know what upset you."

He scowled. "Gu cast the death curse." He rubbed his face. "I guess on top of your hand, it was just too much."

Nanami hesitated, then gently touched the back of his hand with her fingertips. He twisted his hand immediately and clasped hers. "Is that all?" she asked.

He hesitated, not meeting her eyes. Then, "I used one of my mother's nastier tricks on Gu. He tried to blow me out of his residence, so I amplified his fear. And then I felt guilty. He needs help and support, not punishment."

Nanami squeezed his hand. "You feel too much," she told him.

"I don't know how to stop."

She considered that for a moment. "You don't have to stop, but you have to learn how to deal with it besides alcohol. You think Salaana manipulated Gu?"

"Yes. Undoubtedly. And someday he will realize that he's a murderer—that he committed patricide. Will she be able to wipe that away by calling it just?"

Nanami knew the question was rhetorical. She had seen Guleum around the palace, fresh faced and barely pubescent. It was hard to believe he had tried to murder someone. She suddenly decided that if she had any influence in the matter, she would help Jin save the emperor, just so that Guleum didn't become a murderer. Fates curse Salaana. "You faced Salaana down when she took my hand. Why don't you confront her now?"

Xiao squeezed her hand. "Everyone was wondering how I broke her wards—even me. Salaana would kick my ass."

"She shouldn't be able to. You're the scion of two Colors."

"Why does that matter?"

Nanami had never been particularly interested in magic theory, but she obviously understood more than Xiao. She spent a moment to gather her thoughts, then, "The Colors are the nine most powerful beings in our world. An immortal receives all the power of their creation years. The nine of them each appeared one thousand years after each other, but after Hei, immortals appeared yearly. So they are all a thousand times more powerful than other spontaneous immortals. And we, their children, inherit their power. My mother is of a later immortal lineage, so none of my siblings and I are noticeably more powerful than my father. But you are twice as strong as any color."

"Twice as strong as Bai?" Xiao snorted.

"Yes. Don't you know the story of Gang and Olli the Spider?"

"Of course I do. What does it have to do with anything?"

"Gang is also the son of two Colors. The Spider was one of the most dangerous immortal creatures. It almost killed Aka. But Gang defeated it easily and imprisoned it in the Underworld."

"But he was trained by Bai..."

"Even Bai was afraid of Olli. He did not want his pupil facing him. It was power that won the day. If you want to face down Salaana, show her that she should be as wary of you as she is of Gang."

"How?"

Nanami looked around her and reached toward an iris, only to find she had no fingers to pluck it. She stared for a moment at that sad stump, and a feeling trembled its way from her gut to her throat. She managed to swallow it back down. Brusquely, she freed her hand from Xiao's and broke the iris's stalk. As she passed the deep purple flower to Xiao, she said, "Think of what you want, of what it could be. Then will it so."

NANAMI sat cross legged at the low table in Jin's living room. She was trying to sharpen one of her throwing knives and had managed to nick herself twice.

"Do you want me to do that?" Xiao offered, and Nanami glowered at him.

She wasn't sure who frustrated her more—Xiao or herself. They'd been hiding from the Sun Court for over a week now, protected by Jin's wards. (Salaana had attempted to break them once, in return for the insult that Xiao had given her, and Nanami doubted she would ever try again after the humiliation that followed). Xiao lay back on the smooth boards of Jin's hall, slowly shredding some wisteria. If they stayed here much longer, there wouldn't be a purple flower left in Jin's garden, and Xiao hadn't managed to transform a single one of them. He kept insisting that they didn't "want" to be anything but flowers, and Nanami made the mistake of telling him that flowers didn't have desires. He had proceeded to stroke her arms with the flower he was holding as he outlined flower reproduction in shockingly sensual terms.

"The knife is sharp," she snarled at Xiao. "The problem is I need to be able to sharpen it, not that it needs to be sharpened."

"Why? Why not just make a new knife every time this one dulls?"

Nanami sighed. "I could probably do that. After all, I won't need a new one that often. But it's the principle. I should be able to do this. I should..." Her voice cracked.

Xiao sat up and leaned close to her, his arms slipping around her.

She let go of the knife and braced her hand on his chest. This wasn't the first time she had wondered if he might kiss her, but Luye or Yeppeun had always interrupted in the past. Neither was in the residence at present.

Nanami swallowed as she remembered how it felt to be kissed by him in the Wooden Pavilion. Unlike then, he moved slowly, gently, until their mouths met, as soft as butterfly wings. Xiao's hands slid up and down, bringing her tight against him, as his lips grew hot and urgent. Nanami forgot everything and just felt.

He suddenly pulled back, his eyes faraway and his brows knit.

Nanami stiffened, confused and a little embarrassed.

"Something's wrong," he said, and Nanami realized he wasn't even paying attention to her. "Jin's summoning me."

Hot jealousy surged through Nanami. *And how can she do that?* Nanami wondered. *What did you give her of yourself?* "Then let's go," she said aloud. She offered Xiao her remaining hand.

Xiao looked at her other arm. "Are you ready to leave? I can go alone—"

"It doesn't need to heal. Salaana cauterized it even as she burned my hand away. I can adjust anywhere. Maybe it will help, to be somewhere that forces the issue." She continued to offer him her remaining hand.

Xiao hesitated a moment longer, then seized it. She just saw his smile before they moved between.

11

How Jin Was Rescued

JIN was dreaming of falling and falling, surrounded by darkness and damp and cold. Finally she stopped falling but continued to spin. Slowly she opened her eyes, but there was little difference between her dream and reality. It was so dark that she could only see her own hands as pale blurs. She tried to move them, just to confirm that they were indeed her hands, and found heavy metal manacles restricting her movement. Rough stone and straw bit into her cheek. The smell of mold and damp was overpowering, though there was a phantom-like sickly sweetness at the edge of her awareness. When she tried to focus on it, to identify its odd familiarity, the smell disappeared entirely.

She felt damp all over, except for her mouth which felt dry and full of fluff. She tried to draw some saliva into her mouth as she sat up. She managed only the latter, the chains attached to the manacles clanking.

Godsbane, she suddenly thought. *The sickly-sweet smell must have been godsbane.*

When Neela and she had wound their way through the Cold Peaks two thousand years ago, they had stopped very briefly in a valley near Mos Lake, where the ground-covering was a pale yellow and had reeked of rotten fruit. Jin had asked her grandmother if the strange herb was diseased.

"Gang's mother was murdered here," Neela told Jin. "Her death poisoned the whole valley and now this herb is the only thing that will grow."

Neela had used a handkerchief to pick some. "Remember this herb and its smell, Jin. The locals named it 'godsbane' because it harms immortals in five ways. Touching the plant would cause your skin to itch and rash. If it were boiled, the tea would make you vomit for days. If the oil were extracted, its vapors would knock you unconscious. The cut of a blade painted with its juices would put you in a coma. And if you ate the plant, you would die."

Now that the memory had returned to her, Jin touched the faint scar on her cheek, *Was it godsbane that paralyzed me a week ago?* Bai might not be familiar with it. Godsbane grew only in that small valley. It could not be transplanted any more than it could be eradicated. Neela had told Jin that Gang had set a powerful protection over the entire valley to stop beings from harvesting the herb.

"But if that's true, how did we enter?" Jin had asked in surprise.

"With his permission, of course."

Now, in her dark and dank prison, Jin curled as tightly as the manacles allowed. Had Neela done this to her? Had her anger over Jin's perceived betrayal been even greater than Jin realized? Jin grabbed her throat in abrupt panic, but she relaxed when she felt the strong chain which carried both the peacock pendant from Aka and Kunjee. *Surely not NeeNee then.* But perhaps Neela had left Kunjee deliberately, knowing Jin would not teleport away from it?

Jin could quite clearly recall what had preceded the dream of falling. She had left Bai abruptly—childishly, she supposed—when she realized that he was keeping secrets from her as well. She had exited the theatre with the crowd, only to find a little girl crying quietly near the entrance.

Everyone seemed oblivious to the little girl's distress, and though Jin was rather upset herself, she had tried to go to the child. However, the little girl had run away. Jin had hesitated then, but she followed the girl into the small alley next to the theatre, where the girl had hidden her face and continued to sob. Jin had knelt and asked what was wrong.

"Mommy! I need Mommy!"

"We'll find her," Jin promised. "May I pick you up to help you look?"

And then her face had been covered with an oil-soaked cloth that reeked of spoiled peaches.

Whoever planned this knew her well—better than Salaana or Karana. As much as it hurt to contemplate, Neela seemed to be the most likely choice. But Neela knew that Bai was with her—the trap would never have succeeded if he had exited the theatre as well! Could Neela have realized that the play would cause a falling out? Because of the stupid clouds?

Jin shook her head. She felt paranoid and foolish.

She needed to get out of here. She could summon Neela, but if her grandmother was her captor... *Well, so if she is, no harm done, and if she isn't, she will help me.*

Jin focused—she felt Neela, she was sure her grandmother could feel her call. Jin waited five minutes, then ten, but still Neela did not appear.

Maybe she is detained herself, Jin rationalized, but she didn't believe it.

Jin belatedly recalled Gang's pledge to help her. *If he really is my father...*

But something was bothering her.

Gang had access to godsbane. Neela had access to godsbane. Was there anyone else who could get it? If not...

"What does it mean if Gang is my father?" she asked the darkness around her.

It means he hired Nanami.

"That's right—he must have hired Nanami. But that does not mean he wished me ill. Really, it was a nice thing to do for me. And he swore to protect me. If he hurt me, he'd lose his immortality. So why shouldn't I summon him?"

Jin imagined Xiao saying, "His protecting you may not look the way you want it to. What if he wants to lock you in a box so you aren't in danger? What if he wants to protect you from your quest?"

Yes, yes, that was it.

This dark hole was rather like a box. If she'd really been poisoned with godsbane—not once, but twice—then was Gang trying to trap her somewhere until Aka died? But why send her on the quest in the first place?

Because he has secrets. He doesn't want me to know he stopped me.

Jin couldn't be certain of her suspicions, but she really had no relationship with Gang. She couldn't bring herself to trust him.

The only person she fully trusted right now was Xiao.

Jin rubbed the pad of her left pinky. Over three thousand years ago, she and Xiao had made a blood oath—stabbed their pinkies, twisted them together, and promised to always be there if the other needed them. Xiao had suggested it—he had pretended it was a lark, but Jin knew his thoughts had been dark and his feelings bitter. Yet, he had never used it and neither had she. She had never had any need of it before now.

Xiao—Xiao, if you can hear me...

Her connection to him was much weaker than hers to Neela—she couldn't even tell if she had succeeded. Jin stared at her manacles for a moment, still rubbing the small scar on her pinky.

Freedom is beautiful. My blood will free me—I have mastery over blood on both sides. She felt a little ridiculous as she tried to convince herself, but the more she thought about it, the more confidence she gained. Though it was awkward with her arms bound, Jin managed to remove her hairpin—her hair tumbled down in a tangle, and she mused, *Perhaps I should make short hair beautiful.*

Taking a deep breath, she pricked her finger and squeezed until the blood welled up.

You will free me, she told it, forced it to her will.

And though she couldn't easily see, Jin felt the blood changing in her hand. A key was there—it felt heavy and smooth, made of an unfamiliar metal. She fumbled at her manacles, but the key slid smoothly into the lock. Jin heard an audible click and her left manacle fell open. She wasted no time dealing with the right.

Giddy with success, she tried to stand, only to find she nearly fell over with dizziness. She felt the same as when she had collapsed in the market town, and Jin suddenly felt very angry. How dare someone poison her this way!

Her anger gave her strength and she pushed to standing, using the stone wall at her back as support. Slipping the key into her belt, she felt her way around the dark prison. She practically tripped over a wooden ladder that was affixed to the floor. She climbed it until her head pressed against the ceiling. She found a trap door with her hands, but it would not open. It must be locked or blocked from the other side.

Jin folded her hands on the top bar of the ladder and rested her head against it. She could call for help—but surely if anyone was on the other side, they were her enemy.

Several minutes passed with no additional ideas. So she yelled—but there was no response.

Jin went back down the ladder to further explore the room.

She estimated that it was only about six feet by six feet—she found no obvious escape in the walls and turned to the floor, brushing aside the scratchy straw to uncover the stone beneath. She was still at this task, when she suddenly felt as though someone had entered the room with her. Jin froze—then came Xiao's voice. "Jin? Are you here?"

NANAMI took a step in the dark only to leap back when she felt something soft beneath the cloth sole of her shoe.

"Ouch! Yes, that's my hand," came Jin's voice.

"Sorry," Nanami said sheepishly.

"Nanami?" asked Jin. "Did you come, too? Thank you!"

"Don't I get thanked?" groused Xiao.

Jin's laugh chimed. Nanami could hear her rise to her feet— then her eyes adjusted, and she could make out the pale smudge of Jin's face in the gloom.

"Thank you, Xiao. I wasn't sure if my summoning worked."

"What happened? Why are you here? Where's Bai?"

"I was drugged with godsbane, I don't know, and I don't know."

"What?" Nanami could hear the anger in Xiao's voice. "He abandoned you—or planned this?"

"No, no," Jin hastily reassured him. "We fought, and I went off on my own—look, I was foolish and I'll explain, but do you think we can get out of here first?"

Nanami looked around. "You said you were drugged—do you know by who? Or where we are?"

"Not sure. A basement of some sort—there's a trapdoor in the ceiling, but I couldn't open it. The lock is on the outside."

Nanami paused at that. "You speak as if you could open it if the lock were on the inside."

"Yes, I've got a key."

"Then I'll pop out and unlock it—unless there is other danger?"

"I don't know," Jin confessed. "I haven't heard anything, and no one responded to my shouts, but..."

"There might be someone, and they have godsbane." Nanami paused. "What is godsbane?"

"It's an herb that is poisonous to immortals." Jin hesitated. "I thought the only people who could access it were Gang, Neela, and Aka."

Godsbane must be the poison about which Nanami's father had told her. "Well, doesn't that fill me with confidence," Nanami said.

"My money's on Gang," said Xiao.

"You didn't see Neela a week ago," was Jin's reply.

Nanami briefly closed her eyes. She could teleport away from here, and her only problem would be a lost hand.

But that sounded... lonely.

"I still think it makes sense for me to go—I can teleport away immediately if there are guards. But I won't be back for a few hours, maybe a day, if I do."

Xiao's hand touched her arm and squeezed. "I say try it. I will follow you if you don't come back."

"No," said Nanami, maybe just because he offered, "you should stay with Jin. If I can't come back... Jin, do you know how I can find Bai?"

Nanami could hear her fiddling with her skirt. "He said he'd wait for me at the Great Willow—but I don't know how long ago that was, or if he'll still be there."

"Well, I'll start there if I must."

Jin gave her the key, and Nanami almost dropped it. It was unlike anything she had ever touched. It was metal, but it felt... damp.

Nanami moved between.

She reappeared in a dilapidated hut. She neither saw nor heard anyone. She didn't see a trapdoor in the floor but moving some of the debris in the interior revealed it. Completely out of place was a shiny brass lock keeping the door shut.

Nanami took Jin's key out of her pocket and cursed. She should have asked Jin where she got the key. This one—red with an odd gold-blue sheen—clearly did not match this lock.

"Jin? Xiao?" Nanami yelled.

"Yes, we can hear you!" Jin's voice was muffled, but clear.

"Jin, this isn't the right key!" Nanami told her. "I'll try to pick the lock."

"Did you try it? It should work."

Nanami slid the key in and found it did indeed fit the lock smoothly. A quick twist and the tumblers moved easily.

Jin, with Xiao at her heels, crawled out of the basement moments later.

"This key... it's magic?" Nanami asked, examining it more

closely.

"I suppose—I made it."

"From what?"

"My blood."

Nanami dropped the key. "What! Your blood!"

Jin was unperturbed by Nanami's reaction—she just bent over and picked up the key. "Yes, well, I couldn't see the color of anything else in there, and I knew my blood was red." She held up the key as if curious to see what it looked like and Nanami realized that she must be seeing it for the first time.

"What are you talking about?" Xiao reached for the key as well—he stopped just short of touching it. "Since when can you create anything?" There was something almost hurt in his tone—Nanami thought of the long hours he had wasted trying to change a flower petal to silk.

"Since Bai's been teaching me. I've been working on shaping different colors. You should be able to as well, Xiao." Nanami almost wished Jin would be smug about it. Her sincere excitement made Nanami wince. Of course, she had no way of knowing how Xiao had spent the last week and a half. "You ought to be able to shape anything violet or black. Just as Nanami can shape water because of her father."

Xiao's brows were drawn, his eyes narrowed. "Well," he said tightly, "you shouldn't leave things made from your blood lying around. People could use it against you."

Jin tucked the key back into her pocket, and Nanami was distracted briefly from Xiao's frustration. That key could open any lock. And Jin could make a new one easily enough. Perhaps she should...

"Shall we find Bai?" Jin asked, interrupting Nanami's half-formed idea.

"I suppose," grumbled Xiao, "but you'd better catch us up on what we've missed."

Jin smiled. "If you'll do the same."

DAWN washed across the sky, painting gold clouds on a blue canvas, as Bai leaned against the fence ringing the Great Willow. Below, the city of Liushi's entertainment district woke sluggishly, reluctantly, in the form of street sleepers who rose and cringed from the morning light. One of these, a drunk who Bai had watched vomit last night, tripped and fell into him. Bai caught the man by the arms without conscious thought and set him upright again.

"Thanks," the man said before leaning close and peering at Bai's face.

Bai jerked back from the harsh fumes of cheap alcohol and the acrid stench of old vomit.

"Weren't you standing here last night?" the man asked. "I'm for breakfast. Care to join me?"

Bai shook his head and pushed the man away. He needed to wait for Jin—but then, shouldn't he be honest with himself? How long should he wait for someone who might not be coming?

Eager to escape Liushi, but not yet willing to abandon his post, Bai pushed off the cobbled street and landed neatly on the inside of the fence. One more leap brought him high into the Great Willow where the dense white branches and the silver leaves partially obscured him to passersby. If it weren't for his black hair he'd be well-hidden. Bai loosened it from its topknot and attempted to undo whatever Jin had done to darken his aspect. However, though sweat beaded on his forehead, the strands of hair remained too long and too dark. Finally he threw them back in impatience over his shoulder.

Could Jin really have abandoned him because he refused to summon a cloud? He had felt as if he had known her during those lazy afternoons on the Kuanbai River when she sat at his side listening to his stories with shining eyes. But he now realized that he had talked more than listened. Was his analysis of her character just a manifestation of his loneliness and long-suppressed hopes? It would seem she was fickle and impulsive, and he had not thought that of her.

And why did it hurt so much? Had he really opened his heart to her over the past month?

Yes, he had a little bit. He pressed his hands against the bark of the Great Willow, trying to let the rough ridges pull him to the present moment.

Instead, they reminded him of a time long ago, a time when he was just as lonely as he was now, though then he didn't have the words to describe this feeling. After Aka had left him and before he had met any other beings, Bai had cultivated this tree. He had told himself it was in the name of enlightenment, but part of him had known that he was really looking for companionship.

I wonder if Jin would feel the same as Cheng. An unknowable pocket hiding in the world. He thought again how he seemed to fall and drown in Jin's essence when he first saw her.

She won't be far from here, he reasoned. *She won't have teleported away.* Fear—or was it hope?—niggled at him, that perhaps someone else had teleported her, but he quashed it. Jin had overpowered Neela. There wasn't a being in this world with more innate magic than Jin.

And when you find her, whispered an insidious voice, *what*

*will you do? Follow her from the shadows like a dog that doesn't
know it's been abandoned?*

I will force her to say a proper good-bye, he told himself, and
though the thought made him tremble, he sent his power
coursing through the tree, seeking the essence of everything.

First there was Liushi, huge and rambling, full of mortal life
but oddly devoid of plants and animals. It would be a burden
on the environment, he saw, a ravenous creation that would
control its creators, demanding ever more resources to sustain
it. He felt nothing unknowable in its limits.

His power flowed above the sea, finding gulls and terns, and
several fishing vessels but no Jin. He let his power rush ever
further, but his reach was exhausted before he found her.
Worry clenched his gut—had she been threatened? In danger?

He sent his power along the sides of the Kuanbai, and he
found something familiar—Xiao. With him was Nanami,
and... something unknowable. Something that swirled with
red, orange, yellow, and blue, yet defied his categorization.

Bai wrenched his hands away from the tree, cutting himself
off from the world. He swayed slightly at the sudden loss, then
folded his hands together.

This possibility had not occurred to him. Had she
summoned Xiao and changed her plans? He wanted to simply
teleport there and ask, and yet... the idea of demanding she
make a proper farewell in front of her betrothed chafed at Bai's
pride. How Xiao would smirk! And would they repeat it to
their friends, much as Noran had, that Jin had enthralled the
First in just a month? A little slip of a thing that was not even
five thousand years old?

He felt pathetic and embarrassed. And yet, what should he
do—return to the White Mountain too cowardly to show his

face? He straightened his spine and leapt from the tree, teleporting as he did so.

He saw the three companions before they saw him. Jin was a mess for the first time since he'd met her, her face dirty and smudged and her hair tangled about her shoulders.

"... find him?" Jin was asking.

"Do we really need to?" Xiao replied. "We'll accompany you to the Korikami's Tomb."

Jin shook her head. "No! I was angry and harsh. If we don't find him—he'll think—" Jin twisted her fingers unhappily. "Besides, you need to learn to use your powers, Xiao. If civil war is truly brewing..." She looked up then, and her eyes met Bai's. For a moment she froze, her golden eyes gleaming with happiness, a smile curving those plum blossom lips, and, without any magic on her part, Bai suddenly thought she was even more beautiful than he had realized.

Then her face closed, and Bai knew that she was still hurt by him—that his lack of trust had wounded her deeply.

"Why did you come?" The question sounded like an accusation. If Bai hadn't heard her worrying about him just moments ago and seen her smile, that challenge would have cut deep.

"It's my hair," he said, hoping he managed to sound above it all. "I've been trying to change it back, but I can't."

Jin's mouth worked soundlessly, then she glided toward him. One delicate hand stretched out, just faintly brushing his hair. He couldn't see it, but it must have been shorter as it suddenly weighed less. "There," she said curtly. She met his eyes. "And your eyes," she said, her hand drifting toward his temple. He caught it in his, and she went very still.

"I'm sorry," he whispered. "I came because I was worried

and because I couldn't leave things there. Please tell me you'll forgive me."

Her expressive face changed from hope to hurt to uncertainty all too quickly. "I haven't forgiven you," she whispered back. "But I... if—"

"What are you two whispering about?" demanded Xiao, slinging an arm around Jin's shoulders and looking at Bai narrow-eyed.

Nanami elbowed him and Xiao let his arm drop, but Bai barely noticed. "What happened to your hand?" he demanded.

Nanami flushed and held her stump close to her body. "Salaana destroyed it."

JIN forced herself to stop staring at the end of Nanami's sleeve. How had she not noticed that Nanami's hand was gone? It was the first thing Bai saw.

And it was her fault. She had suggested that Nanami become a disciple of Salaana. Xiao had even warned them that Salaana would take Nanami's hand, but Jin had ignored his concern.

Nanami must hate her.

Jin pressed the back of her hand against her lips, trying to calm the bile that was rising in her gorge.

"Jin, are you okay?" Xiao asked.

"I'm sorry—about your hand, I'm so sorry—I should never have suggested being a disciple of Salaana..."

Nanami opened her mouth, but almost immediately snapped it shut. She looked away, and Jin felt terrible. "Ah. It's true, I don't know how I will manage with just one hand... I suppose—"

To Jin's shock, Xiao elbowed Nanami. "Don't tease her! Jin takes everything seriously."

"Hey, handless woman here!" Nanami elbowed him back—which made Jin realize Xiao was right. Nanami *was* teasing her.

Nanami looked a bit sheepish as she turned to Jin and said, "Salaaana has been hunting me for millennia. I knew the risk—it was my own pride and eagerness to trick her eager that made me do it. It's not your fault."

Nanami and Xiao's relationship had changed. Jin wasn't exactly sure what it was right now. She opened and shut her mouth twice before saying, "Still, if there's anything I can do..."

Nanami shook her head and waved her remaining hand.

"So Nanami lost a hand," said Bai slowly. "Is that why the three of you are together? Because of the trouble at the Sun Court?"

"Oh—no," admitted Jin, a little embarrassed to tell him how her foolishness at theatre had led to her abduction. But of course, Xiao and Nanami already knew.

Jin related the story as they walked to Liushi, and the four of them fell in side by side—Bai, then Jin, then Xiao, and then Nanami. Jin worried that Nanami still seemed a bit upset, but she decided it should wait until they could speak alone.

When she showed Bai the key she had made, he smiled slightly and asked, "Now who's scattering miraculous artifacts?"

Jin flushed but met his gaze boldly, and said, "Well, I was taught by the best." Xiao made a gagging sound beside her, and Jin cleared her throat. "I'm sorry I ran away like that."

Bai shrugged and looked away. "You had a right to be upset. I'm more concerned by the fact someone seemed to know you would do that. Someone who knows you well planned the abduction." He looked at Nanami and Xiao. "Did you learn anything at the Sun Court?" he asked.

Nanami and Xiao looked at each other, a silent argument going on between them. Jin picked up some of it and crossed her arms angrily. "I agree with Nanami! Of course you should tell me Gang is my father!" Jin let out a deep breath. "I already knew, more or less, anyway."

Jin glanced at Bai.

"And I also think he was the one who tried to incapacitate me twice. Nanami's right—he and Neela are the only ones who could easily send someone directly to me, and they are the only ones with access to godsbane."

"Godsbane?" echoed Bai.

"It's an herb that grows in the valley where Noran died. It is poisonous to immortals," Jin explained.

Both Nanami and Xiao made exclamations of surprise— another secret that Jin had given away.

"But Gang didn't poison the emperor," put in Xiao. "Gu confessed to me. He did it for his mother."

Jin stopped walking. "But—no—I... I wanted it to be Salaana, even if that meant he deserved the curse."

Xiao stopped as well and pulled Jin into a hug. "Me, too."

"Gu may have cast the curse, but that doesn't mean Salaana isn't responsible," Nanami argued. Jin listened intently as Nanami and Xiao described Guleum's addiction to dreams and the blood he had traded for them.

Bai shook his head when they finished, saying, "You cannot relieve him of responsibility just because he was influenced by his addiction. A being has to own their choices, even if they were vulnerable when they made them."

Jin nodded in agreement, though she did feel angry with

Salaana for abusing that vulnerability.

She pulled free of Xiao's hug and began walking again. "I don't suppose any of this has changed your mind about flying to the Korikami's Tomb?" she asked Bai.

He flushed slightly and cleared his throat. "No."

"Because you aren't sure the curse should be broken."

"The Underworld was dangerous even before it was full of immortal creatures. It would be good to master your powers more, so why not do it as we travel?"

Anger rose again—maybe not as much as she felt in the theater, but close. "Why can't you just answer directly?"

"His point is a good one, though," put in Nanami. "Neither you nor Xiao know much about the immortal creatures. Going there ignorant..." Nanami shuddered.

Jin frowned. "But you and Bai do—unless you aren't planning on entering the Underworld?"

"I am," said Bai, "but wouldn't it be better for you to learn more anyway?"

Jin bit her lip. She wasn't sure if she trusted him or not. She looked at Xiao, only to find her friend was focused on Nanami.

"Are they really that scary?" asked Xiao. "Tell us about the immortal creatures."

Nanami laughed. "There are more than a hundred kinds. And not all are scary but—have you ever heard of the Xuezei, for example?"

Jin shook her head, as did Xiao.

"They are blood drinkers—mortal or immortal, they don't care which. They have fangs and sharp claws and live in packs. When you meet one, you need to prepare yourself for twenty. But they don't care about each other, only for blood. So you can't frighten them off—you must kill every single one. They will suck your blood even if they are severely injured—the only way to be sure they've died is to behead them or burn them. So their viciousness and numbers make them hard to face. Fire is just about the only effective weapon against them—hunters used to corral them with torches and burn them en masse.

"But at least they are obviously dangerous. So if you met them not knowing what they are, you would know to take precautions. That's not the case with the Nisei. They are small and beautiful beings that look like butterflies, and they suffocate you in your sleep." Nanami shook her head. "You and Xiao aren't ready for the Underworld."

12

How Xiao Realized His Strength

XIAO looked out across the endless blue of the ocean, enjoying the warm salt air and the occasional cool ocean spray. He was leaning against the side of the Yanou, a large junk which they had hired in Liushi. Its white sails stretched like fins to the clear blue sky, and the Yanou sliced through the relatively calm waves at a pace that had mollified Jin after Bai's refusal to call a cloud. Believing Gang to be tracking them, Jin had banned other immortals from the Yanou, but the four of them hadn't bothered to hide their immortality from the crew.

Bai's white hair paired with his young face had garnered their curiosity, and all of them bowed and scraped to their passengers. Nanami handled this the most easily, joking and chatting with them effortlessly. Jin surprised Xiao by being the least approachable, her untouchable beauty awing the crew. The crew was almost as shy around Bai, and it would have been natural for the two of them to fall into each other's company, but in the days since Bai had found them by the river, Jin and he had watched each other like wild animals—admiration and yearning accompanied by a wariness, as if the other might suddenly attack.

It was driving Xiao crazy—he could tell their feelings had

developed over the past month and he wanted to just throw the two of them in a locked room and tell them to have sex, and yet... And yet, it was totally hypocritical of him, for was he not circling Nanami in much the same manner?

Logically, he knew that Jin was aware of their attachment, and he knew she didn't care. But he felt uncomfortable flirting with Nanami when he had told Jin he wanted a monogamous marriage. After all, they were still engaged. Nanami was also holding back from him—for the same reason?

He was glad he had told none of them about his sometimes conflicting feelings for Jin. Now that he had seen her again with Bai, he found it surprisingly easy to accept that she and he were only friends. Siblings perhaps, since friends seemed too weak a word. It didn't matter if Jin made him angry or hurt him; he would always be at her side when she needed him. But he didn't need to be her lover. Didn't even want to be. He did, however, want Nanami. If it wasn't for that cursed betrothal...

A throat cleared next to him, and Xiao turned his head to find Bai leaning beside him, looking over the water.

"Can I help you?"

That cursed brow arched. "I thought perhaps I could help you. Jin asked me to work with you."

"You mean you actually talked to her?" Xiao mocked.

Death stared him in the eyes. Xiao didn't believe Bai would hurt him though—it would upset Jin too much. "What is with you? She likes you; you like her. Just apologize and stop this cold war."

Bai crossed his arms. "Do you want to master your power or not?"

Xiao grimaced. "I'm not so desperate as to accept help from someone who dislikes me."

Bai's expression softened just a bit. "I'm sorry if I gave you that impression. It's not you. I dislike your parents."

"We have that in common," Xiao pointed out.

The brow went up again. "I suppose we do at that. They were lousy parents, weren't they?"

Xiao nodded.

"You're full of insecurity. Lost, even."

Xiao turned back to glare at Bai, but the older man didn't even notice.

"That makes me nervous. You're too powerful not to have a purpose, a sense of self."

"So you dislike me because I have mommy and daddy issues? You think I'm weak?"

Bai finally seemed to realize that he had been rude. "Well—"

"I think I'm stronger than you. Because I love people. I love my worshippers, I love Jin, I love Neela, I love—" Xiao paused, and forced himself not to look toward the room where he knew Nanami was.

"Anyway, I may have issues, but at least I'm not afraid I'll go batshit crazy if the people I love die. I'll handle it. I'll mourn and try to honor their memories. How about that?"

Bai's lips twisted. "Do you want to practice your powers or not?"

Xiao nearly growled. "Yeah! Yeah, I do, curse it. I want to make magic keys that open any lock."

Bai blinked stupidly. Xiao far preferred it to the brow arch. "Very well."

The next two hours were extremely frustrating as Bai tried to teach Xiao how to extend his will over shadows on the boat and create something.

"Even just a scrap of cloth would be fine," Bai said, for the millionth time, as if Xiao wasn't already feeling like a complete dolt.

Xiao scowled. "It just doesn't make sense to me. Why on earth should I have dominion over a shadow?"

"Because your father was a shadow."

"Well, that would explain why I could become a shadow, not why I could manipulate one."

Bai scowled and pressed his fist to his mouth, as if trying to hold in an expletive. But a moment later his face relaxed.

"You change yourself all the time, don't you?"

Xiao shifted uncomfortably. He had to admit, he could understand why Aka hadn't liked Bai. The man's constant observations cut a little too close to the core.

Bai stood up, apparently oblivious to Xiao's discomfort. "Do you want to become a crow?"

Xiao stood as well. He should have laughed; how could he become a bird? "Sure."

"Then follow me." Suddenly there was a pure white seagull—only its beak and eyes were gray—sitting on the side of the ship.

Xiao couldn't have explained how he knew what to do, but he leapt into the air as a man and when he landed on the ship's side, he was a crow. He spread his wings, admiring how the light glinted violet off the black feathers. There was a loud exclamation behind him, and Xiao cocked his head to find three crew members prostrate on the deck. Xiao let out a caw of delight and launched himself off the ship with a hop and a flap.

Bai followed him within moments. They ascended rapidly, and Xiao gloried in how easy it was to fly. He was a crow; it was as if he had been a crow his whole life. He lost track of time, the winding buoying him up and carrying away all the worries of Xiao-the-man.

Bai began to fly closer to the water, and at first Xiao thought he was planning on returning to the Yanou. But then the gull became a large white dugong, bigger than Bai himself. The gentle sea mammal disappeared into the water. *Real ones are grayer than that*, Xiao mused. Intrigued, he flew lower, picturing the black and white whales that liked to eat dugongs. He then systematically turned the white markings lavender in his mind.

He slipped into the water, a keen and powerful predator. He surfaced to breathe, then dove deep chasing the white dugong, which gleamed in the murky sea.

Remembering how swiftly Bai had defeated him in the garden, Xiao decided to turn the tables on him and began to harry Bai.

He had but touched his nose to the dugong's side when he felt Bai's power seize him securely. They teleported.

When they re-emerged in the world, they were both men, and they were free-falling through open air. Xiao twisted around and spotted the Yanou below him. He looked at Bai, wondering if they were fighting for real, but Bai just raised his eyebrows calmly.

So Xiao grabbed Bai and tried to teleport back to the ship.

To his surprise, Bai fought the teleport. Stubbornly, Xiao pulled more and more power, forcing the other man to his will. And to his shock it worked—he really was more powerful than Bai. The last thing he saw before they went between was Bai smiling and nodding.

NANAMI woke slowly, fighting the lull of a gentle swaying. She was somewhere dark and warm—ah, that's right, the Yanou. She swung her feet out of her hammock, and then it took her minute longer to stand—it had been a very long time since Nanami had been at sea.

The three other hammocks that the small room held were all neatly stored away, so the others must have awoken already. Nanami folded her hammock against a post and was about to go above decks to find her companions when she noticed a large kerchief of Jin's bundled on the floor.

She wouldn't leave the key in that, would she?

Nanami hesitated a moment, then told herself, *I had better check... Jin is pretty careless about what she leaves around. What if one of the crew took it?*

Awkwardly, Nanami loosed the knotted silk with one hand and spread the large square out. There was a motley collection inside—a spare breast cover and underpants, a pure blue comb, several coins... Nanami chuckled at the spread. Immortals who were used to making whatever they wanted, like Bai and her, didn't bother carrying bags as they travelled. Bai even had the neat trick of shrinking anything he wanted to carry and hiding it in his robes, as he had with his sword, shield, and guzheng.

Nanami pushed the breast cover aside, and her breath caught. She really did leave it.

Reverently, she picked up the key and turned it in her fingers.

The door to the room flew open, banging into the wall. "Xiao just became a bird! Come and see!" Jin was practically bouncing with excitement.

Quickly, Nanami tried to restore the silk bundle, but she was too slow with only one hand.

"What are you doing? You—you're stealing my key?"

"No, no, it just came untied, so I was trying to neaten things up—"

"Don't. Lie. To. Me." Jin pulled the key from the pile, and continued, almost snarling, "I can hear your thoughts. Why would you steal it? I would have given it to you, if you had asked."

Nanami stood slowly. "I shouldn't have opened your things. That was rude. I really wanted to see the key again. I wasn't going to steal it..."

"You were thinking about it. So much for not stealing for yourself. If this is how you treat the people that care about you, I can see why your family sent you away!"

Nanami pulled back. It felt like Jin had slapped her. Then she leaned forward. "I'd rather be sent away than spend my life trying to please terrible people. Your favorite brother burned an entire city to the ground! You watched him murder thousands of mortals, and you still want to be friends with him? Aren't you just a little too eager to please others?"

Jin inhaled sharply, and her already pale face went white. "At least he didn't betray me! Your sister turned you in to justice!"

Nanami scoffed. "No—your brother didn't betray you—oh, because he's not your brother at all! He cuckolded his own father and then avoided his daughter her whole life!" A little voice inside told Nanami that she should stop, but she was too angry. She remembered how Xiao had hugged Jin as soon as they saw her again, and how he had given Jin his blood so she could call him from anywhere. "I guess that's why you think you can ignore others' feelings—you've been playing with Xiao this whole time! He loves you, but you openly flirt with the First!"

Jin took a step closer to Nanami, so they were only a handspan apart. "Openly flirting? You've been interested in Xiao since the first day you met him! You were jealous of me even though I freed you from his spell. I tried to be your friend, but you were really only sticking around to seduce my betrothed, right?"

"At least I stand a chance! Xiao actually likes me! You're clinging to the First when you're just a little girl who reminds him of his lost love!"

Jin's face had changed from white to red. "But he doesn't belong to someone else! At least I'm not a thief who can't even change her ways after she loses a hand!"

Before she realized what she was doing, Nanami raised her arm to strike Jin—but someone caught it. Nanami whipped around and wanted to die. Xiao was holding both her and Jin, Bai behind him.

"Let's calm down," he suggested soothingly. "You are very different people, but you each have your own strengths— "

"Is that why you can't choose between us?" Nanami snarled.

Xiao's mouth worked silently. Nanami's anger faded, replaced by hurt. Could he really not choose between them? She had started to think...

Xiao dropped Jin's arm but continued to hold her own. "I did choose—but Jin is still my best friend." He dropped Nanami's arm too.

"Both of you," Xiao said, "owe the other an apology—"

"Oh, shut up, Xiao!"

Shocked, Nanami turned and looked at Jin. Tears were at

the corners of her eyes, but Jin blinked them away. "Just—just leave me alone!" She ran from the room.

Xiao hesitated, but started to follow her. Bai caught his arm. "I think we should let Nanami and Jin figure this out by themselves." He looked at Nanami. "I trust you won't fight again." Nanami felt like a child.

"No, First," she said meekly.

"We have our own things to hash out," Bai said to Xiao. And then they teleported away.

XIAO didn't immediately recognize the dim room in which they emerged. A fire suddenly blazed up in a hearth, revealing white stone walls with pale live-edge wood furnishings. *He brought us all the way back to his house?*

Bai hung a kettle in the hearth.

"So what do we need to hash out?"

Bai rubbed his forehead, and Xiao realized the older being was making an effort to be patient. "Tea first."

"I'm surprised you are willing to be this far from Jin."

Bai shrugged. "No one can break the ban she set on the ship, and you can find her anywhere in the world. I didn't like leaving, but she needs space and I want to speak with you privately." Bai held up a hand just as Xiao opened his mouth to ask another question. "Please, let me gather my thoughts."

Xiao reluctantly took a seat at the table and waited while Bai set two cups on it.

Finally, Bai said, "I owe you an apology. When we first met, I was dismissive of you." There was a long pause then, and Xiao could see he was struggling for the words. Xiao suspected Bai already knew what he wanted to say—he was methodical like that—but for some reason he couldn't say it.

"And we were both jealous of the other," Xiao suggested. "I was jealous because Jin had fallen for you immediately, when she hasn't been the least interested in me for our whole lives, and you were jealous of me because we are betrothed."

Bai went very stiff. "How can you read my emotions?" he barked.

Xiao blinked in surprise. "They're written all over your face. A little bit of logic, and a lot of experience, it isn't too hard to figure out how most people feel at any given time."

Xiao had finally managed to shock the older being and was in turn shocked himself when Bai bowed to him.

"I have fifteen times your experience, and it is not a skill I have mastered. I have misjudged you."

Xiao burst out laughing. "You have fifteen times my years, but not my experience. I have heard the prayers of mortals every day for the past thousand years. I have had millions of relationships—friendships, lovers, worshippers. Whereas you... well, you spent three times my life in isolation."

Xiao half-expected Bai to be angry, but instead he nodded. "Yes, you're right. I've always shied away from emotion. I was alone when I came to be. For me, it is a habit." He cleared his throat.

"You want to talk to me about Jin?" Xiao guessed. "You apologized because I am her friend?"

Bai looked stricken but shrugged. "If it is so obvious to you, I suppose there is no point in denying it."

Xiao chuckled. "You are wrong. Because it's obvious, you should deny more strongly, but I don't mind. You remind me of Jin, in your honesty. For such an old man, you are a little naive yourself."

Bai suddenly turned away from him and collected the kettle from the hearth—the water was now steaming—and poured some in each vessel. He offered Xiao the cup.

He's being hospitable. I wonder, was he always this clumsy with others, or was his long isolation? Xiao accepted the cup with an inclination of his head, then gulped half of it down.

When Bai had finished swallowing his own sip, Xiao said, "You don't have to do the social dance. Why don't you just spit it out?"

Bai's eyes widened comically, but he managed, "I wish to court Jin."

"But she's betrothed to me."

Bai nodded. "I want to know how you feel about her. About your betrothal." Bai drew in another deep breath. "I don't wish to court someone who belongs to another again."

"Again?" Xiao echoed in confusion.

Bai blushed. "Nanami told Jin, so I had thought she told you as well. My first love was Noran, Gang's mother. She never had feelings for any but Aka."

"But Jin doesn't love me that way—you already know that from Jin herself."

"But when we first met, I thought you were in love with her. I heard you tell Nanami you had chosen between them—I want to hear what you decided, directly from you."

Xiao had met people like Bai before, but he thought it was ridiculous. All that mattered was if his attentions were welcomed by the object of his affections. After all, nobody belonged to anyone else. Xiao drank the rest of his water and decided to humor Bai. He could, after all, break Xiao into little pieces without breathing hard. "Jin and I are friends; that is all we'll ever be. I want to break our betrothal, but..."

Bai nodded. "Your power and your immortality are a fundamental part of yourself. I don't wish to see Jin lose hers either. May I ask, what was the wording of your vow?"

"The emperor and my parents made the vow, and Jin and I agreed to follow it."

Bai, who had been focused on his bowl, looked sharply at Xiao. "What precisely did you and she say?"

"Uh... 'I pledge to honor my parent's vows.'" Xiao thought for a moment. "I think she said the same as I."

Bai's eyebrows flew up, in excitement rather than judgment for once. "But Aka is not Jin's father!"

"I thought about that," Xiao admitted, "But if Jin thinks of him as her father..."

The excitement in Bai's eyes dimmed.

"There is that," he agreed. "Still, if she rejected him as her father, she would be free of the vow."

"And me?"

Bai shrugged. "If anyone involved breaks the vow, it should be voided. But I will admit that side-stepping it might not have quite the same effect."

Xiao drank down the warm water quickly.

"Are you sure it's okay for us to leave them alone together?"

Bai nodded. "They aren't really mad at each other—they were taking out other pain and anger. I think they will resolve it more quickly if we aren't there."

"Because you and I are what is really ticking them off?"

Bai shrugged. "Perhaps."

"You should just talk to Jin," Xiao advised him.

"I don't know what to say," Bai admitted. "When I figure it out, I will."

"I don't understand why you are upset with her," Xiao

prodded. "Like, Jin was pissed that you didn't tell her about the cloud. But she didn't do anything to you."

Bai stared at the fire, and Xiao just had just about given up hearing an answer when Bai murmured. "She left me."

Oh, man, he really was a coward. Xiao was trying to think of a response, when Bai said, "Why don't we stay here tonight?"

Xiao cocked his head in surprise. "You're willing to leave Jin's side that long?"

"You can you track Jin. If they move suddenly, we'll return. This is a good place to teach you."

Xiao didn't think that was really why Bai wanted to stay. He had wanted to come home, to run away from the big, bad world that threatened him with feelings. But he brought Xiao because he couldn't leave Jin without having a way back to her.

Was that stalkerish or romantic?

Xiao touched the ring he had braided of Nanami's hair. He supposed he was in no position to judge.

"Very well," he said, "What else can you teach me?"

XIAO and Bai really did leave them alone, but Nanami avoided Jin as well. She was ashamed and embarrassed by her own words, and she didn't know what to say.

They both slept in their room that night but pretended by unspoken agreement that the other wasn't there. The next morning, Nanami slipped out early and settled herself in the Yanou's prow. To her surprise, Jin stood before her less than fifteen minutes later and bowed.

"I'm sorry. I said horrible things yesterday. And it wasn't because you deserved them—it's because I am angry with my family, and I have been wanting to yell at someone for days."

Nanami chewed on her lips. "I'm sorry, too. I also was taking out other anger on you—I'm upset about my hand, and... I am jealous of the bond you and Xiao have."

Nanami looked away. She felt Jin kneel beside her, and a hand rested on her shoulder. "You really don't need to be. Xiao and I are close, and we love each other, but not the way he loves you."

Nanami focused on Jin. "Why do you say Xiao loves me?"

"Oh, I can feel it. And I—"

"Yes, you love the First. I shouldn't have mocked you. He seems genuinely interested in you—I've never seen him act towards anyone the way he acts toward you."

Jin winced. "I hope that's true, but I'm not sure even he knows how he feels."

Nanami laughed. "That's true. The First is very powerful, but in touch with his feelings—eh, not so much."

"I just wish—this sounds awful, but I keep wishing that the emperor had been cursed just a little sooner, so that we would have embarked on this quest unentangled."

"I think all four of us feel that way." Nanami swallowed, uneasy how much the answer to her next question mattered. "Have you given any thought to breaking the betrothal?"

"Just several times a day since we reached the Lower Kuanbai." Jin's voice was bloated with self-mockery. "If I break it, I'd have maybe fifty years left." Jin shuddered. "That, even more than losing my powers, terrifies me."

"No! No, of course you mustn't break the vow—but there must be some way—some loophole."

Jin shrugged. "I suppose if Father or the Moon Goddess or the Night God broke the betrothal for us—but then they'd suffer the consequences."

To point out that all three deities had no interest in ending the betrothal seemed unnecessary; Jin was surely more keenly aware of that than Nanami.

"Well, there's still eleven months left. Who knows where everything will be then? You seem like a different person from just last week, your powers have bloomed so brightly."

"Yes—actually—well, speaking of powers, there's been something I've been wanting to try, if you'll let me."

Nanami cocked her head in question.

Jin reached out and lifted Nanami's arm—the one without a hand. "I think I could make you a new hand, with your help."

The idea was so inconceivable to Nanami that it took her a few moments to reply. "Come again?"

"A new hand. Have you tried shaping one out of water?"

She had actually. When Xiao had been sleeping, Nanami had gone to the pond in Jin's garden and shaped one. But it had just been self-torture for she couldn't attach it to her body, and she couldn't make it flesh.

Jin nodded. "I think I could help you with that. I could bring your veins and arteries and muscles through it."

"And the bones?"

"Can't you make the bones?" Jin asked. "I've noticed—everything Bai makes is white, but you make things both indigo and silver. I thought…"

Nanami was considering it. "It's because of my mother and her father. He is the Moon Deer, you know, so I have an affinity for both white and indigo. But my power is mostly indigo - I cannot read essences at all. Yet perhaps I could make bone, of a sort…"

Nanami asked a crew member to bring several buckets of seawater, and he practically flew to complete the task. The sailors then stayed well away from the two immortals, sensing that powerful magic was being worked.

Nanami shaped the hand first. This part was time-consuming, yet held the ease of familiarity, as she had done it before. Perhaps an hour later, when the hand looked perfect except for its watery nature, Jin slipped behind her, and it was as if she cocooned Nanami with her own power. Nanami's sense of the world was suspended; time did not exist in the warm, colorful, and bright place that was Jin. Nanami felt lost, a little afraid even, until she found a streak of blue that was almost familiar. Nanami followed that blue streak like a road, and found the hand she had created, only the water sculpture had become flesh and blood. But there was still water inside it—water that needed to be bone. Nanami tried to assert her will over it, but it resisted violently. *Bone is just like deer antlers, isn't it?*

The hand suddenly shredded, horrifically and violently, pierced by silver prongs. Jin was unfazed, changing the bloody, dismembered hand into flower petals that the breeze carried away, leaving only a single silver antler behind.

"Hmm. Shall we try again?"

Nanami felt weak from the creation, as if she had tapped her life force itself for power. She shook her head. "I can't. I can't make bones. I don't have enough dominion over white." Her voice sounded high and strained in her ears.

Jin sagged down. "I'm sorry."

Nanami managed to shake her head, trying to reassure Jin that it didn't matter, but her eyes betrayed her as hot tears spilled out of them.

THEY stayed long enough in Bai's cave that Xiao used the lock of Nanami's hair—or, more precisely, let Bai use it—to track the Yanou before they teleported. Bai noted that the ship was farther east than he expected, a comment that Xiao barely registered until they stood on the junk's deck.

"Where are all the crew?" he asked, his eyes darting first to the sails and then the aft.

"Can't you feel it?" Bai countered. "Nanami and Jin are practically radiating power. The crew has probably hidden from it—most mortals instinctively fear magic." Bai, having regained his sea-legs with no apparent effort, strode across the rocking deck to the prow, blind to anything but the two women.

Xiao frowned at Bai's retreating back. Of course he felt the power that thickened the air like smoke, but he didn't think Jin and Nanami were the priority now. He looked again at the sails, which seemed to him to be adjusting themselves, without a seaman in sight. He almost called Bai back, but then he thought of Bai's easy familiarity with the boat versus his own total ignorance. He didn't remember the sails acting like this in the past few days, but perhaps it wasn't unusual. Still, he'd feel better if he spoke with the captain. Xiao headed for the aft, scuttling like a crab to keep his balance. At least no one was looking.

Xiao opened the trapdoor set in the wood planking and climbed down the steep, narrow ladder to the lower deck. It was dark below and the oil lamp that the crew usually left for their passengers was gone, but Xiao was Laughter in the Shadows. He moved quickly as he was able through the cramped lower rooms, yet it still took a good ten minutes to find the crew.

When he did, he wished he hadn't. The hold had been cleared so that all the crew could lie down, resembling nothing so much as a compass rose with their feet touching in the center and their hands outstretched to form the perimeter. The air felt heavy and the smell of saltwater was strong, even more so than on the deck. Sound asleep, the sailors' lids twitched rapidly, their hands fisting and releasing in awkward jerks. Xiao had granted enough of his own to recognize the signs of a god's dream.

Xiao set to work immediately. Kneeling by the captain's head, Xiao touched his fingers to the man's temples. Xiao scowled—he knew the man had a wife in Bando, but it appeared he did not worship Xiao. Xiao moved on, checking the crew one by one for a worshipper. The third man, a scrawny fellow with gray stubble, immediately relaxed under Xiao's fingers. Xiao smiled. "You'll be rewarded for your faith," he whispered.

The man's dream felt like Nanami—a controlling, old Nanami. Xiao cursed internally. The Sea Dragon must have felt the women's working. Did he know that it was Nanami who had been casting a spell, or was he simply curious about a surge of power within his realm?

It didn't matter either way, Xiao decided. Through the crew's dreams, the ship was now being steered to the Sea Palace, and being trapped in the Sea Dragon's seat of power wasn't in any of their interests. If he was allied with Salaana, as Nanami suspected, then he would sabotage Jin's quest. If he was trying to bring his intractable daughter home—Xiao shook his head.

He considered breaking the dream's hold on the crew, but, given their long and committed worship of the Sea Dragon—

for all sailors worshipped him, though he denied being a god—Xiao wasn't sure there was much he could do. Secondly, he was afraid that bringing the Sea Dragon's attention to them again might result in a worse scenario—perhaps he would turn the seas against them.

Instead, Xiao raced back to the deck, bumping both a shin and a hip painfully in his rush. On deck, he found his three companions in earnest discussion of resurrection. Xiao grit his teeth in annoyance.

"This isn't the time to chat about magic theory!" he overrode their conversation. "This ship is being summoned by the Sea Dragon! We need to get off it."

"What!" Nanami jumped to her feet and Xiao belatedly realized her eyes were red and puffy. Had she been crying? But no, that had to wait.

"Don't you see how fast the ship is moving? And look at the sails! All twelve of the crew are in a god's dream. The Sea Dragon's. We're headed to his palace, as fast as the Yanou can carry us. No, faster—he is using his power to speed the trip. Whatever you did attracted his attention."

Nanami blanched and chewed on her lips.

"You should all teleport away," Jin suggested.

"We can't," Bai told her. "At least Nanami and I can't—Ao is holding us here, and the sea is his territory. If you gave me Kunjee, perhaps you and Xiao—"

"No," Jin and Xiao said together, and Xiao wondered if Jin's flat refusal was for Kunjee or for their companions.

"If I transform into an orca again—" Xiao suggested.

"You'll be putting yourself directly in his element," Bai shook his head. "It's not a good idea." He hesitated. "I will summon a cloud. We can all ride it, at least to the Crescent

Moon."

"Do it." Xiao said. Then he looked at Nanami, worried by her silence. Her lips looked bloodless. Taking a step closer to her, he clasped her elbow. "What is it, Nanami?"

"It's me. He told me never to contaminate his seas again. There's never been any reason too. I—I guess I thought it didn't matter anymore. It was thirteen millennia ago!"

"You can't be sure," Xiao argued, "You said he must be supporting Salaana. Perhaps he wishes to capture Jin—"

"No, it's me." She closed her eyes. "I'm so sick of this. Why—why does he get to have any say over my life? If he wants that then—then—" She swallowed.

Xiao's hand tightened convulsively on Nanami's arm, but she didn't seem to notice. He looked down at her stump. She wouldn't have lost her hand if not for her sister's betrayal. Xiao felt abruptly angry. So angry that his voice shook when he spoke.

"I can teleport in and out of the Sea Dragon's Palace. I could break Bai's hold on me, so I can break the Dragon's too." Xiao didn't even bother checking with Bai for confirmation. He was sure of what he said. "If you want to confront him, Nanami, I will go with you. I won't let them hurt you. I'll take you out of there if need be."

Nanami met his eyes. Xiao wasn't sure what she saw, but the defeated look faded from her face, leaving the confident, pragmatic thief who had stolen her way into his heart.

"Yes. Yes, that's what I want to do. Thank you." Then, in full view of Jin and Bai, she went on her tiptoes and kissed him on the lips.

Xiao was so startled that he blushed—he hadn't known he still could—and glared at Jin, who was smiling slightly, and Bai, whose brow was raised. Those two really were perfect for each other, they were both so predictable.

"Then we should come with you," Jin suggested. "Then perhaps we could rebuild Nanami's hand..."

"Her hand?" Xiao echoed.

"That's what we were discussing when you interrupted—"

"No," said Nanami. "It might not even work, and since you cannot teleport Kunjee, nothing short of an all-out fight would free it from my father's hands once he has it under his power. And they may not consider themselves my family, but I have no desire to see the First slaughter them all, if it comes to that. You and Bai should go on without us."

Xiao looked at Jin. Her duties as a friend and as a daughter sparred on her face.

"I agree," said Bai, and Jin immediately looked at him. It didn't even sting when her face cleared, and she nodded.

"Very well." She took a deep breath then stepped forward to hug both Xiao and Nanami. "May fate smile on you both."

Xiao caught her hand as she pulled away and kissed her forehead. Despite the weeks of travel, her hair smelled of citrus and honey, and Xiao had to smile. "And also on you," he returned her benediction.

Jin smiled back and said, "I'll fetch our things."

As she walked away, Bai clasped Xiao's arm. "Thank you."

"You'll be stuck on a cloud together for a few hours," Xiao told him. "Could be a good time to talk."

Brow arch. Then Bai focused skyward, and wisps of white began to collect around him. Xiao stepped back startled, and Nanami pressed against his side with a wink. By the time Jin returned, Bai was half-engulfed in dense fog—a cloud. Bai mounted the cloud as if it were as solid as rock. Jin handed him two bags and tried to do the same, but it remained insubstantial beneath her foot. Xiao didn't miss Bai's nonplused expression before he pulled her up and settled her in his lap. Bai murmured an apology as Jin blushed. And then they were flying away.

When they were out of sight, Xiao took a breath and turned back to Nanami. "Are you sure you want to do this?"

She punched him in the gut—not hard, though Xiao bent over and groaned.

"Are you sure you're strong enough?" she retorted, and he grinned at her.

"By the way, you need more practice," he told her.

"With punching?" Nanami's brows knitted adorably.

He pulled her flush against his chest and kissed her lips softly, teasing them until he felt her melt against him. He pulled back then and smiled at her. "No, kissing."

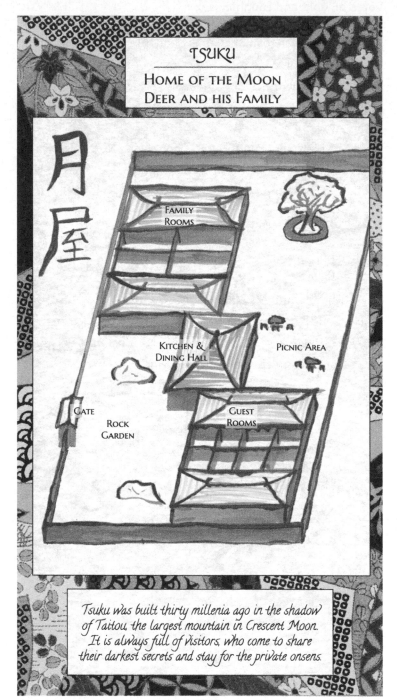

TSUKU

HOME OF THE MOON DEER AND HIS FAMILY

月屋

FAMILY ROOMS

KITCHEN & DINING HALL

PICNIC AREA

GATE

ROCK GARDEN

GUEST ROOMS

Tsuku was built thirty millenia ago in the shadow of Taitou, the largest mountain in Crescent Moon. It is always full of visitors, who come to share their darkest secrets and stay for the private onsens.

13

The Sin of Destruction

THOUGH the weather was mild and the sky blazed blue overhead, a fierce wind carried the small white cloud at a speed the Yanou could never have matched. Bai sat cross-legged, and Jin sat in his lap, her legs dangling in the cold damp of the cloud. Jin didn't mind the damp—put it down to being half flower on her mother's side—but the lap sitting was disconcerting. If she turned her head even slightly to the right, her face would be inches from his, and Bai's arms were wrapped tightly about her waist, pleasant if unsettling bands of heat that secured her against his chest. Jin clutched those arms out of necessity. All that kept her from plummeting into the ocean miles below was Bai.

Although she strived to live in the moment—and never had she better reason to do so, with the danger of falling very real—Jin's mind darted from thought to thought like a minnow searching for food.

When Bai had insisted they travel by boat, he had clung to the excuse that Jin wasn't prepared for the immortal creatures of the Underworld. It had rung true, but Jin now looked for the unsaid whenever Bai spoke, and she was certain there was another reason. Why was it that he had immediately changed his mind when he thought she was in danger?

He was very eager to keep her out of danger. She had spent the last few days on the Yanou turning over their conversations on the Kuanbai. He had said she made him want to live again and that he found her the most desirable being he had ever encountered. Jin had thought that tantamount to a confession of love, but she had realized that he might very well be talking about lust and lust only.

If it were merely lust, why wouldn't he kiss her? Seduce her? Fate knew she wanted to be seduced, even though she hadn't found the courage to do the seducing.

She had thought his reluctance to do more than touch her hand because of her betrothal signaled deeper feelings, but maybe it was simply his own moral code. She wanted to ask him, yet she was afraid of his reply.

Finally she thought of a question whose potential answers didn't make her gut clench.

"Have you never given anyone a ride before?"

"I have," came Bai's reply, a little strangled. At least she wasn't the only one discomfited by their close proximity. "When Gang was my student, we frequently used clouds to survey the land and mortal conflicts."

Jin pictured it—even given that Gang must have been younger and probably slighter, it was absurd to imagine him squeezed onto Bai's lap like this. She snorted, "I shall take comfort in that our ride must be far less awkward than those."

Bai shifted slightly, and she felt his embarrassment. "He didn't—that is, Gang found the cloud quite solid."

Jin frowned. "But that would be because of you, not Gang! Why isn't it solid for me?"

Bai took a deep breath. "I don't know. I'm sorry."

Bai's confession rang with truth, and suddenly, Nanami's words came back to her.

Bai is very powerful, but not at all in touch with his feelings.

Jin realized that the cloud wouldn't support her because it gave Bai an excuse to hold her. *I guess I'm not the only one who uses her powers subconsciously.* Jin wanted to point that out, to bring those feelings into the open, but it was too delicate.

Instead she asked, "Why the Crescent Moon?"

Bai's arms tightened about her waist, and Jin felt his surprise. "Sorry?"

"I mean, why are you so insistent we stop there? Or is it just an arbitrary choice to slow the journey?"

Bai blinked, his smooth face unreadable. "It is not an arbitrary choice, but it may be a fool's errand. A long time ago, the Moon Deer had the most complete records of the immortal creatures. But if Aka was familiar with the collection, it would undoubtedly have been destroyed."

Jin frowned. "Why would he do that?"

"Why would he claim I died serving him?" Bai countered.

Jin hesitated, then she tried to answer the question. "You were a threat to the legend he was constructing. I grew up believing he was the oldest living immortal. Being the oldest seems to imply a right to rule..."

"This collection would also challenge his legend."

"How so?" Jin twisted slightly so that she could see his face.

Bai looked down at her—his eyes grazed her lips and she could feel his yearning for her. But he looked ahead in the next moment, and all he said was, "What do you know about the immortal creatures?"

"The creatures were monsters that harassed immortals and mortals alike."

"Calling them monsters would be like referring to all mortals as criminals. The immortal creatures were of various natures, some good, some bad, some in between, just as mortals—and immortals, for that matter—are."

"Then why lock them away? It seems like an awful lot of work."

"Ambition. Power. Worshippers. All immortal creatures lived on Earth, and many of them were worshipped by their local mortals. Many creatures were dangerous and violent, like the Xuezei that Nanami described or Olli the Spider or the Bulgae. But others were benevolent. The Golden Phoenix protected Bando from invaders and would save children from the Bulgae. The Koch-ssi made the island of Po so fertile that the air smelled like honey. And the Three-Headed Elephant taught the Jeevantians their writing. Aka locked all of them away, both beloved and feared."

"And once their patrons were gone, who better to fill the void than the being who had proven himself more powerful?"

Bai's grey eyes burned into her own. "Indeed."

Jin sought another safe question.

"If the Moon Deer still has his collection, then what? I read and memorize it? How long do you intend us to stay there?"

"Aka's death curse still has more than ten months to go. Why not spend most of that time enhancing your magic—and yes, memorizing the immortal creatures?"

Jin hesitated. "Won't I need that time in the Underworld? To find the black peony?"

Bai shook his head. "I know where they grow—I explored all of it before Aka created his gate and can teleport to the Lonely Island. A month would be ample."

"Why do I feel you are lying with the truth again? You do

want me to look at the collection, and yes, it will have useful information, but that's not why we are really stopping at the Crescent Moon." She faced front and closed her eyes. "I feel so stressed because you don't have faith in me—I want to prove myself to you so badly that it hurts. But perhaps the real question is, why do I have faith in you?"

Bai stiffened, and Jin cringed. "I'm sorry," she quickly recanted, "that wasn't fair. Here you are, carrying me thousands of feet through the air to support my quest and protect me. That's why I have faith in you. Please, pretend I didn't say that."

He made no response.

An hour later, Jin saw Ah on their right, easily recognizable because of its large lake, and then the Crescent Moon came into view. Created by volcanic activity, its steep mountains were covered by forests. The Crescent Moon had relatively few mortals, and its largest city was smaller than Liushi.

As the cloud reached the Crescent Moon, it slowed. Jin supposed that this was the natural effect of passing over land. She soon spotted Taitō, the highest mountain on the landmass, and began scanning around it for the Moon Deer's home, Tsuku. Jin had never been before—like the Sea Palace, Neela was not welcome—but she had heard of it.

"I'm afraid." Bai's confession was so sudden that Jin did not immediately react.

Then she twisted to look at him. "What?"

"I'm afraid," he repeated.

"Why?"

"It's been a very long time since I've really cared about anything."

What was he referring to?

"I just want—I just need a little more time to figure it out."

"And you want to figure it out before we go to the Underworld?" she guessed, still confused as to what "it" was.

"Yes." He cleared his throat. "Xiao is looking for a way to break your betrothal. If—well, that would make it easier."

Jin felt a moment of blinding clarity. "You mean you really care about me? You're trying to figure out us?"

Bai looked like he was choking. His head bobbed awkwardly—a nod.

"But then—shouldn't we figure it out together?"

He shrugged and avoided her eyes. Neither of them spoke again until they reached Tsuku.

BAI directed the cloud to where perhaps ten immortals congregated inside the walls of Tsuku. They watched the cloud descend and were obviously waiting for them. Bai let the cloud dissipate as he assisted Jin to her feet so that they were left standing on the ground. Bai scanned the crowd and felt disappointed. Since the Moon Deer was a friend, he had been here too many times to count, but there were more unfamiliar faces than familiar ones.

A tall, slim man stepped out of the crowd. His full, black-painted lips were quirked in a mocking smile, and his dark eyes were made large and mysterious by kohl. His rich cinnamon skin was smooth and taut; lush raven-black hair hung loose about his shoulders, yet Bai suspected it had been carefully styled. At his wrists and throat, black underrobes peeked out from beneath red robes embroidered with white flames.

"Salaana's been searching for you high and low, little one. How sweet that I should encounter you without the least effort." He spread his arms wide, and Bai was confused by the gesture until Jin flung herself against him. He wrapped her in a tight embrace and swung her around.

"Karana!" she said. Bai barely recognized the stiff and cold woman he held in his arms during the cloud ride; sunshine filled her voice and smile.

Bai touched the shrunken Starlight Sword in his sash before he could stop himself.

A vaguely familiar woman with an oval face and a crown of shining hair stepped forward to greet him.

"First," she said and bowed. "It has been far too long since our hall was graced by your presence. To what do we owe this honor?"

Bai managed to place her as the eldest daughter of the Moon Deer. "Lady Atsuko," he returned the bow. "My friend and I are hoping for the privilege of using your father's library. If it is agreeable, we would stay for some time."

"You and the Sun Emperor's daughter are always most welcome here. Her brother will be delighted to have his sister's company while he confers with my father."

Bai looked again at the handsome man who had set Jin down but continued to hold her hands. He should have listened more carefully when Nanami and Xiao had discussed the Sun Court. This must be the second of the Goddess of Lightning's children. Bai vaguely recalled meeting him as a boy of two thousand years when visiting Gang at the Sun Court. He was the God of Havoc or Devastation or something like that.

Bai stood as close to Jin as manners allowed. After a moment, Karana met his eyes over Jin's head, his gaze frank and cynical.

"Won't you introduce me to your—friend—Jin?" There was

just enough isolation around the label to denote skepticism, and Bai bridled.

"This is Bai. The Great Warrior." Jin looked back at Bai over her shoulder, perhaps seeking his approval for her introduction.

"Most people call me First."

"Bai is fine with me," Karana showed his white even teeth.

Jin laughed awkwardly and Bai realized that while she regretted her brother's rudeness, she was hoping Bai would overlook it. "And this is my brother, Karana, the God of Destruction."

"Her favorite sibling," Karana added.

Jin pulled her hands free from his and poked Karana in the ribs. "You mustn't say such things."

"Don't worry," he said, "I wouldn't if Gu were here—but Salaana and Gang wouldn't care."

A shadow passed over Jin's face, and Bai knew Gang's name had reminded her that Karana was not her sibling—none of them were. They were her uncles, aunt, and father.

"We've actually met before," Bai put in, to distract Karana from Jin's reaction. "When you were just a boy."

Karana smiled. "I remember. You sparred with Gang in the training yard and knocked him to the ground. I'd never seen anyone do that before—or since."

Bai inclined his head in acknowledgement, even as he regretted mentioning it. He should have realized that if Karana remembered Bai, he would associate him with Gang.

"But nobody's seen you in what, seventeen millennia? Most people said you died or slept or whatever it is you do when you grow bored of life."

"I don't believe in growing bored of life," Bai said sharply.

"No?" Karana smiled. "I heard that your friend—Cheng was it?—did."

Bai frowned and his hands clenched.

"Anyway, my apologies if I offended you." The mocking smile didn't seem the least bit apologetic.

"And who was it that told you about Cheng?" Bai said.

Karana's brows lifted. "He hasn't been seen almost as long as you. But I think it was the Moon Goddess who first told me."

Before Bai could question him further, Lady Atsuko cleared her throat. "You and her divinity have been travelling for some time, First. Won't you refresh yourselves?"

And not unsettle our household with rumors of Colors disappearing went unsaid. Bai glanced at the other immortals who had come to greet them. They all immediately looked down.

He smiled at Lady Atsuko. "That would be pleasant. Thank you."

JIN and Karana followed a forest path dappled in sunlight. The new leaves and needles of trees around them were just budding. In another week, this forest would be blindingly green. Bai was still at Tsuku, probably taking advantage of its natural hot springs or visiting with Lady Atsuko. He hadn't liked that Jin had agreed to Karana's suggestion to stretch first—his expressive brows had knit fiercely, and he had bent near to remind Jin that her enemy was still unknown.

But Jin really wanted to talk to Karana now. About everything. After all, even though she thought of Xiao as family, he didn't really understand what it meant to be a child of the Sun Emperor, while Karana did. Also, as soon as she saw him, Jin realized how wrong she had been to keep him on the list of potential suspects. Karana had a temper and could be dangerous, but he was very direct. In fact, as soon as they were out of the Tsuku's gate, he summarized everything that had been unfolding at the Sun Court and admitted he was supporting Salaana against Gang. "That's why I'm here. Salaana is hoping that the Moon Deer and his people will favor her."

"It must help her case that he's the grandfather of Salaana's lover."

Karana blinked in surprise. "It does. But how did you know about Ichimi?"

"Xiao spent a month at court."

Karana laughed and tugged the thick braid that spilled from the crown of her head. "I was very worried about you, Jin, but now I see you aren't nearly as naive as I feared. You sent Xiao to get a lay of the land? But you'll support Salaana over Gang, won't you? I know you and she aren't very close, but Gang never talks to you so..." He trailed off. "Jin, tell me what's wrong. I thought that Bai fellow had hurt you, that's why I was so rude to him, but now... Is it something else? I've never seen you this sad."

Jin hesitated. "There's a couple things."

"I'm listening."

Jin rubbed her nose. She wasn't going to cry. "Okay. Well... we can start with Bai. You know who he is, the oldest immortal, the Scholar, the Great Warrior."

It wasn't a question, but she looked at Karana for confirmation, and to her surprise, he was shaking his head. "Actually, I knew he was the Great Warrior—I do remember him sparring with Gang, and I knew he was older, but—I thought Father was the oldest immortal. That's how he became emperor, isn't it? Is Bai really older?"

Jin nodded, feeling strangely relieved that she wasn't the only one raised in ignorance. "Bai told me that the emperor was once a drop of his blood. That he's the second oldest. And that, unlike Bai, he wanted more power and worshippers. Bai isn't even a god."

"Why do you keep saying emperor instead of 'Papa'?"

Jin stiffened. Then, before she really considered her words, "He's not my father."

Karana stopped walking. "What? Is this something else that Bai told you? I don't think—"

Jin grabbed Karana's arm, which had started to wave wildly. "Neela told me my mother was having an affair, that both I and her unborn child were the results."

Karana was frozen for a few breaths. "So that's why you're less powerful than the rest of us. Wait, is that why he killed her?" Karana's breath hissed out between his teeth.

Jin took "her" to be Aashchary. "You knew!" Jin stepped away from him, dropping his arm.

"I didn't know, no more than I know if he killed our mother, but Salaana has always suspected... we were both away from the palace when our mother died. He told us she committed suicide. But Father married Aashchary only a thousand years later, just before her baby was born. He seduced with the intent of marriage so..."

"So it must have been a matter of days between your mother's death and the seduction of mine." Jin covered her face with her hands. "So did he kill our brother too? The God of Belief?"

Karana became so quiet that she had to lower her hands to

make sure that he was still there. Karana's face was drawn tight, his mouth all but invisible. Jin belatedly remembered Neela's accusation that Karana had murdered Aashchary's first born.

"I am not certain why he died."

The words rang true, but Jin was getting better listening for omissions. "But how did he die?"

Karana rubbed his lips together, before closing his eyes and exhaling slowly. "It was my fault."

Jin stepped closer, but Karana held up a hand as his eyes flew open. "Show yourself," he demanded to the woods at their side. An arrow of red fire formed in his hand, aimed at someone unseen.

Bai stepped out from the woods, looking more embarrassed than anything else. Karana snarled angrily and let the arrow fly.

Bai stepped aside to avoid the arrow and that would have been enough—Karana had a temper, but he wasn't really trying to kill him—but by the time Jin realized that no intervention was necessary, she had already made the flames dissipate.

Karana was slack jawed as he stared at where his arrow had been.

"How did you do that?" he demanded—of Bai. Jin felt sweat break out on her neck. She had just told Karana that Aka wasn't her father, but the power she had shown could only have come from him. Bai told her how serious Neela had been about keeping her parentage secret, and Jin wondered if her friendly brother would change if he knew the truth.

But Bai didn't blink, just cocked one brow. "I think you should finish what you were saying first. How did your brother die?"

Karana's face closed, his eyes narrowing. "I may owe Jin an explanation, but not you."

Bai indicated the air that had swallowed the arrow. "You're outmatched, young one."

Jin, who had been feeling somewhat touched that Bai had followed and that he had kept her secret, suddenly felt cold inside. If Bai could call Karana "young one" in such a dismissive tone, what did he really think of her?

She stepped between the two men and met Bai's eyes. "Please leave," she said. "Karana is not going to hurt me. We need to speak privately—about our family."

THERE weren't words that could have cut Bai more deeply.

Our family.

Bai didn't have a family. He didn't really have anyone. His first love had chosen another man and died. His student had manipulated him to help his rival, and he had made no attempt to reach Bai in the eighteen millennia since. His friend had been missing from the world nearly that long.

Perhaps that was why he had so pathetically latched onto Jin. But he couldn't even do that right because he was so cursed afraid that he would lose her. That another immortal would kill her because of her potential power or that she would be struck down by the dangers of the Underworld.

And yet he didn't have to worry about either of those things if he drove her away himself.

He bowed to Jin and Karana. "My apologies."

He spun and returned to Tsuku via the path, rather than creeping through the woods as he had come.

When the familiar cream plaster walls and dark brown roof of Tsuku finally came in sight, Bai paused. He had been here many times, and there were always long gaps between his visits.

So why did he feel so nervous now, so reluctant to enter the hall?

The first reason that came to him was the people—not the Moon Deer and his two eldest daughters, but the many others. Until Xiao, Nanami, and Jin had come to the White Mountain, he had been alone for a very long time.

He frowned. That didn't make sense; there had been far more people in Liushi. *But those were mortals. These people will still be here next time you visit. They'll remember what you say and do, and gossip about you to others. Soon everyone will know you fell for Jin as soon as you saw her and followed her like a puppy. Just like with Noran.*

No. Not just like. This is mutual. And yet what will they think when I return alone? They all must have realized I followed her.

Jin might like him, but she wasn't his. She was still betrothed to Xiao. She was still undertaking a dangerous quest.

Again Bai thought, *She might die.*

That was the reason he had avoided Jin on the Yanou, speaking to Xiao instead of her. When she disappeared in Liushi, her vulnerability was brought home to him. It was hard to reconcile his fear with his yearning for connection, his wish that she would open fully to him, the idea that he could have a family.

How was it that, after seventy-five millennia, he still had such contradictory emotions and didn't even know what to do about them?

JIN let out a long breath as she watched Bai's retreating back.

"How did you know he was there?" she asked Karana to delay resuming their conversation.

"His emotions. I can usually sense when people are near through them—since our discussion was sensitive, I did a quick scan."

Jin nodded. "But we're alone now?"

"Yes."

Jin swallowed. Now that Bai was gone, part of her regretted not grabbing his hand to hold through Karana's confession, but she knew her brother—uncle—well enough to know that he wouldn't talk with a stranger there.

Slowly, she turned around to face him. "So. The God of Belief."

Karana dragged a hand over his face, pulling his eyes closed, as if he couldn't bear to look at Jin. Tentatively, Jin did her own scan of emotions and felt his turbulent mix of regret and guilt. The words came slowly, as if Karana was dragging them from where they'd been hidden all these years.

"Salaana and I were both very angry then. We had approached Gang with our suspicions about Mother's death, asking him to help us overthrow and imprison Father. He was—is—much more powerful than either of us. But he refused. And then came this new baby, who seemed like he might be more powerful than Gang. Salaana said it was wrong. That it went against the natural order for such a powerful being to exist."

At this, Jin couldn't help but cry, "So you decided to kill him?"

"No. No. We didn't. But what we did decide wasn't much better." Karana covered his eyes with one hand and rubbed them. "I hoped that I would never have to tell you this." He cleared his throat. "There is a virus, borne by mosquitoes, that when contracted by mortals, causes a fever. Those that survive are often blind, deaf, and simple. I released infected mosquitos into the child's room, and I used my powers to enhance the fever—otherwise, most immortals wouldn't even be infected, never mind one as powerful as our brother was. But something went wrong almost immediately. I tried to stop it, but..."

Jin struggled to find her voice. "What do you mean something went wrong?'

Karana dropped his hand and met her eyes. "I'm not sure. I haven't dared to experiment to figure it out. But I think—I think someone else had a similar plan to ours. Someone had given the child something, and he was already weak. So the fever killed him." Karana drew a shuddering breath. "I'm so sorry, Jin."

Jin wrapped her arms around herself and turned her back on him. She had once heard that betrayal turns people into strangers, but Karana didn't feel like a stranger. He felt like her brother. And he had done something really bad, and that hurt her, but—she realized slowly—not as much as it hurt him.

Even though she recognized that, it didn't seem fair that he had escaped punishment for what amounted to the murder of a baby.

"But I was punished—not by Salaana or Father, but by Gang. He beat me so badly, I broke two ribs and an arm. And he told me never to appear in front of Aashchary again. I spent a few years in the Wood Pavilions, recovering under Haraa's care, and then I lived all over."

"You wandered? Like Neela?"

"Not exactly—no caravan. I did walk across Zhongtu by foot. And I lived in Po for a while and in the Hall of the Achamba. I didn't return to the Sun Palace until you were a little over a thousand years old, just before the concubine murdered Aashchary."

"Wait—before? But why did you go back when she was still alive?"

Karana's brow had knit. "Gang invited me home—well, he sent some of the Sun Guard to find me. I was told he wanted an alliance, and that my sins could be forgiven. I think I arrived the night of the murder, though I didn't learn of it until the next morning."

"What happened then? You made your alliance?"

"No, actually. I never learned what it was about—Gang refused to talk to me. That was when he turned old."

"What do you mean?"

"His hair lost its color overnight—went gray. People gossiped about it for a while, said that he had been in love with the concubine that Aka executed."

But it wasn't the concubine for whom he mourned. It had been her own mother, Aashchary. If the secret was so well kept that Karana didn't even suspect the truth, had Aka known that his oldest son and wife had cuckolded him?

But surely he must have, unless Aashchary was sleeping with them both... Jin shuddered at the idea.

Karana slipped a tentative arm around her shoulder. "Now you know all the horrible secrets of our family. Neela worked hard to keep them from you—I was never sure if that made you worthy of envy or pity."

Jin grimaced.

Karana was very quiet, though she could tell he was observing her closely. Finally unable to withstand his silent scrutiny any longer, she probed his thoughts. "Just ask it."

"This conversation started with Bai. Why he's making you sad."

Maybe it meant she was a weak, horrible being, but she leaned against Karana's chest, soaking up his love for her.

"I fell for him. I've never fallen for anyone before."

Karana thought that over. "So you never loved Xiao."

"Not that way."

"Does he mind?"

"I think Bai likes me too. He cares about me, anyway."

"Yes, that was obvious from his stalking just now, but that's not what I was asking. Does Xiao mind?"

"Oh—no. He said we'll find a way to break the betrothal."

Karana tugged her braid again. "Now I definitely feel envy. You've found romance, and your best friend is supportive. So why are you sad?"

"Bai won't—he has a very strong sense of right and wrong, and having an affair with a betrothed being is wrong to him. Sometimes he feels so close, and sometimes I feel like he's unattainable."

"Okay, well, there's something I need to point out, but since you'll be so excited that you won't listen once I do, first you have to listen to a horrible story."

Jin looked up at Karana's face. With his makeup all smudged from his hands and his tears, she suddenly realized that he looked old. Not Neela-old, not even Gang-old, but older than her mental image of him. There were bags under his eyes and fine lines on his forehead. "Okay."

"You saw Xiling burn. Neela brought you."

"Yes," Jin admitted. It had been horrific and strangely beautiful to see the deep red flames consume all the entire city. It had felt so hot, even from the distance where Jin and Neela had watched, that she had thought her face was sunburned. And underneath the crackling of fire and the periodic collapse of buildings, the air had reverberated with mortal screaming. Only a tenth of the population died—Karana had let most of the mortals escape, but some he had held, and no one had told Jin why.

"I burned Xiling for my lover."

"Your lover?" Jin repeated in surprise. "I thought you never took any."

"That's what I prefer people to think. And I never take immortals as lovers—it creates a false promise of forever. But I have taken mortal lovers.

"In Xiling, I loved a woman named An Ning. Her family was wealthy, but not noble. Her father wished for her to marry a nobleman's son.

"I didn't mind that. I loved her, but I understand what it means to love a mortal, and she wanted to please her father. I gave her my blessing. After the wedding, her husband realized she was not a virgin and was outraged by it. Zhongtuese nobility have some strange ideas about such things—I've often thought they've misunderstood the teachings of the Night God."

Karana stopped there, and Jin knew what he had to say next was very, very bad. When Karana waned philosophical, it meant he was avoiding something.

"He had her raped. By many men." Karana made the conscious decision to edit out the details, but they were raging in his mind, and Jin couldn't help but hear them. She pressed her fist against her lips, trying to keep her gorge from rising.

"An Ning went mad. And she prayed to me. She asked me to destroy everything. She wanted—she wanted the world to end.

"So actually, even though some say I went overboard when

I burned Xiling, I think I showed great restraint."

He laughed, and the sound was so painful to hear that tears escaped Jin, even though Karana himself wasn't crying.

"The point of this story, Jin, is people can be crazy for love. Not everybody maybe, but I'm afraid your swain doesn't have the best track record. It's said that he's killed five thousand immortals and a hundred thousand mortals with his own hands, all in a fruitless attempt to undo the death of his first love."

Jin suddenly thought back to The Death of the Great Warrior, and the strange way that someone had known that it would drive her away from Bai. *It wasn't the cloud riding,* she realized. *Someone—Neela or Gang—thought I would be horrified by all the death, all the people he's killed. I was so caught up with the clouds that we never discussed the rest.*

The Bai she knew was so deliberate, so careful, so wise-seeming that she hadn't thought of him as a killer. And that was a mistake.

"Those numbers might be exaggerated," Karana went on, "but he's definitely killed a lot of people. He terrifies me, and he should scare you. I think you should stay far, far away from him.

"But in the end, that's your choice. So that brings me to what I need to tell you.

"If Aka isn't your father, you aren't betrothed. You promised to marry the man your father chose. As far as I know, your father didn't choose anyone."

Jin barely processed Karana's words, as she was still trying to envision Bai as a fighter who had killed more people than she could remember. When she finally registered what he'd said, she pulled back. "I'm not betrothed to Xiao? I don't have to break a vow to end the betrothal?"

Karana smiled lightly. "Have you already forgotten my story?"

"No," she told him, "I'll never forget that story, but to tell you the truth, Karana, it doesn't pertain to me. Your lover was mortal, a worshipper of you. A relationship between Bai and I would be of equals."

"Even given his age? Even given he can make my fire arrows disappear with a blink of his eye?"

That made Jin smile, just a little. "Come, let's return to Tsuku. I need to bathe, and you need to charm the Moon Deer."

BAI'S worry that the inhabitants of Tsuku would mock him for his failure to return with Jin proved unfounded.

Instead, as soon as he passed through Tsuku's main gate, three granddaughters of the Moon Deer cornered him and begged him to play the guzheng for them. One suggested a duet, offering to play her koto, which another immediately criticized, saying that the koto and the guzheng were too similar—she offered to play flute.

Bai politely said he wished to bathe and change before any performance, and all three promptly offered to scrub his back.

He had not quite managed to extricate himself from their flirting when Jin and Karana returned. He watched them pass through the high wooden gate, and though she was twenty feet away, Jin's eyes met his immediately. Then those golden orbs flicked first to granddaughter number three's hand, pressed against his chest, and then to granddaughter number one's fingers, resting on his arm.

A red flush raced across her cheeks. Lady Atsuko approached Jin and Karana, impeding Bai's view of them. The two women spoke quietly, too soft for Bai to hear their words, and then Atsuko led Jin into the hall. Neither of them looked back.

Karana looked as if he wanted to say something, but apparently his vanity was more pressing, as he wiped a smudge of makeup with his hand and then followed the women into the hall.

Bai grit his teeth. He tried several more times to leave the three flirtatious granddaughters until his patience was gone. He abruptly pulled away from them, causing granddaughter number three to stumble—she had been all but leaning against him—and said, "I am going to my room now."

Of course, the result of his rudeness was that none of the granddaughters offered to guide him. He removed his shoes and donned a pair of white cotton slippers in the entry, then wandered to the right, hoping that the guest rooms were still the same. He almost asked an unfamiliar immortal for guidance, but the youth took in Bai's white hair with round eyes and scampered in the opposite direction. However, Lady Atsuko found him soon after, so perhaps the stranger had aided him after all.

Impulsively, he said, "Lady Atsuko, please bring me to your father."

"I'm sorry, First," she bowed, "but my father is asleep."

Bai compressed his lips to seal in a curse. "Please, Lady Atsuko. I have not seen him in fifteen millennia. I very much want to see him today."

Lady Atsuko looked away, and Bai knew she was annoyed by his rudeness. "If you can wait fifteen millennia, can you not wait one more day?"

"I cannot," Bai insisted, even though it thoroughly violated the etiquette of this house.

So Lady Atsuko bowed again and led him through the wooden corridors to her father's room. She slid open the door and gestured.

Bai froze in horror. Was this old man the Moon Deer?

He had been shocked to see Neela's white hair, but she looked like a girl compared to the being on the bed.

The Moon Deer had withered to nothing but bone and loose skin, and though he was sleeping, his breathing was ragged and irregular.

Bai stepped back and Lady Atsuko slid the door closed again.

"I'm sorry," he said to her and made his own bow. "I never imagined..."

"Yes, you seem to be aging in reverse, while my father has compensated for your lost years."

Bai said nothing, feeling ashamed that he had forced her to bring him here.

"I will show you to your room now?"

"Please," Bai said meekly.

"We've put you in the usual one, first, though I'm afraid it is more colorful than you prefer. I redecorated it extensively five millennia ago to suit the God of War. But perhaps—" she caught herself.

Bai gave her a curious look, but the response was the shush-shush of her slippers along the wooden floor. Finally they reached a rice paper door beneath an intricate carving of a woodhawk perched among cherry blossoms. Bai believed it used to be a kind of starburst pattern, but he wasn't sure.

"Its private bath is mostly unchanged—just go through the inner doors," Lady Atsuko said with a bow.

Bai slid open the door and blinked at the vibrancy of the room. Compared to most of the hall, which featured unstained wood with white rice paper doors and cream walls, this room was rich with crimson, gold, and bits of blue. However, as Bai stepped inside and slid the door closed behind him, he found he rather liked the various elements. He paused before a large changing screen with several panels that featured two swallows diving among wisteria branches. The painting was excellent— perhaps rougher than Bai would have done, but it felt more passionate for it—and though its background was gleaming gold, it did not feel ostentatious.

He started to walk around the screen to strip, but paused to examine a patchwork cushion of red, yellow, and blue silks. There were several patterns, yet the odd bits of cloth created a beautiful whole. It reminded him of Jin—it was too bad that this room hadn't been given to her. She would have loved it.

He removed his clothes, folded them neatly, and wrapped a towel about his waist. Opposite him were three more sliding doors, made of pine planks rather than rice paper. A shiver of anticipation ran down his spine as Bai remembered the glorious heat of the Tsuku hot springs, and he slid open one of the doors to reveal a small outdoor courtyard.

He could see steam rising from the corner just past a bamboo thicket. The onsen must have been uncovered in anticipation of his bathing. He substituted his cotton slippers for rattan ones just outside his door and made his across the white stepping stones. When he finally had a clear view of the onsen, he froze.

Jin reclined back against the rocks, completely naked but

for the gold chain that held Kunjee and the peacock pendant between her breasts and her unbound hair drifting around her.

Bai coalesced the steam densely around her, hiding her nudity.

She must have felt the shift in the air, for she opened her eyes. Bai cursed himself. He should have simply turned and left.

Her lips parted, and Bai grew ten degrees hotter.

"Bai?" she looked sweetly confused, and then so hopeful that he would have preferred a punch to the gut.

"A mistake was made. Lady Atsuko apparently put us in the same room."

"Oh." Her lashes swept downward, masking her gold eyes.

"I'll go rectify it," he told her. But he didn't move away yet, still thinking about what the mist hid.

"You don't have to," she told him. "I don't mind..."

"You're betrothed to someone else," he reminded her. "It's different than on the Kuanbai. Being in such close quarters here will lead to all sorts of gossip."

Her lashes swept upward, and then she rose as well. Bai quickly adjusted the mist to cloak her.

"I'm not. Bai, I'm not. I made a vow to marry according to my father's wishes, but Aka is not my father! We could be together."

Bai took a step back. "I'm going to talk to Lady Atsuko."

She frowned. "Didn't you hear me?"

"Yes—because Aka isn't your father, you aren't betrothed to Xiao." He turned, not sure why he wasn't gathering her into his arms instead.

He heard splashing behind him, so he wasn't totally shocked when Jin grabbed his arm. He kept his eyes averted.

"What are you thinking?" When the silence stretched, she cried, "Talk to me!"

He opened his mouth but shut it when no words came.

"Have you changed your mind?" she asked suddenly. "Seeing the immortals here—you have options. Maybe you just want a lover, and I wasn't special after all."

Bai might not be as experienced as Xiao, but even he knew this was the moment where he whirled around, declared his undying love, and kissed her passionately. And he wanted to— at least a big part of him did. But another part shouted that he wasn't ready, that he couldn't bear to fall in love with another woman who was going to die. He pulled away from her, and a moment later he discarded his towels for his clothes. He didn't need to hurry though—she hadn't followed.

When Bai slipped from the room, he didn't go looking for Atsuko. Instead, he broke the Moon Deer's teleportation ban. He reappeared on a snow cap, the top of Taitō, Tsuku and Jin far below him. His hands were shaking, and he was barely conscious of a view that mortals risked their lives to see.

He sat in the snow, welcoming the way the cold brought him to the present. It had been too long since he meditated, and he let his consciousness drift more deeply than he had since Jin broke into his garden and pulled him from his introspection.

His power slid into the snow, which amplified it much like the Great Willow had in Liushi. He felt the world beneath him, all around him, and he started untangling its essence to settle his own mind.

Such was his agitation that it took him fifteen minutes to realize he was trying to know the unknowable—and it wasn't Jin.

SEA PALACE

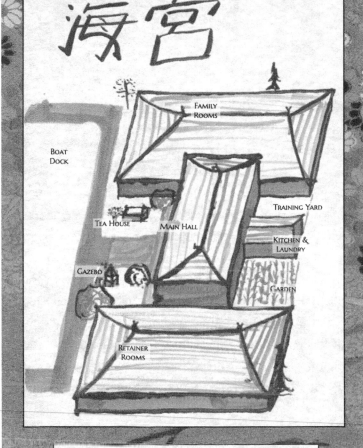

海宮

FAMILY ROOMS

BOAT DOCK

TRAINING YARD

TEA HOUSE

MAIN HALL

KITCHEN & LAUNDRY

GAZEBO

GARDEN

RETAINER ROOMS

The underwater domain of the Sea Dragon, the Sea Palace rests on the ocean floor and is surrounded by a magical bubble of air. Between family and retainers, the palace houses more than fifty immortal beings.

14

How the Sea Dragon Roared

IF the Yanou had been fast when the sailors steered it, it practically flew now that it was under the Sea Dragon's command. The speed dredged up an old resentment in Nanami's breast, one that she had thought long forgotten—how slowly the dinghy that bore her to exile on land had drifted, despite her own attempts to speed it. Her father had wanted her to suffer under the sun, to drag out her agony. The resentment grew so big that it gagged her.

When they were close to the palace, the Yanou began to ride lower in the water and within moments, the sea was even with the deck. Nanami had experienced this far too many times to count, but Xiao's jaw dropped and he grabbed Nanami's arm.

"We need to teleport now!" he said, and he looked adorably confused at Nanami's chuckle.

"The Sea Palace is beneath the waves," she reminded him—or perhaps told him. She was constantly surprised by what Xiao didn't know. "Don't worry—we won't drown. The water around us will become an air pocket, as it is at the Sea Palace."

Because it took her mind off her worries and because she liked to look at him, Nanami watched his expression closely as the prow of the Yanou swung down forty-five degrees. Xiao grabbed the rail with one hand and Nanami with the other, keeping them both from sliding, his jaw clenched. An air pocket silently encompassed even the Yanou's sails. And then the ship continued to sail, just as it had on the surface.

Xiao shook his head in bemusement, his eyes locked on the deep blue water surrounding them, his hands not-quite touching it. "This doesn't make sense. We should float. How..." There were apparently too many questions for him to choose just one.

"But you transforming into a crow makes sense?" Nanami didn't bother to hide her amusement. "The air extends below the boat as well, so we fall into it," she explained idly.

Xiao turned to look at her then, blinking several times. Nanami felt bold and strangely happy. *I should have gone home years ago,* she thought to herself. *Told the old man what I thought of him. It was weighing on me more than I realized.*

She collected Xiao's hand from the bannister and pulled it toward the water. "You can touch it. There's not actually a barrier, just a place where the magic leaves the water alone."

Together their hands pierced the water wall, and Xiao pulled her tighter against him, a seemingly reflexive reaction. It was nice—comforting.

He's mine, and I'm his, in some way we weren't before, Nanami thought to herself. *Even if we aren't 'lovers' yet, we've accepted each other.* Foolishly, the thought made tears prick her eyes, and as she blinked them away, an unwelcome memory intruded.

The sea had been so dark that it had almost been black. Just beyond the air of her boat—nothing more than a dinghy—the water roiled, as if to remind her that she lived or died at the Sea Dragon's pleasure. She had fought tears then too—angry and bitter tears.

Xiao, with his almost unbearably keen awareness, turned Nanami in his arms and one hand cradled her face as the other slipped behind her back. "What's troubling you?"

"I was just remembering—the day I was banished. It wasn't enough for him to scold me in front of the entire household, he refused to let me teleport away. Instead, he sent me away on the smallest, poorest dinghy there was, and I had to ride by myself for weeks before it reached Po."

Xiao's brows knit. "But he gave you supplies...?"

Nanami's smile was bitter. "I'm a daughter of the Sea. It nourished and clothed me."

Xiao pulled her in for a tighter hug, his chin resting on the crown of her head. Even as his embrace soothed the old hurt, a new fear rose in her. Would Xiao be in danger at the Sea Palace? Surely he would be considered too valuable as a potential ally... or would they see him as the enemy?

"You shouldn't have offended Salaana on my behalf..."

Xiao began to run his fingers through the hair loose at her nape. "I may have offended Salaana, but I doubt she's willing to burn the bridge yet. They will want the support of my parents, of course, though it's hard to say if that will offer me any protection. But," and his hand stilled, so that he could tilt her face up, "if it becomes dangerous, I'll get us out. Just stay near me, alright?"

Nanami nodded. Her throat was too tight for words. She captured the hand that cradled her cheek and turned back to the railing. She pointed to a large school of sanma, glinting green blades in the gloom.

Xiao paused a moment, then once more slipped his arms about her waist, and offered a perfunctory exclamation for the sanma. As the Yanou plunged deeper into the ocean, it grew darker, until they were surrounded by the rich indigo that had birthed her father. The dark felt familiar, safe to Nanami, and she could see in the gloom better than most, but it occurred to her that Xiao might wish for light. He refused her offer to fetch an oil lamp though.

"I am Laughter in the Shadows," he reminded her. "The dark doesn't bother me."

She supposed Hei must see in the dark even better than her father.

The fish grew more wondrous, and Xiao's admiration grew more sincere. When a silver oarfish brushed the air pocket near their faces, its body nearly as thick as Xiao's torso and at least three times longer than he was tall, Xiao jumped back, still holding Nanami, and the two of them fell in a tangle.

Nanami laughed, and Xiao flushed, so she leaned forward and firmly pressed her lips to his own. It was the third time they kissed that day, but unlike the first two, Xiao didn't seem inclined to stop.

He smoothly flipped Nanami onto her back, letting some of his weight press her into the Yanou's wooden deck. She grew intensely aware of his body, of his size. Xiao's hand burned its way down her side, his fingers spanning her rib cage. And yet for all the strength in his hand, he moved it carefully, as if she was fragile. She liked that. Nanami wrapped her handless arm around the back of his neck, locking him close to her, then explored the muscles of his back with her hand. One of his thighs slipped between her legs, and a welcome pressure made her gasp with pleasure.

Just as the first time they kissed, in the Wood Pavilions, Nanami felt so overwhelmed by the physical that the world threatened to collapse to just the two of them. This time she welcomed that, living only in the present.

Nanami was abruptly reminded that the rest of creation did in fact still exist when a loud male voice demanded, "What is this?"

XIAO smoothly readjusted Nanami's shirt so that her shoulders were completely covered before turning to face the group that had assembled behind them.

A middle-aged man stood slightly in front of the rest of them, seemingly distinguishing himself as the leader. His dark hair was arranged in a simple topknot, and his soft, round face was sandwiched between a neat square beard and thick wild eyebrows. His robe was deceptively simple. Waves embroidered in the same dark blue as the cloth were barely perceptible, despite the many glowing lanterns that floated around the group. Xiao guessed he was probably brother number six or number eight and offered his most insouciant smile.

"It is foreplay, a prelude to sexual intercourse that makes it more enjoyable. I suggest you pray to me, and quickly, for the sake of any future partners. Then again, if you still can't recognize it at your age, I suppose their existence is unlikely."

Xiao leapt lightly to his feet as the man processed his words, a dull red tinging his round cheeks and his small eyes narrowing to slits.

Xiao was a good head taller than anyone in the group—it seemed slight stature was a family trait—and he could see past them to the predictably indigo walls of the palace. The Yanou was at a dock, of sorts, and the air pocket of their ship had merged with a larger air pocket that enveloped the entire palace. "I see we have reached the Sea Palace," he observed, and was quite pleased that he managed to sound bored, even though the reality of a palace on the ocean floor was, well, awe-inspiring. "You really should work on your welcome," he told the red-faced man.

He half-turned, to offer Nanami his hand. Alarm and amusement were warring for dominance in her expression, so he winked before helping her to her feet. He tucked her stump into the crook of his arm. "My dear, perhaps you would introduce me to these beings, since they seem unwilling or unable to introduce themselves."

Nanami cleared her throat. "This is Kaihachi, the eighth child of the Sea Dragon."

"Seventh!" Kaihachi barked, and Xiao's dislike for the man changed from general to personal.

But Nanami merely agreed blandly, "Seventh. My mistake."

NANAMI'S earliest memory was of baby Kaihachi. He was not quite two thousand years younger than her (each of her mother's pregnancies followed the last as soon as fate allowed) and they had regularly been put down to nap together.

Nanami supposed she had woken first from such a nap, but her memory began when she was kneeling next to Kaihachi in the many futon beds they shared with their parents. He was still deep asleep, his bow-shaped lips slightly parted and his tiny nose rising like a miniature mountain in the sea of his cheeks. Nanami leaned closer and closer until the tip of her nose just touched his. He kept sleeping, and his breath, warm and soft, tickled her face. Nanami wanted him to wake up and play with her, so she moved her head and pressed their foreheads together. Still no response. Nanami sat back on her heels and thought for a few moments before baring his belly, placing her mouth against it and blowing so as to tickle him.

Kaihachi came abruptly awake with an angry yell, and Nanami's mother came running into the room.

"Nanami! Did you wake the baby?" Her fury lashed the air. "Out! Now!"

Mortified, tears leaked down her face as Nanami ran out into the hall. She slid the rice paper door mostly shut behind her, then lay down next to it, listening as her mother hushed the baby. When he grew quiet, Nanami peered around the door to see him nursing. She remembered feeling very jealous—she supposed that at the time she might have remembered nursing herself, though of course she no longer did, and her mother started crooning a lullaby.

> Sleep, sleep, my baby,
> Hush now, my dearest,
> Mama will hold you,
> As long as you rest.
> Sleep, sleep my baby,
> Please don't you weep.
> Mama is here now,
> So please go to sleep.

When her mother had tucked the baby back under a light blanket, she slipped out the door and almost stepped on Nanami, who was still lying on the floor, her eyes red and swollen.

Her mother sighed. "You know better than to wake the baby. Why don't you play with Kairoku if you are bored?"

Nanami made a face. Kairoku always bossed her and took

the best toys. "But I love Hachi-chan the best because he's my baby."

"He'll still be your baby when he wakes up. Now, go play somewhere else." Nanami started to run off, but her mother caught her shoulder. She kissed Nanami's temple. "If you wake the baby again, you'll get a spanking instead."

NANAMI was humming tunelessly, seemingly unaware of it, as Kaihachi and the Sea Dragon's liegemen escorted them across a crescent-shaped dock. Some of their escorts were giving her odd looks, so Xiao dimpled and winked at them. Xiao would like to see them be called before their family after not seeing them for thirteen millennia!

They reached a silver arch surrounded by massive rhododendrons laden with large garnet blossoms. Walking through it, they emerged in an expansive garden. Xiao had to look up to prove to himself that they were really on the seafloor, but fish were indeed swimming in the water overhead. He supposed they were attracted to the light of the palace. He looked around the garden again, curious about the place Nanami had grown up. Had it changed a great deal since she left? Or perhaps she had learned to climb on the pines— carefully shaped trees with bulbous branches and deep green needles— which dominated the landscape? Nanami faltered at his side. She was focused on a large wooden gazebo that seemed in danger of collapsing beneath the weight of a thousand peonies. Her face was full of such longing that Xiao's gut clenched.

WHO had gotten married? Nanami wondered as she saw the peony-bedecked gazebo.

Every one of her siblings' weddings—that she had attended, Nanami amended reluctantly—had been held in that gazebo and Nanami's mother Miko always covered it with more flowers than the time before. For Ichimi, it had been yellow chrysanthemums, but after Ichimi's lying, cheating husband had abandoned her, Miko switched to peonies for Nimi.

Nanami was glad that it was still peonies—hopefully that meant her other sibling's marriages were happier than Ichimi's.

XIAO tucked a strand of hair behind Nanami's ear, bringing her back to him. "You'll have to tell me stories later."

Kaihachi growled at the suggestion, but Nanami smiled and nodded.

More retainers lined up on the wrap-around porch on the front of the palace. There was not a friendly face among the group. Xiao tried to convince himself that these were all new faces, that none of them had been here thirteen millennia ago when Nanami was banished, but he didn't succeed because he saw recognition and hurt in Nanami's eyes.

When they reached the porch, everyone stopped to slip off their footwear and arrange them so that they pointed outward. The residents of the Sea Palace and Nanami did so gracefully, not even needing to sit down, but Xiao plopped right on the porch, provoking several annoyed looks. Actually, he could have easily done as they did, but he wanted to keep their antagonism directed toward him. Nanami watched him with a strange expression as he made a fool of himself, her eyes very soft. She leaned forward, braced her hand on his shoulder, and whispered so that her lips tickled his ear, "Xiao—I don't care anymore. If you want to leave—"

Xiao pressed an index finger to her lips, stopping her words. He didn't believe her; she was just trying to protect him. So he said, "I'm not ready to leave. I want to see the inside of the hall."

Nanami pulled back to free her mouth. "Okay."

The retainers slid open the doors to reveal the hall within. Dark indigo pillars supported the high ceiling and indigo banners with swirls of silver embroidery stretched between them. Low lacquer tables lined the sides of the hall and were filled with staring eyes. Kaihachi and the rest of their escort immediately went to their seats, but there were no empty places for Xiao and Nanami. Xiao stood a bit taller and directed his attention to the far end of the hall where a couple dressed richly in long flowing silk robes of indigo and silver were framed by a wide mother of pearl throne. Xiao examined the man curiously, presuming he was the Sea Dragon.

His long beard was still indigo, and what Xiao could see of his hair was as well—most of it hidden beneath a tall black hat. His brows, also indigo, were bushy slashes that shadowed his eyes. Although he was about fifty feet away, Xiao could tell his skin showed his age and his face was cast in a perpetually sullen expression.

What surprised Xiao the most was how very small the Sea Dragon was—but given Nanami, Ichimi, and Kairoku's petite stature, he supposed he should have realized. Xiao doubted the older immortal would even reach his collar bone. Indeed, although that tall black hat tried to indicate otherwise, it looked as though the Sea Dragon was the same height as his wife, a plump woman who Xiao had heard won the Sea Dragon's affections with her looks alone, but who had sacrificed her luster to bear thirteen children. Tiredness dulled her eyes and not even the swathes of silk that encased her hid the fact that her body had been stretched and deflated many times.

Of course, if either of them smiled—if a hand were extended to their prodigal daughter—Xiao would declare them perfectly pleasant and attractive people, but the censure that emanated from them just made them ugly and sad.

Nanami's arm at Xiao's elbow was trembling, and he looked at her out of the corner of his eye. She was scanning the hall so quickly that Xiao wondered if she was really seeing any of it—and yet despite her almost frantic survey, she was steadfastly avoiding looking at the opposite end.

SO Kyumi was the one who had married. She was sitting next to a handsome young man that Nanami recognized as one of their retainer's sons. She and her husband were still dressed in their wedding finery—had they been married today? After Nanami had been discovered trespassing and the Yanou summoned or before? Not that it mattered. How strange to think Kyumi had just been a newborn at Ichimi's wedding—Nanami, a teenager then and thus not allowed to be an attendant had been tasked with holding her.

Kaihachi's wife was a stranger to Nanami, but they must have been wed for several millennia as two adorable children sat between them. Nanami recognized Nimi's husband at least, and even their daughter, though she was an adult now and the last time Nanami had seen her she had been potty training. Kairoku's son, who had been a baby, was also fully grown.

And there were the twins, Jyumi and Jyuichimi, the first

holding a baby and the secondly visibly pregnant. They still looked so similar that Nanami wondered if their husbands— one short and muscular, the other tall and gangly—ever felt confused.

She scanned the tables thoroughly until she had found all of her siblings but Ichimi, as well as seven new nieces and nephews. Finally, she had to acknowledge there was only one place left to look, but it was as if an invisible hand kept turning her gaze away from the front of the hall. Away from him.

"How dare you, how dare you go to the Sun Court to embarrass my daughter! And how dare you break your exile now! You come here having stolen the Goddess of Beauty's betrothed! Does your shamelessness know no bounds?" his voice was loud, waves crashing on cliffs.

Nanami finally looked at him and was shocked to see how short he was. She supposed he must be the same size he had always been, but in her memories he had loomed like a tsunami. Realizing that he didn't even reach Xiao's chin surprised her so much that a nervous chuckle escaped.

XIAO had only half his attention on the volatile Sea Dragon; the rest of it was trained on Nanami, trying to read every micro-expression that flitted across her face.

But when she giggled nervously, overwhelmed by being here, surrounded by the family that cast her out, her father took offense. Xiao found it expedient to ignore Nanami's pain for a moment to focus on the threat the Sea Dragon offered. He couldn't quite believe that the older immortal would truly harm Nanami, his daughter, but Xiao couldn't remember the last time he saw anyone so angry. The Sea Dragon held all the violence of the sea.

He surged upward from his throne, robes billowing out behind him. They writhed and rippled like eels as the Sea Dragon advanced down the hall, wholly focused on Nanami. Despite having referenced Xiao as Jin's betrothed, and the fact that Nanami had practically glued herself to his side, the Sea Dragon must have dismissed him as useless.

Xiao had no intention of fleeing—that was the last resort. What he really wanted was to show this whole family that they had made a mistake.

About halfway down the hall, the Sea Dragon paused and raised both of his arms. "I brought you into this world and it is time I owned that mistake, as I ought to have done thirteen thousand years ago! I will eat you!"

And then he rippled, as if the millennium of power contained by Ao was suddenly manifesting itself. Almost as soon as the ripple started it finished, and it turned out that the title "Sea Dragon" was literal rather than poetic.

The dragon was as big as the orca Xiao had been days before, if much more sinuous with indigo scales. Its dark mane flared as it raised its head and scraped the ceiling with wickedly sharp horns. Its eyes were the fathomless deep of the sea; the dragon shut them to roar its rage, revealing fangs as long as Xiao's arms. Its sinuous body seemed to shudder with a need for destruction, its tail flickering amidst the pillars faster than the eye could follow.

Xiao smiled. Just as when Bai had become a seagull, Xiao somehow understood exactly what Ao had done, and Xiao unleashed his own power, letting it rip through the fragile shell of his body.

NANAMI was so shocked by her father's transformation that there was no room for fear. She tried to wrap both arms around Xiao, her thoughts almost idle as she wondered if he could really transport them away from here.

But Xiao was gone, replaced by a wave of power that dwarfed her father's.

Perfectly formed scales filled her vision, each beginning as a pale lavender and darkening to a black edge. Nanami turned and found dark violet claws, each longer than she was tall. A horrendous cracking noise drew her attention upward—the ceiling of the hall shattered as the dragon burst through it. Splintered plaster and wood rained down, and Nanami heard cries of terror and desperation muffled by the dragon's body. The dragon lowered its head briefly, examining her with its full moon eyes. Its long black whiskers tickled her as they danced seemingly of their own accord and with great daring, Nanami touched its thick black mane and found it soft and smooth. The mane was pierced by massive horns like growths of amethyst crystal. Those full moons blinked once, and then the head swept away to focus on something hidden from her—her father, she supposed.

Xiao's voice boomed, "Not if I eat you first."

15

The Sleeper's Resting Place

BAI paused in his digging to wipe the sweat off his forehead before it dripped in his eyes. The task of breaking up the hard mountain soil and shoveling it aside had quickly made the mild morning hot, and Bai had stripped down to just his loose white breeches. His bare torso was liberally streaked with dirt and sweat. Bai welcomed that—the solitary labor had brought him the peace of his hermitage and kept his mind quiet for the first time in over a month.

That was half the reason he had not fetched help when he found the unknowable essence halfway down Taitō mountain, buried deep beneath the surface.

The other half was he didn't know what he would find and was loath to expose Cheng to potentially unfriendly eyes. If whatever he was digging toward was indeed Cheng.

He set his shovel next to his pickaxe, both made from snowdrop petals when nothing in the soil responded to Bai's power, and examined the bottom of the pit he'd excavated. He was close to the mystery; Bai would estimate no more than an inch before it was revealed. He'd better stop using the shovel, in case it was fragile.

He changed the shovel into a broom and began to sweep the

360

dirt away. It was repetitive and dull, and Bai's mind, so recently cleared, began to wander.

It wasn't surprising that he was feeling overwhelmed by people when he had been alone for so long. It was more surprising that he didn't find Jin tiring. The flirting of the Moon Deer's granddaughters had overwhelmed him, but he almost entered the onsen when he'd found Jin there.

But he had run away instead. Where had his confidence from their little boat on the Kuanbai gone? He hadn't felt scared then. The rest of the world seemed far away, the dangers of Jin's quest half-forgotten. He had liked working with her, studying with her, watching her elegant movements.

His feelings for Noran had never been comfortable or easy.

The first time they met, at the wedding of Zi and Hei, Noran was already over twenty thousand years old. He had been quite startled by her unique appearance—sunlight hair and gold eyes and delicate fair skin. She had smiled at him shyly and introduced herself. Some point later, Cheng had convinced him that Noran had recognized him instantly, but at the time, Bai had been charmed by her seeming lack of calculation.

He had asked to see her again. Her eyes had widened, and a delicate blush had touched her cheeks. That was like Jin—she blushed so easily, her feelings writ for the world to see. But Bai was fairly sure Jin's were genuine, and not the careful artifice of Noran. Jin had lamented that he didn't trust her, but it was really himself he didn't trust.

Robin's egg blue became visible beneath his broom, and Bai knelt to examine it.

Bai recognized the blue stone as raw turquoise. But surely it wasn't naturally occurring—as Bai scraped away more dirt, the size and purity of the stone became improbable. He started feeling a little ill and worked more quickly to excavate the large stone.

When a head was fully exposed, Bai had to take several calming breaths.

It looked like a statue of a man sleeping. Despite the rough texture of the stone, Cheng's broad nose and pronounced jaw were easily recognizable.

Bai rested his hands on either side of the head, reading the essence of the stone. Even though it encapsulated the unknowable, Bai could read the stone easily enough.

He immediately confirmed his worst suspicions, that the stone had been shaped by Neela.

He tried to remember her exact words regarding Cheng.

I got no answers. Because she asked no questions. Bai's hands began to shake, even though they rested against the stone.

Cheng might not be dead. As former magma, he needed nothing to exist—not air, not food, not drink. He could in theory live forever trapped in a prison of rock like this.

Neela did this. She trapped him in a living hell for eternity. And she chose her words carefully to keep me from suspecting anything.

Bai's first impulse was to destroy the rock. He thought he could, and any sort of release must be preferable to the never-ending confinement. But there was a second possibility.

He would never trust Neela to free Cheng. But Jin might be able to melt away the stone without harming the being within. Taking a deep breath, Bai wrapped his hands around the stone-encased head and pulled it in between with him.

❊　❊　❊

JIN stood before the large changing screen in her room, arms wrapped around her waist, staring at the two swallows as if they might have answers for her. She had painted this screen herself when she had been studying under the Crescent Moon master, but she had no idea how it had ended up here. She frowned at one of the swallow's wings that was all off in proportion—she couldn't see the very proper Lady Atsuko collecting this amateur piece for the art alone.

This whole room felt oddly familiar, and Jin would have liked to discuss it with Bai, but she hadn't seen him since he ran from her last night.

Someone scratched at the door, and Jin hurried to open it, hoping that Bai had returned.

But it was Lady Atsuko. She bowed. "Good morning, divinity. My father is awake—" Lady Atsuko looked at Jin's face and paused. "Was the room alright?"

"Oh, yes, the room is beautiful. I like it very much." Jin brought a smile to her lips and banished her disappointment.

Lady Atsuko nodded. "My father is awake. I will escort you and the First there now if..."

Jin nodded. "Thank you."

Lady Atsuko didn't move. After a moment, she asked. "Will the First be long?"

Jin felt a flush rising on her cheeks. "Isn't he—that is, the First isn't here."

"Oh—then—" She was cut off by several shouts, and Lady Atsuko whipped her head toward the front courtyard.

"Please excuse me," she murmured with a quick bow before hurrying away.

Jin had no intention of being left behind and followed.

They emerged in the large front garden of Tsuku to find a

crowd of perhaps fifteen. They must have been the ones who had been yelling, though it had been replaced by stern argument.

"You cannot teleport here," objected an unfamiliar male voice.

"Except obviously I did, and for good reason." That was Bai. Jin wished she could see through the crowd, but even without a visual, she could tell he was distraught.

Lady Atsuko strode into the crowd, Jin at her heels. People objected to being pushed until they realized who was doing the pushing—then they quickly moved out of the way. Soon Jin and Lady Atsuko were at the middle of the circle, where a man in leather armor was facing down Bai. Bai looked deathly tired, if not ill. He was half naked and filthy, salt and dirt flecking his torso and arms. He was also propping up a massive turquoise statue of a sleeping man.

Jin tried to listen to the argument, but her eyes kept returning to the statue and her hand began to itch and burn with need. Unable to ignore its silent demand, she touched the stone. Without knowing why, she imagined the turquoise dripping away—and then it did, like melting candle wax.

Jin lost track of the people around her—it was just her and this strange statue. But it wasn't a statue at all. When the turquoise had puddled at her feet, a dry, desiccated corpse fell into her arms.

She gently lowered the wasted body. Though she would have expected it to be rigid, the body folded. Jin suddenly realized that the corpse was far warmer than it ought to be.

"Fate be merciful," she hissed. "It's alive."

Bai knelt beside her and touched the not-dead body. He checked its wrist, looking for a pulse, Jin supposed.

It was hardly necessary for the next moment, the eyes flew open and revealed irises the color of hot coals.

"Cheng," Bai said. "You're free."

Cheng? The name bounced around in Jin's head, but she refused to place it.

Cheng's eyes closed again.

Still cradling the body in her arms, Jin looked at Bai for answers. There were none in his shuttered expression.

He reached out and scooped the body into his arms. He lifted the old man and began striding away. Jin hurried after, as did Lady Atsuko.

"That... thing... is Cheng?" Lady Atsuko asked Jin.

Jin hesitated. "Yes. You know Cheng?"

"He was—is—one of my father's dearest friends. But no one has seen him in millennia."

The name finally settled into place, and Jin stumbled. *Cheng. My grandfather. The Color Orange.*

Jin looked at Lady Atsuko and was shocked by the horror etched on that usually serene face.

She thinks he was sealed in that rock for all that time.

Swift on heels of that thought, Jin realized, *It must have been NeeNee who created that prison. But why? Because—because he was the father of her child? But—I don't understand!*

Bai hesitated just inside the hall, and Lady Atsuko said, "Bring him to my father's room. He needs to bear witness—and he'll want to know as—" her voice cracked "—a friend."

They stepped into the room, and Lady Atsuko set about setting up a futon for Bai to set Cheng on. Feeling awkward and useless, Jin looked around the room and found a man staring at her from a raised bed. Propped up by plump pillows, he seemed as frail as a baby bird. White wisps of hair clung to a spotted scalp, and his skin was wrinkled and loose. The only energy in his mien was from his eyes, wide, brown, and moist, like the deer he once was, and rapidly taking in his guest. He lifted one clawed hand and flapped his fingers to beckon her closer. Jin knelt at his side.

"I expected my daughter to bring you and the First," he whispered, his voice whistling and breathy, "but what does he carry?"

Jin clasped her hands together. "That is Cheng. Bai brought him here moments ago, encased in turquoise."

The Moon Deer pressed his lips together, more sad than shocked, and focused on the scene behind her.

Jin turned to find Bai had settled him on the futon and was checking his vitals.

Wholly absorbed by the examination, Bai startled when he finished and looked up to find them watching.

"My friend," Bai greeted the Moon Deer.

"I'm glad to see you looking so well," the Moon Deer said solemnly. "Is that thing really Cheng?"

Bai nodded.

"He's alive?"

Again Bai nodded.

"Is there anything I can get you, First?" Lady Atsuko asked.

"Would ice chips be possible?"

"Of course," and she hurried from the room.

When the door had slid shut behind her, Bai rose and ran his fingers through his hair.

"You're filthy," declared the Moon Deer. "If he's been sealed in stone for the past fifteen millennia, I doubt you taking a few minutes to wash will adversely affect him. Why don't you avail yourself of my bath while the young Goddess of Beauty and I watch over him?"

Bai sighed. "Yes, you are right. Thank you." Bai rose and went through the second set of doors in the Moon Deer's room to his private onsen.

Jin squeezed her hands tighter. She felt like it was her fault that Neela had sealed Cheng in stone.

"So why did you come here?" asked the Moon Deer. "To pry secrets from my head like your Grandmother?"

The accusation didn't match the weakness in his voice, and Jin didn't know how to reply. "Secrets?'

Those brown eyes were pools of sadness as he explained. "That is why mortals and immortals alike come to Tsuku. To confess their deepest secrets and seek absolution. Or, if that is impossible, to make plans for those secrets to be revealed after they pass. Neela is not welcome here, for she has always believed that she is entitled to everything in someone's head." He cocked his head, and Jin had to stop herself from reaching out a hand in support, for it looked too heavy for his scrawny neck.

"You are more like your mother though, aren't you?"

Jin felt her eyes widen despite herself. "You knew my mother?"

"Of course. She came here often with you and your father. The three of you always stayed in the room you are using now. Your father even collected some of your art for it."

Jin's lips parted before she pressed them together firmly. She didn't think the father that the Moon Deer referred to was Aka.

Not knowing what to say, Jin turned and knelt next to Cheng. The wrinkled, pinched face mutely accused her of failing it.

"This happened before you were even born, so why do you look so guilty?" the Moon Deer asked.

"It's just—my grandmother did this. I keep trying to think of something he might have done to warrant it, and I can't." She squeezed Cheng's hand. "Part of me hopes that he did do something truly heinous, so that I can forgive NeeNee, but I also fear that because—"

"Because?"

The Moon Deer's voice was so gentle and soft, that Jin found herself saying, "Because he's my grandfather. My other grandfather did something unforgivable, and I think it would break my heart if he did too." Tears leaked out of the corners of her eyes. Every time she thought she had learned the worst of her family's secrets, another was revealed. She looked back at him, and found the courage to ask, "You know who my other grandfather is, don't you?"

The Moon Deer nodded. There was no judgement in those warm brown eyes, just acceptance of the world and all its vagaries.

Not knowing what else to do, Jin began to hum a children's song, hoping Cheng might hear it and realize he was free of his prison.

BAI scrubbed his face and hair before sluicing water over his torso. From the room at his back, he heard a soft humming. Jin. Jin was humming to Cheng.

Bai sat down suddenly, feeling overwhelmed. She was kind and empathetic. He had seen how horrified she was by Cheng's condition. He almost—almost—regretted finding Cheng when he realized how much it had hurt Jin.

A little over a month ago, she had been the beloved daughter of the affectionate if distant Sun Emperor, celebrating her long-anticipated betrothal. First her father confessed to her that he had trapped her mother into marriage with an unwanted pregnancy. Then she learned one of her siblings hated him so much that they'd placed a death curse on him.

Three weeks later, she found out he wasn't her father at all because the brother she barely knew had in fact had an affair with her mother and it was possible—maybe probable—the Sun Emperor had arranged his wife's death because of that.

But through it all, she had clung to the fact that the woman who raised her, her grandmother, was a good person who loved her. And now she knew that grandmother had trapped her grandfather in a rock for longer than she'd been alive.

What could Bai possibly say to comfort her?

Twenty millennia ago, he would have embarked on a crusade and executed all of these fate-cursed beings. But he no longer believed that was the right path. It would just bring more sorrow.

Bai took a deep breath and returned to the room.

Jin was holding Cheng's hand, humming a lullaby, and crying. The Moon Deer was watching her silently, his own cheeks wet.

He had to face his fears because she needed him now. She was a thoroughly good being, and she had been hurt and would be hurt more. But he would do everything he could to soften the blows.

Bai knelt beside her and took her free hand in his own. Jin stiffened momentarily, then squeezed his fingers.

"I'm sorry I ran away yesterday," Bai whispered in her ear. "I won't abandon you again."

❀ ❦ ❀

BAI'S hand, and more importantly, his declaration, grounded Jin. His emotions and thoughts had clarified, and she could feel his love for her, his trust. They still had a way to go, to become better acquainted and to adjust to each other, but she suddenly was sure that they were going to move forward together and life seemed easier than it had just moments ago.

Jin let all her questions about Cheng and his sudden appearance flow out of her. Bai answered them as best as he was able, but it soon became clear that unless Cheng regained consciousness or Neela appeared to confess, they both had more questions than answers. The Moon Deer listened silently to all of it, and tears dripped from his brown eyes.

Thinking of Aka's painful confession, Jin asked, not really expecting an answer, "Do you think he tricked Neela into becoming pregnant?"

To her surprise, the Moon Deer replied. "Cheng had feelings for Neela. They were friends, but he repeatedly asked her to consider a more serious entanglement. She always laughed off his confessions, preferring her casual affairs. He must have disguised himself to take advantage of that."

"Neela was actively trying to get pregnant—she wanted a mortal father for a child," Bai added when it was clear the Moon Deer had said all he was going to. "I don't know if Cheng knew her intentions or not. I would guess it was bad luck."

"That's upsetting, if you are right," Jin said slowly, "but I still can't feel what she did was justified. It was torture."

"Yes."

BAI tried to think of a way to distract Jin from her worries.

When he finally came up with an idea, he glanced at the Moon Deer. "You still keep secrets?"

"Of course."

"Good. What you see next should be one. Jin, remember how you almost rebuilt Nanami's hand?"

Jin blinked in confusion. "Of course. But...?"

"I think Cheng's body could be restored in much the same way. Would you like to try?"

Jin bit her lip and then nodded. She tugged her hand free of his and settled both of her palms on Cheng's shoulders.

And then a miracle unfolded.

So slowly that it took him several minutes to see the change, Cheng's shriveled skin began to plump and smooth. His hands twitched as the muscles were restored; his hair changed from white to coral to the bright color of oranges. Bai tried to understand what she was doing, trying to read the essence of her power even though he ought to know better at this point. The room disappeared. Colors surrounded him, impossibly brilliant, clashing and complementing each other at the same time.

Suddenly they disappeared, and he sat next to Jin in the room once more, Cheng prostrated before them. Jin sighed and her whole body seemed to fold in on itself. Bai caught and steadied her before she fell on Cheng.

"She rebuilt his body. He aged in reverse," the Moon Deer whispered, his voice sounding even.

"Yes," Bai agreed, momentarily more concerned with Jin than Cheng.

"The body is very colorful," she said dreamily. "It was surprisingly intuitive." Jin glanced at her grandfather and blushed. Bai looked to see what had bothered her. The bits of rag that had clung to Cheng's corpse were insufficient cover for his restored bod, so Bai gently released her to grab a blanket.

"Why hasn't he woken?" Jin asked.

Bai measured Cheng's vitals again.

"He's still comatose, even though his body seems healthy. I suppose his mind must have stopped after all the years..." Bai swallowed sudden emotion. When he trusted his voice to remain steady, he added, "Perhaps that is a blessing in disguise, and when he wakes, he won't remember all of it." "When" was perhaps overly optimistic, but Bai said it anyway.

"What are you doing in here?" demanded the Moon Deer, his voice stronger than it had been all morning. Surprised, Bai turned to see what had upset his friend, and followed his gaze to the door.

Karana was standing just inside the room, the door shut behind him. Bai felt cold. He hadn't even heard the other being come in, he'd been so immersed in Jin's working. "My apologies for intruding, Moon Deer. I came out of concern for my sister, but my knock went unanswered. You were all focused on my sister's working.

"I can understand why, of course. I didn't realize making things beautiful could be so holistic," he said. "Your worshippers would triple, little sister, if mortals knew you could wind back time for them."

"I can't see doing this often," Jin said. "Not only is it very draining, but usually aging should not be undone. This was a special circumstance."

"So this is your friend," Karana said to Bai, and Bai wasn't sure if he'd even registered Jin's words. "Cheng the Sleeper. If anyone can wake him, it will be Haraa. Will you take him to the Wood Pavilions?"

Bai stiffened. "I—" He looked at Jin.

"You can go. I will wait here."

Bai's hands fisted. He was reluctant to leave Jin alone, even in the home of the Moon Deer.

"Would you bring him, divinity?" the Moon Deer asked.

Bai started to say that Jin could not go, but then he realized the Moon Deer was speaking to Karana.

Karana looked surprised then smiled. "For you, Moon Deer? Of course."

Bai stiffened.

"Why does that make you so uneasy?" Karana asked. Reading Bai's feelings, no doubt, with the power he inherited from his father.

Bai didn't fully trust Haraa. She was after all Neela's best friend—might she already know about Cheng's imprisonment? Bai didn't want to believe it, but it was possible.

Jin plucked the thoughts from Bai's head. "Would you watch over him, Karana, and make sure he is safe? He must be protected from Neela until we have our answers. Salaana would do it, in the name of justice, wouldn't she? And if—if he really is dangerous and should be imprisoned, she would take care of that as well."

Karana nodded. "Yes. Jin—I'm sure you're upset that NeeNee would do this, but try not to worry too much until you hear her side, all right? After all, Cheng is a stranger to us."

Jin's attempt at a smile looked painful to Bai.

As for Bai—he didn't trust Karana, no matter how much he obviously cared about Jin. There was nothing in his essence that should alarm him—Bai could sense Karana's deep reluctance to hurt anyone—but Karana was no stranger to plots.

Jin looked at Bai again—he must be thinking very loudly. She smiled in reassurance. "Karana—would you make a vow to seek Salaana's protection for Cheng? To do your utmost to keep his release a secret from Neela?"

Karana considered. "I swear that I shall do everything in my power, short of murder, to protect Cheng from harm and ensure that Salaana, the Goddess of Justice, takes him into her protection."

"Even you should be content with that," said the Moon Deer to Bai. "I believe you can trust Karana."

And what else was there to say?

Sooner than Bai liked, Karana teleported Cheng away.

But Cheng wasn't his only concern, so he turned to his friend. "We didn't come because of Cheng, for I had no idea he was buried near Tsuku. I wanted to show Jin the scrolls I left with you on the immortal creatures."

The Moon Deer met his eyes. "I'm sorry, they are locked away so that they cannot be examined until the Gate to the Underworld is opened, and the creatures can return to this world. Even I can't open them. Perhaps you could break my magic, but not without destroying a great deal of the collection."

Bai sighed. "I see the wisdom in your choice, but it makes things rather inconvenient for us. We are going to the Underworld."

The Moon Deer's already big eyes opened even wider. "Truly? Then you do have the key? But why now?"

Bai looked at Jin and took her hand, pulling her closer to his side. "Those questions are for Jin, not me," he said.

NOT even the excitement of the morning could stop the Moon Deer from his midday nap, and so after about an hour, Jin and Bai left his suite. Jin slid the door closed behind her and looked to Bai. "What now?"

He looked briefly solemn before smilingly lightly. "Lunch, of course."

Jin's own lips quirked up in response. "You know that's not what I meant."

"I know, but both of us will think better with some food."

His hand once again enveloped hers, warm and strong. It was as if now that he had decided to touch her he couldn't stop himself, which Jin didn't mind in the least. They made their way to the central hall of Tsuku. Jin wasn't sure if Bai already knew how meals were done here or if he just followed his nose—the rich scent of oil and onions was drifting from the kitchens to guide them.

Two of the Moon Deer's granddaughters greeted them, though Jin didn't miss their sour glances at Bai and her linked hands. They settled Jin and Bai at large white stone tables in the back garden and soon finely painted earthenware dishes were set before them, filled with rice and fermented soybeans, pickled ferns and radishes, and fresh sprouts.

Last night she hadn't dwelled on the simple, plant-based dinner that had been brought to her room, but now Jin was surprised by the lack of meat in such a rich spread. Bai must have realized her question, for he leaned forward to whisper, "The Moon Deer and his family are vegetarians. They'll eat fish when served it—a necessary adaptation with the Sea Dragon for a son-in-law - but no animals are cooked here at Tsuku."

Jin nodded, thinking that if she had lived a lifetime as a deer, it would indeed be strange to eat meat.

She and Bai were joined by members of the household. She let Bai neatly deflect their questions about Cheng, instead turning the subject to their travels. Jin found they liked to listen to the way she described the Kuanbai and the Great Ladies, even though surely most of them must have visited themselves, for all had at least a few thousand years on Jin.

She was grateful when the meal finished, and Bai suggested they retire to their room for some private conversation.

The first thing Jin noticed when she entered this time was red tea set on a bamboo shelf. She crossed to it and picked it up. A gold sun and the flaring wings of a diving eagle—Gang's symbols. Her eyes began to fill with tears, and her throat closed. Bai's hands settled on her shoulders and she turned into him, the cup trapped between them.

"This is Gang's room," she told Bai.

"Yes, I know. But why does that upset you?"

"I'm not upset exactly." She dragged him to a red silk wall hanging with pink and white peonies. "I embroidered this as a child." She tugged him along to a painting of an adolescent girl dancing. "This is when I was three and half millennia old and I danced at the wedding of the Bandoan king." She dragged him before the folding screen. "And this is the first piece I finished by myself when I was studying painting." She heaved a sigh. "He collected these—he must have watched over me my entire life. But I had no idea. And why would he...

"I thought Nanami was right, that it must be Gang who poisoned and kidnapped me, but I just can't reconcile this room with that. And—and—"

Bai suddenly pulled her close in another embrace. "I don't understand it either. But we don't know that it was Gang who used the poison against you. You are the one who said Aka could not be condemned on hearsay. So let us not condemn Gang either."

Jin nodded, but the tears kept streaming down her face. "I haven't told you what Karana said yesterday."

Bai pulled away and looked her in the face. "I wasn't sure you wanted to."

Jin smiled ruefully. "Because I ordered you away? I knew Karana wouldn't be open in front of you, but I always intended to tell you. If nothing else, I need your help for my quest, so I should tell you everything I know."

Bai lifted his hand and very tentatively tucked some hair behind her ear. "You don't have to do that."

"I want to. But this particular tale is a little difficult." When she finished explaining about her deceased half-brother, the God of Belief, Jin stared at the floor. "Do you—do you understand why I couldn't repudiate Karana? Even though what he did was horrible?"

Bai was quiet. "Truthfully, I probably would have. But you are far kinder than I am, more forgiving and less reactive. I can respect and honor your decision. Jin, you inspire me. I want to be worthy of you, to be more tolerant and accepting. Focused on building a better future rather than trying to avenge the past—"

Jin interrupted him. "I love you, Bai. In this whole mess, you—you've been so important to me..."

Bai leaned forward suddenly and pressed his lips to hers. They were warm and smooth, and Jin was so thrilled that she tried to kiss him back. Instead, she ended up head butting him.

HAVING finally gathered the courage to confess his feelings

and kiss Jin, Bai knew she might hurt him, but he had expected emotional pain, not her skull slamming his nose. Bai had leaned forward for the kiss; he now took a step back, clutching his nose, eyes closed. The pain was fading—he didn't think it was broken, maybe not even bloodied.

"Did I offend you?" he managed after a moment.

Jin didn't reply, and Bai opened his eyes. Jin was staring at the red and gold teacup, her cheeks full of blood. After a moment, Bai released his nose to touch her shoulder. "Jin? I'm sorry, I shouldn't have kissed you without your permission. I misread the situation."

"No! No, you didn't," she blurted, and her eyes darting up at him before returning to the cup. "I'm so, so sorry. I just—I just wanted to kiss you back. I didn't—that is—it's harder than it seems!"

Bai turned that over a few times. "Have you never kissed anyone before?"

She spun around, flinging an elbow over her face. A soft moan escaped her, and Bai understood he had mortified her. His nose didn't bother him at all anymore. In fact, he found a stupid smile curving his lips. He cleared his throat. He reached around and tugged the teacup from her fingers. After he had returned it to its shelf, he pulled her into a hug.

Jin was stiff at first but after a moment, her hands crept around his waist and bunched the robes at his back. Bai had intended to just enjoy her embrace, but he found himself reflecting on Karana's story.

"Jin," he said at last, "Karana and Salaana targeted your brother because he was too powerful in their eyes."

"Yes."

"When Karana saw you restore Cheng earlier, his attitude

bothered me. I felt he was resentful of your power and just a bit afraid."

Jin pulled back slightly and frowned up at him. "He was afraid—I thought he was worried about Cheng."

Bai shook his head. "I don't think so. I think he was afraid of you. If we wish to avoid a confrontation with him or Salaana, I think we need to leave here soon. Maybe today."

Jin bit her lip. "But where do we go?"

He hesitated. "I suppose we should go to the Underworld."

Her brows arched. "What happened to 'you need to study'?"

He smiled sheepishly. "Yes. Well. That was an excuse because I was afraid." He grew very serious. "I am afraid of losing you. But there isn't anything for us to study here. I will teach you more as we travel, but I am beginning to think Earth and the Heavens are just as full of pitfalls as the Underworld."

Jin shrugged. "Then let's go."

He chuckled. Blame his long life, but his "now" and her "now" varied by a few days. "Let us rest here tonight. Tomorrow, I shall summon a cloud."

16

How the Night Dragon Retaliated

THE dragon that was Xiao eased forward. Nanami could see nothing but its large purple-black scales, though she could sense the assembly holding its collective breath. Needing to know what unfolded, even if she was not an active participant in this power war, Nanami made a flying leap onto Xiao's back and then ran beside the frill of his spine until she reached his mane. She wound her hand into those black silky strands, hoping, perhaps ridiculously, that it didn't hurt Xiao.

Xiao had paused when she began her run, and her father took advantage of his hesitation to lunge, teeth aimed for Xiao's throat. They never connected. Instead, Xiao's forelegs shot out and pinned the Sea Dragon to the wood floor of the hall. His massive claws cracked the boards they touched.

"Unfortunately, you're so full of bile, I don't think you'd taste very good. Probably upset my stomach. Why don't you beg Nanami for your life? I would be willing to spare it, if it pleased her."

Nanami's fingers trembled in the mane they held. Who needed two hands when she had a dragon to protect her?

Her father—no, she no longer wanted to think of the old man that way. Ao thrashed against the boards, demolishing the floor that had been spared by Xiao's claws. But he was no match for the larger dragon.

Ao was too proud to beg and too stubborn to apologize, even though it was clear his life was at stake.

But Miko was not.

Miko, the daughter of the Moon Deer, the beautiful maiden who had captured Ao's affections when she was just five thousand years old and who had borne him thirteen children, would not have known how to exist without her husband. She threw herself at the massive violet claws, heedless of the way her voluminous kimono was torn by the struggle, and begged.

"Please, please, Night Dragon, please spare my husband. He doesn't mean it. Our daughter hurt him terribly; it is only because he loved her so deeply that he came to hate her so passionately. He's an old fool, but I love him! Please, God of Love, please spare my heart's mate! I beseech you!"

Xiao went stiff, and then he scoffed, his talon still pinning the Sea Dragon. "I'm afraid you didn't listen. I said to beg Nanami, not me."

Miko looked straight at Nanami for the first time. How old her mother had grown! Her once impossibly smooth skin was now covered by heavy makeup that could not completely hide the lines of her face.

"Nanami," said her mother, "Please, please spare him. We need him."

And then her siblings were gathered around, and their spouses and children. They all looked terrified. Some were even crying, though the Sea Dragon abhorred tears. Nanami remembered being spanked when her pet turtle died and told not to whine. *But maybe it's permissible to cry for the Sea Dragon*, some part of her that was very far away mused.

"Please, God of Love! Please, Nanami! Please spare our

beloved father!"

Nanami had told Bai that she didn't want to watch him destroy her family; who knew that Xiao was as big a threat? But Nanami couldn't believe that Xiao would really kill anyone. He was too kind, and Nanami felt strangely certain that he had never taken a life. He probably let mosquitoes drink from him unmolested because he wanted to make them happy.

It hadn't escaped Nanami's notice, though her family seemed oblivious, that while Ao had tried to bite Xiao, Xiao hadn't even pierced him with a claw. Any damage done to the Sea Dragon was caused by its own thrashing against the broken boards of the hall. Xiao was bluffing them out—and doing it well—all for her. To punish them for hurting her, for abandoning her.

But it hurt him to ignore their prayers—she had felt his shock when Miko called him the God of Love. Nanami had immediately felt the rightness of that address—how must Xiao have felt?

And so for Xiao's sake, Nanami said, "Let him go."

XIAO sat in the garden tea house, a cup of steaming matcha before him. For the moment, he and Nanami were alone. She sat across from him, her eyes on her lap. Her round face was drawn; her full cheeks somehow giving the impression of thinness, as if the struggle between Xiao and Ao had sucked away some of her vitality. She was cradling her stump with her right hand, and that hand looked small and delicate. He tried to recall his first impression of her, when confidence and control had filled her movements. *Nimble, not delicate*, he told himself.

Xiao was sure that the residents of the Sea Palace must be very busy inside its walls, dealing with the damage he had inflicted, but he heard and saw none of them. Probably they were all terrified of attracting his notice.

Nanami's long bangs cupped her cheeks, as Xiao wanted to. He couldn't see her eyes though, and for once he lacked the confidence to touch her without explicit invitation.

"Do I owe you an apology?"

She jerked her head up, at last meeting his eyes. "You saved my life—why would you owe me an apology?"

Xiao spoke slowly. "I terrified your family. And now they fear me, but I don't know if they respect you. That's what I wanted. I realize now I failed."

Nanami stood after a moment and walked around the table until she reached him. She knelt. "Not everything we want in life is possible. This place is no longer my home, and these people are no longer my family. I wish I could say I didn't care that I don't have their respect, but it isn't true—at least not yet. I think someday, it may be." She cleared her throat. "I want...I want you. I," she swallowed, "love you. Would you be my family?"

Xiao turned his head away, trying to hide his tears. Nanami turned it back.

He struggled to find his voice. "For a long time, I was content with marrying Jin. She wasn't interested in me romantically, but she's never been interested in anyone, and she has been my family, more than anyone else.

"It hurt to see Jin fall head over heels for Bai as soon as she saw him. I think...I know this sounds strange, since we're the same age, but I realized that I was waiting for her to grow up, thinking that when she did, she'd fall in love with me. She's always been such an important part of my life and I could—I could have loved her. If she had wanted it, I would have given her everything.

"I'm sorry, I don't say this to hurt you, but because I need to be honest. I want—I need you to understand me."

Nanami nodded slowly, not saying anything, and Xiao worried that he had indeed hurt her. So he hurried on.

"When we saw them on the Yanou, I realized that Jin and I had never fallen in love because we weren't compatible. Jin and Bai are. Just as...just as you and I are.

"Nanami, I love you, too. I want to marry you, to be at your side for the rest of eternity. But..."

She tilted her head.

"If we marry, I'll only have a few decades to live. I'll lose my powers. So I don't know...do I marry Jin, just so we can follow the letter of our vow? Would you accept me..."

Nanami leaned forward and kissed him. Her arms wrapped around his back and she pressed against him.

This is it. This is all I need.

Nanami ended the kiss. "I would accept you on any terms. I don't need a wedding or the promise of forever. If you choose to be with me now, I would be very happy."

Xiao shook his head. "Don't ever say that again. You have the rest of my life, and you better say the same to me!"

Nanami's lips parted softly in surprise. Then she nodded and laughed, so Xiao kissed her again.

A soft cough came from the entrance of the tea house.

Note to self, the Sea Palace is terrible for trysts. Nanami's siblings always interrupt us.

Nanami settled at his side, smoothing her clothes, as Nimi and her husband entered the teahouse. They were followed by

Kairoku and his wife.

"Our mother sends her apologies. She must tend to our father," announced Kairoku.

When Xiao had released the Sea Dragon, he had bled profusely from ten deep scores, one for each of Xiao's claws. Xiao flexed his now small, relatively harmless human hands now, remembering the feeling of the Sea Dragon writhing in them. Xiao wasn't entirely sure if he had cut the other dragon deliberately—he had to hold him tightly because of the Sea Dragon's struggles. However, Xiao had never wanted to hurt another being so much in his life, and he couldn't say for sure if the way he had dug his claws in near the end had been necessary or not.

Xiao supposed that the fact Nanami's family had even sent four people to speak with them was a good sign. After all, the tea house was too small to hold many more and the main hall too damaged. Not to mention, he had terrified them so thoroughly that none of them wanted to be near him.

"Your divinity, may we ask how long you plan to stay?" ventured Nimi.

Xiao looked at Nanami. "That is up to Nanami."

He half-thought she would say they weren't staying at all, but she seemed to seriously consider it, as hurt, hope, confusion all danced across her face.

"We will stay until we know if Ao will live or die," she declared. She looked at Nimi. "I didn't know that he could actually become a dragon. Did you?"

Nimi looked at Nanami with a blank face, her hands fisted on her thighs.

When no answer seemed to be forthcoming, Xiao said, "Why aren't you answering her?"

"Father forbid speaking to her—"

Xiao slammed his fist on the table, and the tea things all clattered.

Nimi swallowed. "But I always resented that order and see no need to follow it now. Mother told me that he could transform himself, but I had never seen it. I do not think he has transformed since Ichimi was born." Nimi stared down at her hands.

"The first millennium that you were gone, we all thought you'd come back. Father said when you arrived to beg on our doorstep that we were to let you in, and he would forgive you. It was only after he heard about your apprenticeship to He Who Walks in Shadow that we were forbidden to ever speak to you or acknowledge you in any way." She cleared her throat, and Xiao realized Nimi was crying. He wasn't quite willing to stop despising her though. "I'm sorry about your hand. Ichimi shouldn't have done that—even if—she's changed, you know, since falling in love with the Goddess of Justice. She sees everything in absolutes now."

"Is Ao supporting her in the war for the throne?" Nanami asked.

Nimi nodded, while Kairoku made a strangled noise.

"You shouldn't—" he began, and Xiao turned a baleful glare on him.

Kairoku shut up.

Nimi hesitated. "Has the God of Love decided on his candidate for the Sun Throne?"

"Stop calling me that. And I thought you people didn't like being ruled," Xiao said. "Why would you support anyone?"

Nimi and Kairoku looked at each other; Nimi bit her lower lip.

"Ah. Your sister will be consort. Since it benefits your family, you've changed your tune."

"Salaana will be a just arbitrator! She is far more deserving of the position than Aka," Kairoku argued.

"She will certainly be decisive and adhere closely to her moral code. But she doesn't understand others' perspectives.

"Don't misunderstand. I'm not arguing against a Sun Emperor. Maybe I would have, if anyone asked me before Aka became one. But now millions of mortals worship him. He holds dominion over the gods and keeps immortals from feuding with each other. Someone has to do that job. But I wouldn't choose Salaana."

"I suppose you'd support Gang, since he's a freak like you!" jeered Kairoku.

"Freak?" echoed Xiao, and Kairoku flinched. "Because we're more powerful than you? Perhaps you're right. But doesn't that power give us the right to rule? What do you think, Nanami? Would you like to be the Moon Empress?"

Nanami swatted Xiao on the arm. "Don't tease them. They don't know you like I do."

Xiao laughed. Then he looked back at Kairoku. "I'll support whomever Jin chooses."

Kairoku's brow knit. "Who's Jin?"

"His betrothed," Nimi told him. "The Goddess of Beauty." She stared at them. Then, "I once saw the third Sun Empress with the God of War at my grandfather's home."

Xiao couldn't quite hide his reaction.

Nimi nodded slowly. "Well, I daresay the Heavens will be a very exciting place in the coming months."

AFTER Nanami and Xiao had been assigned to a guest room, Xiao left for the baths, leaving Nanami alone in the chamber. She knelt before the tokonoma, a small, recessed space containing a brown vase with flowers and a black ink painting of a thrush on a pine tree.

She couldn't quite believe she was here. That she had been welcomed—not for her own sake, but for the sake of her lover. Who her family openly acknowledged as engaged to another woman. The Sea Dragon scorned illicit affairs, and yet enough power changed everything.

A soft scratching sounded at the door, and Nanami stiffened. "Come in."

The rice-paper door slid to reveal Miko. Her hair was loose, swinging down her back, and she had replaced her elaborate kimono with a simple brown one meant for chores. She slipped into the room almost as a servant would, and Nanami couldn't find any words, even though there was so much she wanted to say.

Miko knelt next to her and silently regarded the tokonoma as well, as if the only reason she had entered was to contemplate its arrangement.

"I'm glad to see you, Nanami, even under the circumstances."

"Mother—"

Miko pressed the back of her hand against Nanami's lips.

"I'm sorry, but you must not call me that. Your father renounced you and struck you from the family tree."

"So why have we been invited to stay?"

Miko smiled sadly. "Did we have a choice in the matter?"

Nanami wanted to shake her, this small woman who was completely dominated by her husband.

"I would never forsake any of my children, even if their father did!"

Miko was very quiet. "The God of Love seems like a good choice for you then. He would fight for those he loved against anything."

Even though the title suited him, Nanami asked, "Why do you keep calling him that? He is the God of Pleasure."

Miko shook her head. "A conceit of Zi and Hei. They named him wrongly. But children can break free of their parents to become who they were always meant to be—look at you."

Nanami whirled on her mother then. "If you aren't here to say you love me, that I'll always be your daughter, why did you come?"

Miko pleated the skirt of her robe over her thighs. "Did you notice that in dragon form, Xiao was at least five times bigger than Ao?"

Nanami was so surprised by the question that it took her a few moments to respond. "Well, I wasn't thinking very actively about it, but certainly I noticed he was much, much larger."

"The dragon form is a manifestation of a being's power. In truth, any immortal can become a dragon. Ao taught me when we first wed. I was only the size of myself though—much less intimidating than your father. Would you like to see how I look now?"

Nanami shook her head, bewildered. "If you wish to show me."

Miko rippled and suddenly a small white dragon with silver horns and a mane like mist was next to Nanami. It was about the size of a kitten, and just as elegantly, it climbed into Nanami's lap and curled into a ball.

Gingerly, Nanami caressed its scales. Tiny and delicate, it was like petting a snake. The little dragon spoke.

"No one worships me, and I never had very much power to begin with—I think that's why I notice every time power trickles away from me. As it does with each birth in our family.

"It is widely said that born immortals inherit the power of their parents, but it is more literal than most people realize. By the time Sanmi was born, I had realized that a family's power is finite, and we all share the same power. When I met Ao, I already shared my power with my father and sisters. Between my children and my nieces and the grandchildren, that same power is now pulled in over forty directions."

Nanami was shocked. "Does—does Ao know this?"

"Of course. Why do you think he controls his children so tightly? When you use magic, his own is reduced. That's why he stopped transforming into the Sea Dragon after Ichimi's birth - he realized he was smaller. He didn't fully understand why, then, and he was afraid of losing standing."

Since his children literally had his power, he viewed them as extensions of himself.

"If—I have trouble believing that Ao would willingly share his power. Why didn't you stop having children?"

Miko the dragon slipped off Nanami's lap and became herself again. "We wanted to have a big family. He found that if his will is the strongest, he can keep most of the power for himself. And of course, he figured out how to supplement by taking mortal worshippers."

"But he isn't a god..."

Miko made a noncommittal gesture with her right hand. "He isn't called one, but he is worshipped. How else could he control the sailors on your ship?"

Nanami pressed her fists to her forehead. "This is all very interesting, but I don't understand why you're bringing it up."

Miko's hands came together, stroking each other as if she needed to be soothed. After a moment, Nanami grasped her mother's two hands in her one and squeezed them.

"I married a man a thousand times more powerful than me. I have tried to arrange more equitable alliances for my children. Xiao has access to the power of two Colors, while you have only one—and you must share it with two dozen others."

And then Miko tugged her hands free of Nanami, and her eyes became distant.

"I will convince your father to lift your exile, but this isn't your home anymore. We aren't your family. You are free of us, and all the vows you made as a daughter of the Sea Dragon. But please, don't come back. Take your lover away. Leave us in peace."

Nanami stared at the tokonoma, too hurt and angry to answer. How dare Miko claim they weren't family when their shared power proved otherwise? After the silence stretched unbearable, Miko rose and left.

Miko's warning, that there was too great a disparity between her power and Xiao's, seemed to indicate her mother still cared for her, but Nanami felt that care was wholly misguided. It was her father's personality that made him override his wife so wholly, not his power. And if Miko really cared about Nanami, she wouldn't reject her like this.

Some time later, Xiao returned. He stopped just inside the door, and Nanami knew he was reading her like a book, just like always. That was good because she didn't want to explain herself.

He lit a lamp, then pulled her into his arms.

"Who came to see you?"

"Miko."

"And she begged you to take your big, bad dragon and never return?"

Nanami laughed, though it wasn't a happy sound. "Yes. She said that they are no longer my family, and this is no longer my home. I am free of them, and all the vows I ever made to the family." She began to cry, and Xiao offered her his sleeve, which she soaked.

"Why does it still hurt?" she asked him. "It's nothing I hadn't realized. I knew this already. I said it to you, that you will be my family now. So why does it still hurt?"

"If you want, I can destroy this whole place."

Nanami shook her head. "No. I still want... I still want..."

"Them to be well? To be happy? To be safe?"

"Yes," she admitted.

Xiao stroked her head; then his hand suddenly fisted, pulling her hair.

"Ow! What was that about?"

"Oh—I am sorry—but..."

"What?"

"What did you say your mother said? You're free of them and the vows? What vows?"

"Ah—as children we all vowed to protect the waters of the world, to give mortals safe sailing, unless they were wicked. The Sea Dragon considered it our duty as his children. I suppose that is what she meant."

"And so, because you are no longer his daughter, you are released from your promise."

"Yes...why? Is it important?"

Xiao opened and closed his mouth twice before saying, "I

think it's time for you to meet my parents."

Nanami sat up, feeling very confused. "I have met them, you know. Before you were born."

Xiao looked at her blankly. "You have? When and where and why?"

"Several times actually. We saw them—not regularly but sometimes—before the immortal creatures were all trapped. The time I remember the best was my four thousandth birthday party."

"Your coming-of-age celebration," Xiao mused.

Nanami nodded. She was glad to talk about the past. It was easier than dealing with the messy present.

"Tell me about it," he demanded.

So Nanami leaned against him again and accepted his fingers running through her hair, letting them pull away her sadness.

She fell back in time remembering how she felt the morning she came of age. She had awoken alone in her room, but her handmaiden had soon come to help her dress.

"I can't imagine you wearing anything that requires a second person to put it on."

Nanami snorted. "Not with my current life choices, but I wore a gown as impractical as Miko's yesterday," she told him.

"What color was it?"

"Not indigo," she said, and Xiao kissed her forehead. She'd been allowed to choose the material herself, so of course she had decided on whatever would get her the most attention. "It had white and silver fans with green pine trees embroidered on a really gorgeous coral silk." She remembered being disappointed when she put it on though—the pretty fabric hadn't suited her, and she had looked dumpy.

"Nanami? What's wrong?"

She opened her eyes to find him bent over her, his engaging features no less appealing for being upside down. "I didn't look pretty. I don't have perfect dimples or a chiseled jaw," she teased, touching those features of his.

"Ah, but you are Nanami, so you don't need those things. Round cheeks," he cupped them, "and delicate brows," his thumbs stroked them simultaneously, "suit you splendidly."

"Charmer," she said.

"Naturally," he winked. "So who was invited to this shindig?"

"Hmmm." she closed her eyes, and his hands began to massage her scalp. "It was large—the main hall was packed. Bai came, and I remember Ao being angry that he brought the God of War—he was of course, the only child of Aka at that time. Both of your parents and the Sleeper."

"You're older than Salaana." Xiao shook his head. "I guess I should have known that, but for some reason it never occurred to me before. That's so weird."

Nanami slapped his arm and he dimpled at her. He said, "I'm surprised Aka and Neela weren't there."

"Father hates the Sun Emperor. Father isn't that fond of Neela either, and he never invites her when my grandfather— the Moon Deer—will be here."

"So did you speak with my parents? Did they give you a present?"

"Mmmm, that feels good," she told him, referring to the magic his fingers were working without any power at all. Unless...

"You're not spelling me to feel better, are you? I have some resistance to influence, but you are very powerful."

Xiao's hands stilled. "No. I would never. Not without your permission anyway."

Nanami's cheeks heated, and she opened her eyes again. "I'm sorry if I offended you. I didn't mean to sound accusatory. I just can't believe how much better I feel. I haven't had someone to...take care of me like this in a long time."

"I know," he said. "Now stop delaying! What happened with my parents?"

"Oh—right. Let's see—they did give me a present, I'm sure, but I don't remember what. Probably something very pretty that took a hundred years or so to make. That's what most people gave. But I do remember what your mother said to me.

"'Ao is blessed with his children! You are so beautiful and talented. It makes me yearn for a daughter.'"

"That's it?" Xiao asked. "I'm surprised you remember that."

Nanami met his eyes—his beautiful lavender eyes. "It may seem like nothing much to you, but I was rather upset by it. No one really thought I was beautiful. Nor particularly talented. I was neither musically nor artistically inclined. The only thing I've ever been really good at is stealing—creeping, sneaking."

WHEN Xiao returned from his bath to find Nanami distraught over her mother's visit, he had set out to comfort her. In some ways, it had been easy. Her long repressed need for physical affection meant she responded disproportionately to his touch—a fact he enjoyed immensely.

But when she revealed her insecurities, he didn't know what to say. She was such a source of strength—someone he admired so deeply that he had trouble comprehending that she might not see herself the same way. He mulled over her words, that she had felt neither beautiful nor talented when she came of age.

"I'm sorry," he said at last. "I'm sorry that you ever felt that way, and I'm sorry that my mother caused you pain. But I'm not sorry that you have become who you are—that you are so strong and independent and unique—because of it. You've given me courage, inspired me, set me free, and I feel so grateful for you being just as you are."

Nanami was still staring into his eyes, her head in his lap, his hands cradling her skull. "Thank you." Then she cleared her throat. "I went off on this tangent because you said you wanted me to meet your parents. What were you thinking of?"

"Well," he kept his tone to be light, "I'd guess, no offense, that my parents might not even remember that exchange you had. And since I'm going to marry you, I think they really ought to know who you are."

Xiao could see the moment she processed what he had said. She sat up quickly and shifted onto her knees. "Marry? But Xiao—"

He pressed a finger to her lips. "You're worried about my breaking a vow, but what you don't know is my vow is only to honor my parents' wishes. Bai pointed out to me two days ago that if Jin stopped thinking of Aka as her father, she would be released from her promise. And when you told me what Miko said, I realized that was true for me as well, even though they're my biological parents."

Nanami's lips parted beneath his finger. Then she smiled and threw her arms about his neck, her lips smashing into his.

Xiao chuckled. "You like the idea, then?" he murmured against her mouth.

But a moment later she pulled back, her brows knit. "But

Xiao, do you really want to emancipate yourself? You won't regret disowning your parents? I don't want—"

Xiao tackled her to the tatami mats, pinning her wrists with his hands. "Nanami, it would be a dream come true, even if I didn't get to marry you. You're just a bonus."

She stuck her tongue out at him, so he pulled it into his own mouth. He couldn't help but chuckle when she gasped in surprise and arousal.

When Nanami broke their kiss yet again, Xiao growled his displeasure. "Just one last question, I swear, and then you can have your wicked way with me." Her voice quavered slightly on the last words, and Xiao knew she was nervous.

"We don't have to—"

"Shush," she said. "We most definitely do. I have twenty-thousand years of pent-up sexual frustration to release."

Xiao's head spun a little just thinking about that.

"But first, I want to know, can your parents wait until I've spoken with my father?"

Xiao blinked. "Yes, of course. We won't leave here until you are ready—regardless of what anyone else wishes."

Nanami smiled, then lifted her head for another kiss.

NANAMI woke slowly, appreciating the warmth that enveloped her. She knew immediately that the smooth skin against her own belonged to Xiao, and her lips curled up without conscious thought. Her head was pillowed by his shoulder, and if she listened carefully, she could hear the steady beat of his heart.

"I love you so much it frightens me," she whispered and then immediately tensed—what if he weren't asleep after all?

But he did not respond, his heartbeat slow and steady.

She would have liked to go back to sleep, but thoughts were rushing into her head, faster than she could process. She hoped Xiao was right and they would have forever. Fear that they wouldn't was one of many things weighing on her. Another fourteen were her forsaken family members. Maybe she shouldn't stay any longer. Part of her felt guilty for making love with Xiao in their guest suite. Was it asking too much to stay and accept their hospitality?

Someone scratched at the door and Nanami went stiff. She waited, hoping she had imagined the sound, but it came again. With a sigh, she sat up. The thick coverlet fell to her waist, and Nanami shivered in the cool air.

"Mmmm?" Xiao whimpered. "Wha-" he yawned, "happening?"

"Either someone else has come to ask me to leave or Ao is ready to see me."

Xiao sat up as well, and despite the person at the door, Nanami took a moment to appreciate his glorious torso.

"What are you looking at?" he smirked.

"My lover," she said boldly, poking his belly.

He flinched from the jab and smiled. The scratching came again.

"Hold your horses," Xiao scolded the scratcher. The two of them dressed quickly.

When Nanami went to open the door, Xiao put a hand on her shoulder. "Let me."

Nanami had been expecting Nimi, or, hopefully, a conciliatory Kaihachi, and she couldn't quite stop herself from stepping back when Xiao slid the door to reveal the Ao himself.

He wasn't scowling for once. Nanami swallowed and

stepped forward again, stopping at Xiao's side.

"You're well enough to talk then?" Nanami asked, feeling a bit ridiculous.

He nodded once. Nanami tugged Xiao out of the way and used her stump to direct Ao into the room. His eyes rested briefly on where her hand should be, but he stepped into the room without saying anything.

Nanami arranged three zabuton cushions, and Ao immediately took a seat. She supposed he must still be in a great deal of pain to put his comfort before his pride.

Nanami and Xiao sat as well. She glanced at him for reassurance, and he winked at her. It was quick and his face was so devoid of expression that she might have imagined it, but she felt reassured anyway.

"What do you want?" demanded Ao.

"I want an apology," Nanami said.

He snorted. "I'm sorry you became a thief, living off of others' honest achievements."

Nanami's brows snapped together. "That's not what I do—I steal only when it is justified."

"Oh? And how was the theft of your aunt's hair stick justified?"

Nanami grit her teeth. "That was different—"

"But you said you only steal when it's justified."

"Now! Back then I just wanted to see what it would take to get someone to notice me!"

"Such pride," scoffed Ao.

"And who did I get it from?" returned Nanami. Her hands fisted. This wasn't going the way she wanted. She wanted to have a calm, adult conversation. But instead she felt just as she had thirteen millennia ago when she'd been caught stealing

Aunt Atsuko's magic hair stick. Of course, no one would have even noticed if it hadn't been magic. If it hadn't been, maybe she would be unhappily married by now, popping out children to honor her parents.

No, she would have just stolen something else, have kept stealing until she was caught.

"I'm glad—I'm glad you kicked me out, so that I could be me instead of the Sea Dragon's seventh child!"

"Then what are you still doing here?" he growled at her, brows beetling.

Nanami stared at him. "Wasting my time," she finally answered. "Xiao, please, I'm ready to leave now."

Xiao wrapped his arm around her waist and effortlessly moved between.

17

How Four Fears Were Faced

NANAMI regretted her impulsive request to Xiao as soon as they reappeared in New Moon Manor. She should have told him to take them somewhere else first, so they could prepare. Zi, the Moon Goddess, and Hei, the Night God, sat on thrones of silver, amethyst, and obsidian. The whole room gleamed, a depiction of the moon's phases on silver walls that would never dare to tarnish. The air was thick with lavender and star anise incense—prayers, Nanami supposed—but it did not obscure her messy hair or sloppily tied tunic. Zi's eyes had touched upon both as soon as they appeared in the room.

Nanami should have created a new kimono for the occasion, a formal one that would make her look like someone impressive. She now knew how to make them so that they flattered her slight figure.

Hei rose and offered his hand to Zi. She accepted it, and the two of them advanced toward their son. Zi had a dozen or so large silver hair ornaments in her elaborate updo—Nanami's head ached in sympathy—and layers of chiffon and silk floated about her tall, slim form like a violet cloud. Hei wore his hair shockingly short and with no adornment. His robes looked like cotton, unrelieved black matte, and did not go past his ankles.

Despite their thoroughly contrasting appearances, they were unnervingly in sync, partners in a way her parents would never be.

"Laughter in the Shadows," said Zi, "You have been remiss in your filial duties. We have not seen you since your betrothal. Who is this woman?"

"Why, you don't remember meeting her, divinity?" Xiao's voice was overly cheerful. "This is Nanami the Thief. And she is very good at what she does—I'm afraid she has stolen my heart."

Zi's eyes narrowed at her son, while Hei assessed Nanami. "I don't care where your heart is, as long as you do your duty to your parents and marry Sunlight turns Petals Gold in ten months."

Xiao very gently nudged Nanami away from him. She moved to give him room, and as he stepped forward, his hands spread.

"See, I've been thinking about that. Duty to parents, I mean. And I decided, being filial isn't all it's cracked up to be. So how 'bout we cut ties?"

"Elaborate," ordered Hei.

"I'm no longer your son, and you're no longer my parents."

"We don't find that acceptable," said Zi. "It appears you need to be punished—the next ten months in confinement while you study the virtues of filial piety."

Xiao rippled, and soon the black and purple Night Dragon filled the silver hall—but this hall was much larger than her father's, and the ceiling arched above Xiao's head.

Nanami had expected Zi and Hei to back away—to gasp in surprise, if not fear. But they barely seemed to notice that their son had become a massive dragon.

Instead, threads of raw power emanated from them, purple and black blending into twilight shadows. The threads wrapped themselves around Xiao, and he roared in pain, as if they scalded him.

XIAO was excited to face his parents, to make them acknowledge him at last. He wasn't a scared child any longer—he was the Night Dragon, the God of Love.

As he let his power pour outward, Xiao loomed over his parents. But to his disappointment, his parents were unmoved by the revelation of his power. As if they had been expecting this for years, they immediately moved into action, threads of twilight and shadow flowing from their fingers and wrapping around his neck and legs.

Xiao couldn't tell if the threads were colder than ice or hotter than the fire, but either way the pain threatened to overwhelm his ability to think. He pulled and bucked against the threads, but they might as well have been made of steel.

They are stronger than me, Xiao realized, and he looked at Nanami. He had rescued her from her father's wrath only to bring her into worse danger. After his parents defeated him, what would they do to Nanami?

He roared, trying to tell her to flee, to get out of there, but she just stared back at him.

The teleportation ban, he realized. *She can't break it.*

Suddenly Nanami disappeared. He wasn't sure how she had managed to go, but he was grateful that she had.

HOW are they so much more powerful than he is?

Nanami looked for a way to help.

Her gaze was drawn to the incense; its smoke fed into the threads, making them thicker and stronger.

They have more worshippers than he does.

Someone needed to steal their power if Xiao was to stand a chance—good thing Nanami was the second-best thief in the world.

Zi and Hei weren't paying her much attention anyway, but Nanami grabbed the pouch of nishikai powder to shrink herself. There wasn't much left—she'd have to find more or visit the Sanctuary Caves to return to normal size. But better to risk being stuck small for a few days than to fail Xiao in his moment of need. She used the last of it to shrink herself smaller than a mouse, making it child's play to sneak through the hall and take the incense.

Zi shook her head when Nanami broke the sticks, but she didn't turn around to see what had happened. Hei didn't even react.

Nanami looked at the threads again. They were still absorbing other power.

This isn't enough, she realized. *If only Jin or Bai were here—they might be able to counter this.*

Nanami looked at the threads of power again. *Or maybe not. They must have millions of worshippers.*

Nanami looked at Xiao, a writhing mass. She could feel his pain so clearly that her nails dug into her palms.

XIAO tried to teleport himself, but he was caught fast in the web of his parents' power. It was strange—everyone had told him that he had the same power as the two of them, but as he pitted his will against theirs, it was obvious that they were far stronger. Running away seemed the best option, but the thin whips of power that wrapped around his legs and neck wouldn't snap. He tried biting them. They blistered his mouth, but he persisted, and yet all he accomplished was feeling smaller.

Or maybe he really was smaller? He seemed to be shrinking—the hall loomed higher overhead and his parents no longer seemed miniscule compared to him. These whips—the pain they caused was not purely physical, they were actually siphoning off his power. The harder Xiao struggled, the more pain he felt. He laid down, trying not to struggle at all.

When he no longer actively fought them, the whips stopped stinging so badly but they thickened and glowed, more power than ever flowing down their lengths. Xiao began to shrink more rapidly, and he belatedly began to struggle again, but too late.

One moment he was a small dragon, the next he was in his natural form. He lay splayed on the floor, too weak to even sit up. The cords of twilight and shadow disappeared.

NANAMI concealed herself in the skirts of Zi's voluminous robes. She hoped that Xiao didn't think she had abandoned him.

It was torture to hide while Xiao roared in pain, but nothing compared to how Xiao must feel, so Nanami grit her teeth and bore it, waiting for an opportunity.

Xiao's cries abruptly stopped. Peering through the gauze of Zi's skirts, Nanami found him sprawled on the ground, once again a man. Zi and Hei let their power whips fade, and both stepped close to Xiao's head. Nanami was both relieved to see him closer and horrified at the wanness of his face. His eyes were closed, and she wondered if he were conscious.

"Should we call someone to carry him?" Zi asked.

"No, I'll do it myself," Hei replied.

Xiao was about the same size as his father, both in height and build, so it was a very awkward business of grunts and heaves for Hei to pull Xiao up on his back. Zi had to help prop Xiao up, and they shuffled down the hall like a crippled beast. At the door, Zi went out first, and she told a disciple to clear the hallways. They encountered no one as Hei dragged Xiao through the corridors.

They stopped before a pair of double doors and Zi opened them. Hei stumbled through, banging Xiao against the frame. Nanami winced and decided that Xiao must indeed be unconscious—he didn't so much as moan, never mind open his eyes.

They managed to get him in the bed. They both stared at him a moment, and then Zi arranged his limbs in a more dignified manner, even removing his shoes, and pulled a blanket over him. Nanami had trouble believing this was maternal kindness and decided it was a distaste for awkward things. At least it gave Nanami a convenient moment to disengage from her skirts and conceal herself in Xiao's clothes.

"We'll talk about this when you are recovered," Zi announced, as if Xiao could hear her, and she and her husband left together. When the door shut, Nanami heard the falling of a lock's tumblers. She slipped out cautiously and examined the room.

It was oppressively dichromatic, with violet wall hangings and lots of black ceramic.

And on the windows were bars of black iron.

But wasn't this Xiao's bedroom?

Suddenly Nanami remembered how Xiao had gripped the bars of the bamboo cage she had made, glaring at her and throwing insults.

At the time she had thought him unable to handle any hardship. Now...

Now she realized that he was used to being in cages and that she had triggered his childhood trauma.

Nanami pressed the back of her hand to her mouth, pushing back her emotions. How had he been able to forgive her? Become her friend and then her lover?

She ran up his body to his face.

"Xiao! Xiao!" There was no response, and Nanami sat down on the bridge of his nose.

"I'm sorry. I should have saved the nishikai powder for you—I should never have agreed to come here. I'm so sorry."

She stayed like that for several hours, overwhelmed by guilt, begging fate to smile upon him. Her thoughts were tumbling, chaotic as she tried to think of something, anything she could do to help him.

Finally, as the sun set and threw the room into darkness, one idea clarified into coherence. *If anyone is to have a chance at rescuing Xiao, I need to stop the prayers from reaching the Moon and Night deities. I need to steal the incense burners from their temples.*

She stood and examined his face once more. She didn't want to leave him—she still remembered the way he had nearly panicked when she teleported away to sink the Infinite Jug, and that situation had been far less desperate than this one. But she couldn't just sit here and do nothing when he was suffering.

She tried teleporting, just in case, but indeed the ban here was far beyond her strength. Knowing it would be all but impossible to return unless she succeeded in her task made it that much harder to leave. She walked down Xiao's nose and planted a kiss between his brows. Then she slid down the side of his head. She paused at his ear to say, "Wait for me, my love. I will rescue you."

It took her a ridiculous amount of time to climb down the intricately carved bed, cross the room, and crawl under the door. She doubted that she would make it to the gate of the manor before sunrise, and she felt quite thirsty and tired already, but the fear of discovery kept her alert and fast.

Probably because everyone assumed her already gone, Nanami made it through the manor undetected. Even after slipping through the cracks at the edge of the iron gate, she was still unable to teleport. With no other way to escape, she jumped off Zi and Hei's heavenly territory.

She had to test the teleportation ban periodically as she plummeted, but finally she passed its boundary and moved between.

XIAO woke slowly, his head pounding and his limbs heavy.

"I shouldn't have drunk so much," he groaned.

Then he realized where he was. The most hated place in the whole world. His room.

Not that he had slept here in, oh, maybe a whole millennium. Why would he choose to be here when there were so many other beds that welcomed him?

He sat up slowly, but the room spun around him. To steady himself, he focused on the violet wall hangings and black pottery that had nothing to do with Xiao's taste and everything to do with his parents.

He hadn't drunk anything after all. The aches he felt were because of his parents' power whips draining away his magic.

Xiao lurched across his bed to vomit on the floor, but his stomach was empty and only produced dry heaves. He slipped out of bed, and found his feet bare against the basalt floor. Whoever had carried him here must have removed his shoes.

Xiao stumbled to the door. It was locked. He hadn't doubted that it would be, but he still had to make sure. He looked around the prison of his youth, complete with black iron bars blocking the windows of the outer wall. He closed his eyes and checked in with his body.

He wondered how long it had been since his parents had siphoned away all of his power—his whole body ached, as if the power whips had bruised his muscles. Every slight movement scraped his skin. He pulled back a sleeve and saw the whips had in fact left burns.

I was a fool to come here. But... at least I achieved my purpose. I have disowned them and am free of the vow.

He knew that with the same certainty one could tell which way was up and which way was down. He had felt the vow break; he had felt the tie to his parents dissipate. He wondered if Nanami was actually free of her family, since she hadn't mentioned such a feeling.

He breathed deep, checking in with himself and calming the gut-clenching anxiety that was starting to build. Even though he hadn't been locked in this room since he was a child, he still remembered it well enough that being here made him nauseous. For the first time in nearly a month, he found himself thinking of the Infinite Jug, but he pushed that aside.

His power was trickling back, and he thought the physical weakness was merely a side effect. With great effort, he walked slowly but smoothly to a plush silk rug depicting irises in full bloom. He sat cross-legged and began to meditate the way Bai had shown him when they went to the White Mountain. His body began to relax, and what power he had flowed evenly within him, welcoming more.

Bai was right. I will recover much faster this way. And it was almost as good for his anxiety as a cup of wine.

Nanami had left, somehow. He touched his pinky with his thumb and found the ring of her hair. His parents hadn't noticed it or maybe didn't realize what it was. He stroked it now and reassured himself she was well. He could call her with it, summon her, but what good would that do either of them? His parents had made it impossible for him to teleport out of here and would Nanami even be able to teleport back? Not that he wanted her in danger but...

Now that his fear for her was less immediate, his fear for himself was growing. He had hoped earlier that she would abandon him and live well, but now he thought surely she wouldn't have. He needed to believe that. Was she trying to gather an army to come save him? But he couldn't imagine Nanami leading an army.

She'll be plotting, he soothed himself. *Even now, she's developing a scheme to save me. She'll get Bai and Jin, and they'll bust me out of this jail.*

I don't need anything to survive, just to lie here and exist until I'm rescued. I can manage that—I have before.

"SO this is it?" Jin stood before the large red gate atop the

Korikami's Tomb, her right hand fisted about Kunjee. Bai wasn't sure if she realized she was holding it or not. They had disembarked from a cloud just moments ago—this time, Jin had found it quite solid.

"This is it," he agreed mildly. He hesitated a moment, then put his hand on her shoulder. "Are you ready? We can wait, maybe until Xiao and Nanami are able to come."

Jin had tried to summon Xiao when they arrived at the gate, but he had not responded. Presumably he and Nanami were still at the Sea Palace.

Jin turned to Bai, shaking her head. "We've talked about this. It's better to go now." She collected his hand from her shoulder and gave it a squeeze. "I'll never be ready compared to you—at least, not within the timeline we have. We don't really know what awaits us either way. I don't want to study anymore."

She shivered under Bai's gaze—this island wasn't called the Land of Winter for nothing. It was almost summer, but the mountain was covered in deep snow and the air was frigid.

"You're cold?" Bai asked. He would make her a shawl from the snow.

"I'm fine. Maybe it will be warmer wherever we end up," she said with a smile and tugged his hand. "Let's go."

Bai interlocked his fingers with hers, and they stepped through the gate together. Bai came out the other side, the blue sky of Earth above him and the snow-covered ground of the Korikami's Tomb beneath him. Jin, however, was no longer holding his hand.

Bai blinked. "Jin?" He stepped back through the gate, as if that would undo whatever had happened. Had Kunjee unlocked the Underworld only for her? How did he follow?

He laid his hand against the bright vermillion wood of one column. The gate resisted him—he was firmly locked out. He pushed the gate further; his pool of power was as deep as Aka's was when he made this gate.

The gate shook against his hand, and the soil shivered under his feet. Bai pulled his power back. Sweat beaded on his forehead as he realized how close he had come to destroying the gate—and blocking any movement between the Underworld and this one. With Aka unconscious and dying, who knew if anyone would be able to recreate it.

The shaking that had threatened the gate seemed to have transferred to Bai. Maybe Jin would walk back—surely once she realized he wasn't with her, she would return for him, and they would figure out how to make Kunjee work for both of them. Maybe they should have hung the chain over both their necks...

Curse it, did he know the essence of things or not? He should have realized it wasn't like teleporting!

He paced in circles around the gate, trying to think of something to do.

And then suddenly he was not alone.

About a hundred women surrounded him, all dressed in white saris edged with blood-red silk.

One woman stood slightly ahead of the others. She was tall, maybe taller than Bai, and her reddish hair was bound by silver to form a tower. With her rich ochre skin and rust-colored eyes, she ought to have been beautiful, but her face was cold and haughty.

She looked very like Karana, if with much less make-up.

"You must be the First," she said, and her voice chilled him more than the wind. "Karana thought you intended to go through the gate with Jin. No matter."

And lightning shot from her fingertips, arcing toward the gate.

It was foolish of her to use lightning—that white light bent to Bai's will and bounced back, melting the snow at her feet.

"And you must be Salaana. If you are intending on destroying the gate, I'm afraid you're about to be disappointed."

She smiled—at least, her mouth curved upward.

"I only see one army here," she said, "and it's mine." She waved her hand, and her disciples drew their swords.

Bai wasn't sure if they intended to use them on him or the gate, but he found both options equally unacceptable. "I'll kill anyone who comes within six feet of this gate."

Two women charged together. Bai molded the snow in front of them into pikes and pierced both women's hearts.

And then the fight really began.

JIN emerged in darkness, and she immediately noticed that her hand was empty.

"Bai?" she said softly. There was no response. She spread her arms in front of her and turned slowly. She touched nothing, but by the time she finished her rotation, at least her eyes had adjusted.

There was no obvious source of light, but it was about as bright as being outside when the moon was not quite full. Unfortunately, she didn't see Bai anywhere, just rough stone all around, as if she were in an underground cavern. There was a path forward that faded into gloom as well as a path behind.

"Bai?" she called, more loudly this time. His name echoed

back to her, but there was no sign of the man himself.

Perhaps he didn't make it through the gate. She stepped back the way she had come, but there was no sudden change in her surroundings, nothing to indicate there was a gate here at all. Jin swallowed.

Of course! She shouldn't have spun in a circle. She probably was walking the wrong direction. She tried the other way, and then she tested the walls. Impulsively, she leapt for the ceiling, but all she got for her trouble was slight scrape on her palm.

A whimper escaped Jin, and she forced herself to slow her breathing. Apparently stepping through the gate on Earth didn't bring one to the gate in the Underworld. Or maybe there was a different key to open it from this side. She didn't know. She didn't know anything about this place at all! She had been relying on Bai to be her guide—foolish, foolish.

"I might not even be in the Underworld!"

Once again, her cry echoed around her, and Jin hugged her arms. *Don't cry. Just pick a direction and start exploring. Maybe Bai is nearby, he just can't hear you or you can't hear him.*

"Oh, you are definitely in the Underworld," came a voice at Jin's back. She whirled and pulled her tessen from her belt.

There was a giggle at Jin's side. "And we're so glad you are."

Jin could make out at least five pale blurs around face height around her, and bodies as well, darker than the walls.

"You smell lovely," she was told, and Jin clutched the heavy metal base of her tessen tighter.

"Who are you? What do you want?" Jin asked.

"You," followed by more giggling. It was nearly impossible to distinguish the speakers, though she thought there was more than one. Jin felt a rush of air at her back, and she whirled just in time to strike another of them with her tessen.

"Ow! She hurt me!" complained her would-be attacker.

Jin did not like these odds. There were at least six of them, if not more, given the way they appeared out of the shadows. They must surely be immortal creatures, and even if she was able to identify them, she knew so little that it probably wouldn't help her. Why couldn't she have run into benevolent ones like Bai had described?

"It's probably been a while since you've seen any immortals," Jin threw out, wondering if it was possible to delay the confrontation and somehow gain an advantage.

"We don't mind not seeing you," came the disembodied response, "we mind not *eating* you."

"What did you do to your hand?" asked another. "We don't want to waste any of that lovely blood."

Jin fisted her scraped hand—it was indeed bleeding a little.

She had set out to distract them, but she was the one distracted. Something bit into her cheek, and she felt the most horrendous tugging sensation. It was sucking her blood.

Jin sliced at the creature with her tessen, and she heard something fall to the ground—an arm, perhaps. The creature released her with a scream that echoed painfully.

Blood-drinkers—could these be the Xuezei that Nanami told us about?

Jin shuddered at the idea. Nanami had described mortal corpses covered in wounds and bled dry when Jin had pushed her for details about the Xuezei.

"The Xuezei were totally merciless creatures that live only to satiate their endless hunger," Nanami had said. "They lived in packs of a dozen or more and would slaughter whole villages in a single night."

They could be beheaded, but the better weapon against

them was fire. The pack Nanami had seen in action had eventually been lured into a village to feed, then trapped and burned to death. The people inside had known that would be their fate as well, but they had accepted it to save their families.

Fire. I can make fire.

Jin didn't know what to set on fire, but as she felt another Xuezei land her, she settled for herself.

An inferno engulfed her, burning away her clothes and the Xuezei. It screamed as it died. Through her blaze, Jin could now see its companions clearly.

Their faces, pale as ivory, were surrounded by thick black manes that extended down their bodies. Needle-like teeth filled their mouths, clearly visible as the Xuezei hissed at her.

Two more ran at her, either not believing she could sustain the fire or perhaps their greed for her blood overwhelmed their need for self-preservation. Jin burned both to ash.

The others then ran from her, and Jin let the inferno shrink to a small blaze, wearing it around her body like the clothes it had destroyed.

So I don't know where I am, where I am going, or where Bai is. I'm surrounded by unfamiliar creatures of power, many of whom will want to kill me because it's in their nature. I better not mention that I'm trying to save Aka, the man who locked all of them here.

And then Sunlight Turns Petals Gold, the most powerful being to ever exist, walked into the darkness.

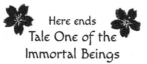

Here ends
Tale One of the
Immortal Beings

Glossary

Aarti—the third justice disciple.

Aashchary—Born to Neela 82,000 years after creation, Aashchary became the Goddess of Thought through her own efforts. She was noticed by Aka, who wished to marry her. She took him as a lover but only accepted his proposal when she discovered she was pregnant. During her marriage, she held the title Sun Empress. She was murdered under mysterious circumstances while pregnant, leaving behind one living daughter, Jin. A blue and orange immortal.

Ah—a large island south of the Crescent Moon.

Aka—Once a drop of blood, Aka became the first red immortal 26,000 years after creation. Aka became the first God shortly after mortals appeared in the world, and eventually the Sun Emperor, ruler of all, after he confined the immortal creatures to the Underworld. He has been married three times (see Goddess of Lightning, Aashchary, and Goddess of Flight) and has had six acknowledged children (see Gang, Salaana, Karana, God of Belief, Jin, and Guleum). His first lover (though they never married) was Noran, and she is the mother of his eldest son.

Ao—Once part of the midnight ocean, Ao became the first indigo immortal 31,000 years after creation. Ao is famous for turning into a dragon and is called the Sea Dragon. He is worshipped by mortal sailors though he denies being a god. He is married to Miko and has thirteen children and more than twenty grandchildren. He disowned Nanami 86,000 years after creation.

Atsuko—daughter of the Moon Deer, sister of Miko, lady Atsuko has run her father's household since her mother's death. A white immortal.

Bai—Once a piece of white quartz, Bai became the first white immortal 25,000 years after creation. He is known as the First because he was the first being to appear in the world. He invented writing, art, music, and mathematics and is so known as the Scholar. He became obsessed with martial arts after the death of his love, Noran, and was also called the Great Warrior. After he retreated from the world, many immortals believed he had died. Bai has pure white hair and gray eyes; he is slightly above average height and is extremely fit.

Bando—the peninsula separated from the Zhongtu region by the Byeong Mountains. Bando is a mortal nation as well as an immortal region and claims an unbroken line of rulers for 40,000 years.

between—how immortals refer to the time lost during teleportation; between is remembered only by the sense of time passing.

black—the ninth color, black magic changes the essence of things. See Hei.

blue—the sixth color, blue magic reads thoughts. See Neela.

Bulgae - immortal creatures that resemble dogs made of fire.

Byeong Mountains—mountain range that forms the border between Zhongtu and Bando.

Cheng—Once magma, Cheng became the first orange immortal 27,000 years after creation. He has not been seen since 83,000 years after creation and is called the Sleeper.

Cheolmun Pass—a narrow pass in the Byeong Mountains, which form the border between Zhongtu and Bando; Bai famously killed 300 mortal soldiers here.

Cold Peaks—a mountain range forming the border between Zhongtu and Ehkoron.

Colors—how the first nine immortals are known collectively. Also, the way the essential natures of immortals are categorized. All immortals can identify their natures by a set color, though it is only obvious in the appearances of the Nine Colors and their offspring.

Crescent Moon—a long island east of Bando; the Moon Deer lives here.

deity—an immortal who has mortal worshippers. The beliefs of those worshippers amplify the power of the deity but can also limit their abilities if the mortals specifically believe a deity cannot do something. Disciples of a deity thus spend much time ensuring the worshippers' beliefs align with their deity's goals. Deities are properly addressed as "divinity."

disciple—immortals who follow and learn from another immortal are called disciples; most deities have disciples.

diviner—a mortal who can read other beings; they can see a being's essence, thoughts, feelings, and sometimes future.

Earth—one of the three realms in the world, the others being the Heavens and the Underworld.

Ehkoron—the northernmost region of Earth, north of the Cold Peaks.

Eun-ji—the 48th justice disciple. Color unknown.

Forever Child—a mortal whose cognitive ability does not

surpass that of a child around age five or six; they usually are quite short with facial features that remain childlike as well.

Gang—Full name Sunlight Glints on Steel, Gang is the son of Noran and Aka and the first born-immortal. He was declared God of War at his birth 57,000 years after creation. He was trained in martial arts by Bai between 4,000 and 15,000 years of age. A red and yellow immortal.

Gate to the Underworld—a red gate made by Aka to control passage between the Underworld and Earth; to open it, one must have the key Kunjee.

god/goddess—see deity.

God of Belief—the son of Aashchary and Aka born 92,000 years after creation, he died as an infant; his full name was Mind Brighter than Sunlight. A red, orange, and blue immortal.

God of Destruction—see Karana.

God of Pleasure—see Xiao.

God of War—see Gang.

God of Wind—see Guleum.

Goddess of Beauty—see Jin.

Goddess of Flight—mother of Guleum, she is the current wife of Aka and the current Sun Empress; she is an orange immortal who was once a bird.

Goddess of Justice—see Salaana.

Goddess of Lightning—the first wife of Aka, and the first Sun Empress, she was a white immortal who was once lightning. She committed suicide. Her children are Salaana and Karana.

Goddess of Thought—see Aashchary.

godsbane—an herb that grows in the valley where Noran was killed that can poison immortals in five ways.

Godsmarket—a marketplace in the Sun Palace where immortals sell and trade goods.

Golden Phoenix—an immortal creature that was once the patron of a Bando.

golem—a magical construct that has a singular purpose.

Gomi—the fifth child of Ao and Miko, she is married with children. A mostly indigo immortal with a little white.

Great Ladies—a mountain range that forms the border between Zhongtu and Jeevanti.

Great Willow—A magical willow made by Bai 29,000 years after creation. It amplifies power. and is worshipped by mortals in Liushi. Tea made from its leaves grants clarity and insight; it is particularly popular with scholars and magistrates.

Great Warrior—see Bai.

green—the fifth color, green magic heals. See Haraa.

Guleum—The youngest son of Aka and the Goddess of Flight, Guleum was named the God of Wind at his birth 97,000 years after creation, but he does not yet have any mortal worshippers as he has not yet reached his majority. His full name is Sunlight through the Clouds. A mostly red with some orange immortal.

Haraa—Once a leaf, Haraa became the first green immortal 29,000 years after creation. Haraa is known as the Warden and is the ultimate doctor for all immortals. She is the mistress of the Wood Pavilions, which has only one rule for its many guests: Do not damage the plants.

Heaven - one of the three realms in the world, the others being Earth and the Underworld.

Hei—Once a shadow, Hei became the first black immortal 33,000 years after creation. Hei is now known as the Night God and invented marriage with his wife, Zi, 46,000 years after creation. He has one child, Xiao. He is the master of New Moon Manor along with his wife.

He Who Walks in Shadow—the best thief in the world and Nanami's onetime master.

Ichimi—the eldest daughter of Ao and Miko, Ichimi is also Salaana's lover. She is skilled with a tessen and considered both beautiful and tactful. She was once married, but her husband left her when she suffered a miscarriage. A mostly indigo immortal with a little white.

immortal being—a being that will not (it is believed) die of old age; the oldest immortal being is Bai, who is 75,000 years old as of this tale. Immortals can be formed spontaneously, from anything, when they persevere in existing. The oldest nine immortals (the Colors) each formed 1000 years apart; after that, an immortal appeared spontaneously each year. It is commonly believed that this change accounts for the dramatic decrease in power between the first nine and all subsequent immortals. All power an immortal has can be categorized as one or more colors. Immortals can also be born if at least one of their parents is an immortal. In this case, the born immortal gains access to their parent's power pool. If the family members compete for their pool of power, it comes down to will and need. Immortal pregnancies last 1000 years and born immortals reach adulthood after 4-6,000 years. As adults, Immortals age due to trauma, stress, or grief.

immortal creature—(almost) all immortal creatures were locked in the Underworld through Aka's efforts; the first to be locked up was the Korikami 75,000 years after creation and the last was the Golden Phoenix 82,000 years after creation.

indigo—the seventh color, indigo magic nullifies yellow (influence thoughts), violet (influence emotion), and black (influence essence).

Infinite Jug—an artifact made by Hei which dispenses limitless alcohol.

Jamyang—A Forever Child who Jin helps.

Jeevanti—The westernmost region of the world, it is known for a colorful aesthetic and rich, spicy food. Neela, Haraa, and the Goddess of Lightning (the mother of Salaana and Karana) all came to be in Jeevanti.

Jin—Full name Sunlight turns Petals Gold, Jin was declared Goddess of Beauty at her birth. She was born 95,000 years after creation and has been worshipped since becoming an adult at four thousand years old. After the murder of her mother, Aashchary, the second Sun Empress, Jin was raised by her grandmother Neela. When she came of age, her father Aka insisted that she return to the Sun Palace to live. Of average height with an idealized figure, gold eyes and black hair, Jin is considered the most beautiful living immortal.

Jyuichimi—the eleventh (or tenth, excluding Nanami) child of Ao and Miko, she is married; Jyunimi is her twin sister. A mostly indigo immortal with a little white.

Jyunimi—the twelfth (or eleventh, excluding Nanami) child of Ao and Miko, she is married with a child; Jyuichimi is her twin sister. A mostly indigo immortal with a little white.

Kaihachi—the eighth child (or seventh, excluding Nanami) of Ao and Miko; Kaihachi is married with children. A mostly indigo immortal with a little white.

Kaijyusan—the thirteenth (or twelfth, excluding Nanami) child of Ao and Miko. A mostly indigo immortal with a little white.

Kairoku—the sixth child of Ao and Miko; Kairoku is married with children. A mostly indigo immortal with a little white.

Karana—Full name Sundered by Sunlight, Karana is the younger child of the Goddess of Lightning and Aka. He was declared the God of Destruction at his birth 78,000 years after creation. Except for the Cult of Karana in Jeevanti, Karana is not worshipped by mortals. Instead, statues of him are made with closed eyes, so that his attention will not fall where they are placed. A mostly red immortal with some white.

Kuanbai River—"The wide, white river," the Kuanbai starts in the Great Ladies and ends at the Double Bay. Bai's spring is a tributary of the river.

Koch-ssi—an immortal creature with an affinity for plants.

Korikami—the first immortal creature that Aka locked in the Underworld.

Korikami's Tomb—once the home to the Korikami, this large volcanic mountain now holds the Gate to the Underworld.

Kunjee - Kunjee is the key that allows one to pass through the Gate to the Underworld. It is a vermillion sun pendant.

Kyumi—the ninth (or eighth, excluding Nanami) child of Ao and Miko; she is married. A mostly indigo immortal with a little white.

Land of Winter—a large island north of Crescent Moon, it is dominated by the Korikami's Tomb.

Laughter in the Shadows—full name of Xiao.

Light Hands—the name for disciples sworn to Salaana.

Liushi—coastal city in Southern Zhongtu on the Kuanbai River; contains the Great Willow.

Luye—the second beauty disciple, Luye was a born immortal whose parents tried to win favor with the Sun Emperor by sending her as a concubine to the Sun Court. Color unknown.

magic—the word immortals use for their associated powers. All magic is categorized by the color over which it has dominion and comes with an associated ability. The first nine immortals—originally known as the Colors—have significantly more magic than all other immortal beings, but all immortals have some magic.

Maoyi—city on the southern tip of Zhongtu region famous for its street food.

Mind Bright than Sunlight—full name of the God of Belief.

Miko—the third daughter of the Moon Deer; according to legend she was seen by Ao while swimming in the sea, and the two immediately fell in love; she married to Ao 70,000 years after creation and is called the Sea Queen by mortals. She has thirteen children and over twenty grandchildren. A white immortal.

Moon Deer—a white immortal (many to believe the second,

after Bai) who will remember and keep all secrets told to him; his home is Tsuku. His wife died long ago; he has three daughters, notably Atsuko, who runs his household, and Miko, who married Ao, and many grandchildren. A white immortal.

Mount Korikami—see the Korikami's Tomb.

Mos Lake—a large lake in the Cold Peaks where Nanami hides the Infinite Jug.

Nanami—also known as Nanami the Thief. Once the seventh child of Ao and Miko, born 74,000 years after creation. Nanami was disowned after she was caught stealing her aunt Atsuko's magical hair stick 86,000 years after creation. She was the first disciple of He Who Walks in Shadow until they had a falling out 94,000 years after creation. Short and slight, Nanami has navy hair and eyes, a round face, and favors plain trousers and tunics. A mostly indigo immortal with a little white.

Neela—Once a dayflower, Neela became the first blue immortal 30,000 after creation. She had one daughter, Aashchary, and has one surviving grandchild, Jin. Neela travels Earth as she wishes in a caravan and is called the Wanderer.

New Moon Manor—the residence of Zi and Hei, New Moon Manor floats in the Heavens; it was made of shadow and twilight 40,000 years after creation.

Nika—the 42nd justice disciple. Color unknown.

Nimi—the second daughter of Ao and Miko; she is married with children. A mostly indigo immortal with a little white.

Nine Colors—see Color.

Nisei—immortal creatures with butterfly wings.

nishikai powder—A magical powder made from nishikai

shells. Nishikai are immortal creatures that escaped Aka's attention for they exist only in the deep ocean. They are harvested by the Sea Dragon and the powder of their shells can make anything grow or shrink in size.

Noran—Once a grain of yellow sand, Noran became the first yellow immortal 28,000 after creation. She was Aka's lover, the mother of Gang, and Bai's unrequited love. She was killed by mortal bandits 58,000 years after creation.

Olli the Spider—an immortal creature that was defeated by Gang.

O'o—the largest city in Crescent Moon.

orange—the third color, it nullifies the powers of white (knowing the essence), red (feeling emotion), and blue (reading thoughts). See Cheng.

Po—a large island south of Ni.

red—the second color, red magic feels emotion. See Aka.

Salaana—Full name Sunlight's Allure, Salaana is the oldest child of the Goddess of Lightning and Aka. She was declared Goddess of Justice at her birth 76,000 years after creation. She is a fierce deity who is known to be harsh and decisive, making her equally revered and feared among mortals.

Sanmi—the third child of Ao and Miko, she is married with children. A mostly indigo immortal with a little white.

Scholar—see Bai.

Sea Dragon—see Ao.

Sea Palace—the underwater residence of Ao, the Sea Palace is contained within a magical dome of air.

Sea Serpent—an immortal creature that Bai rode.

seer—a mortal who sees the past and the future; this sight interferes with their sense of reality and they often struggle to communicate and coexist with others.

Sleeper—see Cheng.

Sonam—mother of Jamyang (the Forever Child who Jin helps).

Sowon Gold—an artifact made by Noran; mortals will do their best fulfill the wishes of anyone holding Sowon Gold.

Sun Emperor—see Aka.

Sun Empress—the title of Aka's wife. There have been three, the Goddess of Lightning, Aashchary, and the Goddess of Flight (current).

Sun God—see Aka.

Sun Court—the immortals who live in the Sun Palace.

Sun Palace—the city in the Heavens that contains Aka's residence and those of his children; it was made of light from the setting sun 46,000 years after creation.

Sundered by Sunlight—full name of Karana.

Sunlight Glints on Steel—full name of Gang.

Sunlight Turns Petals Gold—full name of Jin.

Sunlight through the Clouds—full name of Guleum.

Sunlight's Allure—full name of Salaana.

Taitō—the largest mountain in Crescent Moon.

teleport—the word immortals use when they magically move from one place in the world to another. Teleporting takes a great deal of power; the average immortal can only teleport once a day and it takes them about an hour. Bai is famous for being the best at teleporting—he can teleport in five minutes and has teleported as many as thirty times in a single day.

Three-Headed Elephant—an immortal creature.

true dream—an immortal dream that revisits actual memories that an immortal rejects as their history. It is accompanied by a high fever, can last indefinitely and can be deadly, particularly to immortals who need to eat or drink.

Tsuku—in Crescent Moon, Tsuku is the home of the Moon Deer and his family.

Underworld—one of the three realms in the world, the others being the Heavens and Earth.

violet—the eighth color, violet magic influences emotion. See Zi.

Wanderer—see Neela.

white - the first color, white magic knows the essences of things. See Noran.

White Mountain—Bai's origin and home, the White Mountain is the tallest mountain on Earth and is perpetually snow-capped. It is on the border of Ehkoron and Zhongtu.

Wood Pavilions—The home of Haraa, the Wood Pavilions are a section of forest with twenty-odd copper-roofed buildings. They are known for wild parties and hedonistic living but is also the best place to go for healing.

Xiao—Full name Laughter in the Shadows, Xiao was declared God of Pleasure at his birth. He was born 95,000 years after creation and has been worshipped since he came of age. He has no disciples but is popular with mortals. Most of his parents' temples have a small shrine to him. Tall and lightly muscled, Xiao has long black hair and lavender eyes. He is usually smiling, and his dimples are famous. Xiao, along with Jin, is called a useless god in the Sun Court.

Xiling—Once the capital of the largest mortal country within the Zhongtu region, Xiling was burned to ash by Karana for reasons known only to him.

Xuezei—immortal creatures that drink blood.

yellow—the fourth color, yellow magic influences thoughts. See Noran.

Yeppeun—the first beauty disciple, Yeppeun was a mortal courtesan who ascended to immortality after dying of a fatal disease at the age of twenty. Color unknown.

Yonmi—the fourth child of Ao and Miko, she is married with children. A mostly indigo immortal with a little white.

Zhongtu—the largest region on Earth, to the east of the Great Ladies and the south of the Cold Peaks; the Wood Pavilions are here.

Zi—Once twilight, Zi became the first violet immortal 32,000 after creation. Zi is now known as the Moon Goddess and invented marriage with her husband, Hei, 46,000 years after creation. She has one child, Xiao. She is the mistress of New Moon Manor along with her husband.

A Note About Language

The immortals speak a divine language and understand all mortal languages spoken to them. There are as many mortal languages in this world as in our own; because I am more interested in studying existing languages than creating my own, I drew names from the real-world languages whose cultures and myths inspired elements of this world. The cultures in the book are very loosely derived from ones in our world. Zhongtu is derived from China, Tibet, and Thailand; Ehkoron from Mongolia; Jeevanti from India; Bando, Po, Ah, and Ni from Korea; the Crescent Moon and the Land of Winter from Japan.

Just like in our languages, words shift and change. When I write a name in English—such as the White Mountain—the characters know what it means (just like the name Joy has a clear meaning in English). When I use a different language—such as the Kuanbai River - it represents a meaning that has shifted or is no longer used, and the characters may or may not be aware of its roots (just as only linguists and history buffs will know a town called Chester was probably once a fort). Some names I took wholly from a language (Bai means white in Chinese), while others are variations I created (Salaana, whose full name is Sunlight's Allure is derived from "phusalaana" or allure in Hindi). Others have ambiguous etymologies—Gang means steel in Chinese and his children have pseudo-Chinese names, but being named by Noran, I think Gang is really a shortening of "gangchoel" which is steel in Korean. I wanted to convey different characters' self-identification with different cultures or regions of their world—which is why Ao and his family, who feel tied to the Crescent Moon, all have pseudo-

Japanese names while Zi and Hei associate with Zhongtu. Some characters have transplanted themselves—Haraa is from Jeevanti (Haraa means "green" in Hindi) but lives in Zhongtu. And a few names I created without regard to their meaning—the city Xiling could have a few meanings in Chinese, but I choose it for its sound rather than its possible meanings.

Xiao and Jin have full names (Laughter in the Shadows and Sunlight Turns Petals Gold) with obvious meanings, but their nicknames (Xiao being Laughter 笑; Jin being Gold 金) are not immediately clear (even to Chinese readers since I used Roman characters without diacritics). However, you now know the title of the book refers to the vow that they make in chapter two and all that unfolds because of it. At any rate, if I have made a mistake in my use of various languages, please forgive me and know my intent to celebrate and reference the influences on this book.

Acknowledgments

Thank Joshua Pawlicki for brainstorming with me, listening to long rambles, and reading almost as many iterations as I did. Thank you to Gail Hanson for your unending encouragement. Thank you to Helen Luk for really enjoying the story and bragging about it to others. Thank you to James Hanson and James Zola for your excellent magic system suggestions and analytical questions. Thank you to Wanxi Yang for your discussion on endings and character arcs. And thank you to Margaret Ball for your close reading, dozens of grammatical corrections, and wonderful suggestions for the glossary and end note.

About the Author

Edith Pawlicki lives in Connecticut with her husband, twin sons, dog, and rabbit. She fell in love with words in fourth grade and finds writing necessary to free the worlds and characters in her head. When she isn't busy being a mom and author, she enjoys cooking and crafts. In addition to the Immortal Beings series, she has also written a YA science fiction novel, Minerva. Find her and her books at edithpawlicki.com.